"Frantz's in-depth historical research combines with her fascinating characters to create a gripping romance that kept me turning pages late into the night. I highly recommend *Love's Awakening*. It is a rare find."

—**Serena B. Miller**, RITA Award–winning author of
The Measure of Katie Calloway

Praise for *Love's Reckoning*

"Stunning. Heart-wrenching. Breathless. Not since *Gone with the Wind* have I read an epic novel that has stolen my heart, my breath, my sleep to such a jolting degree. *Love's Reckoning* marks Laura Frantz not only as a shining star in Christian fiction today but as a shooting star who soars skyward to the glittering heights of Rivers and Higgs."

—**Julie Lessman**, award-winning author of the
Daughters of Boston and Winds of Change series

Praise for Laura Frantz

"You'll disappear into another place and time and be both encouraged and enriched for having taken the journey."

—**Jane Kirkpatrick**, bestselling author of
All Together in One Place and *A Flickering Light*

"Laura Frantz portrays the wild beauty of frontier life, along with its dangers and hardships, in vivid detail."

—**Ann H. Gabhart**, author of *The Blessed*

"Frantz paints a vivid picture of the tough life out in the wild, and yet her characters demonstrate that it was possible to have a wonderful life."

—*RT Book Reviews*

Love's Awakening

Books by Laura Frantz

The Frontiersman's Daughter
Courting Morrow Little
The Colonel's Lady

THE BALLANTYNE LEGACY
Love's Reckoning
Love's Awakening

the
Ballantyne
LEGACY 2

Love's AWAKENING

A NOVEL

LAURA FRANTZ

R
Revell
a division of Baker Publishing Group
Grand Rapids, Michigan

© 2013 by Laura Frantz

Published by Revell
a division of Baker Publishing Group
P.O. Box 6287, Grand Rapids, MI 49516-6287
www.revellbooks.com

Printed in the United States of America

Library of Congress Cataloging-in-Publication Data
Frantz, Laura.
    Love's awakening : a novel / Laura Frantz.
        pages cm. — (The Ballantyne legacy ; Book 2)
    ISBN 978-0-8007-2042-1 (paper)
    1. Families—Pennsylvania—Fiction. 2. Domestic fiction. I. Title.
PS3606.R4226L65 2013
813′ .6—dc23   2013015726

Scripture quotations are from the King James Version of the Bible.

Published in association with Books & Such Literary Agency, 52 Mission Circle, Suite 122, PMB 170, Santa Rosa, CA 95409-7953.

13 14 15 16 17 18 19   7 6 5 4 3 2

To my beloved grandmother,
Catherine Fay Cleek Feagan

They that trust in the LORD shall be as
   Mount Zion,
which cannot be removed, but abideth
   for ever.

PSALM 125:1

Who clings to God in constant trust
As Zion's mount he stands full just,
And who moves not, nor yet does reel,
But stands forever strong as steel!

PSALM 125:1,
OLD SCOTTISH VERSION

Prologue

BENJAMIN FRANKLIN

PITTSBURGH, PENNSYLVANIA
OCTOBER 1793

"You've a visitor, sir. Just wanted to warn ye." The young apprentice at the office door stood in the glare of autumn sunlight, the brilliant blue Monongahela waterfront behind him.

Silas Ballantyne thanked him and looked out the door he'd left open to see a woman stepping carefully around cordage . . . and seeming to court the stares of every boatman in her wake. What was it about Elspeth Lee that made even a lad of twelve take notice and feel a bite of warning? Silas could hardly believe it was she. He'd not seen her in years. And now the bitter past came rushing back with a vengeance, dredging up unwelcome emotions.

She stepped into his office without invitation and looked about with appraising blue eyes, her beauty undimmed by the passage of time. He gave no greeting. The tension swirled thick as the sawdust in the boatyard beyond the open door.

"Well, Silas," she finally said, lifting her chin and meeting his grudging gaze. "I've come to see my sister and wish her well."

Wish her well?

He felt a sweeping relief that he'd not wed this woman. The sweetness he'd experienced with Eden couldn't be measured. Those sultry days following their July wedding had been the happiest he'd ever known. He'd not even gone to the boatyard at first. They'd kept to the bridal suite at the Black Bear Hotel, as if to make up for all the time they'd been apart, emerging only for meals or to ride out to New Hope. The house was half finished now and would be done by the time Eden delivered their first child in April. But he wouldn't tell Elspeth that.

"Eden is indisposed." The words were clipped, curtailing conversation.

Her eyes flared. "Indisposed?"

He didn't mean ill, he meant unwilling—yet she seized on the other. "My, Silas, you're hard on a wife. 'Tis glad I am that I didn't become Mistress Ballantyne." She looked about as if getting her bearings. "I suppose I shall bide my time here in Pittsburgh till she recovers and can have visitors—"

"Nae. You'll be on your way."

She assumed a surprised petulance, eyes sliding back to him. "That's hardly the welcome I expected from my new brother-in-law."

"You'll get no greeting from me now or in future. But I'll gladly pay your return passage back to York on the next stage." He took a slow breath. "And if there's any harm done Eden between now and then, any loss to my property or business, I won't bother bringing you before the Allegheny Court. You'll answer to me."

Though carefully stated, the words held a telling edge, sharp as the dirk that lined his boot. He had enemies aplenty in Pittsburgh, namely the Turlock clan. He wouldn't be adding to their numbers with this woman. But his most pressing concern was Eden, already aglow with the babe inside her, the harm done her in York a fading memory.

"I'll have my head shipwright escort you off the premises— and I'll make sure I'm present to see you leave Pittsburgh on the first stage tomorrow. Now if you'll excuse me, I have work to do."

Back stiff, she stood on his threshold, malice hardening her every feature. "I'll be back, Silas Ballantyne. You can't keep me away from Eden—or Pittsburgh—perpetually."

Their eyes locked, but hers were the first to falter when he said, "Say what you will. I'll not welcome you. Ever."

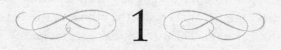

1

*The city of Philadelphia is perhaps
one of the wonders of the world.*

Lord Adam Gordon

Allegheny County, Pennsylvania
April 1822

*Elinor Louise Ballantyne is an agreeable
young lady with a fortune upward of twenty
thousand pounds . . .*

Nearly wincing at the words, Ellie fisted the latest bulletin from the Matrimonial Society of Philadelphia, hiding the paper beneath the generous folds of her pelisse. The kerseymere fabric was too warm for an April day that had begun in an overstuffed coach and was now stalled on the Pennsylvania turnpike to Pittsburgh, but she'd chosen the nondescript garment for a purpose.

She *was* an agreeable young lady.

She *was* traveling alone.

And she *was* indeed worth a fortune.

These three things were a tempting combination on any day, but here in the wilds of western Pennsylvania, they were potentially lethal. Hadn't she just seen a handbill warning of highwaymen at the last stage stop?

Emerging from the coach, she stood in a patch of sunlight slightly apart from the other passengers and tried to ignore the oaths coming from beneath the vehicle as the driver dealt with a broken axel. The other passengers looked on in consternation, some muttering epithets of their own.

"Miss . . . ?" The inquiry came from a robust, heavily rouged woman to Ellie's left, her hazel eyes appraising.

"Elinor," she replied with a hint of a smile, clutching her purse a bit tighter.

"Care to walk with us? We might well make it to Pitt ahead of the driver. It ain't but a dozen miles away, so the marker there says."

Relieved, Ellie glanced at the stone pillar alongside the road before falling into step with the others. A little walk would hardly hurt, given she'd been cooped up in a coach for days on end. Her travel mates had boarded just twenty miles prior, far fresher than she but just as anxious to see the smoky valley that was Pittsburgh, its three rivers entwining in a silvery knot.

They'd walked but a mile when the sky cast off its blueness like a discarded dress and clad itself in shades of Quaker gray. At the first stinging drops of rain, Ellie quickened her steps, the thin soles of her London-made slippers padding along in dusty protest. Merely a *gandiegow*, her Scots father would say. A heavy shower.

Or . . . worse?

Worse.

Hail big as goose eggs began pelting down, giving rise to grunts and cries as all ran for the cover of the woods.

14

Thankful for the broad brim of her bonnet, Ellie huddled beneath a sturdy oak and fixed her eye on the western rim of the horizon. There a funnel cloud was whirling, black as pitch and sounding strangely like a waterfall. Grabbing hold of the tree's rough trunk, she squeezed her eyes shut against the swirling debris, the scent of damp spring earth suffocating. Twice the storm nearly upended her, prying her fingers free from their fierce hold. She felt fragile as a butterfly about to be shorn of its wings, certain the tempest would tear her to pieces.

Lord, help me get home . . .

When the whirlwind finally departed, sheets of cold rain took its place, soaking the mass of her waist-length hair now matted with twigs and leaves. Nary a hairpin remained, to say nothing of her bonnet.

The road was oozing with coffee-colored mud and downed trees. Through the haze she could make out a few of her traveling companions ahead, scrambling for a light in the distance. It beckoned like a star, promising shelter and peace.

The Widow Meyer's? The last stage stop just shy of Pittsburgh?

When she stumbled toward its broad wooden steps, she found the yard as littered as the road, full of stranded coaches and damaged wagons and hysterical horses, its cavernous public room just as chaotic. Night was falling fast.

What a strange world a tavern was!

Standing on the threshold, she could almost believe she'd left Philadelphia for good. No more Madame Moreau. No tedious lessons in French or embroidery. No performing harp solos in stifling assemblies or declining dances at society balls. And most importantly, no more being hounded by the Matrimonial Society of Philadelphia.

Her reticule was gone, pickpocketed by the wind, just like

her bonnet. No coin. No comb. No proof of who she was. The realization edged her nearer the hysteria rising all around her. Looking up, she noticed the western portion of the tavern roof was missing, shingles agape. Rain was pouring in like water through a sieve, drenching a far corner and sending people scurrying.

"The storm of the century!" someone shouted amidst the din, raising the sodden hair on the back of her neck.

Hot and cold by turns, she unfastened the braid trim along her collar, shrugged off her pelisse, and draped it over one arm, mindful that one too many men were watching. Unbidden, a memory crawled through her benumbed conscience and turned her more wary. Something had happened to her mother in a tavern long ago, the murky details never broached. What she most remembered was her father's aversion to such places and his insistence she stay clear of them.

Oh, Father, if you could see me now . . .

Toward dawn, Jack Turlock and a collection of the most able-bodied men finished clearing a three-mile path from the tavern toward Pittsburgh. The storm had touched down slightly west of Widow Meyer's before blazing a new trail east and inflicting the most damage. By lantern light they worked, thankful the rain and wind had abated, all relieved to see the sun creep over the far horizon in reassurance the world had not ended after all.

He moved slowly, the heavy canvas of his trousers mudmired to the thigh, his boots soiled beyond repair. He'd misplaced his coat in the melee, and his grimy shirt had snuck past his waistband and now ended at his knee. Rubbing the crick in his neck, he remembered his cravat was adorning someone's broken arm as a sling. It had been a very long night.

A gentle wind was stirring all around him after a dead calm, reminding him of his near escape the night before. In the thick of the storm, a falling oak, broad as three men, missed him by mere inches. The crashing thud of it echoed long in his thoughts, and on its heels was the voice of his former schoolmaster.

Pulvis et umbra sumus. We are dust and shadows.

He tried to shake off the memory, but the tempest inside him lingered, of far greater fury than the storm now bearing east. He ducked beneath the low lintel of the tavern's main entrance, and a hush ensued. At the mud-spattered sight of him? Or his family's reputation? Likely the latter. In the keeping room of this very tavern was cask after cask of Turlock whiskey.

He entered warily, the stench of spirits and unwashed bodies colliding in a sickening rush. Slightly light-headed from hunger, he began assembling women and children, keeping families intact for travel. A few genteel ladies murmured in complaint at being made to wait, but he gave them no notice other than a cursory reassurance they'd not linger long. The room had emptied by half now, and he could better assess the situation.

"Mr. Turlock, sir, ain't like ye to tarry." The stable boy at his elbow shifted from one bare foot to the other, looking befuddled beneath his many freckles. "What d'ye want me to do with Cicero?"

"See that he gets an extra nosebag of oats." He pulled a coin from his pocket and flipped it into the air, and the lad caught it with a grin. "I hope to leave come morning."

Truly, he rarely overstayed his welcome, his restless nature never settling. He only needed a tankard of ale. A meal. Maybe a bath. Aye, that was a necessity. His mother tolerated no mess at Broad Oak, nor did her housekeeper. Glad he was that he had a change of clothes in his saddlebags.

It was twilight when the last of the wagons and coaches pulled away and he arranged for a room. Only a few men and a handful of women remained, eating and making low conversation at the surrounding tables. As he stood by the counter, sipping from his tankard, his attention was drawn repeatedly to a corner cast in shadows. Had he overlooked someone?

A young woman sat alone, back to the wall. He'd noticed her earlier helping with the children and assumed she was part of a family. He drew closer, breathing past the tightness crowding his chest.

Aye, he'd overlooked someone. But he couldn't believe it was she.

Although Ellie had kept her eye on Jack Turlock if only to stay clear of him since he'd first set foot in the tavern, she now looked away. Toward the gaping kitchen door where roast goose and apple tansy and bread she had no coin for mingled with the smell of pipe smoke and spirits. Folding her hands in her lap, she sat as erectly as she could despite spending the previous night in a chair, her backside as stiff as the splintered wood.

Mercy, it couldn't get any worse, her sister Andra was wont to say.

But yes it could, and he was coming straight for her.

She'd not seen Jack Turlock in years. Last she heard he was touring Europe, taking inventory of distilleries in Scotland, Ireland, and France, or so the papers said. In that time she'd almost forgotten all about him. Clad in mourning garb due to his grandfather's passing, he'd cut a sober if striking figure on the streets of Pittsburgh. As the younger son and not the heir, he wasn't nearly as interesting as his brother, Wade, at least to meddling society matrons.

As he walked her way, their many childhood encounters came rushing over her like the rivers at flood stage. She felt like a little girl again, about to be struck with a stone or at least belittled by his terse tongue. They'd often faced off at the creek dividing Turlock and Ballantyne land back then, her brothers Ansel and Peyton the same age as Jack and Wade. Sometimes Andra had been there, and Daniel Cameron. As the youngest, Ellie had escaped most of their wrangling. The look on his face assured her she'd not escape now.

He stared down at her, his low voice skipping any pleasantries. "Why didn't you tell me you were here? I'd have put you on the first wagon."

"There was no need. I'm not injured." Her gaze fell to her lap.

I'm simply a bedraggled mess, without coin or comb.

As badly as she wanted to be home, she did not wish to be singled out. This preferential treatment was what she was running from. Besides, Rose usually handled all the details for travel. Without her maid's plucky presence, Ellie hardly knew what to do.

She raised wary eyes to his, finding him more mud than man, his clothes in tatters. He managed to look bemused . . . somewhat mocking. Leaning into the table, he motioned to a serving girl in a checkered cap and kerchief.

"Tea," he said quietly. "Some bread."

With a smile the girl disappeared, as if taking orders from the inn's owner. But the owner was busy serving Turlock whiskey behind a long, scarred counter hedged with a cage. Business, from the looks of all the thirsty gathering there, was brisk.

"You're in want of a room," he told her. "Then we'll leave in the morning."

"We?" Her mouth formed a perfect O as she said it.

His sharp gaze pinned her so there would be no mistaking his meaning. "You're in need of an escort to take you home—a chaperone."

"I'm in need of a chaperone?" she echoed in disbelief.

To keep me safe from the likes of you.

Humor lit his gray eyes and warmed them the color of pewter, as if he well knew what she was thinking. "I'll return you to New Hope myself, out of respect for your father."

My father? The man who jailed you countless times?

Speechless, she felt a rush of gratitude override her surprise as the requested tea and bread arrived, the latter slathered with butter and honey. Her stomach gave a little lurch of anticipation, but she pushed the plate his way. He'd not said they were hers, so she'd make no assumptions.

With a long, grubby finger, he pushed the plate back toward her, along with the steaming tea. Famished, she bent her head and breathed a quick prayer before biting off a corner of bread, a cascade of crumbs spilling down her wrinkled bodice.

"I can do little about how you look, but I can certainly feed you," he said drily.

She stopped chewing, heat creeping into her cheeks, and remembered her trunk. Had the coachman ever repaired the axle and gotten this far? Or was he still stuck, hemmed in by countless fallen trees—or worse? Concerned for his safety, she nevertheless rued the loss of her belongings. Perhaps she could beg a comb. Some hairpins. Taking a sip of tea, she felt immediately better. Tea was comfort. Tranquility. Civility.

"I can walk home," she said, setting her cup aside and brushing the crumbs from her dress. "'Tis but a few miles more. I don't need an escort."

Quirking an eyebrow, he looked beneath the table at her feet. Ever-practical Jack. Quickly she drew her sodden slippers beneath the muddy hem of her skirt.

"Five miles and you'd be barefoot. Ten and you'd end up begging a ride. There's a sidesaddle in the stable—or a coach."

Those were her choices then. Since her riding clothes were in her trunk, she'd have to take a coach. Only she had no coin . . . "My belongings were atop the stage that broke down a few miles east of here. The driver—I trust he's all right—"

"There's been no loss of life that we know of, just injuries. But I'll send someone back that way to be sure."

Relieved, she confessed, "My pocketbook is missing—lost in the storm."

"Why aren't you in Philadelphia?"

She winced at his bold question. Her father would soon ask her the same, only his tone would be more gracious, surely. "I—I'm done with finishing school. 'Tis time I return home."

"You picked a poor time to do it," he murmured.

She took another sip of tea, unable to refute this fact, glancing toward the kitchen but snagging on his profile instead. He was looking up at the men repairing the roof, the feeble light framing him as it spilled through. His coloring shocked her, so deeply tanned one would think he was a common laborer and spent all his time outdoors. His features had always been sharply handsome, almost hawkish, his hair the color of summer straw, not whiskey-dark like Wade's. That he was a worldly man there could be no doubt. He even moved with an ease and agility far removed from the stiff formality of society's drawing rooms. He was, in a word, different. And dangerous.

Father would not approve.

2

A low voice and soft address are the common indications of a well-bred woman.

HANNAH MORE

Somewhat miraculously, Jack Turlock delivered both coach driver and trunk. Ellie thanked him and went above stairs to the room he'd arranged for her, feeling uncomfortably in his debt. Now, with baggage to manage, she let go of her ludicrous plan to walk, finally agreeing to the coach he'd hired. He'd ride alongside her, he said, the remaining miles into Pittsburgh and out the Greensburg Road to New Hope.

Getting into the coach the next morning, she sighed. Traveling together was as appetizing as last week's she-crab soup.

Settling back on the seat, she lifted the leather window shade to survey the damage from the storm, an unwelcome thought piercing the fog of her discontent. Was her home as badly damaged? Though New Hope was brick solid and even the chapel was made of stone, the devastation unfolding all around her seemed to whisper a warning. She was barely aware of the sudden shift of clouds overhead, so fixed was her gaze upon the ground.

Enormous trees lay toppled like kindling, requiring the coach to weave and lurch in crazy fashion, bringing nausea to the back of her throat. As thunder growled and lightning lit the sky, disbelief pummeled her. At least there was no wind, just gray sheets of rain that marred her view and soaked Jack Turlock to the skin. Though she disliked the man, she didn't want him dead. Slamming shut the shade, she raised a gloved hand and thumped on the lacquered ceiling. The coach slowly shuddered to a stop, and her escort climbed inside. When another flash of lightning lit the landscape an eerie white, she almost expected the coachman to follow.

Uttering a curse, Jack Turlock settled on the seat opposite, wet as a woodland creature and twice as riled. "Pardon my profanity."

The apology startled her more than the oath. The Turlocks were notoriously unrepentant, not given to admitting wrong. She dug for her handkerchief and dangled it before him like a white flag of truce, wondering if her family had erred in writing them off. Might there be some spark of redemption here?

But the aggravation in his eyes snuffed her hopes, though he did take the embroidered linen and mopped his brow. Rain beaded the darkened ends of his hair and dripped onto his muddy shirt. Handing the handkerchief back to her, he gave a vicious shake of his head, splattering her in the process.

Just like one of Father's sheepdogs.

"Mr. Turlo—"

"Jack," he corrected, locking eyes with her.

Her chin lifted. "I'll not call you anything but Mr. Turlock."

"And I'll not call you anything but Ellie. This foolish formality is more aggravating than the weather. We've grown up alongside each other for twenty years or better. My mother, if you remember, nearly married your father."

A near catastrophe, she didn't say.

Isabel O'Hara Turlock was a force to be reckoned with at fifty. Ellie could well imagine what she'd been like at twenty. The Turlock matron and Mama were as different as paste jewelry and gemstones.

"Actually, our ties are more long-standing than that," she said, in the mood to contradict him. "My father built New Hope in 1793—"

"And River Hill was established sixteen years prior," he interrupted. "Without my grandfather's backing, your father wouldn't have had the land for New Hope to begin with."

Her chin lifted a tad higher. "So the Turlocks say."

"I suppose the Ballantynes—and Camerons—say otherwise."

"And always will."

He rolled his eyes. "At least we agree on something."

She wouldn't ask but wondered what he was doing at Widow Meyer's Tavern, if he was on his way to River Hill. Upon Judge O'Hara's death, he'd inherited the sprawling estate along the Monongahela River, while Wade, the heir, resided at Broad Oak, a few miles west of New Hope.

Leaning back on the seat, he crossed his arms. "Where is your maid?"

His familiarity nicked her. "Where is your manservant?"

"I have none."

"Nor do I have a maid," she replied, pinched by Rose's loss. "She eloped a fortnight ago."

"I've seen you with her in Philadelphia."

Oh? Did his taste run to tavern wenches *and* ladies' maids? "I've never seen you in the city."

"I have business there on occasion." At her frown, he added with no levity, "The devil's business."

At this, she almost gave him a knowing smile, for that was

24

exactly what she'd been thinking. "I wouldn't have encountered you, I suppose, as we don't frequent the same places."

"No doubt." Clearing his throat, he produced a sodden paper, his voice a bit mocking. "'Elinor Louise Ballantyne is an agreeable young lady with a fortune upward of twenty thousand pounds . . .'"

She looked on, disbelieving. The Matrimonial Society bulletin? How had he gotten that?

"The Society erred, of course, in their calculation of family fortunes," he told her. "With your father's holdings, you're worth a good deal more than stated."

"What?"

He turned the paper over. "Aye, specifically the 'Table Showing the Exact Situation in Life and Personal Qualities of Known Marriageable Ladies.'"

Leaning forward, she snatched the bulletin from his hand. She fisted it, opened the coach window, and tossed it out, to his obvious amusement. "What do you know about the Matrimonial Society?"

"Enough to avoid it."

"I don't suppose they issued you an invitation?"

"They did but I declined, though it was tempting once I saw the heiresses offered, you being one of them."

"You're jesting."

"Nay, I've long been smitten with you, Ellie. Ever since you crossed the creek years ago and brought me a sheepdog pup to replace the one I'd lost."

Smitten? She wouldn't succumb to that foolish notion. Yet his expression, for the barest moment, was so serious she knew he spoke the truth about the puppy, though she had no recollection of it.

He shrugged. "You'd have been about four to my ten. Too young to remember."

Truly, she only remembered the sticks, stones, and spats. "'Twas probably Mama's doing to give you the puppy. She was always trying to mend hearts."

"It wouldn't have been Andra," he said bluntly.

No, not Andra. Her older sister's heart was half stone.

The patter of rain on the roof grew louder, and they rode on in stilted silence, locked in the still, semidark interior of a coach far inferior to what Ellie was used to. She almost groaned when the contraption lurched to a halt and nearly spilled her onto Jack Turlock's lap. While he exited to investigate, she held her breath, praying they'd continue on. Pittsburgh was so close . . .

Long minutes passed before the coach door cracked open again and he motioned her out, his horse near at hand. Shock scuttled through her. He wanted her to ride? She looked heavenward as if seeking answers. But the fickle spring sky was now a robin's-egg blue, backing up his startling invitation.

Beside them, the coachman mopped his sodden brow and glowered at the immense elm blocking the road from stem to stern ahead of them. Muttering, he turned and began unhitching the team, intent on returning to the tavern.

Ellie felt the pressure of a callused hand as Jack mounted the fine, dun-colored stallion and pulled her up after him. With her skirts hitched so, her stocking-clad ankles showing above hopelessly soiled slippers, she frantically worked to assume a ladylike posture—impossible when not riding sidesaddle. They were soon careening down the mud-slicked road over brush and round impediments as if the devil was on their heels, rattling her very bones. Was Jack . . . liquored? The faintest hint of spirits wafted back to her as her thoughts began an agonized rotation.

Father cannot see me like this. Even the help will be scan-

dalized. I'll make Jack leave me at the gate—no, the lane—
before reaching home . . .

Heaven help her, why the worry?

She wouldn't live to see New Hope!

New Hope's immense front gate was surprisingly plain
with a bold *B* affixed in the center. Wrought in iron, it was
a reminder of the Ballantynes' humble blacksmithing roots.
Pittsburgh had been raw wilderness back then, and New
Hope a poor Scotsman's dream, not the jewel crowning the
Allegheny bluff that stopped river traffic midstream. Like
a pearl in an oyster, the main house rose in gray-bricked
splendor, a spacious veranda with ivory columns soaring to
the second story on all sides, Palladian windows abounding.

No wonder Ellie Ballantyne wanted to come home. Now,
in spring, all the lushness of the season held sway. Fields
unfolded around them, worked by Ballantyne hands—not
slaves but indentures and free blacks—and Jack's eye was
drawn to a large garden and orchard sprawling to the south,
the trees full of fragrant blossoms. He tore his attention from
the stirring sight as Ellie shifted in the saddle behind him.

Parched from their twelve-mile ride, his throat felt like
river sand, though Ellie hadn't complained. He'd stop at a
nearby creek to drink if refreshments were denied him, and
he wagered they would be. Not once had a Turlock set foot
at New Hope. If the Ballantynes entertained, the Turlocks
weren't invited.

Moving beyond the gate, he started down the drive, dismay
sitting square in his gut at the sight of once-towering oaks
and elms felled as if by an ax, their massive roots a muddy
stain upon the glistening grass. Alarm ticked inside him. Was
River Hill the same?

He sensed Ellie's shock as she rode at his back. Though she'd made a feeble protest as they'd turned in the gate, telling him she could walk the rest of the way, he'd ignored her, and her pleas had become whisper-thin. When he finally dismounted and helped her down after him, he felt a jolt at the tears welling in her eyes. But she dashed them away with a quick hand as a figure emerged on the porch.

Jack's hopes rose, then extinguished like candle flame. He'd expected the housekeeper, though he'd dared to hope Silas Ballantyne would be waiting. Everyone from Pittsburgh to Philadelphia knew Ellie was the apple of her father's eye. Jack figured he'd scored quite a victory rescuing her as he'd done. And he was honest enough to admit he wanted to ingratiate himself with the most respected man in Allegheny County by bringing his beloved daughter home unharmed.

Instead he faced Andra, the fire of dislike in her eyes, her posture soldier-stiff. She gave him no more than a disdainful glance as she focused on her little sister, who, Jack noted with grim amusement, was missing a shoe.

Ellie's narrow, stocking-clad foot hovered over the wet stone walk. She looked down in surprise and then up at Jack, open blame in her blue eyes. He'd ridden hard and fast to get her here—his horse was lathered and drooping behind them and in dire need of a drink. But from the set of Andra's jaw, he knew he'd get no water or welcome.

"I'd invite you in," she said with a voice that bore a burr of her father's Scots speech, "but since River Hill is so close, I'm sure you're anxious to assess the damage to your own home place."

Close? River Hill was miles more and likely littered with a blow-down the likes of which he'd never seen. But he wouldn't give the righteous Andra the privilege of seeing his disappointment. Schooling his emotions as he'd done at every

Ballantyne snub, he turned without a word and mounted Cicero, intent on the nearest creek, and tried not to smile as his horse wheeled round and slung mud on the skirt of Andra's fine dress.

Andra waited till Jack Turlock was out of earshot before wheeling on Ellie, face berry-red and tone blistering. "Elinor Louise! The shock of having you arrive home without warning is enough! You didn't have to bring a Turlock to boot! And now my dress!"

Bare foot forgotten, Ellie winced as Andra began shouting for a maid, summoning Peyton in the process. He stepped onto the battered veranda smeared with wet leaves and broken branches, impeccably dressed and seeming oblivious to the mess. His familiar chuckle set her at ease, though he made no move to hug her. No doubt she'd soil his suit.

"So, little sister . . . did you get off on the wrong foot with Andra?"

The pun was not lost on Ellie as Andra pushed past them, still fuming. "Where's Father? Mother?"

"Downriver in New Orleans. They'll be back the end of June."

A whole two months more? She swallowed down her disappointment. By then Andra would have exhausted every means to return her to Philadelphia. "And Ansel?"

Peyton cocked his head and raised a brow. "Don't you hear him? He's in the music room at the moment, and the door is open."

The trill of a violin sent her scurrying past into the still, shadowed foyer. Here everything was as calm as it was chaotic outside. Fine wood paneling and Dutch and Flemish paintings gave the impression of a grand country house, the parquet floor and timeworn furnishings a genteel reminder of another century. She kept walking toward the last door on the left, tucked behind an immense curving stair. Of all the rooms in the house, this was the most beloved, at least to her and Ansel, the home of her harp and his violin.

The sight of him by a window erased the sting of her arrival. Taking a seat at the large concert harp, she placed her hands on the strings, praying the instrument was in tune. It wasn't. Her fingers plucked a discordant note before falling to her lap. Everything else had been a disaster since dawn. Why would this be any different?

Ansel swung round, his obvious delight at seeing her an antidote for all that had gone wrong. "El?" Setting aside his violin, he pulled her to her feet and smothered her in a bearish embrace. "Tell me you've come home for good."

She nodded and fought back tears, weariness making her emotional. Only Ansel knew how homesick she'd been in Philadelphia.

Holding her at arm's length, he studied her. "How did you get here?"

"It seems the Lord brought me home in a whirlwind . . . atop the devil's own horse."

"What?" He looked down at her, a puzzled light in his eyes.

She forced a smile, still stinging from Andra's rebuke. "Jack Turlock just left. We met at Widow Meyer's Tavern during the storm. He took it upon himself to bring me home."

Surprise rode his features—and raw alarm. "Gentleman Jack?"

Ellie nearly cringed at the long-standing nickname, spoken derisively by most. "The same."

"Good thing Da is downriver. *Wheest!*"

Da. She'd been away so long, the Scots word seemed a bit strange. "No, Da wouldn't approve," she murmured, thank-

30

ful her father couldn't see what a muddy mess she was. "Our dear sister just sent Mr. Turlock packing."

"Did she now?"

"I thought it rather rude of her, but I wasn't much better." She felt a twinge of conscience. "If Mama had been here . . ."

"She would have insisted he stay for supper, and the old Ballantyne-Turlock grievance would be buried forever." He gave her a quick wink. "Don't be too hard on Andra. She's none too happy that a funnel cloud lifted the roof of her room and ruined her new French wallpaper. Don't you hear the hammers?"

The faint tapping of workmen from on high reassured her all would be well. Still, the damage she hadn't seen was what most worried her. "I wasn't sure I'd ever get here. There are trees down everywhere. I wonder about our neighbors . . . Pittsburgh." But even as she said it, her concern narrowed to the figure in front of her. She studied her brother, finding him much changed. The sun lines about his eyes seemed more pronounced, indicative of his time outdoors. And his russet hair—could it be?—was silvered at the edges. The transformation shook her. He was but five and twenty.

"I spoke with the neighbors at dawn before riding into town, and all is calm. The mercantile and glassworks withstood the storm well enough, but the boatyard is quite battered. I didn't have time to walk the length of the levee." He rubbed his brow, thoughtful. "A stable on Water Street suffered damage and some horses got loose. The Baptist steeple went down. Thankfully, the mayor and aldermen have all in hand. I came back here half an hour ago to see if the farm manager has resumed the fieldwork and got distracted."

Distracted by his music . . . this beautiful room. He hadn't changed in that respect.

"I'd keep to the house for the next few days." His tone was

light, but his eyes were grieved and looked as deep a blue as Mama's in that instant. "Don't go into the garden—or out to the chapel."

A tight knot was expanding inside her, and she felt somewhat sick despite his gentle warning. She sensed he was withholding something, but a gentleman, as Madame Moreau said, always spared a lady's sensibilities. And a lady, in turn, never fished for details. The damaged roof was easily dealt with, but the chapel Da had built for Mama surrounded by all those heirloom roses . . .

"I'm needed at the stables." He moved toward the door, shrugging on a coat. "Da's prize mare foaled last night. A bit of good news amidst the bad. We'll talk more at supper, aye?"

Supper? Queasy as she was from the day's events, Ellie didn't think she'd eat for a week. But a bath was in order, at least.

3

Truth does not blush.
TERTULLIAN

Since learning of Ellie's homecoming, New Hope's cook had turned into something of a funnel cloud in the kitchen, making such a din Ellie could hear her on high. All afternoon, enticing aromas wafted to the upper floors, rousing her from her nap, and she considered eating after all, if only to spare Mamie's feelings. Soon a linen-clad tray was set before her, Mamie's smile brimming with indulgence as if to make up for Mama's absence.

Chicken and dumplings nested in a glazed blue bowl, its rim cracked—the very one she'd used in childhood. Thin slivers of pears from the hothouse and thick slices of Cheshire cheese from the cellar were layered temptingly on a china plate. A fluted glass held cherry pudding.

Ellie bent her head and gave thanks over the artfully arranged meal, grateful the storm hadn't destroyed New Hope's kitchen.

In moments, without so much as a knock, the bedchamber

door swung open and Andra entered in a clean India cotton gown, no hint of the Turlock mud in evidence.

"Mind if I join you? Peyton was quite put out you didn't come down for supper."

Peyton? More likely Andra, wanting to waylay her at table and pepper her with questions. "I was sleeping . . . after spending a night in a tavern chair."

Andra bent down and kissed her cheek before taking a seat, enveloping her in a subtle rose-carnation scent and the welcome she'd been denied hours before.

"I'm sorry for spoiling your homecoming. 'Twas just such a shock to see you ride in like that, without warning—and without Rose."

Ellie forked a dumpling to her mouth, depriving Andra of the elaboration she so obviously wanted. She smiled up at Mamie as the woman poured a second cup of tea and then left them to an awkward silence.

Andra added sugar to her cup, expression thoughtful. "Where *is* Rose?"

Pensive, Ellie sampled a slice of pear. "Probably in Boston by now."

"Boston?"

"Last winter Rose met a young tradesman—a printer. They spent the Sabbaths ice skating on the Schuylkill River and fell in love." Looking back, Ellie could hardly believe the turn of events. Her comely maid hadn't had to go hunting for a groom. Tradesmen abounded in Philadelphia, all hers for the picking. Ellie envied her the simplicity of the match. "They decided to marry and move farther east."

Andra's fair eyebrows arched, giving an impression of petulance. "But she was devoted to you—and was bound to fulfill the terms of her contract."

"I freed her from her indenture document in writing and

gave her my blessing." Doing so had felt bold, but hadn't Father done the same when circumstances required it? If anything, Ellie rued the fact that she'd not written to ask his permission first. "Besides, who am I to deny her happiness? She'd fulfilled four of her five years and was more friend to me than maid."

Taking a sip of tea, Andra raised jade eyes. "You're too soft, just like Mama."

Ellie shrugged away the criticism. "Da and Mama simply wanted Rose to act as a chaperone—be a companion to me while I was in Philadelphia. Now that I'm home I hardly need a maid."

"Well, you'll have need of another soon enough. Best begin making plans to return to Madame Moreau's before Da comes home."

Ellie looked away, trying to gather courage. "After four years of finishing school, I feel quite . . . finished."

"But Da has such hopes for you. He wants you to have a Philadelphia connection, marry well."

"Does he?"

"He wants one of us to wed." *And it shan't be me*, her tone seemed to say.

"One of us? Or all of us?"

Andra's corset-stiffened figure seemed to wilt against the Windsor chair. "You know he's cast all his hopes on you. Mama too. You're lovely. Accomplished. Gracious."

Ellie shifted uncomfortably in her chair. It wasn't like Andra to flatter. Ellie much preferred her plain speaking, even her criticism. "I'd expected Da would be here when I arrived so I could explain things."

"I'm glad he's in New Orleans, and not only because of the storm. If he'd seen you ride in with Gentleman Jack, looking like the two of you had just eloped—"

"Shush," Ellie whispered, losing what little remained of her appetite. "I suppose we were quite a mud-spattered spectacle, but that's all it was. I haven't seen any of the Turlocks in years."

Andra's chin tipped up in fresh offense. "I have a mind to send that gown he ruined to River Hill for recompense. My maid said she'll never be able to remove the stains. He did it on purpose. You know he's never liked me."

"'Tis mutual, isn't it? You never cared for him. Or his brother."

At the mention of Wade, Andra shuddered. "Outright rogues, the both of them."

Ellie started to give Jack his due. *If not for Jack Turlock, I'd still be stranded on the Pennsylvania turnpike.* But the words seemed to stick in her throat.

"So . . . how did the two of you happen to cross paths?" Andra poured more tea, feigning a disinterest she was far from feeling, Ellie guessed. Her animosity for the Turlock clan was matched only by her curiosity.

"I took the stage and was nearing home when the storm broke. I never expected to meet up with him. I nearly didn't recognize him."

"What do you mean?"

"He—" She weighed her answer, not wanting to compound Andra's ill will for him. "Ja—Mr. Turlock was supervising a group of men clearing the road." For all the Turlocks' faults, shirking work wasn't one of them, unlike the majority of entitled men she'd met who sat on their hands and waited for the bulk of the family fortune to fall into their laps. The air of authority he'd had baffled her. She remembered him as quiet, stoic, always in the shadow of the brash Wade. "He was surprisingly considerate of the women and children."

"Especially the women," Andra murmured disapprovingly.

36

Especially to me.

Ellie blinked as if doing so would dispel the virile image in her mind. Stubborn, it wouldn't budge. Despite his flaws, Jack Turlock had a certain *je ne sais quoi* that was undeniable. Amidst her usual musings involving books, flowers, and music, he didn't fit.

"You still haven't explained why you left finishing school."

Relieved at the change in topic, Ellie set her fork aside. "My studies were at an end. All my friends had married and moved on. There was little left for me to do in Philadelphia. Coming home seemed . . . right."

"It might be all right for days, a few weeks. But there's little at New Hope for you to do. Mama and I manage the house, the help. Actually, Mama is so often at the orphan home in town, I'm seeing to most everything now. And Ansel and Peyton and Da tend to the boatyard and other business."

There's simply no room for you.

Ellie heard the underlying message loud and clear, noted the stubborn set of Andra's features. "Perhaps I can be of use at the mercantile—"

"Da won't let you near the mercantile. 'Tis too close to the levee and all those blasphemous river men."

"Perhaps the glassworks, then."

"Doing what?" Andra laughed. "Speaking French? Dancing?" She rolled her eyes, much as Jack Turlock had done in the coach. "Elinor Louise, you've no head for business. That's why you were sent east in the first place."

Bruised by the slight, Ellie struggled to keep her composure. Obviously Andra's opinion of finishing school and feminine pursuits as frivolous hadn't altered. It was no secret she wished Ellie wed and off the premises, familial ties or no. "What of society? Making calls and the like?"

Andra shook her head. "Social niceties aren't what Pittsburgh is known for, unlike Philadelphia. Calling cards and afternoon visits simply aren't profitable. There's precious little of anything civilized here except for an occasional dance or two. This town is all about industry. Period."

Finished with her tea, Andra stood and surveyed the room they'd once shared before the new wing had been added a few years before. The mint-green walls were a tad faded, and the Queen Anne furnishings, though still lovely, had an antique look about them. Even the white dimity bed hangings seemed a trifle childish, unchanged since childhood.

Ellie withheld a sigh. "Perhaps I'll begin work on my room."

At that, Andra's tense face melted into relaxed lines. "Now *that* should keep you busy, little sister."

Broad Oak was as solid and enduring as its name, made more memorable by the immense trees that shaded the long drive with an everlasting rustle of limbs and leaves. As Jack rode down the muddy length of it, his level gaze took in the house's stone façade with the wide portico so typical of riverfront properties, a place where his mother sometimes sat with his sister to escape the summer's heat. But no one was on the porch today, and his gaze tripped on something else entirely.

Nearest the house, as if split by lightning, the oldest and largest oak had fallen, leaving a gaping crater that resembled the dismay carving a hole inside him. The revered old tree had stood a century or better and was his favorite, almost majestic in its height and reach. He had a sudden urge to turn round and ride straight to River Hill till a feminine voice stopped him, pointed in its displeasure.

"Jack . . . that you?"

He slid from the saddle, his boots making a smacking sound as the heft of him landed atop stones and mud. "Chloe?"

His sister circled the felled oak, wearing battered brogans and a man's shirt and hat, silvery eyes glistening like newly minted coins, nose freckled, mouth planted in a pout. She looked like an unmade bed. The only feminine thing about Chloe was her name. He guessed he and Wade were to blame, always treating her like a little brother.

"Look at this cussed tree! Daring to fall—my very favorite for climbing!" There was a telling wetness about her eyes that belied her indignation. "Yours too, if I remember."

Sympathy softened him as he tugged the unsightly hat off her fair head. "Be glad it didn't fall on the house." The memory of his own mishap along the turnpike, still vivid, nearly made him cringe. His six and twenty years had almost ended in the dark Monongahela woods. If they'd buried him, what would they have said?

"Son of whiskey scion succumbs to storm"?

He shook off the thought and tied Cicero to the iron hitching post, which stood slightly askew. A casualty of the storm, most likely.

"It'll make good firewood, I guess," Chloe admitted grudgingly, kicking at a gnarled branch, "or staves for whiskey barrels."

"None of that talk, Daughter." The voice, firm and far-reaching, drifted down from overhead. Chloe and Jack looked up, but Isabel Turlock's eyes were firmly planted on her secondborn son as she leaned out an open window. She couldn't tolerate a daughter who talked trade, her stern countenance reminded. Whiskey was taboo, though they wallowed in its profits.

"How is River Hill?" she demanded, the worried cast of her features hinting she expected the worst.

"I've not been there yet," Jack told her.

"Well, when you do, send word that all is well. But before

you go, I need to speak to you—in your father's study." With that, she shut the window so hard the glass rattled. Jack half expected it to shatter. It wouldn't be the first time . . .

"Ma has a bee in her bonnet," Chloe warned. "You'll be sorry you've come."

She grabbed her hat from him and spun away, skirting the fallen oak and heading for the summer kitchen. There she'd pour out her angst to Sally, their Negro cook, the woman who'd been more mother to them than the tiny woman who soon stood before him. What Isabel O'Hara Turlock lacked in stature, she made up for in spirit. She raked him with a glance and motioned him inside as soon as he set foot on the porch.

"There's more than the weather to worry about," she murmured, the fine lines in her face deepening when she frowned.

He followed her down the hall, his gaze scouring the elaborately painted ceiling for signs of damage. Unscathed, the plump, harp-playing cherubs surrounding a bearded Father Time smiled down at him benignly, as they had a quarter of a century or better. Everything was polished, echoing, empty. Mrs. Grimm, the housekeeper, was a stickler for tidiness—and well deserving of her dour name.

Isabel's voice wafted back to him, as clipped as the rap of her heels on the polished floor. "You look like you've been in another brawl."

"I've been clearing the pike," he said, reminded of his wretched clothes. Though he'd changed at Widow Meyer's, they were now as soiled as before. "Where are Pa and Wade?"

"That's what I want to talk to you about. They're in the quarters. Four of the slaves are missing. They took advantage of the storm and fled."

"Which four?"

"The ones fresh from Kentucky. You know the ring leader

well enough—Big Jim, so hot-tempered he could boil beans."
She rounded his father's desk and began searching through
stacks of papers, her ringed hands flashing with amethysts
and diamonds, her favorite gemstones. "He's been upset ever
since your father sold his wife downriver, as if he had a choice.
She was as surly as Jim. Together they made more mischief
than the other fifty slaves combined." Taking up a pen, she
signed a document and thrust it toward Jack. "Here are the
transfer papers for Jim's brother, Ben. We want him off the
property in case he's tempted to run too."

"What about Sally?"

Isabel raised a hand to sand-colored hair that didn't hold
a hint of gray, eyes hardening. "What about her?"

"You're bound to stir up a hornets' nest separating Sally
from Ben."

"It should have been done long ago. Sally's indulged that
boy far too long, treating him like a house slave when he
belongs in the fields."

"You can hardly blame her, as he's her youngest grandson."

"I need no reminding. Just take Ben with you as you go.
I'm sure you have work for him at River Hill."

"Aye, in the stables. But I'll have a talk with Sally first."

"That's hardly necessary." Her voice held a hint of hostility. "I don't consult the slaves before making decisions and
neither should you."

Folding the paper, Jack bit back a retort, temper simmer-
ing. Weary as he was, he was in no mood for his mother's
fits and whims. Likely she'd want Ben back tomorrow. "All
right, I'll take care of it."

"I know you will. If I ever want something done, I start
with you. Wade is much too preoccupied with the distilling.
As for your father . . ." She set a crystal paperweight down
with a thud, her voice fading to a thread of disappointment.

Jack well knew what she was thinking but didn't give it voice.

"There's another matter." She raised weary eyes to his, somewhat entreating though still hard as glass. "The social season has begun, what little there is of it in Pittsburgh. The Pressleys and Nevilles have sent invitations—"

He grimaced. "No doubt they want to recover their losses from the Panic of 1819 and are desperate enough to wed a Turlock to do it."

"What am I to tell them? That you and Wade prefer tavern wenches?"

"That fact is well known," he said flatly, curbing his irritation as best he could. It was a well-worn subject, always sore, and one he'd dodged repeatedly in the past. "You needn't say anything at all."

"You should reconsider, Jack. 'Tis not too late to think of an heir. If I could only get Wade to ponder something beyond horse racing and gambling and that infernal distilling . . . "

Her voice trailed after him as he turned away. Leaving the ornate study, he passed through the shadowed foyer and out the back door, thankful when a ray of sun slanted down and left him wishing for his hat. He'd lost it on the way here, like Ellie had her shoe. The memory lifted his mouth in a near grin, easing the dread of what he was about to do.

The summer kitchen, cast in stone, was connected to the main house by a narrow colonnade made bright by wisteria vine. Despite the rising whine of flies and mosquitoes, the door was open, and Chloe's excited chatter overrode the usual kitchen din. Jack filled the doorway, waiting till Sally looked up, her dark face wreathed with a near-toothless smile.

"Why, Master Jack, you come through the storm to my kitchen?"

"Aye," he said, smiling past his misgivings. "I need to borrow Ben."

"Ben? Oh, he'd like that real good."

"Well, I don't." Chloe swung round on her stool, a small sugar cake in hand. "Ben and I have plans to go fishing."

"You can come to River Hill and do the same," he reminded her as Sally brought him a cake of his own. "I need some help in the stables. Ben is the best choice, able hand that he is."

Sally fetched him cider next, clearly pleased. He felt a wide relief. There was a right way and a wrong way to manage people. He'd witnessed the wrong way all his life. Still, he felt rather duplicitous. His mother might, in a fit of temper, tell all. Likely Sally didn't know about the runaways just yet. His father liked to keep things hushed, as it tended to cause such unrest in the quarters.

He took a bite of cake, nodding his thanks.

"You need a cook at that lonesome house of yours?" Sally asked, studying him.

Chloe's smile was thick with mischief. "Jack needs a wife."

Swallowing, he shot her a wary glance. "Wives are troublesome creatures. We're talking about Ben, remember."

Sally chuckled as Chloe stuffed the last of the cake into her mouth, spilling crumbs down her front and reminding him of a famished Ellie at the tavern.

"I'll be back on the morrow," he told them. "I've yet to see the damage to River Hill."

Sally followed him outside, her amber eyes taking in the downed limbs and leaves. "Law, but I thought my kitchen would blow clear to next week when that wind hit. The very breath of the Almighty come down, seems like. But I'm ready to meet Him when it's my time."

The words slowed Jack's steps and he paused, wanting to ask Sally just what she meant, tell her about his near-fatal mishap in the woods. Then he changed his mind. He was done with distractions. He needed a bath. A shave. Clean clothes.

And a means of forgetting Ellie Ballantyne.

Six hours later, as the sun spent itself in a glow of scarlet and gold beyond the study's west window, Jack laid his quill down and tugged off the spectacles he always wore while working on accounts. Their fragile lines gave him a scholarly look, his mother said, reminding him of her father the judge. Jack raised his gaze from the jumble of numbers in the ledgers before him to the portrait of Hugh O'Hara above the oak mantel. Formidable. Determined. Respected.

Of all the rooms at River Hill, this one felt the most like the man he'd so admired. His grandfather's tobacco-laden, bergamot scent still lingered, perhaps because nothing had been altered since he'd died six years prior. The study had a shabby, old-world grandeur Jack liked. While other people were papering their rooms with French toile and hauling in ornate Empire-style furnishings, he hadn't so much as replaced a pewter candlestick.

Snuffing the candelabra atop his desk, he looked toward the door, glad supper was over and he could walk. He normally rode Cicero, choosing a different route each evening, but the wind had picked up and he didn't want a skittish mount if a second storm hovered. Signs of damage were everywhere, and he passed the aging dependencies of the estate with a wary eye, most of them empty, like the old spinning room and summer kitchen. Only a few were still in continuous operation since his grandfather's time, namely the stables and icehouse.

He made his way along River Row, which had housed his grandfather's slaves in the previous century, each cottage's hollow-eyed windows staring back at him with a strange poignancy. He didn't like the reminder of the trouble brewing at Broad Oak with the runaways, so he moved on, preoccupied and more than a tad uneasy. The river was his reward, a shimmer of fire as the sun set. Here the grass was knee-high as it hugged the riverbank, the lushness of spring begging a second look. And every inch was his, as far as the eye could see—more than a thousand acres.

His grandfather had been a shrewd man, one of Pittsburgh's founders. As he'd had no son, River Hill had passed from daughter to grandson, and Jack was the beneficiary. Wade, the firstborn, would inherit Broad Oak, and though Jack never said so, River Hill was superior in every way.

He picked up a smooth stone and skimmed it over the Monongahela's fiery surface, watching it ripple and disappear into the deeps. River traffic was light, for the storm had churned up a nightmare of muck beneath the now-calm surface, though a lone packet made a cautious trek downriver bearing the Ballantyne flag. He turned away, wanting no reminder of Ellie. She was, he'd be willing to wager, thinking the same of him.

4

Peace and rest at length have come,
All the day's long toil is past,
And each heart is whispering,
"Home,
Home at last!"

—Thomas Hood

Early the next morning, Ellie donned a light linen dress and came down the curved staircase in muted expectation. With her parents away, New Hope seemed hollow, even lonesome. Had they been home, she would have breakfasted with them both in the small morning room, its sunny yellow walls reflecting the light that dawn cast up to the east-facing windows. Mamie's customary ham and eggs, biscuits, and honey from New Hope's hives would be waiting, and they'd say grace and discuss the coming day.

It had been this way for as long as Ellie could remember, and she never wanted things to change. But change, she was learning, was everywhere. Hammering and sawing and the drone of men's voices had roused her long ago. There was a push to repair the storm damage before the steamboat bearing her parents returned from New Orleans.

This morning Mamie seemed to have forgotten about her and no breakfast graced the sideboard, perhaps because Ellie was so seldom home, but most likely because Andra had the cook busy elsewhere. Restless, Ellie felt like a ball as she bounced from door to door across the empty, gleaming foyer, just as she'd done as a child, searching for her parents.

Parlor. Music room. Dining room. Study. At last she stepped into her father's domain, taking stock of his personal effects, if not him. A massive desk dominated the room, and the surrounding bookcases rose to the ceiling, requiring a rolling ladder to reach the utmost heights. When younger, she and Ansel would jump from the highest rung and land atop the lush bearskin rug spread before the hearth, avoiding the ornate andirons fashioned by their father's own hands. That he'd once been a poor blacksmith she couldn't quite fathom. If not for his branded thumbs, indicative of another life, she'd not have believed such. By the time she was born, it seemed Silas Ballantyne owned half of Allegheny County.

Her fingers trailed across the dustless mahogany desk, up and down mountains of paperwork and ledgers and legal documents, to a crystal inkwell and a box of pens alongside sealing wax. An old Gaelic Bible lay to one side, heavily marked in the margins, open to the twenty-third Psalm. Since she couldn't read Gaelic, she didn't tarry long.

Across the royal blue Axminster carpet was Mama's bower with its small French writing table embraced by three curved windows, something of a novelty when the house was built. A faded jumble of rose petal potpourri, still faintly fragrant, filled crystal bowls here and there. Ellie sank down atop an upholstered chair, eyeing the stack of letters attesting to Mama's voluminous correspondence with friends in Philadelphia.

Opening the drawer, she extracted a crisp sheet of paper, shook a bottle of verdigris ink, and pondered the idea that had come to her in the night. This was surely the answer to Andra's perplexity at having her home—and the remedy to the blank days that stretched before her. Inking the tip, she scrawled:

> *The subscriber begs leave to inform the public that she intends to open a day school for young ladies; she therefore hopes parents will be kind enough in sending their daughters. She flatters herself she shall be able to give entire satisfaction, as no care or expense on her part will be wanting. Her days for teaching are negotiable . . .*

She wrinkled her nose, dripping ink onto the pristine paper. The words sounded rather formal, a tad high toned. It pained her she was skilled at dancing and little else. She'd been abominable at French. Though she loved geography, it didn't return her affection. Arithmetic eluded her. Deportment came somewhat easily, for she'd been reared to be a lady. Ah, embroidery! She had a gift for needlework, like her mother before her.

"Elinor, where are you?" Andra's voice, a touch heated, jarred her into action. Ellie folded the paper and pocketed it as her sister came through the door, small leather basket in hand containing keys to unlock every room and dependency at New Hope.

"Ansel told me to remain indoors," she confessed, sensing Andra's exasperation at finding Ellie sitting, doing little, while the rest of them labored.

Andra nodded. "That's just as well, otherwise you'd be underfoot."

"I'd rather help. There must be something—"

"Take out your paints or play your harp, if you like. It might well soothe our nerves." Andra sighed and dug for a key in her basket. "Everywhere we look there's damage to be dealt with. The smokehouse and dovecote are in splinters, the garden a shambles. Pittsburgh fared worse—and some of the finest homes along the rivers are missing roofs and chimneys . . ." She paused, a half smile easing her aggravation. "I can only hope Broad Oak and the Turlock distillery were blown to bits! 'Twould be just punishment, don't you think? For distilling on the Sabbath—and worse!"

The venom in Andra's voice gave Ellie pause. There were many distillers among them. Did she wish them all ill? The surrounding river valleys were known for producing the finest rye and corn that made whiskey the lucrative enterprise it was in Pennsylvania, though the Turlocks had turned it into a small empire.

"I'd hoped we could all sit down together for supper tonight," Andra said, surprising her with the turn in conversation. "But Peyton and Ansel are preoccupied in town. 'Twill just be the two of us, after all."

Long after the lonesome supper hour, Ellie snuck into the garden, wincing at the creak of the old wrought-iron gate. Beneath a waning moon, the damage was better dealt with, its harsh effects muted. Still, her heart hurt. She was hemmed in by bushes stripped of every bud and leaf, a sundial overturned, the arbor in a shambles. Early spring flowers that had danced on slender stems were shorn and snapped. To her grieved eyes it looked like someone had turned loose the livestock.

Oh, Mama, I'm glad you're gone.

"Miss Elinor?" A coal-oil lantern cast light in her path as New Hope's aged gardener wandered out of the stone cottage he called home.

"I couldn't bear to look by day," she said, her voice cracking with vulnerability.

He nodded his shaggy head, shoulders bowed. "Some of these roses were planted the year the master married the mistress. Some of the trees too." He waved a hand toward a prized magnolia now uprooted. "I don't know as I can set it to rights, but I'll try."

"Do you need any help?"

"You been asking me that since you were knee-high, Miss Elinor. And I been telling you no. Those pretty hands of yours are made for finer things, like harps and gloves."

He moved away, and she drew her shawl closer as a breeze lifted its lace edges, her eyes drawn to the cupola. High above, Ansel was tending the lantern atop New Hope, his lean shadow in stark relief. She'd always been amazed a single beacon could shine so bright. The large lantern was an invention of their father's, with a mirrored back that reflected twice the light. It spilled over the shingled roof and down the sloping ground to the river and was extinguished at dawn.

Soothed by its familiar presence, she took a seat on a stone bench, glancing in the direction of the chapel. Her parents had begun their married life within its walls. The house had been built soon after, the gardens laid out. New Hope was a mirror of their hearts, their hopes and dreams.

She thought of her own home in years to come, wanting it to be much like this, safe and solid and enduring. But a home necessitated a husband, a well-thought-out betrothal beforehand. Like any Pittsburgh or Philadelphia belle, Ellie was expected to marry and marry well. And her father, though he'd never said so, had one man in mind and one only.

Daniel Cameron.

The movement in the garden below caught Ansel's eye. Ellie made a slight shadow in her ivory shawl, the lace embellishments shining beneath the light of moon and lantern. His heart twisted. She'd come home unaware of what New Hope had become in her absence. A haven. A refuge. Well deserving of its name. He wanted to tell her, but he didn't want her touched by the depravity of it all. Let her wander in the moonlight like the innocent girl she was. He wouldn't be the one to disturb her.

He'd stood in the shadowed cupola a good half hour before minding the light, adjusting to the fading of day, alert to every shadow, praying for the harried souls waiting to cross the river. Tonight he could barely see the far shore. A ghostly outline in the mist, it bore a great many bushes and trees. He and his father had secured boats there—small crafts hidden in the tangle of growth—to help them cross. To a new life. To freedom. Some never survived the journey. That was what haunted him night after night as he wondered how many would come. If they would make it.

Bowing his head, he breathed a desperate prayer. Lately he was becoming more conscious of the danger. His hands seemed to shake when they touched the wick and turned it blazing, mayhap due to a tremor of inadequacy as he thought of his father. Da never trembled, never looked back. Jaw set, Silas Ballantyne lit the lamp and looked out across the wide river, resolute.

Would that he could be his father.

With a gentle pull of the reins, Ellie turned toward Cameron Farm, thinking how the tall stone chimneys set against the clear blue sky were like bookends framing the unassuming stone house. Her mare, Dolly, loped along and shook its mane as if gleeful of their destination. Both she and the horse could find their way blindfolded. Oddly, the land looked as pristine as when she'd last seen it. Not a leaf seemed disturbed, nary a fencerow down. Some benevolent hand had spared the Cameron clan all damage. If only the same could be said of New Hope!

The freshly painted door—a bright, berry-red—invited her to raise the brass knocker straightaway once she arrived. Still, trepidation ticked inside her as she thought it might well be Daniel who'd appear. But it was Mina who burst through the front door as soon as she'd dismounted, arms open wide.

"'Tis you, Ellie? Oh, I scarcely believe it! Your mother said you'd not be home till midsummer." Embracing her, Mina led her into the cool recesses of the hall. "Tell me why you've come."

Smiling, Ellie removed her bonnet and followed her into a small parlor. "There simply wasn't any need for me to stay in Philadelphia. I've decided to tutor the girls of local families, advertise my services in Pittsburgh instead."

Surprise played across Mina's fair features, and she pushed at a stray curl sneaking from her cap. "'Tis admirable, though I wonder why you don't just help your mother with the new orphan home or one of the charities."

"That's Mama's doing. I need to make my own way. Besides, the only day school for young ladies closed over a year ago. Why not bring a little Philadelphia polish to the West? Families would no longer have to send their daughters east."

"Sound reasoning, but do you think anyone would accept?" Her brow furrowed in a way reminiscent of her late mother. "People are recovering from the last financial panic. So many lost their businesses and homes and are in dire circumstances still."

"I'll charge very little. It would be more of a service—a ministry." She almost flinched at the word, thinking how sanctimonious it sounded. The bitter truth was best. "The sooner I find my place, the better. I'm going into town this very afternoon to post an advertisement and was hoping you'd join me. I'm afraid Andra has little need of me at home."

"Ah, Andra." Mina gave a sympathetic nod then brightened. "Of course I'll go, if you're quite determined. There's a new confectionery on Market Street just down from the *Pittsburgh Gazette*. Need I say more?"

Ellie laughed. "You *are* looking noticeably more rounded. Hardly the broomstick I remember."

"I daresay you notice more than that brother of yours." She sighed at the mention of Ansel, brown eyes assessing. "Speaking of waistlines, you're thinner than when I last saw you. Have you been ill?"

"I'm afraid Philadelphia didn't agree with me."

"You're not nursing a broken heart, I hope."

"Hardly that. Just fleeing the Matrimonial Society."

"I've never heard of such." Mina looked almost envious. "Why would you flee that sort of thing?"

"You'd have fled too, if you'd been subject to their assemblies." Ellie took a chair, setting her bonnet in her lap. "The girls at Madame Moreau's were required to attend monthly or else. A bulletin of sorts was sent out to eligible gentleman and the finer Philadelphia families detailing which females would attend and the state of their fortunes. All in the name of matrimony."

"Oh, fortune hunting! It sounds . . . splendid." Mina gave a wicked wink. "Would that we had such a society here! Why don't you scrap your plans for a day school and found the Pittsburgh Matrimonial Society instead?"

Ellie's smile faded. Obviously Mina was no nearer a betrothal than when she'd last seen her. At five and twenty, her friend was on the verge of spinsterhood and wanted to be wed with all her heart. She ventured carefully, "You . . . and Ansel . . . are you not . . . ?"

Mina gave a shrug. "I don't know what we are, Ellie. Friends? A bit more at times? I'm never sure. Ansel keeps so busy and . . . well, with Mama gone, I have so many things to manage here." She started for the door. "You must be in need of a little refreshment. Then we can go to town."

The tea tray was brought out—a charming assortment of mismatched cups and saucers, some prized silver spoons, and a Wedgwood pot from England. They filled an hour talking of everything their frequent letters hadn't touched upon, delicately skirting the issue of Ansel, though Ellie sensed it was all Mina thought of.

Noting the time, Mina reached for the empty teacups, but Ellie intervened. "I'll return these to the kitchen and meet you at the stables when you're ready."

Picking up the tray, Ellie moved toward the hall. Sadly, Cameron Farm was not the same without its mistress. Though she'd succumbed to consumption two years prior, Anna Cameron's presence still lingered in the colorful samplers of Scripture adorning the walls. She'd hoped to see her only son enter the ministry, but Daniel had other ambitions. Ellie thought of it now as she washed the cups in the stone sink.

Beyond the window, a quaint wooden gate was ajar. The housekeeper was likely in the garden, for she was the cook too. Though the Camerons were prosperous farmers, they hadn't the means to afford more than this. The bulk of their hired help were men who worked the land alongside Mina and Daniel's father, Cullen. But someday, her father had said more than once, that would all change. Young men like Daniel Cameron would leave a lasting legacy.

"Daniel is away touring factories in the East now that his apprenticeship has ended," Mina had said over tea. "He's working on another of his inventions, this one involving pressed glass. He's due home in July."

July was but three months away. Pondering it, Ellie went out the back door, traversing a stone path that circled a pond, a large timbered barn in back of it. The doors were open wide, and she felt a tickle of apprehension as she stepped inside, half expecting Daniel to materialize before her very eyes.

Today the sun slanting through weathered cracks swirled with dust motes, and the empty structure sighed in the wind. Ellie wasn't sure if she was more relieved or disappointed. Her rare meetings with Daniel always left her upended. Perhaps it was the unspoken expectations placed upon them, the uncertainty of whatever was in store.

Hearing Mina's distant call, she pushed aside her musings, anxious that her advertisement be printed in the very next copy of the *Pittsburgh Gazette*.

Hours later, feeling like she needed to tiptoe, Ellie entered the newly refurbished anteroom adjoining Andra's bedchamber. The lovely French wallpaper, a dusky rose and silver, had been rehung in one corner, the crown molding repaired. Elegant and bursting with new furnishings, it seemed to state Andra had no intention of moving or marrying, ever.

Ellie moved over the rich floral rug toward the far windows, eyes drawn to the sheep pasture beyond. She'd come to confess she'd just placed her advertisement in the *Pittsburgh Gazette* but nearly forgot her mission when greeted by the clutter atop her sister's normally neat desk. Papers were scattered across the tambour top, several sheets crowded with lines and a great many names. A dim memory kindled. Andra's passion was genealogy. Had she taken it upon herself to keep the family records?

"Elinor! What are you doing?"

Ellie spun round, feeling like a little girl caught snitching something. "I thought you might be here and just didn't hear my knock."

"I was below with the maids." Depositing her leather basket on a windowsill, Andra shook her head in consternation. "Sometimes I don't know if I'll ever get those girls trained. They seem far more inclined toward the stable hands than they do the dust in the parlor."

"They're very young—and very pretty."

"I think I'll make sure the next ones are plain as grain sacks." Sighing, she pulled out her desk chair, gesturing for Ellie to sit opposite. "I'm glad you've come. I've something to discuss with you."

Dismay sat squarely in Ellie's stomach. Did Andra know of her plans? Or have something that would upend what she now had in place? The advertisement had already gone to print.

"I'm at a standstill with my research." Andra's attention returned to the family tree she was constructing, her flowing script missing in several noticeable areas on the genealogical papers. "I wanted to see if Mama might have revealed anything to you over the years that might help with the family record."

Relieved, Ellie leaned back in her chair. "Mama rarely speaks of the past."

"Precisely. Which is why I need for you to rack your memory." She surveyed her work, a disgruntled look on her face. "Da's Scottish roots are more easily traced, but the Lees' . . ."

"I know Mama has a sister named Elspeth and a brother named Thomas."

Nodding, Andra identified their names on the papers. "There was another brother—a baby—who died. I'm in dire need of his name, his dates of birth and death."

"She's never spoken of such to me."

"Mama only mentioned the babe once to me. Strangely, there's no baptismal record in York County—or certificate of death." She sat back, clearly perplexed. "I've been thinking of writing to York for answers. 'Tis been so long since we've had a letter from Grandmother Lee. She wasn't well, you know, last time Mama wrote her. I don't know that we ever received a reply."

"Mama has always sent packages to her—dry goods and comfits from the mercantile."

"But Mama never goes to York herself. Don't you find that strange?"

Did she? Ellie lapsed into silence. She'd never given it much thought. Their father was as closemouthed about the Lees as Mama. "'Tis quite a journey to York, almost as far as Philadelphia." She glanced again at the paperwork. "Did you ever find out about Da's brothers?"

"I confirmed their names from the manifest of the ship they sailed on from Scotland to Philadelphia before the Revolution."

"And Da's sister? The one who died in childbirth?"

"Naomi Ballantyne? I know little but her name, though I remember Da saying you look just like her." Andra studied her as if trying to imagine the resemblance. "I hate to ask him anything else, as he turns so silent and melancholy when she's mentioned . . . which only increases my curiosity."

Ellie held back a sigh. "Perhaps all this genealogy is not a good thing."

"What? Unearthing family secrets and skeletons and the like?" Andra's expression turned impish. "'Tis just my cup of tea."

"Meddling, you mean."

"Genealogy isn't meddling!" Andra began straightening the papers. "More like preserving. 'Tis important to preserve the past for future generations."

"Generations?" Ellie sent up a silent prayer on Ansel and Mina's behalf. "There may not be any, given the fact none of us are as much as betrothed."

Andra chuckled, green eyes smug. "Well, we plan to remedy that now that you're home, little sister."

All thoughts of the day school vanished. The "we" she spoke of was definitely a worry. Ellie said quietly, "I've no more intention of marrying than you do."

"Well, I wonder what Daniel Cameron will have to say about that."

"Very little, given he's in the East."

"And due home by your birthday, or so Mina tells me."

"He only wrote one letter to me while I was at finishing school," Ellie admitted, reluctant to say she'd thrown it away. "Once in four years. That hardly qualifies as a romance."

"Daniel is quite busy—too busy for penning poetry to a sweetheart. He's nearing a patent, Da says, and wants a position at the glassworks. And more."

And more? Feeling hemmed in, Ellie groped for a decidedly safer subject, that of deceased relatives. "Tell me about Da's brothers."

But her mind remained on Daniel.

5

Death at one door, and heirship at the other.

SCOTTISH PROVERB

By candlelight, Jack stood at the study's open window and looked past open fields and fencerows toward New Hope. From Broad Oak, New Hope's cupola could be seen beyond a distant thicket of trees like the spire of some towering cathedral, a hazy, golden orb in the darkness. Welcoming. Beckoning. Reminding him of Ellie Ballantyne. But here at River Hill, miles distant, he could only imagine the sight. Contemplating it, he felt restlessness steal over him and made his way back to his desk. But before his backside connected with the leather chair, the abrupt snap of a pistol pulled him to his feet.

Wade.

The long, tree-lined drive was peppered with gunfire, a ruckus usually reserved for the shadowed alleys of Pittsburgh. Brother Wade was inebriated—in the words of their whiskey-abhorring mother—or riled. Or both. Here there was no Allegheny County sheriff to rein him in, just two alarmed faces poking out of the sole occupied cottage on River Row—those of Solomon and Ben. Jack felt a blistering irritation. Lately Wade didn't seem to know if he was afoot or on horseback.

Jack stepped onto the veranda, where the evening shadows encroached and fireflies swirled thickly in the sticky air. He felt a strange heaviness at his brother's approach, so at odds with his usual expectation. True to form, Wade rode his black stallion past the aromatic tangle of lilac bushes and up the muddy steps right onto the veranda. The huge horse huffed at Jack as Wade waved a pistol in the air, a smirk on his scarred face.

Though Wade was the eldest by two years, Jack was the largest. With a long, hard arm he grabbed Wade by the back of his coat and dangled him like a puppet before wresting the pistol away from him. It fired again, lodging in an ornate column, and Jack nearly swore. He searched for a bullet bag and returned the gun. "Someday you're going to hit more than the house and find yourself a permanent place in jail. Or the cemetery."

Wade snorted and jerked away, smoothing his finely tailored coat. "I didn't ride ten miles to hear some straitlaced lecture."

"State your case then." Jack slapped the horse's flank and sent it off the porch.

Two hard, blue-gray eyes took him in. Normally his brother's best feature, they were marred by a nose broken in too many brawls and tonight were a telling red. "I'm riding to town to post a handbill about the runaways. Thought I might stop at Teague's Tavern before I'm through and see Delia."

"The road is a shambles. You might not get there."

Wade shrugged and slanted a hand through unruly chestnut hair. "There's a full moon and I have little choice. Pa wants more bounty hunters." The last words slurred slightly, and Wade leaned into the nicked column. "Usually you're saddled at the mere mention of Teague's. You and Janey have a fight?"

Jack ignored the question. "Why more bounty hunters?"

"Two more slaves ran away this afternoon—Adam and Ulie."

Only two? It didn't surprise him. Broad Oak's overseer, James Marcum, was as hard a man as he'd ever met, even harder than the overseer they'd been used to at the Turlock plantation in Kentucky.

Wade ambled on. "You know Marcum, can't stay away from the still when the day's done. He got into it with Adam again over Ulie. He's long been smitten with her—"

"Ulie belongs to Adam."

Scowling, Wade shot down the notion. "Ulie belongs to Broad Oak, and Marcum thinks he has every right—"

"Get to the point."

"There was a bit of a fight . . ." At Jack's scrutiny, he averted his eyes. "Things got ugly. Marcum pounded a block of wood into Adam's mouth in a drunken rage."

"*What?*"

"All that matters is that they're gone and Pa's grieving the loss of his property. He wants you with me when I ride into Pittsburgh and talk to the McTavishes."

"All right, I'll go," Jack said, turning toward the stables and weighing this latest complication.

The two-mile ride to town was something of an adventure, complicated by skirting downed logs and mud sloughs by the light of a brilliant moon. Wade drew a plug of tobacco from his pocket and tucked it in one cheek, casting a wary glance at the wall of woods on both sides of them. "I never liked riding this road at night. Too many thugs and the like."

"Aye, us," Jack replied wryly.

Wade let out a cackle, his features less taut as the lights of Pittsburgh came into view. "What's first, business or pleasure?"

"Since you smell like a barrel of rye already, I say business."

Grumbling, Wade reined his horse toward Water Street. "Chloe begged to come."

"Chloe?"

"She's bored, missing Ben. All through supper she lamented him being at River Hill till Pa put her in her place." Wade was rambling now, his tongue too loose. "Should have been a boy, our Chloe. Strangest little sister I ever saw. There are times when Delia and Janey show more feminine graces." His horse veered again toward the waterfront, to the glittering hulk of Teague's Tavern.

Reaching out, Jack gave a rough tug to the stallion's bridle. "The bounty office is this way."

Spitting a stream of tobacco juice into the street, Wade said merrily, "Just gauging how sober you are, little brother."

"Stone cold," Jack answered.

Truly, tonight he couldn't slip into his usual *joie de vivre*, as a great many things clawed at his conscience. Wade was looking at him, his expression such a study of bewilderment in the moonlight that Jack's own perplexity deepened. He couldn't tell him about his near accident in the woods. He had no words for how he'd felt since it happened—the chill of memory, the inexplicable sense of warning, his inability to shake free of its grip. Wade would likely laugh—or punch him.

The bounty office was before them, a sole light burning in one grimy window. Though Jack despised the place and the abrupt barking of bloodhounds raked his already fractured nerves, he slid off Cicero's back and tied him to the hitch rail with a terse "Let's get this disagreeable business over with."

Though the shingle out front said TANNERS, the McTavish brothers engaged in a host of nefarious activities, one of which was tracking fugitives fleeing Kentucky and other slave states. Jack leaned against a wall, letting Wade take the lead in providing details about the runaways—height, weight, brands, and other defining marks.

Although slavery had ceased being legal according to state law and legislation had been enacted for its gradual abolition, its grip on Pennsylvania lingered. More than a few Allegheny County residents owned slaves, the Turlocks being the largest holders with fifty-six. Forty-nine, Jack mused silently as a few coins and bills crossed the counter. The remainder of the bounty would be paid upon the runaways' return.

"What's the matter, Jack?" Clive McTavish pocketed the money and squinted Jack's way. "Rather be at the tavern?"

"River Hill," Jack answered, pulling open the door in a bid for fresh air. Stepping outside, he stood by Cicero beneath the light of a whale oil lamp and felt the stallion's warm breath as he nosed Jack's arm.

Just across the mud-mired alley was Ballantyne Boat-works, its long, storm-damaged levee snaking alongside the Monongahela and crowded with vessels. A month before, he'd watched from afar as the *Elinor*, a Ballantyne-built steamer, departed for New Orleans in a haze of rain. It was every bit as fetching as its namesake, with three graceful tiers, the newly painted hurricane deck open to the heavens, and the jack staff flying the black-and-white checkered flag denoting the Ballantyne line.

The *Andra* and *Eden* lay at anchor and weren't half as fair, being older. Jack's longing to have been at the *Elinor*'s christening still lingered. There'd been quite a celebration—a throng of well-wishers, colored streamers, a small band. If his grandfather was still alive, Jack liked to think Hugh O'Hara would have been foremost among the crowd.

Once, when Pittsburgh was more of a frontier village, the judge and Silas Ballantyne had been business partners and friends. Before Jack's mother had sullied the connection and then severed it altogether. The closest Jack had ever gotten to Silas was in jail. Color crept into his bewhiskered cheeks—he could feel its heat—as he tried to put down his unsavory past.

"Jack—you there?" Wade was at his back, done with the McTavishes. "It's not yet midnight. What do you say to a quick game of draughts? If the tavern's still standing."

Too tired to argue, Jack simply nodded, sure he'd leave Teague's alone. Wade spent almost as many nights in town as he did at Broad Oak.

Untying Cicero, he swung up into the saddle, trying to summon some enthusiasm. But tonight he simply felt empty. Drained. Soulless. The memory along the turnpike was too fresh.

At the soft clatter of a tray sliding onto his desk, Jack came awake. Sunk into his leather chair, boots splayed outward, arms crossed, he mumbled his thanks as Mrs. Malarkey slipped away. Quiet as a mouse—he didn't think she'd said a dozen words to him since he'd inherited River Hill—she was getting so gout-ridden she could barely cook and clean.

Pulling the tray nearer, he surveyed the offering with surprise. Toast, a trio of eggs, grits aswirl with butter, and fried apples adorned the immense china plate, all indicative of her Southern roots. First he sipped the steaming coffee, black and bitter—just the remedy for spending the night in his study.

Half a dozen candles were guttered in wax-hardened holders around him, no longer illuminating thick ledgers detailing Turlock whiskey accounts. He couldn't understand why desk work tired him more than field work—how he could till over an acre a day with a moldboard plow and a team of oxen, stopping only to scrape the heavy earth free of the metal plowshare with a paddle staff—and yet a few hours of paperwork laid him low. Out-of-doors he felt alive, even as sweat plastered his shirt to his skin and mud climbed to the tops of his boots.

As he ate, he eyed the latest copy of the *Pittsburgh Gazette* at the edge of the tray, the headlines a bold tapestry of black.

Storm takes down new Allegheny bridge.
Damage to livestock and buildings incalculable.
River traffic slows.

He leaned back in his chair, his gaze drifting past the glass-fronted bookcases to a near window. The slant of the sun as it filtered past heavy drapes foretold eight o'clock. He needed to speak with his farm manager about the new variety of rye they'd planted. See how Ben was faring with Solomon at the stables. Check the notices of auction for farm implements.

He turned the paper over, his attention snagging on an elaborately fonted advertisement. A day school was opening for young ladies.

And the teacher was . . . *Ellie*?

Surprise skittered through him. A Ballantyne for hire? Though the clan was known for their benevolent bent, this seemed sort of odd. Or maybe right on target. A smile tugged at his mouth as he recalled Ellie tossing the Matrimonial Society paper out the coach window. Obviously she was as opposed to marriage as the headstrong, imperious Andra— and was opening for business instead. He wished her well. She was certainly qualified. Four years of finishing school had undoubtedly left their mark. Pittsburgh was in need of a lady's academy. The academy for men had opened its doors in 1794, and though Jack had wanted to enroll, his father forbade it, calling it a foppish retreat.

Leaving the paper on his desk, Jack started for the door,

practically colliding with Chloe as she charged in, the tip of her parasol poking a small hole in his chest. "Are you here to see Ben?" he asked, angling the point away from him.

"No, you!"

He took her in from head to toe in one dismayed glance, from the too-short hem of her dress to her mismatched shoes and stockings and ridiculous hat. Shutting the door, he gestured to a chair, finally wresting the parasol away from her after calling it a public nuisance.

Agitated, she slumped in her seat, the silk violets atop her bonnet trembling.

"How did you get here?" Jack asked warily. She'd never come so early, nor been so riled.

"I rode Shadow."

Not sidesaddle, Jack knew. The mare was likely in a lather. Chloe smelled like horses, had hay in her hair. Who had suggested that ridiculous dress?

"Ma called me into Pa's study this morning. She wants Silas Ballantyne's daughter to take me on as her pupil."

"Take me on" was certainly the right wording. From the rigid set of Chloe's features, she wanted nothing to do with it. A knot of alarm tightened in Jack's gut. He ran a hand across his whiskered jaw and groped for a sensible solution.

"Nay," he said.

"She's posted an advertisement about some blasted day school—"

"Nay," Jack said more emphatically.

Tears glinted in his sister's eyes, blunting her anger, and Jack saw beneath the surface to the heart of the issue. Chloe knew she was a failure at femininity, that she, of all Allegheny County girls, was in need of some polish. But he suspected their mother had ulterior motives, and this was what worried Jack most. Likely she wanted to enroll Chloe in this so-called day school only to declare it a failure, withdraw her daughter in a public display, and cast reproach on the Ballantyne name.

Jack was no seer, but their mother's bitterness had led her to seek countless confrontations with the Ballantynes over the years, one of the reasons the Turlocks were never invited to New Hope. Chloe was obviously the latest pawn in a humiliating game.

"Elinor Ballantyne is nothing but a bluestocking!" Chloe tore off her hat and flung it onto the floor, looking like she might trample it. "Next we know she'll be heading up the local temperance society we keep hearing about."

Though he wanted to chuckle, Jack had no wish to pursue the matter. He walked across a frayed rug to a tall chest and withdrew a cedar fishing pole. He could feel Chloe's mood lighten with his every step. She shadowed him, near reverence in her tone.

"Was it Grandpa O'Hara's?"

"Aye." Jack felt a twist of sentiment saying so. "Tell Ben he can spend the morning fishing if he tends to the horses this afternoon. I promised him a trip but haven't had the time."

Her lip quavered again. "What about Ma and the day school?"

"I'll handle that," he said, ruing the interruption. He was expecting a bottler from Pittsburgh. A large order of seed from the East. His confrontation at Broad Oak would have to wait. "I'll ride over and see Ma at suppertime and settle matters then."

She smiled and looked like she wanted to throw her arms around him in gratitude, but the fishing rod was between them, crowned with a particularly menacing hook.

"Try not to drown yourself—or Ben," he cautioned as she made her way out the study door.

"I can outswim you nearly!" she replied, admiring the hook, her fury forgotten.

He forced a grin, though he wasn't lighthearted. Chloe's mishaps were well known. Not long ago she'd gotten stuck in a corn crib, emerging so mouse bitten it seemed she had the measles. Another time she'd sampled a bottle of horse tonic found in the stables and became gravely ill. A dozen other calamities flashed to mind, but he simply watched as she ran past the lilacs toward the stables, bellowing for Ben like a wharf-hardened river man.

"God help her," he breathed.

It sounded remarkably like a prayer.

6

I do perceive here a divided duty.
WILLIAM SHAKESPEARE

Ellie sensed Andra's displeasure in her furious footfalls as she traversed staircase to foyer to music room. Letting go of the harp strings, Ellie's hands dropped to her lap and the ethereal music faded. She removed her foot from the harp's pedal and tried to smile as the door she'd left ajar swung wide open with the force of a strong wind. Andra swept in—there was no other way for Andra to enter—linen skirts swirling, every line of her taut with tension. She clutched a paper—*the* paper—bearing Ellie's advertisement.

"Elinor!" Sinking down atop the ottoman opposite, she shook the *Gazette* in agitation. "Peyton laughed, Ansel applauded. But I'm outraged! First you return home un-announced, without your maid and a Turlock in tow, and now . . ." She paused for breath, voice trilling higher. "*Now* you advertise your services like a common tradesman. I can only hope no one responds to your ridiculous offer should they have the misfortune of reading it!"

Biting her lip to still a hasty reply, Ellie was drawn to the figure in the doorway. For a moment she thought it was her father, as the tall, lithe outline was so familiar, but Peyton had a swagger Da lacked. His deep voice resounded across the room, stemming Andra's tirade. "Bravo! A masterful performance. I've been thinking you should audition for the new theatrical company in town, and now I'm convinced."

"Shush!" Andra stood, fisting the paper. "What will Da say when he returns and finds his beloved youngest daughter employed—"

"I ken he'll admire her enterprising spirit. You seem to forget our humble beginnings. Poor Scots blacksmith and all that." Going to the pianoforte, he banged out a few discordant keys. "Have you any replies to your post, little sister?"

"Only two." Ellie forged ahead. "The Dennys and Wrenshalls have enrolled their daughters, and I'm meeting with the Negleys tomorrow. I hope to hold lessons in the girls' homes two afternoons a week and then meet for a dancing lesson here. The parents seem particularly eager for their daughters to learn the latest steps."

He nodded. "Who will play for you? Provide the music?"

"Ansel volunteered, though at the moment he's far too busy. I'm hoping for more students, enough for partners, at least. Mina said she'll help."

"Mina?" The censure in Andra's tone said she was none too happy with that either. "You shouldn't involve so many in your scheme. We'll simply be fodder for gossip." She wadded up the paper and deposited it in the cold hearth. "When do you begin?"

"Day after tomorrow." A stitch of nervousness threaded through Ellie's middle. "I've decided any earnings will go toward the orphan home."

"Well, at least Mama will be pleased." Andra's strident voice eased somewhat, though she still looked vexed.

"The more pupils I have, the busier I'll be," Ellie told her. Surely Andra could rejoice that she'd not be underfoot.

"You'll need a groom to take you into Pittsburgh and back," Peyton reminded her. "You remember how adamant Da is about that. A lady—particularly a teacher—should have an escort."

Ellie looked at him, surprised. "If you insist, though I rather like driving my own rig."

"It's no longer safe to travel alone. Highwaymen, ruffians, and the like." Peyton and Andra exchanged a glance. "Da would never forgive us if something happened to you. We'd not forgive ourselves." Stealing a look into a near mirror, he started toward the door. "I've been away from the mercantile long enough. Thankfully, river traffic is returning to normal and the boatyard is busy again. Don't wait supper on me. I have business in town tonight."

The click of the door as it closed returned the music room to a strained hush. Andra was looking after him as if she wanted to call him back, worry crimping her brow and calling out a wrinkle. Sympathy—and second thoughts—tugged at Ellie. Her sister was preoccupied with a great many things yet would share the burden with no one. Ellie felt a tad guilty adding to it but held fast to her plan to teach. Now home for keeps, she needed to find her place, wherever that might be.

Of all the rooms at Broad Oak, the dining room was Jack's least favorite—the place of heated eruptions, stilted silences, and seemingly endless disputes. The dark wood paneling lent an oppressive air, the heavy drapes were always closed, and the immense table seemed to reinforce the distance between them. Jack's father occupied one end while his mother favored the other, a good six seats down. Wade and Jack usually sat on opposite sides while Chloe preferred eating with Sally in the kitchen.

Tonight Wade was missing, still at their offices in town or spending another night at Teague's, and so Jack sat discussing runaways in the glow of candlelight when all he wanted was to settle the matter of Chloe and the Ballantynes once and for all. He was acutely aware of how much wine his father had drunk and the way his mother glared at the help as they entered and exited on nervous feet through the side door to the kitchen.

As usual, Sally's cooking was faultless. Her blancmange was his reward for the prolonged silences between courses, though he much preferred meals at River Hill, where a simple tray brought to the library sufficed. By the time coffee was served, Jack had managed to steer the conversation away from the subject of escaped slaves back to business.

"So, Jack, are you prepared for a fall trip downriver to St. Louis?"

Jack paused, caught off guard. "I thought you wanted me to go east."

"Nay, I've just signed a contract with the Missouri Fur Company. Eight hundred gallons of whiskey need to be delivered to one of its posts before the rivers freeze, and I'm in need of an escort."

"Isn't there a ban on importing spirits in Indian country?"

"A mere formality. Most of the Indian agents are opposed to any restrictions on the whiskey trade—and the few who would enforce it are powerless to do so. Boatmen and fur traders are still allowed to bring in personal supplies in as great a quantity as they like." Henry took a drink of Madeira and motioned a servant to bring him a cigar. "In fact, I'm considering transporting the necessary equipment up the Missouri River and building a distillery there. We won't import whiskey. We'll circumvent the ban by making it on-site."

Jack schooled his surprise. "In hostile territory?"

His father smiled a tight smile. "Not so hostile once the barrels are rolled out. I've heard prairie dirt is capable of producing forty bushels of wheat or a hundred of corn to the acre." With a shrug he lit his cigar. "We've nothing to lose."

Nothing but our scalps, Jack thought. He'd read the reports in the papers—of Indian unrest and the halfhearted attempts to regulate trade in the newly christened state of Missouri. Chaos reigned. It was one thing to transport— ship—whiskey illegally. They'd been doing it for years. Making it on the premises was another matter altogether.

"You're not opposed to going west, I trust?" Henry posed the question and drew hard on his cigar.

"I'd planned on going east."

His father's level gaze took him in, hard and glossy as frosted glass. "The West calls for a cool head and a steady hand. Wade will handle established accounts in the East."

A snort from the far end of the table drew their attention. "I don't know how you expect to manage that. Captain Ames nearly refused to let Wade board our very sloop in Philadelphia last fall." Isabel's voice was low and annoyed as she toyed with her dessert. "I have a feeling it was more his paramour in every port than his imbibing that dismayed the captain."

"The captain is in our employ, remember. He'll do as I tell him, inebriated son or no. I'd let Wade go by land, but he seems to find worse trouble there. Besides, no sense traveling all that way by coach or horseback when you can sail along the coast from port to port in half the time. The sloop is currently in Martinique but should dock in Philadelphia in late July. Captain Ames requested you come, Jack, but I think you're needed elsewhere."

Isabel sighed and motioned for coffee. "We can expect better from Jack. And he'll not risk any accounts either."

"That's precisely why the West is Jack's territory. Missouri—and beyond—has become far more important than eastern accounts. The West is, simply put, our future." Pushing aside his empty plate, Henry Turlock eyed the candelabra at the table's center. The flickering light called out the deep grooves in his weathered face, which had always reminded Jack of furrows in a freshly plowed field. "You've not been to dinner here in some time, Son. I have a feeling you have something else to discuss."

Jack nodded. He never fooled his father for long. "My mind isn't on business but Chloe," he admitted, grieved by the sudden shuttering of his mother's fair features. "I heard there was some talk about enrolling her in a day school."

"Chloe's schooling? That's something I know little about." Henry rose abruptly. "I have a shareholders' meeting tonight at the Alexanders'."

His exit was prolonged, slowed by the rheumatism that plagued him, reminding Jack of the fifteen-year difference in his parents' ages. Isabel looked after him, her irritation fading to melancholy. "Another meeting. This happens virtually every eve. I know these outings are nothing but a pretense for the valley men to gamble and make fools of themselves. Or worse."

Or worse. Henry's infidelities were no secret. They seemed to grow more brazen over time. He'd even begun appearing in public with his latest paramour.

Jack fixed his gaze on the candle flame and said quietly, "We need to talk about Chloe . . . why you want her to go to New Hope."

She stiffened visibly, jet earrings trembling. "At the moment your sister is the farthest thing from my mind."

As usual, Jack didn't say. He leaned forward, couching his words carefully. "I propose a different plan. For the summer, anyway. Let Chloe come live at River Hill."

"River Hill? Why? I'd rather take advantage of the Ballantyne girl's services and have her tutor Chloe here." She met Jack's eyes with her usual resistance, and he detected a slur in the word *girl*.

"Since the French governess you hired didn't last a fortnight," he said, "I doubt any other arrangement would be much different."

"That was more your brother's doing than Chloe's," she countered, confirming Jack's suspicions of Wade's unwanted attentions. "As for the Ballantyne girl, surely four years at the finest female academy in Pennsylvania amounts to something."

"This has more to do with Chloe's unwillingness than Elinor Ballantyne's capabilities," Jack told her. "Personally, I think such a pairing would be a disaster."

"And so you want your sister underfoot at River Hill?" Her tone assured him she expected another defeat there as well. "You know I've had little time for a daughter. She was born so late—an afterthought." Jack tensed, ready to correct her if she used the word *mistake* as she sometimes did. "And then when I tried to make something of her, I realized I was trying to make a sow's ear into a silk purse. We can lay the blame at your father's door. If she's willful and unladylike, it's because he treated her like a third son and never corrected her—"

"I'll keep her with me." Jack's calm overrode her complaining. "She can visit Broad Oak as often as she likes. Or you can come to River Hill."

"Would that I had never left it." The words were a mere whisper, but Jack had heard them before. She looked at him, eyes still clouded with doubt. "How on earth will you keep her occupied?"

"I'll begin by opening the judge's library to her. Some required reading should be in order. And since she seems to have a head for figures, I'll introduce her to accounts—"

"All masculine pursuits, which is why I want Elinor Ballantyne. She's advertised needlework, French, dancing."

Ignoring this, Jack took a sip of coffee. "I'll have my housekeeper take Chloe to a seamstress, see about a new wardrobe. Maybe arrange for a trip downriver."

"To Louisville? New Orleans?" Isabel all but rolled her eyes. "Now that sounds disastrous. I can just see her falling overboard—or worse. You're of a sensible bent, Jack. Don't do this." Yet even as she uttered the words, he saw through her exasperation to the relief beneath.

He shrugged. "And if I fail? It won't be for lack of trying."

She expelled a frustrated breath. "Perhaps it will be of some benefit. With the slave unrest and the storm and whatnot, we're all in need of a change."

"Perhaps you and Pa should take a trip, then. See to accounts farther south and combine business with pleasure." Pausing, he gauged her reaction. "The new steamer, *Naomi*, is set to launch in July."

"If you're suggesting I take a Ballantyne-made vessel, I'd sooner walk on water." Coldness crept into her fair features, deepening the lines and years, making her look as old as Henry. "Besides, steamboats are fraught with danger. A boiler is always exploding, crew and passengers killed. Europe is far more to my liking. There's some interest in Turlock whiskey on the continent, your father says."

"We can't compete with the Scots and Irish distillers, at least in Europe," he murmured. "We'd best set our sights on the American West."

When she frowned, he let the matter rest, wanting to return home to River Hill and tell Chloe the news. Excusing himself, he started for the door, aware his mother would be left alone just as she had so many nights. The thought was sharp as a knife's blade, the knob of the door cold beneath his hand.

He turned back to her. "You're welcome to come to River Hill whenever you like and see Chloe. It was yours before mine, and I've not forgotten."

7

Unbidden guests are often welcomest
when they are gone.

WILLIAM SHAKESPEARE

Would the spring hold nothing but storms? From her open
carriage, Ellie eyed the unsettled sky as dark thunderheads
shut out the sun altogether. She hoped the weather was better
in New Orleans. Her father was in need of a respite, absorbed
by business as he was, and sometimes Mama's charitable
spirit seemed careworn too. Still, she missed them and wished
them back. New Hope wasn't the same without them. Peyton
and Ansel were overwhelmed with work at the waterfront
and rarely came home, and Andra's temper seemed to fray
at the slightest provocation.

Though repairs were being made and dependencies restored, the incessant sawing and hammering shattered the
usual birdsong, encroaching on what had always been a peaceful place. Ellie knew better than to look out her bedchamber
windows onto the garden and chapel. The sound of falling
timber from its direction grieved her. The chapel had always

been the spot she'd gone to be quiet, to pray. Without it her prayers seemed small and scattered, without a home.

"Keep count of your blessings," Mama always said.

Mindful of this, Ellie ticked them off one by one. She was back in Allegheny County. Free of Philadelphia. Earning her keep. She now had four girls to instruct—and four sets of pleased parents—and had begun teaching this very afternoon. All her finishing school years were fading. Though she missed Rose dearly, the future seemed bright.

With a squeal of wheels, the carriage slowed to a stop, and the groom helped her down. Ellie stood for a moment atop the large mounting block, slick from moss and rain, and eyed the unfamiliar horse hitched to the iron post a few feet away. Her stomach swirled.

Daniel Cameron?

Impossible. Mina said he was in the East. As if sensing her disquiet, the handsome animal reared its proud head and snorted so loudly Ellie started. Chuckling, the groom regained his seat as Andra came onto the porch, her expression no more friendly than the glowering skies above. Ellie wanted to climb back inside the carriage, but it was lumbering away to the stable down a shaded side lane.

"Elinor, you have a . . ." Andra paused, her face florid. "A *caller*."

A maid usually announced visitors, not Andra. Ellie's alarm peaked. "Where is Mari? Gwyn?"

"Trying to keep our guest out of mischief. She's been here half an hour and can't seem to sit still. She's already let Feathers out of his cage!"

"*She?*" Ellie refused to go another step till the visitor's name was divulged.

"Chloe Turlock." The words were hissed as if announcing the devil himself.

Ellie felt her features go slack as she mentally raced to put together her tattered memories of the youngest Turlock. All she recalled was a pudding-faced lump of a girl, following after her older brothers with none of their natural graces and all of their flaws.

"In the parlor?" Ellie asked.

"Yes—with Feathers!" Andra ground out the canary's name between clenched teeth, as if demanding Ellie do something.

Following her into the foyer, Ellie removed her gloves and bonnet and set them on a nearby chair. "I'll try and rescue Feathers . . . and send Miss Chloe on her way."

Andra eyed the closed parlor door warily. "You'd do well to remember what Peyton always said. Never turn your back on a Turlock."

"I believe he was referring to Wade." Ellie swallowed, unwilling to say Jack's name. His kindness to her along the turnpike—if that was what it was—returned to her and raised her color a notch. She touched the parlor door with some trepidation, mindful Feathers might be winging about. Both Mari and Gwyn were standing guard just inside.

"You can go now," Ellie said, summoning a smile. The maids fled, leaving Ellie to spy Feathers atop a tall bookcase, preening and enjoying his newfound freedom.

"I—I'm sorry about the bird. I didn't mean to release him. I only wanted a closer look."

Ellie's gaze settled on a girl in the shadows—boyishly slim, brown as a chestnut, and clearly ill at ease. "Never mind Feathers. I only hope he performed for you after all the fuss."

Before her last syllable was uttered, the canary burst into song, and its sweetness seemed to banish all awkwardness. Chloe looked from Ellie to the bookcase as if she'd pulled a string and gotten the bird to do her bidding or concocted some sort of magic.

Ellie touched her sleeve. "Just raise your arm like this. He'd much rather perch than return to his cage."

"I've never seen such a cage."

Ellie smiled. "Too grand for a bird, you mean? My father made it. He was once a city smith—a blacksmith—and fashioned one like this for Benjamin Franklin in Philadelphia. You've heard of Franklin and his inventions, I suppose."

Chloe didn't answer, obviously far more interested in the canary now moving from its lofty roost than Philadelphia history. Her lips parted in surprise when Feathers flew to a nearby sofa and then landed on her extended arm.

"Meet Feathers," Ellie said. "Now if you'll be so kind to walk toward the cage, my sister will be forever grateful."

Chloe's expression soured. "Your sister tried to send me away."

"Yet you're still here," Ellie whispered with a wink. "So who won that battle?"

A conspiratorial smile played about Chloe's mouth. She inched across the carpet to the brass cage, where she imprisoned the canary once again and locked the small door.

Nearly singing with relief herself, Ellie smiled her brightest smile. "Would you like refreshments? Something to drink . . . eat?"

Shrugging, Chloe sat on the edge of the nearest chair as Ellie tugged a bell cord. When Mari appeared she requested gingersnaps and orange ice from Mamie in the kitchen.

Chloe's eyes were on her again, questioning, wary, unsure of her welcome.

Ellie took a seat on a near settee. "While we wait, why don't you tell me why you've come?"

Taking a breath, Chloe fiddled with a wrinkle on her skirt. "I . . . I saw your advertisement in the newspaper."

Had she? So Chloe Turlock was literate, at least . . .

"I'm in need of a teacher, Ma says, and it's true. I should be doing more than fishing and riding horses. I'll soon be thirteen—yet I can't sew a stitch or speak a word of French or dance a step."

The lament in her voice seemed sincere, yet Ellie still felt a niggle of doubt. She stayed silent, letting Chloe tell her what she would, trying not to stare at her disheveled dress—a sad affair of linen and ruffles in a style more suited for a three-year-old than one nearly thirteen.

"Ma wanted me to come and talk to you last week, but Jack intervened." Her silvered eyes held Ellie's, reminding her of his. "You remember my brother—the younger one? Not Wade."

There was an unmistakable grimace at Wade's mention. Ellie could only surmise that Jack was the favorite. "I remember them both."

"Jack told me not to ask you, but I keep wondering if you might teach me . . . make him change his mind."

For once Ellie was wordless. Jack's reasons for refusing intrigued her, in light of Isabel Turlock wanting her services. Yet one long look at Chloe convinced Ellie some intervention was overdue. Best proceed cautiously. She sensed a snare but couldn't discern just where.

The ices were brought in, mounded in crystal glasses, a sprig of fresh mint atop each. Chloe took up her spoon with relish, delight softening her solemn features. "I'm so thirsty I'm almost spewing feathers, as Wade says."

Hiding a smile, Ellie sampled the ice without really tasting it. "So you want me to talk to your brother Jack. What makes you think he'd change his mind?"

Chloe raised an eyebrow. "He likes your pa."

I can't imagine why, Ellie almost said. Jailed as many times as Jack had been when her father was temporary sheriff . . . "I could send a note round."

"That's the coward's way out, Jack says."

Chagrined, Ellie set down her spoon. She could imagine Jack Turlock feeling that way. He seemed more a man of action than letters. "Why does your brother have the final say in your education, Chloe? More so than your mother and father?"

"Because I'm living at River Hill."

At that, everything slid into place. Chloe was Jack's ward now? Why? Ellie had been in Philadelphia far too long to be privy to the latest happenings at Broad Oak, but she sensed all was not well. "All right, then. I'll ride over in the morning."

"Promise?" The blonde head lifted, and Chloe's eyes were awash with gratitude—and something else Ellie couldn't name. "I'll try to keep Jack to the house. Sometimes he's hard to pin down."

A telling statement, Ellie thought. In the meantime she'd tell no one of her mission—and try to summon some courage.

Standing before a full-length mirror, Ellie glanced at the small clock ticking the time across the room. Half past nine. She'd been trying on one garment after another for over an hour, dismissing each as too fancy, too plain, too snug, too childish. When meeting Jack Turlock, it was paramount she looked the part of teacher—even if he denied her request and sent her packing. Another quarter of an hour passed, and she wanted to send a note round instead. Why take such pains? Was it Chloe's solemn face that made her press on? Or something more?

She finally decided on a simple yellow day dress and blue paisley shawl, a bit dated but sufficient. She needn't worry about Jack Turlock being fussy about fashion. When she'd last seen him, he'd shunned proper attire for the most common breeches and boots. Still, she pinned her hair carefully into a looped knot high on the back of her head, securing it with a silk ribbon. It wasn't as fine as the coiffure Rose would have done, but it would suffice.

The plan was ridiculously simple. She'd arrive at River Hill—a place she'd heard about but never seen—and there Jack would deny her request, and she'd continue on to Pittsburgh. Since her lessons didn't begin till early afternoon, she'd visit the boatyard and see Ansel, perhaps hunt for a new hat at one of the shops along Market Street.

Too nervous to eat breakfast, she'd simply sipped a cup of tea, wrapped the biscuit Mamie had sent upstairs in a napkin, and deposited it in her reticule. Her driver showed no surprise at her destination, covering the miles to River Hill at a steady pace now that the roads were clear of debris. When their carriage passed through unfamiliar iron gates, Ellie's anxiety rose a notch, as did her curiosity.

River Hill was known to be old, elegant. A step into the past. Her parents had met again here after years apart, ending the eight-year association between Hugh O'Hara and Silas Ballantyne. The blacksmith turned industrialist had wanted to wed Eden Lee, and the jilted Isabel O'Hara had eloped with Henry Turlock, leader of the infamous Whiskey Rebellion, soon after. Sometimes entire fortunes—and futures—were made in mere minutes. She was thankful Providence had decided in her favor. Being a Ballantyne was far better than being a Turlock in anyone's estimation, surely.

The long drive unwound like gray ribbon through copses of lush trees and meadows brightened by wildflowers before cresting a magnificent hill. Her pulse climbed along with the lumbering coach. She was increasingly unsure of her mission, the careful speech she'd rehearsed in shreds. The sight of the main house, immense and aristocratic, snatched away her last shred of poise.

"I won't be long," she told her groom.

Just long enough to be refused . . . humiliated.

But she couldn't deny Chloe's unusual request. It had taken a great deal of courage to arrive at New Hope unannounced and manage Andra till Ellie had come in. The least Ellie could do was take the poor girl's plea to River Hill, lost cause though it was.

She stepped down onto uneven cobblestones, and for a moment the crush of lilacs stole her breath. Fragrant spires of thick blossoms—burgundy, blue, white, and creamy yellow—waved in the breeze in double clusters, releasing an intense perfume as they crowded the walkway and steps. The house was of the same gray brick as New Hope, the windows of old manufacture but the best crown glass. Ornate shutters, once a lively green, framed countless windows fronting the river. It had a faded grandeur that warmed Ellie's heart and gave her a bittersweet glimpse of a bygone era.

Had Mama come up these same steps and into the ball-room that ushered her into Da's life again? Wonder stole her concentration, and Ellie failed to notice the elderly woman in gingham and wrinkled apron at the door. So River Hill had a housekeeper?

"I'm here to see Mr. Turlock," Ellie said, half hoping he'd be away. Praying. Her palms were damp beneath her gloves. Her breath was coming in ragged bursts like she'd walked all the way.

"Is he expecting you?" The woman's mouth firmed with disapproval. She was taking Ellie's measure as if she were as forward as a fallen woman.

Heat bloomed in Ellie's face. It *was* pretentious to arrive unannounced—uninvited. A note should have come first. She took a step back, all resolve seeping away. "If Mr. Turlock's not available, I'll call at another time."

She turned toward the carriage and saw the groom jump down from his perch. But before she took a step, a quiet voice carried across the veranda.

"I'm here, Ellie. And there's no better time than this."

Jack.

No social niceties. No hello or greeting. Slowly Ellie turned around. The groom regained his perch. The housekeeper vanished. Ellie found herself wishing Chloe would appear. But it was just she and Jack. Alone. An arm's length apart. Nothing stirred on the veranda but the heady scent of lilacs in the wind.

He was looking down at her, making her feel even smaller and more awkward. She'd forgotten how intimidating he could be. His skin was darker than she remembered, his hair more sun-streaked. His gaze like granite.

"We could walk in the garden," he said.

She felt a burst of relief. Yes, out in the open, not shut away in the house, giving cause for scandal. She nodded and followed him down mossy stone steps, wondering if the housekeeper watched from a window. A crumbling brick wall enclosed the garden—or what was left of it.

"I'm sure it bears little resemblance to yours," he murmured.

She caught his low words as shade trees swallowed them and her eyes adjusted to the play of light and shadow. A dry fountain stood at the garden's heart, surrounded by barren flower beds begging for color and beauty. Buds clung to a few neglected rosebushes, decaying leaves scattered all around.

"Actually, it looks very much like ours," she said.

He glanced at her. "After the storm, you mean."

She nodded, wanting to take a seat on a near bench and still her unsteady legs, but he turned down a side path with a river view. The garden hadn't been tended for years, but one look at the expanse of shimmering water beyond the sloping lawn and it hardly mattered.

"Is Chloe here?" she asked, eyes on the fitful Monongahela, so different from the serene Allegheny she'd been raised beside.

"Fishing," he said.

Awkwardness crept over her and nearly closed her throat. Jack Turlock wasn't in a talkative mood. Best state her case and dispense with any pleasantries. "I'm here on Chloe's behalf. I'd like to school her."

His eyes were on her now, shining with amused, half-mocking light. "Her French governess only lasted a fortnight. What makes you think you'd fare better?"

Beneath his scrutiny she tried not to cower. "Chloe gave her consent yesterday when she came to New Hope. Surely that counts for something."

"She came to see you?" The words held the ring of surprise. Clearly, Jack wasn't privy to his sister's whereabouts at all times, even if she was his responsibility. "Are you lacking students, Ellie?"

"I have four pupils so far. Chloe would make a fifth." She read outright skepticism in his face and strove to counter it. "I instruct each girl individually in their homes. They also come to New Hope for a dancing lesson once a week."

He grimaced. "My sister . . . dancing."

She felt defensiveness take hold. "I watched her ride away yesterday. She's very graceful on a horse. If that's any indication . . ."

"Horses and waltzes are an odd pairing. I can't dance a step but I ride like the wind."

"Oh?" She couldn't check a smile. "Then perhaps you'd better come for lessons too."

His stony gaze shot down the notion. "I'm better suited for the stables."

"So is your answer aye or nay? For Chloe's sake?"

"Nay."

The strand of hope in her heart snapped. "Don't do this, Jack." She hadn't meant to say his name, or beg, but she had his full attention, at least. "I didn't thank you properly for bringing me home after the storm. Think of it as repayment—"

"So this is a charity case?"

Exasperation ticked inside her. "I do charge for my services—a small fee—"

"Expenses be hanged. Money isn't the issue, ever."

His boldness made her bold in turn. "Then what is?"

Impatience sharpened his features. "You'll likely end up with Chloe and lose all your other students, once they learn you're schooling a Turlock. I'm simply trying to save you the trouble—and spare her the hurt."

She'd not thought of this and had no ready answer. She wouldn't tell him her genteel pupils didn't need her or that their time together was pleasant—and decidedly dull. They stitched samplers and stifled yawns, conjugated French verbs and fluttered their fans inanely.

"I care little about what others think," she said softly, eyes on the sunlit path at her feet.

"Well, I do, for once." Turning his back on her, he began walking toward the house without a word of farewell, violating every single tenet of good behavior. But then Gentleman Jack was no gentleman. Though they'd known each other since childhood, how wide the chasm was . . .

She felt oddly hurt, and her discomfort doubled when Chloe appeared and blocked his path. Jack reached out to her, laid a hand on her shoulder. Though she couldn't hear him, she guessed he was explaining his refusal. The slump of Chloe's shoulders confirmed it. Sensing that staying any longer was futile, Ellie disappeared down a side path, skirting a brick wall, till she reached the porte cochere where her carriage waited.

"To town, please," she said without enthusiasm as the groom opened the door.

The clatter of wheels atop muddy stones sounded in her ears, and she looked back at the old house through an open window. Jack watched her go, a formidable shadow on the sun-dappled veranda, Chloe at his side. The vision of River Hill vanished from sight, if not from memory.

8

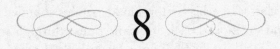

The high trill of a fiddle began a simple country dance, the girls stepping lightly and avoiding toes. Soon they were laughing more than dancing, the ballroom floor noticeably scuffed, and Mamie was bringing a tray of raspberry ice up two flights of steps to the third floor. The lesson had gone on long enough this May morn, Ellie decided, and her students needed to return home. With Andra hovering at the door intermittently—and Mina flirting with Ansel while he attempted his bowing—Ellie couldn't keep her mind on the lesson.

"You have a letter, delivered but an hour ago," Andra told her when the ballroom emptied.

"A post?" Her finishing school friends wrote her often enough. Likely it was one of them. Ellie pocketed the paper, wanting to read it in privacy, aware of her sister's probing eye.

"And there's also word from Mama." Andra sank down on a chair beside an open window and unfolded a letter. "Seems like they're having a lovely time in New Orleans."

90

She studied the familiar script. "She writes, 'The city is the same—humid, hurried, yet ever fascinating.'"

"We should have gone with them." Ansel swiped his brow with a handkerchief before putting his violin away.

"You and Peyton, perhaps," Andra said. "Da won't let Elinor or I set foot on a steamer. And I don't want to. They're too dangerous."

Ellie took a seat beside her. "They likely don't know about the storm, I suppose, being so far away."

"They may by now," Ansel replied. "News travels fast along the river. By the time they return, everything should be in order again, Lord willing."

"At least we can live vicariously through their letters." Andra returned them to the matter at hand.

> *New Orleans is quite unchanged. Its citizens spend the Sabbath drinking, dueling, partying, and presenting slave dances to African drums in the public squares. We cannot help but notice and pray for them on our way to church . . . Magnolias are abloom everywhere . . . Your father and I have become quite fond of the local fare, gumbo, a French dish made of meats and mingled with rice and seasoned with chopped sassafras and okra. Perhaps Mamie could make a fair rendition in the kitchen . . .*

They listened to the remainder in thoughtful silence, and Ellie felt a keen craving to have her parents home. "How long does it take for a steamer to travel upriver from there to here?" She was half ashamed she couldn't remember, having been away so long.

Ansel winked at her. "Two thousand miles? With Da at the wheel?" He shrugged. "Overnight."

They laughed and went down to an early supper, a quiet affair without Peyton present. Ellie pushed her chicken fricassee around her plate as Andra talked endlessly of repairs and what needed to be done on the morrow. The mysterious letter, momentarily forgotten, seemed to burn a hole in Ellie's pocket.

Excusing herself, she made it to the staircase landing, pausing long enough to examine the post. The sepia wax seal bore a bold *T*, but the hand that had penned her name was sprawling and uneven. Still, the words bore a surprising eloquence, if misspelled.

> *Miss Ballantyne, my brother Jack has given*
> *purmishin for you to tutor me at River Hill.*
> *Cum whatever afternoon you wish.*

> *Chloe Turlock*

Clearly, Miss Chloe was in need of a penmanship lesson or two. Why, she wondered, didn't Jack send a note instead? But she knew that required good manners. Something he didn't have nor was the least concerned about.

Climbing the remaining steps to her room, Ellie smiled. What had transpired in the week since she'd come to River Hill and he'd refused her?

Chloe's timing was perfect. Tomorrow was blank as a piece of newly minted writing paper.

Sometime in the night, Ellie awoke to a child's crying. Just a dream? She lay completely still as an old memory unfolded from childhood. When Mama was a little girl, living on the edge of the Pennsylvania frontier, she'd been near enough to an Indian encampment to hear a baby cry. Indian children rarely cried, Mama said, for they were trained not to. But this child . . .

Her eyes fluttered closed as the sound ebbed, only to fly open at the creaking of a door above. Her senses grew taut. Someone was humming . . . a hymn? The familiar melody tugged at her, and the darkness seemed almost unfriendly, harboring secrets. In all honesty, the house hadn't felt right to her since she'd come home. Something other than the storm and her parents' absence was at play, she felt certain. The babe's cry was proof.

Fumbling her way from bed to dresser, she shrugged on a dressing gown and moved into the hall. Light from the cupola high above splashed through the large landing window, gilding the rug beneath her feet. She began a slow, silent climb to the third floor and attic and then stopped, surprise shackling her. Ansel's voice drifted down—and then another she knew but couldn't name. It seemed to echo in her head, taunting her, prodding her to memory.

"The leg will mend. I've given him laudanum to ease the pain. But his mouth is badly damaged. He may never talk normally again. I'm afraid Broad Oak's overseer is responsible."

Dr. Brunot?

Ansel's reply was smothered by the baying of hounds—at first distant, then hellishly close. Someone cried out in the darkness. The sound lingered, rose above the baying. Ellie pressed herself into the velvety fold of drapes at the landing window and stood stone still. Muffled footsteps tread past in the dark, and she caught Ansel's subtle bergamot scent. Panic churned inside her as he went below. The distinctive snap and click of a rifle being loaded met her ears.

Through the balustrade, she had a clear view of the foyer two floors down. Andra emerged from the study, candelabra in hand. Still dressed despite the late hour, she flung open the front door just ahead of Ansel and stepped onto the porch, venom in her tone. "You McTavishes are encroaching on Ballantyne land, which carries a hefty fine—mayhap a court appearance or jail time."

"There ain't no hidin' anymore, Miss High and Mighty." The deep voice was just as vitriolic yet held a taunting streak Andra's lacked. "Tonight there's a trail of blood clear to your door, and I dare anyone to deny it."

Another voice sounded, a bit hoarse but more reasonable. "We just want to search the house and grounds, see for ourselves. The law is on our side—"

"The law? Nay. You have five minutes to get off Ballantyne land or I'll fill your hide with buckshot and bury your dogs."

Ansel? Never had she heard such mettle in his voice. For a moment she thought it Peyton, home from town.

The silence stretched long and excruciating, finally broken by the jostle of horses and riders as they turned away. Light-headed, Ellie released a breath, unaware she'd been holding it. The front door slammed closed and was bolted. Dr. Brunot came quickly down the stairs, clutching a satchel. He, Ansel, and Andra went into the study and shut the door.

Beneath her nightgown, Ellie's heart beat an irregular pattern as she hurried up the stairs. Reaching the attic landing, she pushed at the glass knob leading to dark, dusty rafters. The door gave way. The crowded attic of old had been swept clean, former furnishings and trunks missing. Ellie smelled blood and medicine—and unmistakable fear.

A man lay on a narrow bed, his leg and his mouth cocooned in a swell of linen, eyes closed. Was he drugged? Or simply sleeping? A woman sat in a rocking chair beside him, a baby in her arm, the child's hair a fuzzy halo in the lantern light. Her troubled gaze met Ellie's own.

What had Dr. Brunot said? Were these Broad Oak's slaves?

Though fear wove its way across her chest, she tried to smile reassuringly as the pieces of this strange puzzle fell into place. "'Tis all right," she whispered. "The men who came looking are gone."

Gone, yes, but for how long? The McTavishes were of ill repute. Feared. Shunned. And on their very doorstep.

The woman's worried face creased in a small, grateful smile as Ellie eased the door closed and tiptoed back to bed.

And a long, sleepless night.

The next morning a lukewarm breakfast awaited her on the sideboard. Taking a plate, Ellie spooned some scrambled eggs onto its shiny surface and took a biscuit from a covered basket. Mamie served tea, her dusky features a study of serenity. Born of a French trader and an Indian mother at Fort Pitt the century before, she was a free woman.

Unlike the people in the attic.

With no one else at table, Ellie wanted to ask her about the goings-on upstairs. But 'twas likely they didn't want her to know. Yet how was it possible to sleep through such a ruckus? Something told her these weren't the first escaped slaves beneath their roof—and wouldn't be the last. She'd thought home was safe. Civilized. Unchanged. She'd been in Philadelphia far too long. New Hope had become something else in her absence.

Buttering a biscuit, she pushed down her shock, but the moving scene in the attic stayed steadfast. Where were these people going? How did they end up at New Hope? The child was so small, the woman so thin. The man had been shot, his mouth severely injured. Somehow Broad Oak was involved.

Since her family had never owned slaves, and most of the Negroes in Philadelphia and Pittsburgh were free, she'd given such matters little thought. But all at once, like awakening from a dream, everything came clear. The weariness Ansel wore like a second shirt—was it from countless sleepless nights? And Andra's temper? Was it frayed not only from the storm but from frequent fugitives?

"Morning, El." Ansel came into the sunny room, taking a chair opposite as if nothing unusual had happened. "It's early. I thought you'd still be abed."

She started from her reverie, rattling her teacup as she returned it to the saucer. "You know what Da says—early to bed and early to rise . . ."

"Makes a man healthy, wealthy, and wise." He reached for the sugar bowl and glanced at the sideboard. Mamie appeared and poured him coffee, as he'd never liked tea, before padding away on moccasined feet. "Did you have a sound night?"

She stirred a sugar lump into her cup. "Well enough. And you?"

"I'll sleep better when things return to normal."

Amen, Ellie thought, wishing he'd mention the night's events and include her. But he simply drank his coffee and eyed the *Pittsburgh Gazette* spread open on the table, the headlines still swelling with reports of storm damage.

She forced a lightness she was far from feeling. "I wanted to thank you for coming to the dancing lesson yesterday. I'd forgotten how beautifully you play."

He looked up, regret in his gaze. "I'm surprised it was worth hearing. I don't practice as much as I used to. Business, ye ken."

Business. Had his whole life become one of work? Her heart gave a little lurch. Where was the quick-to-smile, affable Ansel she so loved? The one who was happiest amidst reams of music and plans to craft a violin?

A shadow filled the doorway, and Andra came in, looking equally preoccupied as she fastened fretful eyes on him. "Pey-

96

ton needs you at the boatyard but I told him to wait. One of the carpenters wants you to have a look at the smokehouse first." She cast a glance at Ellie. "Are you teaching today?"

"This afternoon," Ellie murmured, praying Andra wouldn't ask where. She wasn't ready to divulge that her newest student was a Turlock just yet.

"Mamie could use your help sorting seeds and planning the kitchen garden this morning. Jacob is busy with a shipment of roses and shouldn't be bothered."

"Of course. I'm almost done with breakfast." Poor Mamie, eyesight ebbing, had been in their employ long before Ellie was born. Jacob, the gardener, was no better, unable to decipher the tags that identified manifold plants shipped from the East, even with his spectacles on. But her father, out of loyalty and affection, wouldn't let them go. New Hope was their home till they died, if they so wished, and they would be buried in the family graveyard beyond the chapel.

Ansel finished his coffee and got up, his breakfast untouched, his voice a low rumble. "Don't leave without an escort, El. Da's orders, remember."

The words assumed new meaning. Because there were slaves in the attic—and slave catchers at their door—and everything had turned perilous? Though she'd been insulated from such matters all her life, she now felt thrust into the very thick of it.

"Sabbath services are on the morrow, the first time since the storm." Andra's voice cut through Ellie's musings. "We'd do well to attend."

Ellie gave a nod. Andra somehow made churchgoing sound as appealing as encountering bounty hunters. She took a bite of egg, but the forkful seemed to stick in her throat. Ansel and Andra left without another word.

The scent of old leather and tobacco embraced Jack as he entered River Hill's study. Every crack in the worn floorboards, every nick in the paneled walls, he knew like his own name. He'd been schooled in this very room by his grandfather. No reason Chloe couldn't do likewise. A woman's mind was no less agile than a man's, therefore the curriculum would be the same. Latin. Geography. Arithmetic. Forget the fancy needlework and French. And since no one would be inviting Chloe to any dances, dancing lessons seemed frivolous as well.

Opening a cabinet, he took out his old lap desk, the top scarred and worn. A gift from his grandfather on his eighth birthday. The judge had wanted him to pursue a career in law. Since Wade had been commandeered for the whiskey trade, their parents had let Hugh O'Hara take their secondborn to River Hill. Jack spent more time there than at Broad Oak, nearly taking up residence. No one protested the arrangement, least of all Jack.

"You're so like my father," his mother had once said. "You might have been his son. You belong at River Hill."

Jack often wondered what she meant. He'd been studious. Thoughtful. Dutiful. Until the day his grandfather died. Then his moorings had come loose and he'd run pell-mell into trouble like a scow snagged midriver. All that Turlock wildness had threatened to sink him—and might still.

His knuckles grazed the spines of countless leather-bound books as he perused one bookcase after another, dismissing *The American Distiller* and *The American Brewer and Malt-ster* in search of more acceptable fare. He'd start slowly, as he wasn't sure his patience—or Chloe's—was up to the task. Myriad responsibilities weighted him, and he was faced with travel come fall. But he'd do what he could till that time.

Half an hour later he'd made his selection and was riffling

through the lap desk, emptying it of childhood memories—
stubs of pencil, a slingshot, yellowed sheets of penmanship
and arithmetic. He grew pensive at the passing of time.
Though his grandfather had been gone for years, his legacy
lingered. A king's ransom of books. A crumbling, ivy-coated
house. The unmistakable essence of leather and tobacco and
brandy. But Jack most remembered a broken old man with
broken dreams. And a daughter who'd destroyed them.

Glancing up, he took in the front drive through a bank of
open windows, wondering where Chloe was, how long he'd
have to look for her. Likely she was in the stables or fishing
again. He left the study and traversed the cool hall, nearly
colliding with Mrs. Malarkey as she exited the parlor.

"Mr. Turlock, sir. I didn't see you."

He couldn't help but smile. He stood well over six feet and
could hardly be missed. Little wonder dust decorated every
corner and spiderwebs spanned every crevice. She couldn't
see those either. "I'm looking for Chloe."

"Chloe? Oh yes, she's here somewhere. On the veranda.
Riverside."

There were two verandas—the one fronting the shimmering Monongahela, rarely used, and the one facing the drive.
Chloe, in perpetual motion, never lingered long on either. He
nodded thoughtfully and watched his housekeeper sans cook
make her way down the hall as carefully as if she was walking
a tightrope in a circus. Blast, but the woman was blind! She'd
seemed old and in need of replacing when he first came to live
at River Hill. But if he turned her out, where would she go?

Passing through the ballroom shrouded in dust cloths for
twenty years or better, he caught sight of a bent head through
a near window. The image seemed to tease him, the fetching
hat aflutter with navy ribbon. Not Chloe . . .

Ellie.

On his veranda.

He felt the same breathless wonder he'd felt along the turnpike when the tree had fallen and missed him by a hair. Pushing open a French door, he stepped out so quietly she didn't look up, preoccupied as she was with the book in her hands. Kohl-black hair, shot through with glints of red, was gathered beneath her straw hat, a few curls escaping.

He couldn't recall the color of her eyes, but when she looked up at him, they struck him hard with their blueness. A half smile softened her pale, heart-shaped face, so fetching he glanced at the river as if to stop it from reaching his heart. It was rude not to greet her, but his thoughts were in such a tangle all good manners escaped him.

"Chloe went looking for you." Her voice was as tentative as her smile. "I wanted to thank you for allowing the lessons after all."

"For allowing . . ." *What?* He felt a deep sinking in his chest as the realization took hold. They'd both been tricked. By a thirteen-year-old snip of a girl. Only Ellie didn't know. He swallowed hard, trying to harness his surprise. "Are you . . . finished?"

"With today's lessons, yes." She stood, smoothing the skirt of a finely made green dress edged with lace. "We've been deciding on a course of study. I'd like to capitalize on Chloe's interests."

"Other than fishing and riding?"

Again that fleeting smile. "You might be surprised at what swims round your sister's head."

"No doubt," he said wryly, wishing Chloe back if only to wring her conniving neck.

"I was hoping we could meet once weekly, perhaps more."

"You and Chloe . . ." he said slowly. At her nod, he shrugged. "Meet whenever you like. I'm often away on business. Mrs.

Malarkey will be here to let you in." He couldn't believe he'd just agreed to the deception. Feeling stubborn, he said, "But there'll be no dancing, understand."

Her smile strengthened and bordered on teasing, or so he thought. "Have you never danced, Jack? Because I believe, if you had—"

"No dancing, Ellie."

Their eyes locked, held fast, till pink touched the tops of her cheeks. Seconds ticked by, slow and sweet. He looked toward the river again, and her voice reached out to him.

"Chloe seems to have gone fishing." She made a move toward the door, clutching the book to her chest, making him wonder what the title was. "I'd best be on my way."

"Your rig is out front?"

She nodded, looking suddenly vulnerable.

"Don't ever come alone," he cautioned.

Her gaze swung back to him, troubled. "My father forbids me to ride by myself, much as I'd like to."

"Wise man, your father."

She left then, climbing into a finely appointed carriage. The driver was crisp and efficient in his actions, reassuring Jack she'd arrive home safely. As soon as the wheels met gravel and pulled away, Chloe appeared, an impish look on her usually straight face.

Jack wrestled with his temper. "I should send you back to Broad Oak for such a trick."

Her smile dimmed.

"I seem to remember you not wanting any tutoring, and yet today I find Ellie Ballantyne on my porch."

Thoughtful, she bit her lip and looked up at him with a telling shine in her eyes. "I didn't ask her here for me, Jack. I asked her here for you."

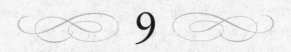

9

A great fortune is a great slavery.
SENECA

Ansel stood on the levee with Peyton, eyeing the skeleton of a ship on the scaffolding taking up a good hundred feet of waterfront. William Mason, the sailmaker on Water Street, was there to take measurements, his mouth pursed in contemplation as they reviewed the dimensions. It was a task Ansel had overseen countless times but never without his father near. The questions that had arisen were ones he couldn't answer. Lately New Orleans seemed as far away as the Orient, and he found himself wishing his parents would materialize. But the only sight that met his eyes was an aging packet coming up the storm-swollen Ohio, almost limping along, hardly a Ballantyne steamer.

How different it had been last winter when fifty boats had lain locked in ice, unable to break free till the spring thaw. Now that it was mid-May, a great many vessels were taking in cargo bound for Nashville and St. Louis and intermediate ports. Places he'd never seen but wanted to, their mystery gnawing at him with fresh ferocity. Standing there, sweat beading his brow, Ansel listened to the drone of Mason's voice and wrestled down the desire to roam till it was no bigger than a fleeting wish, snuffed like a candle flame.

Around them the whole of the levee was dotted with drays and wagons, freight stacked high as a man's head in manifold bales and barrels and hogsheads, all in "beautiful disarray," as Peyton called it. Shouting seemed to come from every quarter—shippers, porters, draymen, and more. He could hardly hear himself think.

Passing a hand over eyes stinging from the water's glare and lack of sleep, Ansel marveled that Peyton was already chafing at returning to the mercantile that swallowed the street behind them. It had just expanded to accommodate more supplies needed to send settlers west. They were coming in a steady stream as summer began, and Peyton, most obliging, kept doors open from dawn till dusk.

And then there was the glassworks, the mining on Coal Hill, and the endless string of properties about town that needed tending. His father had a hand in everything and managed to stay atop it all. Not so his sons.

It was nearly noon when Ansel received a summons to come to the mercantile. Accustomed to interruptions, he left the boatyard office and entered a timbered building redolent with coffee and spices and brimming with clerks and settlers. The only thing they didn't carry, Ansel mused wryly, was spirits, specifically Turlock whiskey, though every traveler seemed to desire it, if only for medicinal purposes.

Distracted by the hum of activity, he slowly worked his way to a back room that resembled a ship's galley, narrow and shadowed but for a few small windows and hanging lanterns. Peyton stood at the far end of a counter, shoulders squared, the rigid set of his features giving a warning. Lately he was unbearably short-tempered, barking orders, making the apprentices cower. None were present today but stayed busy in the adjoining warehouse, taking inventory and stocking endless rough-hewn shelves.

"I've just learned that you signed off on some cargo that was missing valuable content." Peyton tossed aside his quill and turned toward him, tense with fury. "But I suppose you have an explanation for such an oversight."

Ansel stopped mid-aisle. "Aye, I've been awake half the night transporting freight about the county, something you'd know little about, as you've taken rooms in town."

"*Freight?* Call them what they are. *Fugitives.* And don't talk to me of rooms in town. I'm weary of your excuses—and they don't mend accounts."

Leaning against a low counter, Ansel struggled to keep his voice even. "I've told you before, I'm too busy at the boatyard to help here. You have clerks to do the same. If you'd take pains with your apprentices and train them properly, you'd not have me to reckon with." He started to turn away, but Peyton's low lament stopped him.

"Sometimes I wonder what we're working for—if we're little better than the fugitives in the attic, enslaved right here working for Da and standing the risk of losing it all." He reached for a newspaper on a near stool and fisted it. "Have you heard the news? Another abolitionist ruined, his business seized, his house burned to the ground, this one in Washington County."

"Aye, the risks are well known. Yet Da won't be moved."

Peyton let the paper drop. "Nay. He feels his whole life—this business harboring slaves—is in God's hands. That he has divine approval."

"Aye. But not yours."

Their eyes locked. This was the very heart of the matter,

something Peyton couldn't deny. He could only respond in heated protest, raising his hands in futility. "Da's risking our futures—our very inheritance. Yours and mine. Elinor's and Andra's. Everything he's worked for—all we're working for. Are you at peace with that?"

"I'm at peace with God," Ansel replied. "That's all that matters."

"By heaven, to be so glib." Peyton shook his head, regret in his gaze. "I wish I shared your faith. As far as I'm concerned, this battle is Da's, not ours. Not mine."

Ansel looked toward the door to make sure it was shut and lowered his voice. "You don't have to continue the work. The understanding is that once you're wed, you'll leave New Hope and inherit your own land, your own share of the business."

"Aye, but it's still a gamble. I'm a Ballantyne, and Da's sentiments about slavery are becoming known. He's just joined the new abolitionist society, all in secret, though these things have a way of spreading. A great deal of his capital goes to the cause. Besides, there's no one I wish to wed—or who'd wish to wed me, given our involvement. There's too much danger."

"No one?" Ansel could count half a dozen women who were smitten with Peyton, abolitionist activity or no. But his brother was blinded to his matrimonial prospects. "There's more than one woman who'd be glad to further your acquaintance, given the chance."

"Oh?" His surly mood sharpened. "How am I to notice, buried as I've been?"

"When Da returns, you'll have more time." His own tone was more gruff than reassuring. Lately all Peyton did was grumble. "At least look up now and again. You might be surprised at what's waiting."

"That's what I'm afraid of." Peyton raked a hand over the stubble marking his jaw, the day's growth glinting copper in the noon light. "There's talk of a group—a ring of proslavery activists and professional slave hunters, even local lawyers and city constables—at work in Pittsburgh much as they are in Philadelphia, the Turlocks foremost. They mean trouble to every abolitionist."

"You mean the Pittsburgh kidnapping ring? The ones who sell free blacks into slavery?"

"Aye."

"There's always been fierce opposition, especially in a border state like Pennsylvania."

"But never in Allegheny County till now. Rumor is they're not above targeting women they believe to be sympathetic to the cause. I worry about Mother. Andra and Elinor."

Coldness crept over Ansel at the words. "Only a rogue would stoop so low."

"We're dealing with Turlocks and their ilk, remember. They seem to know no bounds. I can't stomach the thought—"

Peyton's words caught and hung in the air as the door groaned open. Ellie appeared, cheeks flushed, her smile bright. Ansel felt a crushing anxiety at the sight of her. For a moment he couldn't so much as return her greeting. Even Peyton stayed silent.

Andra could hold her own if needed. Even their mother was made of sterner stuff than her ladylike demeanor suggested. But Ellie . . . Ellie was unassuming. Innocent. Unaware of all that was at stake. She should never have left Philadelphia.

I will both lay me down in peace, and sleep: for thou, Lord, only makest me dwell in safety.

Ellie shifted atop the feather mattress, finally putting the pillow over her head and meditating on the Psalm heard at church that very morning. But there was little sleep to be had this night. Her body tensed as the baby's cries reached a crescendo, loud enough to be heard throughout the house—and throughout the entire county—summoning the bounty hunters to their door once more. Or so she feared.

Footsteps sounded on the landing and stair. Ansel? Something other than the frantic wailing was stirring, and this returned her to the attic. Pushing open the small door, she found Andra on her knees by the bed, salving the man's facial wounds before applying linen cloths. A thick tension spread over the room. Ellie could see fierce determination in her sister's expression as she worked, as if time was against them or she might explode at the child's incessant fussing. Ellie's sudden appearance only raised Andra's ire, judging by the hasty glance tossed to her.

Was the babe hungry? Colicky? Sick? The lone lantern revealed little, but Ellie felt the child's resistance as she took her from her mother.

Leaving the attic, she descended to the third-floor landing. A hymn spilled out of her, though it was her harp she wanted, thinking it might lull the babe to sleep. Barely a year old, she guessed, and smelling of her mother's milk. The blanket was one of Andra's doing, as it was new flannel from Mama's sewing chest.

Though it took a few minutes of jostling, humming, and pacing, the child finally quieted, her tiny mahogany fingers splayed across Ellie's dressing gown where they'd clutched it frantically before.

Behind her, Ansel reached the top step and set a candle on a low table. "You remind me of Mother. She's especially good with the children."

"There have been others, then—more than these." Ellie kept moving lest the babe wake. "That's why the bounty hunters were here."

He gave a nod. "We started taking in runaways several years ago, right after you left for finishing school. Most are from Kentucky and Maryland. Some come farther."

"How do they know to make their way to New Hope?"

"Our place can be seen for miles along the river. Word spreads as to who can and can't be trusted."

"And the cupola light—is it a signal for them to come?"

"Aye, on the nights it's deemed safest to cross the water. We have small boats hidden in the brush on the opposite shore."

She felt a chill at the words, knowing he meant when bounty hunters and their bloodhounds weren't about.

"We feed and clothe them, help the sick. If they're here long enough, Mother and Andra teach them to write their names and read."

"Where do they go next?"

"Farther north to safe havens—Quaker settlements. Most head to Canada where they can live free. Sometimes Da transports runaways on Ballantyne boats coming up from southern ports to Pittsburgh."

She stopped pacing. "What?"

"Aye, it's somewhat risky. Just last fall, port officials in Louisville searched the *Elinor*, where a dozen fugitives were secreted. But they were so well hidden among the cargo they weren't found."

Somewhat risky? Smuggling slaves? Fear and surprise lashed her. "Is that what Da's doing now in New Orleans?"

"He never says. That's another thing you need to know. Everything is cloaked in secrecy. There are other abolitionists in Allegheny County and elsewhere, but we don't know them by name other than Dr. Brunot."

"But aren't they breaking the law?" The question seemed to stick in her throat. Her beloved father, pillar of Pittsburgh, elder in the Presbyterian Church . . .

He hesitated as the attic door opened. Andra appeared, rags and a tin of liniment in hand. Her eyes rested on the child in Ellie's arms, as if not quite believing the crying had ceased.

"I'm sorry to involve you in this, Elinor," she said. "But you're home now and it can't be helped. 'Tis becoming quite dangerous."

"If things become more so, we'll move them to the gristmill." Ansel's tone was resigned. "They'll be safer there than the attic. Till the harvest anyway. Then the mill is in full operation and of no help hiding them."

Without another word, Andra moved past them, a stiff-backed shadow descending the stairs.

Tired as she was, Ellie couldn't rest till she had answers. "Isn't Da breaking the law?"

Resignation kindled in Ansel's eyes. "Aye, federal law."

"And the punishment?"

"El, I won't lie to you. But I'd rather you not ask."

"Ansel, 'tis not a secret any longer. I would be informed."

He swallowed as if even talk of it was bitter to the taste. "The punishment for harboring fugitives is harsh. Da could be fined or flogged or imprisoned. Mayhap worse."

"And the slaves who come here?"

He looked toward the closed attic door. "Death."

10

Farmers, I have before remarked, ye
are the Lords of this lower creation.

AN EARLY HANDBOOK ON
AMERICAN FARMING

In the years since his grandfather's passing, Jack had tried
his hand at a great many things, but nothing satisfied like
working the land. Some of his best thinking was done amidst
the fervor of seedtime and harvest. Now, standing in a field
at dusk, the grain knee-high, he listened as his farm manager
spoke of crop rotations, the new variety of rye they'd just
sown, and plastering the lower mow lands with manure. Jack
knew the details firsthand, having tilled and planted several
acres himself, combing the fields to uproot cull growth, watching for disease, and calculating the yield as the strengthening
summer sun warmed his shoulders. Wade laughed at him,
called him a fool for doing what he had slaves to do in his
stead, and even their father had looked on in silent disapproval. Jack's kinship with the land couldn't be explained.

River Hill sprawled along the Monongahela River for miles,
some of it forest, most of it field, the plentiful grain they

grew fueling Broad Oak's gristmill and distillery. When his grandfather manumitted his slaves upon his death, Jack had contracted indentures from the British Isles, mostly Irish. These men and their families lived as tenants on River Hill land, farming large tracts in exchange for their eventual freedom. Though Jack was far more involved in the daily aspects of agriculture than most landowners, his absences from River Hill were increasing, and he would soon see Missouri, all in the name of the expanding Turlock whiskey enterprise.

He chafed at the possibility he might miss the harvest, that his unpredictable father might send him west sooner than planned. Little surpassed swinging a scythe over a gilded, fragrant field from dawn till dusk. The challenge of the gleaning was what he lived for. He longed to be lost in his labors, not sunk in dismal reflection like he'd been since the storm.

A sliver of guilt drove his thoughts home. Tonight Chloe would be waiting for him to return from the fields, their unfinished conversation dangling between them. Was it just a couple of weeks ago Ellie had surprised him on the veranda? And Chloe's confession rendered him speechless?

I didn't ask her here for me, Jack. I asked her here for you.

He'd avoided his sister ever since, trying to bury her words beneath a blur of work, but they stuck to him like pitch. Even now they stole his appetite. He sought another distraction, but all that came to mind was town and Janey. Shrugging aside his misgivings, he finished with his farm manager and gave in to the temptation to head for the stables.

He headed west on Cicero, finally turning down Water Street, where the acrid smells of tanneries and slaughter houses stung his senses. Pittsburgh was fast becoming a city, a pall of soot and grime obscuring the rivers and hanging like a shroud over boats and buildings, making him itch for clean air and clear vistas. Maybe the West wasn't such a bleak prospect after all.

Around the corner, Teague's Tavern loomed, still a bit battered from the storm with shingles and shutters askew. He tied Cicero to the hitch rail in front and entered, the swirl of tobacco smoke obscuring his view of the corner table he preferred, now commandeered by Wade. Janey hovered, serving drinks, and Jack tried to mask his stark surprise when she moved away in a flurry of plum skirts and revealed Wade's companion.

Peyton Ballantyne.

The heir. Harvard educated. London dressed. As striking as his father yet . . . different.

Jack veered toward the tavern counter, expecting Wade to motion him over like he usually did. But Wade was obviously too engrossed in the company he kept to give him any notice. To Jack's knowledge, Peyton Ballantyne had never set foot in Teague's Tavern. He preferred the gentleman's club farther in town.

Without waiting for him to ask, the barkeep served him a tankard of ale. Mumbling his thanks, Jack sought a shadowed alcove, the day's labor catching up with him. He learned back in his chair, glad when Janey's ample form blocked his view of Wade and Peyton and theirs of him.

"I ain't seen you in some time, Jack." She smiled wearily, the gentle rhythm of her words a reminder of her Virginia roots. "Where you been?"

"Plowing and planting. It's spring, remember."

"The seasons don't seem to change inside these four walls." She reached for his hand and turned his callused palm over, studying it with such intensity it seemed she was about to tell his fortune. "You're in need of a respite, a good meal . . . and more."

As usual, Janey was not one to miss a proposition. He extracted his hand and ran it over his unkempt hair, feeling downright shabby next to the impeccably dressed Peyton.

Her beleaguered eyes held his. "I'd begun to think you were gone again—to New Orleans."

"I'm done riding the river," he said. The very mention brought to mind one too many sordid recollections he had no stomach for. "Standing on solid ground is more to my liking."

"I never did figure you for a roustabout." She got up, the heady scent of her perfume cloying. "I'll bring you a plate."

When she moved away, his view broadened. The truth was he'd never cared much for the eldest Ballantyne. With his ruddy Scots coloring and hair, Peyton reminded Jack of Silas. But Silas had an uncommon clarity of countenance that Peyton lacked. Peyton was arrogant, guarded. Jack preferred the affable, unassuming Ansel. No guile, just guts. He worked the levee like a seasoned river man, whereas Peyton didn't like to get his hands dirty, confining himself to mercantile and office.

Janey set down a plate and awaited his reaction. Roast pork and potatoes, pickled beans and warm bread. He nodded his thanks and lifted a fork. She moved away among the other patrons as if sensing he was in no mood to talk, leaving him to eat in peace. If peace could be found in a crowded tavern.

Wade was doing the lion's share of the talking now, animated by another round of drinks, Peyton listening intently. Jack couldn't fathom what had brought them together. All he could think about was Ellie, who wouldn't want her brother in such a place. He attempted a few halfhearted mouthfuls before leaving a gold piece beneath his plate and passing out the back door.

The uneasy feeling followed.

Beyond the tavern's entrance, the Monongahela waterfront shone like polished pewter beneath a gibbous moon. All around him the clip of carriages sounded and laughter burst from doors and windows. All was the same as it had ever been. Once, it had been enough. What had changed? When?

Now, like a coin that had been flipped, he craved the familiar confines of his study . . . Chloe's impudent chatter . . . the sight of Ellie on the veranda, dark head bent over a book.

The black edges of the night weighted him on every side. He much preferred a new day kindling at the rim of the horizon like yellow candle flame. Night reminded him of his misdeeds. His mistakes. The dark moment along the turnpike. Shrugging aside the grim memory, he untied Cicero and mounted. He was nearly to the edge of town when a voice rang out like a gunshot.

"You there! Jack!"

Standing in his stirrups, he looked back over a lumbering wagon to a cadre of horses and riders, bloodhounds at their heels. Bounty hunters. The McTavishes foremost.

"We need to talk, Turlock." The words were slurred, rum-soaked. "There's been a spit o' trouble."

Jack turned into an alley and waited for them to join him, anxiety brewing in his belly. The leashed hounds were yelping and sniffing, latching onto a plethora of scents the city streets offered, most of them unsavory. One of the men leaned over and spat tobacco juice onto the cobblestones, barely missing Jack's boot.

"Talk, then," Jack said, unable to keep the aggravation from his tone.

"We think we've found what you're looking for—you and your pa and Wade. But it'll require more coin, as there's bound to be trouble." Clive McTavish paused and tucked tobacco into a sun-wrinkled cheek. "We tracked some of them runaways onto Ballantyne land two nights ago."

Jack shifted in the saddle, ice lining his spine.

"We suspect it's your man Adam and his Ulie."

"They're not mine. They're Broad Oak's."

Clive shrugged. "The dogs led us to New Hope. There

may even be more runaways there. We ain't sure but we aim to find out."

Another man, Jared Sparks, maneuvered his horse closer to Jack, a smugness lining his heavy features. "This calls for a little mischief. With Silas Ballantyne downriver, the time's ripe for it. I say we harass them, hide out, and watch their comings and goings. Give 'em a scare. The eldest daughter, she's something of a wildcat, but the younger one . . ."

A muted whistle of appreciation turned Jack's head. Clive McTavish muscled his way into the conversation again. "You mean the pretty, dark-haired gal? The one fresh from Philly? I saw her around town the other day. Word is she's downright docile. Might be a good candidate for some of that mischief you mean to make—"

Jack had no memory of leaping off Cicero and taking a McTavish with him. Fists full of fabric, he shoved Clive hard against a timbered wall, epithets crowding his throat. "If there's any trouble with the Ballantynes, I'll send some bounty hunters after *you*."

In the gleam of moonlight he read surprise—nay, outright shock—on all their faces. Straightening, never taking his eyes off Jack, Clive adjusted his hat and backed away. Few could outfight a Turlock, sober or otherwise. In the past Jack had wrangled with them, not against them, and now a somber mood ensued.

Sparks's tone turned surly. "What do you want us to do about the search, then?"

"The search?" Jack cast him a menacing glance. "Call it off."

"What?"

"You heard me. The bounty expires now. Keep the coin my brother paid you and say no more." Mounting Cicero, he left the alley, his breathing labored, his stomach clenched. Hearing Ellie bandied about so coarsely left him sick. Ellie

. . . docile? That hadn't been his impression. More demure. Determined.

And no match for these men.

He knew what the McTavishes were capable of. The law was often lax in a western settlement like Pittsburgh. Allegheny County had many criminals who were never caught or punished for their crimes but simply pushed farther west to commit more.

He rode hard all the way home as if to outdistance his tangled thoughts, glad when Ben met him at the lantern-lit stable and saw to his lathered horse. "You gave Cicero quite a run, Mister Jack." The boy's toothy smile shone wide and reassuring. "You goin' to turn him into a prize racehorse with all the night ridin' you do."

Jack simply clamped him on the shoulder in response, throat too tight for their usual banter. With a low call, Ben led the stallion away as Jack turned toward the house. The scent of lilacs, unbearably sweet, ushered Ellie into his thoughts again. Was she part of the slave harboring the bounty hunters suspected at New Hope? Having been away in Philadelphia for so long, she'd likely returned and stumbled into her family's abolitionist activities, if there were any.

The foyer was empty and felt strangely lonesome. Mrs. Malarkey liked to retire early since she rose at dawn. He took the stairs two at a time, following the curve of the banister, the hallway lit by a single sconce. When Chloe had chosen her bedchamber from all the rooms on the second floor a fortnight before, she'd surprised him. It was their mother's suite she'd wanted, untouched since she'd married and left home more than thirty years ago.

Jack had an almost eerie feeling when he entered, as if he'd stepped back in time. Fashion babies lined a deep windowsill, dressed in their eighteenth-century best. A writing desk held

Isabel's favorite girlhood books alongside a framed black velvet silhouette of her mother. Through an adjoining door was a dressing room containing a great many old, unfashionable garments. Everything reinforced his belief that his mother had been more of a child when she'd made the rash decision to wed his father.

Asleep atop a feather tick, Chloe looked carefree like the child she was, or he wanted her to be. Not an afterthought. Not an accident. Just a girl who'd had the misfortune of being born to an embittered mother who couldn't embrace the present because of the past, whose unhappiness spilled over to those closest to her in increasingly callous barbs.

The sudden, overwhelming urge to reach out and brush back the hair obscuring Chloe's flushed features—to be gentle and not harsh—struck him hard. His fingers extended. Faltered. He was unaccustomed to any tenderness, any fine feeling. Turning away, he felt a twist of regret. But the old Turlock pride and stubbornness won out.

"I want you to take me fishing."

Looking up from her lap desk, Chloe regarded Ellie with a sort of bemused wonder. They sat on the veranda, riverside, the table between them spread with books and papers.

"I've never been fishing," Ellie persisted. "And I'd like to learn."

"Seems like you've done everything else."

"Not everything, Chloe." She didn't want to give the impression she was *that* accomplished. "There's a great many things I've never done. Like travel by steamboat. Or tour Europe. Or have a suitor." At this, she had Chloe's full attention. "Nor have I ever," she added with a slight smile, "tasted Turlock whiskey."

Grimacing, Chloe cleared her throat and spat into the near bushes. "Oh, it's dreadful stuff. Fit for a spittoon." At Ellie's raised brows, she said in a little rush, "Pa makes me take a sip at Christmas, but I just about cast up accounts doing it. He even gives me the special cinnamon whiskey women prefer, but I still hate it."

"I'm glad fishing is more to your liking." Ellie closed her book, signaling an end to lessons. She made a silent vow to go slowly, sensing Chloe's patience was thread thin and would snap if too pressured. Though she did need to put in a stern word about spitting . . . "So, shall we?"

Two wide gray eyes shone with surprise. "Dressed like that?"

Ellie looked down at her sprigged muslin gown. "'Tis not good enough for fishing?"

Chloe smirked. "I'm afraid you'll fall in." Standing, she looked about, lingering on the stables. "Can we take Ben?"

"Ben?"

"Yes, Ben." She hesitated, perplexity playing across her sunburned face. "He's my . . . friend."

With a nod, Ellie included Ben. Whoever he was, Chloe was fiercely fond of him. "Don't forget your bonnet," she said gently.

Chloe made a face. "I'll go find Ben if you'll ask Jack for the rods."

Rods? Reading her blank expression, Chloe grinned, but it was so full of mischief Ellie wondered if she was up to more than fishing.

"Jack keeps the fishing gear in his study. It was my grandfather's."

"Judge O'Hara?" Of all the skeletons in Chloe's closet, the judge was the most respectable by far. "I wouldn't want to bother your brother—"

"Oh, you're far less a bother than I am." She was already off the veranda, moving past the lilacs toward the stables. "Just ask Jack for the rods and he'll hand them over."

Ellie began stacking books, mulling her request. They'd had but three lessons, and despite Chloe's agile mind, restlessness and a lack of confidence undermined her natural abilities. If they interspersed study with fishing and other diversions, their time together might be a success. It was important Chloe not fail in her family's eyes. Or her own. Nor did Ellie want to be dismissed like the French governess . . .

Or beg fishing gear from Jack Turlock.

In moments Chloe returned, a wiry, homespun-clad boy in her wake, and a little dog in his. "Where are the rods, Miss Ellie?"

"Still in your brother's study."

"I suppose ladies don't pester gentlemen . . . though Jack's hardly that."

Stifling a chuckle, Ellie smiled at Ben. His close-napped hair was a deep auburn, his skin coffee dark. Full of feature and wary of gaze, he reminded her of someone in the attic— Adam. Might they be related? She didn't dare ask.

Chloe nudged him with her elbow. "This is Ben." Looking down at the little dog, she added, "And Max."

But Ben hardly looked Ellie's way. His attention was fixed on the stack of books atop the table, a small tower of them. Sensing his interest, she passed him *Gulliver's Travels* as Chloe's earlier perplexity came clear. Ben was a friend but far more. A slave, albeit a favored one.

"Do you like books, Ben?" Ellie asked.

"Ben can't read," Chloe said when he hung his head.

Ellie's heart twisted. She searched through her supplies and handed him a primer. "You're welcome to this one too. There are illustrations—pictures on every page."

Grinning his thanks, he tucked the books into the band of his breeches, as pleased as Chloe.

"I'll get the rods." Whirling, Chloe nearly collided with the object of her mission as he came out the front door.

Jack stood before them, gear in hand. "I heard something about fishing."

She squinted up at him in the glare of sunlight. "We'll need another pole for Ell—"

"'Miss Ballantyne' to you," he corrected, then turned toward Ellie with a questioning smile. Slight and unexpected as it was, it warmed her inside and out. "Fishing? Is that on the curriculum?"

"It is now," she said, smiling back at him.

"You digging for worms too?" he asked her.

"No, Mr. Turlock, I draw the line at that."

He relinquished the poles and left to get a third, Ellie's gaze trailing after him. Today he was in typical dishabille, without coat or waistcoat, just rolled up shirtsleeves, riding breeches, and boots. Finely wrought spectacles rested atop his head as if he'd pushed them up and forgotten all about them. She lowered her eyes when she realized Ben was watching.

Chloe started off the veranda. "Ben and me—"

"Ben and I." Looking up, Ellie softened the reminder with a smile.

"Ben and I will dig the worms. You wait here with the rods."

Ellie sank down in her seat, wondering if Jack would accompany them. But it was Mrs. Malarkey who appeared instead, a tray in hand. "I thought you'd like a spot of tea." She uncovered a plate, her tone turning a touch prideful. "I've made some scones, my mother's recipe. The peach preserves are from the orchard here—what's left of it."

Thanking her, Ellie gave her attention to the garden, where

the worm digging was in progress. Mrs. Malarkey poured the steaming tea and left Ellie to sample a scone. Her teeth almost rattled at first bite. Hard as lead. Afraid of offending, Ellie pocketed the scone and tasted a spoonful of very sour jam just as Jack reappeared with the promised pole. He cast a grim glance at the tray.

"The tea is very good." Ellie took a second sip, sputtering as he reached into the basket and tossed the last scone to Ben's dog. Her gaze darted to the door. "Jack, please . . . Mrs. Malarkey might see."

"That's the trouble, Ellie. She can't. You might well be poisoned eating these. For all I know she used plaster for flour."

Laughter bubbled in her throat, easing her anxiety at having him so near. "Well, don't poison poor Max."

But Max was looking askance at the scone and then ran off to bury it beneath a far oak, tail wagging. Jack took the chair opposite Ellie, lowering his spectacles and examining a hook and string. For a wisp of a second he looked like the boy she remembered. Focused. Intense. Strikingly handsome. Never in her wildest imaginings had she thought they'd share a veranda, a light moment. The sticks and stones of childhood passed away . . . or had given way to more mature, precarious matters.

She still didn't trust Jack Turlock.

His sudden reversal puzzled her. He'd been adamant about refusing Chloe's schooling at first. Why the change? Could it be because he wanted to learn more about her? Because he suspected her family of hiding slaves? His family's slaves? Thinking it, she felt suddenly foolish, as if he'd somehow ensnared her without her knowing.

She sipped her tea, trying to dismiss her suspicions, eyes on the decrepit garden beyond the low brick wall, imagining it as it once was fifty years before. The pride of Pittsburgh. "Tell me about Ben. Chloe seems very fond of him."

He continued to examine the length of string, pausing to tie a knot. "Ben belongs to Broad Oak."

Belongs. The word cut deep, pointed as the shining fish hook. Adam and Ulie belonged to Broad Oak too. Broken and battered, Adam might never speak normally again, all because of an overseer's cruelty. While he healed, Andra had begun teaching Ulie to read. Literacy was a powerful weapon, she said. A free, literate ex-slave was a force to be reckoned with.

She kept her voice light, disguising the challenge beneath. "Might Ben like to learn to—"

"No, Ellie. I know where you're going with this and it's not a good idea."

Disappointment doused her hopes—and fueled her angst over Adam. Perhaps it wasn't wise to press the issue. Jack might think she had abolitionist leanings. Place her family in more danger.

"Ben is only here for the summer, as I'm in need of an extra hand. He's confined to the stables."

She withdrew reluctantly. "Tell me about River Hill then."

"What do you want to know?"

"Its history. I'm interested for Chloe's sake."

He glanced up, and his intensity seemed to banish all pretense. "Your family's part in its history, you mean."

She traced the delicate contours of her teacup with a finger, offering him a slightly sheepish smile. She always felt he was one step ahead of her. Was that borne of his being worldly?

He continued examining the rod. "The land was bought before the Revolution. The house was built in 1777 of local brick, the same as Fort Pitt. My grandfather was an officer there. He hired John Bartram and Sons of Philadelphia to design the garden for his bride, my grandmother."

Romantic, Ellie thought, a bit wistful it had fallen into disrepair. The Bartrams were noted botanists, renowned in

Philadelphia and elsewhere. If they'd left their mark here, it was truly a tragedy the garden had turned to weeds.

"She died when my mother was born." Jack spoke without a trace of emotion, as if reciting rote facts, not family history. "My grandfather never remarried, just turned his attention to Pittsburgh and raising Isabel." He set the rod aside and looked toward the garden. "Your father used to come here often."

"He said River Hill's library is the finest anywhere."

"Aye, and there he met my mother . . . who was no match for yours."

She heard a hint of bitterness in his tone and sensed they hovered on shaky ground. "My parents seldom speak of the past."

"Mine seldom speak of anything else. My mother, anyway."

Ellie finished her tea as a dozen questions clamored for answers. Did Isabel have regrets? Did Henry? For a few fleeting seconds, Jack had thrown open a window on the Turlocks' turmoil before it slammed shut again, his features stoic.

He stood and handed her the fine birch rod as Chloe and Ben came round with a pail of worms.

Chloe eyed the transaction, slack-jawed. "You're letting Ell—Miss Ballantyne use your prized pole?"

"A lady should always have the best of everything, aye?"

Still, Chloe gaped. "Are you going to hook her worms too?"

"Nay, Ben is." Again that charming, disarming smile. "But any fish she catches are mine. Understood?"

Ellie stepped off the veranda. "You have my word." She didn't look back. She didn't dare.

Lest Jack Turlock reel her in.

11

They speak of my drinking, but never think of my thirst.
<small>SCOTTISH PROVERB</small>

The scent of the contents of the largest Turlock storehouse, a quarter-mile long and two stories high, wafted thick and rich on the warm June wind. The tang of spirits emanating from hundreds of charred oak barrels met Jack long before he'd reached the door that seemed more like the dark, cool entrance to a cave. As a boy he'd had a profound fear of this place, afraid the barrels stored on their sides in ricks would shift and fall and he'd drown in a whiskey bath. The stuff even had a fragrance he didn't find palatable. Though Wade could down it like water, Jack had never acquired a taste for it, much to their father's chagrin.

Much had changed since those early days. The Turlock clan had come to America a hundred years before, rich from illicit distilling and smuggling in Ireland. They'd possessed a mere hundred acres of land but a hundred thousand in capital, most of it ill-gotten. His father, quick-witted no matter his faults, had eventually installed grain-handling equipment that could do the work of thirty men. The endeavor was a huge risk but one that had paid off in spades, shutting down the competition clear to Kentucky, where their greatest rivals operated on a smaller scale.

Remembering, Jack took in the swiftly changing landscape, marveling that each time he came, something new seemed to be in evidence. The present operation was a village in itself with the four-story malt house, drying kilns, saw and gristmill, and more. The cooperage where oak casks, staves, and hoops were turned out had recently been enlarged, and they'd had to bring up more slaves from Kentucky to manage the livestock fattened off the copious mash.

He'd ridden to Broad Oak that morning on the pretense of examining the still newly arrived from the British Isles—a behemoth containing ten tons of copper that would allow them to make greater quantities of whiskey at considerably less cost. It gleamed like a jewel on its bed of limestone, no worse for wear despite its long journey, already being petted and fretted over by Wade and master distiller Josiah Kilgore. They didn't look up at his approach, engrossed in examining every seam, tube, and rivet like a father might a newborn child.

Eyeing the huge contraption, Jack tried to summon some enthusiasm, but his interests lay at the start of the distilling process, not its end. Cultivating the finest corn and rye and experimenting with new varieties of grain fascinated him as much as it bored Wade. At least they weren't coveting the same things. Wade was firmly fixed as heir, and Jack was glad to be second in command. He could do as he pleased while his brother was tethered to Broad Oak. Forever.

Wade swung round, his bloodshot eyes raking Jack in a glance. One arm was in a sling. From another brawl? "So, Jack, think she's worth her weight in gold?"

"I'll answer that once you've put her through her paces."

"We'll soon be swimming in whiskey." Wade's boast fell flat as Kilgore pointed out a dent in the copper tubing. Deeming it a minor flaw, Wade returned his attention to Jack. "Our estimation is that we'll soon be averaging fifteen hundred gallons per day, depending on the availability of grain."

"We should glean the first wheat in early July, barring bad weather. Ninety or so bushels to the acre." His gaze held Wade's. "But I've come to discuss other matters. Like what you were doing at Teague's the other night with Peyton Ballantyne."

Wade's sudden smirk was confirmation that the liaison boded ill. "I may have found a chink in the Ballantyne armor. Peyton seems willing to ship some whiskey if the price is right."

Jack schooled his surprise. Their own father had tried to finagle such a deal for years, but Silas Ballantyne wanted nothing to do with their lucrative enterprise, so they'd been forced to rely on less desirable transport instead. "While his father is away, you mean. Without Silas's consent."

"I told him we'd pay double, that we're simply shipping grain to garrisons and fulfilling army contracts. Once the papers are drawn up, there'll be no way for them to back out or reconsider." Wade glanced at the cooperage, where a great many empty barrels were being loaded onto a wagon. "Now with greater quantities of whiskey being made, we'll be relying more on river travel instead of sending over land like we've been."

"You know the courts will back Ballantyne if he finds you lied and wants out of the contract."

Wade's grin turned sly. "Maybe, but I'm willing to risk it. We'll soon have an attractive cover with Ballantyne backing. It'll make your mission all the easier when you go west."

There was no denying this. The frontier was their future, their fortune. Be it over land, by boat, or by rail, Turlock whiskey would one day cover the entire continent, their father boasted. It hadn't hurt that Lewis and Clark had taken a hefty supply of Turlock spirits with them on their trek west, thus making a way.

"I'm simply looking to the horizon, Jack. Trade with New Orleans has never been better, and soon the West will be the same. The government can't restrict the sale or distribution of spirits forever. There's simply too much demand."

"If we aren't shut down first, you mean."

Wade shrugged. "Let the authorities nose around all they like. I'm not above a little intimidation, nor is Pa."

Nay, not the notorious Turlock clan, who had a history of burning down buildings in Pittsburgh and tarring and feathering its citizens. And worse. Jack passed a heavy hand over his whiskers. Though their guilt had never been proven, suspicions still lingered. He wasn't proud his father and grandfather were the instigators of Pennsylvania's Whiskey Rebellion the century before, nor was he oblivious to the fact Henry Turlock's name still inspired fear in the most stalwart of men.

Except Silas Ballantyne.

When Jack and Wade had been jailed for brawling and public drunkenness and their father had come round posting bail and making veiled threats, Silas, the temporary undersheriff at the time, had not so much as flinched.

Wade pulled a flask from his pocket and took a long sip. "Speaking of intimidation, what's this I hear about a bounty hunter being flung against a wall?"

Jack shrugged. "The search is off."

"I don't remember calling it off." Wade was studying him, his smug mood shifting. "I paid the bounty. It expires when the job is done."

"The McTavishes were murmuring about the Ballantynes. Considering something stupid." The very mention turned Jack cold right there in the warm June sunlight. Bounty hunters and slave catchers were known for their brutality, and it wasn't limited to the prey they caught. He fixed his gaze on the small pot stills that Broad Oak's slaves tended beneath a wooden awning, the women's heads bound with bright kerchiefs, the bare-chested men slick with sweat from the steam of the distillation.

Wade shrugged. "I'd hate for a McTavish to get in the way of a deal with Peyton Ballantyne. Maybe it's better those slaves stay missing after all."

Jack nearly sighed with relief, glad Wade didn't press him for particulars. He had no wish to label the Ballantynes abolitionists. He refused to even mention Ellie's name. Lovely, intriguing Ellie. Who would soon tire of Chloe and move on to other things. The memory of the fish she'd caught with Chloe and Ben almost made him smile. Though she'd reeled in two praiseworthy catfish, she refused to touch them, handing them to Jack in a bucket, her dainty nose wrinkled.

He'd fought down the inclination to ask her to stay for supper. He, Chloe, and Ben had built a fire on the riverbank and cooked the fish as dusk crowded in, only returning to the house when a sliver of moon denied them enough light to linger. Even then in the privacy of his study, buried in ink and ledgers, Jack felt his thoughts repeatedly go astray, as hard to rein in as wild horses.

Ellie. The jewel of her father's heart.

And now . . . his.

Ellie paused on the landing as Andra's voice rose from the foyer below. The two maids slipped past, silent as shadows, eyes downcast. Ellie knew little but their names, Mari and Gwyn. Twin sisters from Wales. Mama had rescued them from a tannery along the waterfront months earlier when they'd been orphaned at barely fifteen. Ellie couldn't tell them apart, but Andra could, and her tone knotted with impatience as she addressed them.

"Mari, the silver needs polishing in the pantry this morning. Gwyn, you may spend the day mending and ironing linens." She paused and consulted her list. "I have a feeling Mother and Father will arrive home at any moment, and we'd best be ready. I don't want them to think we've been remiss." Starting up the stairs, she looked back as if to ascertain they were moving in the right direction before focusing on Ellie. "Sister, we need to talk."

In Andra's hand was a letter. From Mama? Ellie felt a spark of excitement before the worried slant of Andra's mouth snuffed it altogether. Had Chloe sent a second note? Her light step turned heavy. She'd still not told anyone where she was spending her Wednesdays. Andra rarely asked about lessons, preoccupied as she was and somewhat disapproving, so Ellie had stayed silent. No one knew she went to River Hill save the stable hands, and they, like all New Hope's staff, were notoriously closemouthed. They simply took her there and returned her home four hours later.

As Andra's bedchamber door clicked closed, Ellie breathed in her unmistakable essence. A rose-carnation scent pervaded every inch of the utterly feminine room, even saturating the anteroom where Andra now led her.

"We've a letter." Andra lay the post down, turning it so Ellie could read the watermark. *York, Pennsylvania.* "'Tis marked urgent, and I think we should open it."

"But it's addressed to Mama—"

"And I'm acting in Mama's stead." Andra broke the seal with a swipe of a letter opener. Her expression was rapt—even hungry—as if some delicacy had been set before her and she couldn't wait to devour it.

"Are you . . . sure?" Ellie hovered between expectancy and dread. Mama seldom mentioned York County. And letters rarely came from there.

"'Tis from Aunt Elspeth." Andra sighed, scanning the page. "Grandmother Lee is failing and has asked Mama to come."

"To York?"

"Yes, to York." Andra set her chin in contemplation. "How unfortunate Mama isn't here. I wonder . . ."

"You're not considering going in her stead?"

"What an interesting thought! But how could I? With runaways in the attic and a household to manage . . ." Her voice trailed away, yet Ellie could see the temptation had taken hold. "I'm certain I would get my questions answered there."

"What do you mean?"

"My queries about Mama's family. She's not very forthcoming, I'm afraid. Just look." Laying the letter aside, she gestured to her genealogical papers. "I've nearly completed Da's side of the family, barring a trip to Scotland, but Mama's . . ."

Ellie could see the empty places on the Lee register begging to be filled. "I sense Mama's childhood was not a happy one. Why else would she stay silent?"

"All that aside, it's important for these names and dates to be known. They're our history—our heritage."

"I'm not sure about you going to York." Ellie's voice was soft. "But that may be better than worrying Mama about it."

Their eyes met and held, Ellie growing more alarmed by the minute. She could feel Andra's mind spinning, calculating distance, coin, timing. "I could take the stage . . . be there in days. Perhaps it would be a comfort to Mama since she's not here to do the same. Perhaps the Lord wants me to go in her stead."

Ellie nearly rolled her eyes. Rarely did Andra invoke the Lord's name unless it was her own will she wanted done. Suddenly even Ellie's homecoming held providential purpose.

"You're here now and can assume things in my absence—manage the household, continue teaching Ulie. I'll convince Ansel not to light the cupola till I return."

"Shouldn't you consult Peyton first—"

"I doubt I'll see Peyton to ask him." Andra's irritation returned. "He's so burdened with business he forgets to come home."

"Ansel says he's taken rooms in town."

"Rooms. I wonder. He'd not do such with Da here." She took up the letter again, brow creased in question. "Haven't you ever wondered what Aunt Elspeth looks like? *Is* like? Or Thomas, Mama's younger brother, who inherited the smithy when Grandfather Lee died? And then there's Grandmother Lee. You're named after her, you know."

Elinor Louise. Ellie knew it well enough. Still, she felt a whisper of warning. "Perhaps your going to York would be wrong. What if they only want Mama and don't welcome you—"

"A hearty welcome is not what I'm looking for. I simply want names. Dates. Answers."

"But Grandmother Lee may be dying. 'Tis not the time—"

"Well, *you're* the one who broached the idea!" Andra stood, looking like a general contemplating battle. "I've decided to go. For Mama's sake."

"When will you leave?" Ellie asked, warming to the idea despite her worries.

"Day after tomorrow."

"Shouldn't you have an escort?"

"Don't be silly. I'm perfectly capable of looking after myself."

Ellie studied her sister with quiet wonder. Once Andra made up her mind, there was no turning back.

The Ballantyne steel, their father called it.

12

Those who forgive most shall be most forgiven.

JOSIAH BAILEY

Standing in the polished foyer clutching the small leather basket holding all of New Hope's keys, Ellie felt decidedly skittish. If she rose each morning by five and supervised all the household needs, then tended Adam and schooled Ulie, her afternoons would still be free for lessons.

If all went well.

An arm's length away from her stood Mari and Gwyn, looking decidedly more cheery now that the door had shut in Andra's wake. On the mahogany sideboard to her right were pages and pages of instructions, some in Mama's hand penned for Andra and some in Andra's hand penned for Ellie. She gathered them up, feeling armed for battle and somewhat prepared, except for the matter of Adam and Ulie.

She was ever mindful that from his cupola perch, Ansel had seen shadows—movement—along the riverbank and woods. Slave hunters or slaves? The giant lantern hadn't been lit for a fortnight or better. But as soon as the crossing was less treacherous, the light would shine again.

"Adam's spirits are improving despite his injuries," Ansel had told her at daybreak. Sadly, the damage to his mouth was far less encouraging despite their frequent ministrations. "When he's better, Dr. Brunot will come and transport them to the next station."

Station. Yet another hiding place, she guessed. She dared not ask more questions because she feared the answers.

Lord, protect them, bless them, cover them as they go north to freedom. Cover us.

Her relief at the thought of their leaving was short-lived. Soon others would come and take their place. An endless string of them, Ansel said, empathy shining in his eyes. Even now Da might have a Ballantyne boat steaming north, more fugitives hidden among the cargo.

"Pardon me, miss. Are you all right?" Mari's Welsh accent reached out to her, ushering her back to the foyer and the unsullied summer morning.

"Yes, thank you. Where were we?" Glancing at the papers, Ellie tried to recall the thread of conversation. "If you both could see to the parlor, clean Feathers's cage, and dust the study, that should be a fine start. I'll be planning menus with Mamie in the kitchen should you need me."

They nodded in tandem and disappeared, each bearing a feather duster and rags smelling of lemon oil. Leaving out the back door, Ellie let the warm morning air wrap round her. Her favorite task was walking the grounds at dawn and unlocking every dependency, the day new and untouched.

She became reacquainted with everything while making the rounds in Andra's stead, rediscovering all the little details she'd forgotten. The tang of the smokehouse. The potent henhouse. The chill of the larder, where meats were packed in Portuguese salt. The busy washhouse, brimming with color and lye, manned by three of the tenants' wives. Only the spinning house, where Saxony wheels and carders had once hummed industriously, now sat idle.

Ellie stayed clear of the stables, the staff quarters, and storehouse. This was Ansel's domain, as was the gristmill on Rogue Creek half a mile away.

Her final stop was her favorite. As she traversed the colonnade to the summer kitchen, passing myriad posts smothered in climbing roses, her worries of the night passed. On such a summer morning, it was hard to believe evil could exist.

"You hungry, child?"

Child. Is that all she'd ever be to Mamie? Ellie smiled and accepted a biscuit layered with ham from Mamie's outstretched hand. She took a bite, gratitude filling her as the woman poured a cup of hyson tea. "It's a fine mornin'. You goin' to your lessons?" In the bright light flooding the tidy kitchen, Ellie detected another question in Mamie's eyes.

"Not till this afternoon." Ellie reached for the cream and sugar and eyed a shelf clock. "It only takes half an hour to get there."

Mamie nodded, hands busy paring potatoes. "Where's 'there'?"

Ellie almost choked on her tea. There was simply no evading Mamie. Shifting on the stool, she weighed her answer. "River Hill."

Mamie's eyes flared. "What you doin' at River Hill?"

"Schooling Chloe Turlock."

Her gaze grew wider. "Who's the master there? Gentleman Jack? I s'pect he's in need of some tutorin' too."

A chuckle rose in Ellie's throat. "Perhaps."

Shaking her head, Mamie moved to a corner where a

chicken hung. "How long is it goin' to take with Miss Chloe? Reckon you can finish before your daddy comes home?"

"Sometimes I don't think Chloe will ever be finished." The confession slipped out, truthful and a touch unkind. Chloe was rough as a gravelly riverbank, like all the Turlocks, and had some stubborn habits. "Once I correct her spitting—"

"Spittin'? I bet those brothers of hers taught her that." Mamie's hazel eyes held a warning. "I remember them boys throwin' rocks and ugly words around when you was small."

"'Twas long ago, Mamie."

"Now their deeds go darker. Deeper."

Did they? Despite the day's warmth, the words brought goose bumps. What all did Mamie know? But Mamie had turned away, scalding the chicken, the smell of feathers heavy in the air. Ellie finished her biscuit, sipped her tea, and watched sunlight spackle the blue Spode dishes in a far cupboard. She fought her heaviness of heart, wondering if her prayers for Jack and Chloe reached no further than the ceiling.

Mamie's shoulders sagged as she began to pluck the scalded fowl. "I'd be ashamed to give voice to such deeds. And I shudder 'bout what your folks will think when they find you rubbin' shoulders with Turlocks."

"I couldn't turn Chloe away," Ellie said quietly. "She came here wanting something more, something better. Who am I to refuse her?"

"Doesn't Scripture say the good Lord visits the iniquity of the fathers on the children to the third and fourth generations of those that hate Him?"

"But doesn't it also say the son shall not bear the iniquity of the father if he turns from his sins?" She looked at Mamie entreatingly, clinging to the Scripture she'd taken to heart. "'Have I any pleasure at all that the wicked should die? saith the LORD GOD: and not that he should return from his ways,

135

and live?' It's not too late for Chloe or any of her kin in God's eyes, is it?"

A softening soothed Mamie's features. "You have your mama's heart, that's for sure. I just wish you had a measure of your daddy's good sense."

Ellie tried to smile. She'd always been a bit impetuous, led by her feelings.

Heaving a sigh, Mamie wrestled the plump chicken into a pot. "The Turlocks were always bad to the bone, right from the start. I remember them comin' to Fort Pitt when I was young as you and cookin' for the soldiers there. They'd been makin' their whiskey in Ireland and set up a still outside fort walls, dousin' the Indians with it when they came for treaties and to trade." She hesitated, lip atremble. "My own pa—he took to the whiskey and never did right himself."

A dozen images lit Ellie's mind concerning the little she knew about Mamie's past. Drunkenness. Beatings. Coin squandered for liquor over food. She wanted to shut the hurt of it away, but Mamie's pain was grafted on her wrinkled face. "When your daddy came to Pittsburgh as a blacksmith, Judge O'Hara owned River Hill, and I was cookin' for Jean Marie's tavern atop Grant's Hill. The whiskey tax soon caused an uproar in the county, and the Turlocks and their ilk began makin' more mischief for those who supported the tax. Word was one of the Turlocks tried to kill your daddy. No one suspected the judge's own daughter would run off with the worst of 'em."

Ellie knew the worst of them was Jack's father, Henry. As for the threat against her father . . . Shaken, she rose from her stool, mindful of the tick of the mantel clock as it pulsed past noon, toward the forbidden. Why did she always feel the need to defend Chloe? Jack?

"Mr. Turlock has never behaved unseemly. Granted, he's

rarely there when I come. I expect he'll be away today." Once
again she fought down her inexplicable disappointment of
late at finding him gone. "I'll be back for supper. 'Twill just
be me and Ansel tonight, unless Peyton appears."

Mamie gave her a lingering look, as if she feared she might
not return. "I feel some better, knowin' it's just you and Miss
Chloe."

Ellie hugged her tight. "And there's Mrs. Malarkey, the
housekeeper, who could take a few baking lessons from you.
Though she's a lovely Southern lady, her biscuits are hard as
Fort Pitt bricks."

Mamie chuckled, but the worry in her eyes remained. "I'll
be lookin' for you 'bout suppertime, then."

Ellie tried not to be *too* pleased that Andra was away,
though she was finding it hard to keep up with her myriad
responsibilities. Housekeeping was indeed tedious business.
She lacked Andra's knack for following after the help and
making sure everything was done, dusted, and put away—
and scolding if it wasn't. Moreover, her sister's canary was
worrying her to no end, as it was suddenly refusing to sing
and plucking out its feathers with an agitated beak, hardly
deserving of its name.

"If he expires—or becomes bald—we'll hear no end to
the matter." Ansel stood by the cage, arms crossed, as if he
could glare the bird into submission.

"Perhaps you can coax Feathers to sing by playing your
violin," Ellie suggested.

He grinned. "Or silence him forever."

They laughed and moved to the music room, though they
did leave the parlor door open. As Ansel took out his case,
Ellie felt a delicious intoxication. They'd played together but

twice since her homecoming, and both times they'd grown
so lost in the music time had melted away. Only Andra had
halted their reverie, reminding them it was midnight. But
today, just past noon, neither she nor Peyton were at home.
The only audience was Adam and Ulie and the baby, who
carefully kept to the attic.

Seated at her harp, Ellie felt a nick of fear. If trouble came,
they wouldn't hear the jostle of horses and barking of dogs,
sequestered as they were in the music room with its thick
walls. She groped for a snatch of Scripture, a favorite from
Psalms, to settle herself. *Praise Him with the psaltery and
harp . . . praise Him with stringed instruments*. This they
would do, danger or no.

She waited patiently as Ansel riffled through sheets of
music, some of his own composing. In profile his hair, so
ruffled from his habit of raking his fingers through it, reminded her of their father. Pensive. Handsome. Intense.

"Does Da ever play?" she asked.

He glanced up from the mahogany music stand. "Only
when Mother asks him to. He's none too fond of these violins.
The tone, he says, is far inferior to his own."

"The Guarneri he sold years ago?"

He gave a nod, the set of his jaw telling her it was still a
sore subject. She pressed on gently. "Have you given up trying to locate it?"

Taking up his bow, he applied rosin to the strings till a
white cloud fell over the stand. "The trail stopped cold in
Paris two years ago."

"Paris?"

"I've written to serious collectors in Europe, and everything points to its sale somewhere along the Petit Champ
after it left Da's hands in Philadelphia. But I have no name.
No contacts."

"You've not looked since?"

"I've no time for it. Ballantyne interests are always expanding. You've heard about the new ironworks, I suppose."

"Yes, Peyton talks of little else, but I'd rather hear about your music. When I left for finishing school years ago, you'd begun making a violin in the workshop above the stables."

"Child's play." He struck a string and winced. "I should have apprenticed with one of the master luthiers in Europe by now."

Sensing his frustration, she fell silent, turning back to her harp. They began a piece by Handel before moving to a Scots strathspey. Discordantly. Full of starts and stops. When Peyton came in unexpectedly, his expression a grimace, they stopped altogether, though Peyton, for all his accomplishments, couldn't play a note.

He took the chair nearest Ellie and began loosening his cravat. "Don't stop on account of me. From the sounds of it, you two need plenty more practice." Ellie stuck her tongue out playfully and he smirked. "Though truthfully, I prefer the harp to the violin and always have."

Ansel shot him a knifelike look, and the tension in the room raised a notch. Ellie moved on to a piece by Haydn, sensing a confrontation coming that had little to do with the music.

Over her soft playing, Peyton said to Ansel, "You're needed at the boatyard. Something about copper sheathing on that schooner to protect it from shipworms in southern waters."

Ansel's bowing stopped. "I left the head shipwright specific directions about the hull. Why did he come to you?"

"Because you were here when you should have been there, and he had other questions." The censure in Peyton's tone made Ellie cringe.

"There's more to my being home than making music."

"That's not what it looks like."

"Dr. Brunot's due any minute."

Ellie plucked a wrong note and recovered, directing her gaze to Ansel.

He continued in an undertone. "If you'd seen all the signs along Rogue Creek . . ."

"Slave catchers, you mean," Peyton murmured.

Her hands stilled and both brothers looked at her.

"On second thought," Peyton said, all animosity gone, "rotting schooners can wait."

He got up and went out, leaving the door to the music room ajar. Ellie heard the gun case beneath the stair open and close. In moments he'd returned with a pearl-handled pistol. "Our little sister is in need of some shooting practice."

Ansel gave a nod while Ellie's eyes widened. "Today—right now?"

"Why not? It won't be a long lesson if you prove a fair shot. Andra certainly is."

Ellie didn't doubt it. Andra seemed to master anything she put her mind to—except matrimony.

The pistol felt cool and heavy in her hand despite its diminutive size. Yet rather than allay her fears, the weapon stoked them. And Peyton's intensity only fanned them further.

"This is Mother's gun. Andra took hers to York." He led her outside, onto the back veranda, showing her his own pistol tucked inside his greatcoat. "We'll use some old bottles from the glassworks as targets," he told her, "though I'd prefer a Turlock or two."

13

Though she be but little, she is fierce!
WILLIAM SHAKESPEARE

"Jack, I do believe you're avoiding me!"

The scolding in Chloe's voice made Jack smile. In tone she sounded like their mother, but in her exasperation she was still a child. He didn't so much as glance toward the stable door, where his sister stood in cross-armed defiance. He simply continued examining saddles and harness, muttering a Latin phrase beneath his breath: *"Qui se excusat, se accusat."* He accuses himself who excuses himself.

It wasn't Chloe he was avoiding but Ellie. And he supposed his actions betrayed him. But there was no sidestepping Chloe. She circled round till she stood in front of him, looking like she might snatch a near horsewhip and lash him. "I don't know a lick of Latin, Jack, so stop your mumbling. Miss Ellie is teaching me French. And I've learned enough from her to know a gentleman doesn't keep a lady waiting—and she's waiting for you in your study! *Dépêchez-vous!*"

Hurry up?

Letting go of the leather trappings, he started after her,

albeit reluctantly, following the blue swish of her skirt as she left the stable. A new dress? Recently she and Ellie had been shopping in Pittsburgh. After an afternoon at the milliner's and dressmaker's—and untold damage to his bank account—Chloe appeared to have left childhood far behind.

She turned back to him, blatant disapproval in her eyes. "Really, Jack, you look like you've been jumping in the hay mow!" As they climbed the steps to the house, she plucked some straw from his shirtsleeve. "And you reek of horses!" Nose wrinkling, she dug in her pocket and thrust a small vial toward him. He looked askance at the offering.

Caswell Massey Number Six?

"This," she announced, "is what a gentleman should smell like."

Disgusted, he tucked the cologne in his pocket. "I'm no gentleman."

Fire lit her eyes, and her voice was a poorly disguised whisper. "I've told you that Miss Ellie isn't for me . . ."

She's for you.

He stopped her right there in the hall, a stone's throw from his study door, his voice a low hiss. "I've gone along with your little scheme so far, but it stops *now*. Ellie Ballantyne is here for you and you alone. Understand?"

"That's not true, Jack! Even God agrees with me—'It is not good for man to be alone . . . go forth and multiply,' and all that!"

His hand clamped her shoulder. "Listen hard, Chloe—"

But she simply shook him off and headed the other direction. "I think I hear Mrs. Malarkey calling."

He watched her go, raking a hand through hair he hadn't bothered to comb in days, though it was clean, at least. He'd swum across the Monongahela and back at daybreak, just as he did nearly every morning save in winter. Pausing, he retrieved the cologne from his pocket and deposited it in a liquor chest in the hall before opening the study door.

Something told him Ellie awaited to give notice, that she'd tired of playing tutor to Chloe. Or her father had returned and forbidden it. Just as well. Time the charade ended once and for all. He was becoming far too aware of her—the profound emptiness he felt in her wake, the stranglehold she had on his senses.

Her gentleness disturbed him.

He swallowed down any disappointment he felt for Chloe as he stepped into the room, but nothing could prepare him for the picture Ellie made as she waited for him. Patiently. Expectantly. And heartrendingly lovely in a pale blue dress that fluttered to her ankles in an alluring flounce. Her back was to him, the knot of curls that crowned her head cascading to the nape of her slender neck, the paisley shawl she wore slipping off her shoulders, its fringed end swaying gently as she turned round.

The smile she gave him was nothing short of glorious. Did she smile that way at everyone? So broadly a dimple appeared in her left cheek? For a moment he couldn't even recall his own name. "I—my sister said—"

Her gaze was unblinking. "Chloe told me you wanted to see me."

The tightness in his chest soared.

Duped again.

But Ellie was obviously none the wiser.

"Chloe says a great many things," he muttered, unaccustomed to the heat creeping up his neck. He moved to his desk, shuffled some papers, and tried to salvage the situation. "I was simply wondering—how are the lessons going?"

"Very well. Her penmanship is improving and she's quite fond of reading. I was hoping we might borrow a few books."

He glanced at the bookcases. "Borrow as many as you like."

"I was thinking of George Whitefield's *Journals* and a Bible."

"Whitefield, the British evangelist?"

"You've heard of him?"

"My grandfather once heard him preach in Philadelphia." He walked to the far side of the study, pushed aside a rolling ladder, and opened a glass-fronted case. "His *Journals* are in here."

"Do you know where everything is so readily?"

There was teasing in her tone as they surveyed what was, at last inventory, over ten thousand tomes. "I've a ready explanation. The books are grouped by subject. The Bible you're wanting is in my bedchamber."

She took the leather-bound books from him. "I won't trouble you about the Bible, then, especially if it's in use."

"Your father gave it to me . . . the last time I was in jail."

Color pinked her cheeks, but her gaze held steadfast. "Then it must be having some effect, given you've not been back since."

He nearly smiled as she looked down at the borrowed books. She was so close his every sense was heightened. Lemon . . . lavender . . . talc. Her subtle fragrance rivaled the lilacs at River Hill's entrance. He wrestled with wanting to reach out and touch an inky curl to test its softness.

Like the rogue he was.

Turning her back to him, she began perusing the shelves while he sat down, scuffed boots up on the corner of his desk. Try as he might, he couldn't keep his mind on the words at hand.

"What are you reading?" she asked, looking over her shoulder.

"*The American Farm and Garden.*"

She nodded thoughtfully. "Speaking of gardens, I have another request. 'Tis Chloe's, actually."

He removed his glasses and rested his book atop his chest, not bothering to lower his boots.

"Might we have a small corner of the garden? A sunny place to plant some flowers?"

The request, so humbly and hopefully stated, tugged at him.

Just a corner? I would give you all the garden if you would ask, Ellie.

"Aye, if you like," he said.

Her petition was so small. Couldn't she sense he'd give her anything? Anything at all?

All but his heart. That he kept locked. Behind bars.

"I have some seeds from Hope Rising—perennials mostly. Gardening holds some good lessons, and your garden was once so beautiful. The talk of Pittsburgh, Mama said. I heard it rivaled the King's Garden outside Fort Pitt."

"That was before my time or yours." He regretted his abruptness but wanted to bring a close to the conversation. He needed to talk to Chloe—reiterate what he'd said in the hall. Absent himself. "You're leaving now, I'd wager."

"Yes, we're done for the day. I just need to give these books to Chloe."

He got up and took them from her hands, feeling an insatiable desire to read them himself. "I'll see that she gets them. And I'll walk you to your carriage."

Now what had made him say that?

It sounded almost . . . gentlemanly.

Jack rode Cicero hard, skirting the fringes of River Hill, hoping to outride the knot festering inside him—or at least loosen its frayed edges. All around him, endless fields of grain bowed low in the warm night wind. His land. His bounty. Tonight they failed to bring the usual pleasure. He was weary. Hungry. Flummoxed.

When Ellie's carriage had disappeared through River Hill's imposing gates that afternoon, he'd found Chloe in the southeast corner of the garden, already overturning a plot of soil. He wrestled the shovel away from her, his aggravation at fever's pitch. "Should a lady be digging like a common laborer?"

"I'm wearing gloves—see?" She held up canvas-covered hands already blackened with dirt. "Miss Ellie said you can't call a garden your own unless you tend it, which is what I'm doing."

"I'll help you, then." He thrust the rusty tool into soft soil, unearthing loamy ground, rocks, and a tangle of worms.

She stood and watched him work, expression perplexed. "I know you didn't come out here to help me, Jack. You look mad enough to spit nails."

"Aye, I'm here to fix your flint once and for all in regards to Ellie." He gave her a black look before another shovel thrust. "No more double dealing, understand? No more conniving or manipulating or—"

The surprise on her face was sharp. "But that's what you and Wade and Pa always do!"

Aye, best take a long look in the mirror, Jack.

He felt he'd been hit broadside with the shovel. Tears wet Chloe's eyes and spilled down her dress front. She looked like a little girl again, and it didn't help that Ben was watching, his own eyes damp and round as marbles as he peered at them over the garden wall.

She swiped at her eyes with a dainty sleeve. "I asked her here for you, Jack. You're all alone. You need someone like

Miss Ellie." Her words were all a-warble. "She's pretty and kind. She even likes to fish. She's not a strumpet!"

"Chloe Isabel . . ."

"What's more, she seems to like me—and Ben. I-I can't tell if she likes you yet. She never says."

He tossed the shovel aside. "A lady like Ellie would never consider a Turlock, no matter how much conniving is done. If she comes here at all, it's out of pity. A mercy mission. Don't expect it to last. She'll soon move on."

Turning away, he left her with Ben and returned to his study, only to find that Ellie's lingering presence drove him out again. He finally sought refuge in the stables, taking deep breaths, his pulse racing inexplicably. Cicero whinnied in welcome as he led him out into the waning sunlight, not bothering with a saddle, just sinking his fingers into the horse's tumbled mane and riding bareback.

Stepping out of a cottage, his farm manager tried to intercept him, but he waved him away. He was in no mood for small talk or fielding trouble with tenants. His feelings were too raw, ready to spill over into a brawl. All because of Ellie Ballantyne.

He took a backwoods route to Broad Oak, arriving in record time, disgruntled when his mother met him on the porch. Her eyes narrowed as he tied Cicero to the hitching post. He rarely arrived at dusk, and she likely sensed trouble. "You're just in time for supper."

"I'm not hungry." The words were flat, gruff, much like her welcome. "There's a storm brewing and I need to hurry. I'll not be long."

Thunder underscored his words and sent a shiver up his back. Ever since his brush with death along the turnpike, the mere threat of rain haunted him and seemed to carry a second warning. He brushed past her and went into the house, slowing impatiently when her voice trailed him, tethering him.

"If it's Wade you're looking for, he's not here. He's in jail . . . alongside Peyton Ballantyne."

He stopped as if lightning-struck, turning in time to see blatant satisfaction, even triumph, cross her aging face. "Apparently, Wade became intoxicated and tore up the gentlemen's club in town. Peyton was jailed for inviting him in, among other things. Something to do with gambling . . . a threatened duel."

"Has bail been posted?"

"Not yet. They're such a lovely pairing, I urged your father to let them sit it out." She smiled coldly, her sarcasm at its peak. "Of course, Peyton might be released by his brother or one of his father's business associates once word gets round. But the damage is done. It's sure to be in all the papers come morning."

There was no measuring her glee. Disgusted, Jack pushed open the door to his father's study and found him leaning back in his chair, cigar in hand. Josiah Kilgore stood by a window and gave Jack a cursory nod as he came in. Gauzy spirals of smoke curled toward the elaborate plasterwork ceiling. A celebratory cigar? His father's ill will toward the Ballantynes was just as deep as his mother's, and he looked equally pleased.

Jack rued his timing, relieved when the door closed behind Kilgore and he and Henry were left alone.

"Well, Jack, you've no doubt heard the news. It's sure to be the talk of all Allegheny County shortly."

Jack took a chair, misery twisting inside him. Though he had no fondness for Peyton, he regretted the turn of events, if only for Ellie's sake. And he had no wish to discuss it further. "I'm here to talk about going west. To Missouri and beyond."

Henry studied him through the smoke. "When I first broached the matter, you weren't what I'd call willing."

"I've changed my mind." The words were terse and far too obliging, revealing a desperation he'd not intended. "I'll leave whenever you like."

Immediately his father's hackles rose. "You're not in any trouble, are you? In town? With that slattern Janey?" He leaned forward, displeasure deepening the furrows in his face. "I'll not have another illegitimate child on my hands, not after Wade's debacle with the women at Teague's Tavern, both of them claiming—"

"Nay," Jack cut in. "I tend to learn from Wade's mistakes, not repeat them."

Henry's gaze hardened. "I don't care what you do just as long as you don't get caught doing it."

The warning chilled Jack to the bone. Though he'd been hearing the admonition all his life, tonight it seemed more wounding. He fixed his attention on a brace of dueling pistols in back of his father. "I'm considering selling River Hill, using the profits to push west and establish a distillery up the Missouri River like we planned."

Jack sensed his father's surprise in the silence that followed. Henry raised a hand and smoothed his mustache, his stare unwavering. "That's all well and good. But those eight hundred barrels that need escorting won't be ready till autumn. Besides, with Wade residing in the county jail more than Broad Oak lately, you're needed here."

"Autumn, then. Time enough to bring in the harvest." Yet even as he agreed, his anxiety deepened. Months yet.

His father nodded. "I'm certain our new venture in the West will prove profitable, given your oversight. We should finish the fall run by October. By then you'll be on your way west before the rivers freeze. You can winter at Fort Bliss, scout the best land, prepare for spring planting."

"You've no objection to the sale of the estate?"

"Not as long as we can lease the land and continue to grow grain. But your mother might not be so agreeable to the plan. It was her home, after all." He snuffed his cigar and stood, hesitating long enough to check the timepiece in his waistcoat pocket. "Care to join us for supper, Jack?"

"Nay, I need to get back to River Hill. Chloe."

Henry nodded and started for the hall. "How is your sister?"

Jack mulled his answer. He wouldn't mention Ellie. The less said, the better. "She seems content."

"Well, she's enough like her mother that it won't last." The words were spoken at the very entrance to the candlelit dining room, loudly enough to set Isabel smoldering.

Jack could hear the soft clink of china as a skittish maid prepared to serve the first course, careful to not offend her mistress. The tension was as thick as the gravy being set upon the sideboard in its crystal dish. Isabel looked ready to pile on the agony as Henry joined her at the immense table.

Without another word, Jack turned on his heel and left the house. He walked into the damp, lightning-lit night, more pent-up than when he'd come. Perhaps peace could be found in Missouri.

It had always eluded him here.

14

A lost good name is ne'er retrieved.

JOHN GAY

Twilight found Ellie sorting seeds in a warm corner of the hothouse and wrapping them carefully in wax paper. On the outside of each packet she wrote the name of the plant, what month it flowered, and how high it grew. A catalog of John Bartram and Sons of Philadelphia lay open to a lantern's lambent glow. June was fading fast. If she and Chloe started soon, at least a portion of River Hill's garden would be abloom by late summer.

Head bent in concentration, she didn't hear the slight footfall beyond the open door.

"Ellie?"

Looking up, Ellie took in the familiar silhouette, surprised at seeing Mina at such an hour. "Please, come in. Are you . . . all right?"

"I'm fine, Ellie. Ansel asked me to come. He's gone to town with my father. There's been a bit of trouble."

Ellie stood and held the lantern higher as if to shed more light on the matter. "Trouble?"

151

"Peyton is—well, he's . . ." Her voice dropped a notch. "In jail."

Jail? The very mention sent Ellie's stomach swirling. She didn't even like to utter the word. Jail was darkness. Misdeeds. Lostness. Peyton wouldn't . . . couldn't . . .

Mina's face, usually so animated, was ashen. "Something happened with a Turlock at the gentleman's club."

Ellie's thoughts spun to Jack. She'd left River Hill but hours ago. Had he gotten into trouble since? Or was it Wade?

"You know those Turlocks—never idle for a minute, but they're making mischief," Mina said, reaching out to touch a lemon tree's waxy leaves.

Ellie clamped down a warm retort in Jack's defense and ached to know more, but Mina seemed preoccupied with the hothouse's lush interior. A far cry from the drama at the jail.

"Papa went with Ansel to post bail. I'm not sure when they'll return." Mina turned back to her. "I'll stay with you till they do."

How long did it take to free someone from jail? Ellie wished Jack was near enough to ask. Speechless, she followed Mina into the house, where they sat in the parlor and sipped tea. The whole evening seemed odd . . . off-kilter. Even Feathers was strangely silent in his corner cage.

Mina tried valiantly to distract her with chatter and eventually succeeded. "Daniel is coming home."

Though her thoughts stayed pinned on Peyton, Ellie managed, "I've not seen your brother in two years or better, not since your mother's passing."

"Far too long," Mina pronounced, reaching into her pocket for a letter. From Daniel? Opening it, she scanned it briefly before reading, "Tell Elinor I expect a dance—and I promise not to step on her slippers." Mina looked up. "Has he ever called you Ellie?"

"Never."

"Well, he's ready to take a position at the glassworks. There's some excitement over an invention of his involving lead and sand. Your father thinks it may revolutionize the way glass is made not only in Pittsburgh but elsewhere."

"He's getting nearer a patent, then."

"One would hope. After ten years or better . . ." She placed the letter on a table. "He has no interest in farming like Father. He thinks the future is in glass, industry."

"Sounds ambitious."

"Oh, he's always been fiercely competitive. Don't you remember?"

Ellie didn't. Amidst the excitement of her homecoming and all that was happening, her old memories of Daniel Cameron had been shelved like a tin of stale tea. "I'd rather talk of you and Ansel."

It was Mina's turn to flush. "There's precious little to discuss on that score."

"I thought—hoped—the two of you had set a date."

Mina shook her head, eyes downcast. "The only dates Ansel thinks about are launch dates. I'm afraid I'm the only one pondering a honeymoon voyage aboard one of your father's vessels."

"Honeymooning on a steamer sounds very romantic."

"So you aren't opposed to the idea?"

"What? Steamboat trips?"

"Becoming a Cameron."

For just a moment Ellie succumbed to the notion. "I suppose now that I'm home, it's expected that I'll settle down. But I still don't feel . . . ready."

"Ready?" Mina repeated.

"I want to know Daniel cares for me." Frustration tinged her words. "It has to be more than something unspoken . . . expected."

"He's cared for you since childhood. He even spoke with your father about you when he was last home."

Had he?

Overhead came the sudden shutting of a door. A baby's cry. Ellie tensed, praying for quiet.

Mina's gaze fixed on the ceiling before drifting down again. "I know about the people in the attic, Ellie." She squeezed Ellie's hand. "Ansel told me some time ago. Perhaps we should go into the music room. I'll be glad to accompany you on the pianoforte if you like."

Ellie nodded, desperate to mask the attic sounds. To ease the pain she felt over Peyton. To quell the flutter of anxiety at the mention of Daniel's name.

To forget Jack Turlock.

In all his five and twenty years, Ansel had never set foot in the Allegheny County Jail. Though his father had once been temporary sheriff and the building was a respectable-looking establishment on the corner of Fourth Street, he'd never crossed its threshold till now. Sheriff Ramsay met him and Cullen Cameron at the door, surprise and regret on his weathered face.

"Ansel, Cullen." With a nod to them both, he returned to a wide desk lit by a single candle. Behind him yawned a narrow hall with barred cells leading to a dead-end brick wall. Skeleton keys hung nearby from a rack. "I suppose you've come for Peyton."

Ansel nodded, trying to stem the stench of urine and spirits and worse, his breathing labored from the effort.

The sheriff took out some paperwork and inked a quill. "Bail is set at the amount written. Sign here and make payment. Then I'll release him. But you might have trouble getting him to sit his horse. He's that drunk."

Ansel winced. Richard Ramsay wasn't known to mince words, but this was one time Ansel wished he would. He'd never seen Peyton drunk. Even the thought seemed ludicrous. He almost didn't believe it.

"Well, there's a saying in Ireland about that," Cullen murmured with forced levity. "A young man's got to make his hay before the sun sets, whether rich or poor. I expect your brother has now done so."

The words failed to lessen Ansel's disquiet, though he appreciated the older man's efforts. Ramsay counted the money Ansel laid out—once, twice—before reaching for the keys. "Follow me, as there might be a bit of a ruckus. The jail's full tonight, so I've had to combine two and three to a cell. If any try to rush the door, you'll have to help me keep order."

With that, he cocked a pistol, holding it aloft, keys in the other hand. Ansel's angst thickened. *God in heaven, I'm glad Da isn't here to witness this.* It was shame enough to share the burden with Cullen Cameron, a godly man and elder in the Presbyterian Church.

When they reached the last cell, past shouts and curses and spirit-sated laughter, Ansel felt as filthy as the floor he walked upon. A lone candle was affixed to an end wall, otherwise the cells were cast in darkness. Like hell, Ansel thought. Hell was surely full of such vile smells. And sounds.

"That you, Ballantyne?"

A man lunged at the bars, rattling them so hard Ansel thought they might bend. He hated that he started. But even Cullen looked wary as he turned toward the sound. Someone was spewing epithets their way—and more. A wad of spit slicked the back of Ansel's neck, and he groped for his handkerchief in the darkness.

"Take that, you pious upstart!" a man shouted.

"Mind your tongue, you heathen Hennessey," the sheriff

spat back at him. "Ye'll find no favors trying to bust out or belittle sober citizens. Get back to your cot."

A rattle of keys. The whine of bars swinging open. Ansel tensed at the sight of Peyton's drawn face in a dark corner, revealing bloodshot eyes and soiled clothes that would never come clean.

"Bail's been posted, Ballantyne."

Peyton stood—or tried to—and then listed a bit. A solid figure rose in back of him, grabbed his coat collar, and heaved him toward the opening.

Wade Turlock.

Ansel's gaze shot round the fetid cell for a second shadow, sure Jack was there too.

"That . . . you . . . Ansel?"

Peyton's words, hopelessly slurred, brought more shame. Ansel had to shoulder him out as the sheriff slammed the door behind them, his voice overriding the din. "I have his personal effects up front—a pistol and the like."

Ansel gathered up Peyton's belongings while Cullen led him outside. How they would get him home was a mystery. He clearly couldn't sit his horse. Tonight the few miles to New Hope seemed one too many.

15

More things are wrought by prayer
than this world dreams of.
ALFRED LORD TENNYSON

Long after the music had faded, Ellie lay awake, listening to the house settle, trying not to think of jail and the strange matter of bail. 'Twas all too easy to ponder River Hill instead and wonder whether Chloe was abed, or whether Jack . . . Stifling the thought, she turned on her side, the linen pillow slip smooth against her heated cheek. Old houses seemed to have noises that only came alive at night. Though she didn't believe in ghosts, she felt River Hill and New Hope a fine haven for them, full of dusty memories from another century.

At midnight the Edinburgh-made clock in the foyer far below struck a resounding twelve notes like little chimes. Ellie felt a ripple of unrest at another sound. Approaching horses. Her heart seized. Bounty hunters?

Lord, protect us, please . . .

Mina slept alongside her, her breathing deep and even. Tonight Ansel wasn't home to throw open the door, rifle in hand, Andra in his wake. Just two helpless women. Getting up, she reached for her dressing gown and felt her way to the door, dredging up Scripture to keep her knees from knocking. *The Lord is my rock, my fortress . . .*

A key clicked in a lock. The front door swung wide as she peered into the foyer below.

Peyton looked up at her, bewhiskered and red-eyed, Ansel silent and serious behind him. She hovered on the top step, wondering what Andra would do in such a moment. Lambast Peyton, most likely. She felt a rush of gratitude her parents couldn't see their firstborn so . . . undone.

Hurrying down the stairs, she read a question in Peyton's eyes. Unable to bear that querying look, she did what her heart bid and slipped her arms around him in an awkward embrace. He stiffened, unused to her touch, clearly uncomfortable with any display of affection. Or far too inebriated to appreciate it.

Ansel's frown deepened as Peyton pulled away and moved past them, treading up the stairs like lead lined his shoes, gripping the balustrade to stay his swaying.

"It's all right, Ellie." Ansel's words held wry exasperation. "His pride is damaged. But he's got plenty left."

"What happened?"

"The sheriff told of a bet, a brawl. Someone insulted Wade and a duel was threatened. The men's club is a bit of a wreck as a result. Damages will have to be paid."

"Was Wade's brother involved?"

He looked at her, surprise sketched across his features. "Gentleman Jack? Why do you ask?"

"I . . . I've been . . ."A small thread of hope tightened round her heart. "I've been praying for him."

"About his drinking and carousing, you mean?"

She nodded. "Da used to visit him in jail. He even gave him a Bible."

"Jack? And he kept it? Didn't pitch it in the river or gamble it away?" He looked bemused at the thought. "I wonder how many of those Bibles that Da's given out are ever used?"

Ansel was studying her, and a wave of guilt swamped any high feeling. He didn't know she went to River Hill. No one knew but Mamie and the stable hands. What would Ansel say? Keeping it secret seemed devious, but she wasn't comfortable sharing it . . . yet.

She changed course. "Your sweetheart is above stairs."

He nodded absently as if he'd forgotten. "And Adam and Ulie?"

"I took supper up to them. They're ready to leave with Dr. Brunot when it's safe."

His face clouded. "I'd meant to send word to Brunot tonight. But there's still some sign of bloodhounds and slave catchers along the far shore."

Hearing it, she felt small and overwhelmed. "I'll feel better when Da is back—and Mama."

"They'll soon walk through that door to find you here—and Andra gone." He released a pent-up breath. "I wonder what Da will have to say about that."

Ellie was more worried about Mama's reaction, especially where Andra was concerned. She had more to pray about than Jack and Chloe Turlock, truly.

Dr. Brunot came the next eve, pulling the carriage known as a liberator into the lantern-lit stable at nearly midnight. Adam and Ulie were waiting, knapsacks brimming with food and clothing to see them north. Ansel had taken care to fit them with new shoes, and Ellie wondered how many miles they would go to find freedom. The Quaker settlements were close, but Canada seemed a world away.

Handing Adam a Bible, Ellie was touched by the sheen in his eyes. He couldn't yet speak, but he'd begun to read, and his appreciation was unmistakable. Ellie hugged Ulie and the baby as Brunot opened the trap door in the false bottom of the carriage. Surely a more cramped, uncomfortable ride couldn't be found. Ellie felt an overwhelming need to know they'd be safe, that the next haven would indeed be welcoming, but the night held few guarantees.

Removing his hat, Brunot bowed his head and offered up one of the most heartfelt prayers Ellie had ever heard. When the coach clattered away into the night, Ansel lingered in the stables while Ellie returned to the house.

She lay awake in her bedchamber long after the coach had departed, but the sound of its wheels atop the drive didn't seem to fade. She would never forget the cruelty of Adam's injuries. Or all that Ulie had suffered at the hands of the Turlocks' overseer. While her heart was too full for sleeping, the attic was all too empty.

Mamie served strawberry ice for breakfast the next morning as the sun poked fierce spokes across New Hope's grounds, banishing the dew by seven o'clock. "Summer is here," she crowed in satisfaction, standing amidst her kitchen garden. Old Jacob had been working night and day to restore the physic and formal gardens to their former glory, while Mamie labored over her own humble patch. "Look at these herbs already flowerin'. Glad we took two tons of ice from the river last winter, or this heat would curdle all my cream."

'Twas the end of June. Ellie felt time slipping through her fingers like river sand. She went about her morning duties as if driven, thoughts on River Hill and afternoon lessons. A wheel was being repaired on the coach, denying her the usual transport, so she asked a groom to ready the two-wheeled chaise. Peyton, fully recovered from the debacle with Wade yet tight-lipped about the lapse, had left for the levee at dawn with Ansel. Only Mamie eyed her with concern as Ellie placed her bundle of flower seeds and sewing basket beneath the seat, the pearl-handled pistol hidden within.

Mamie gestured to the rear platform where a groom usually perched. "Where's your escort?"

Ellie stepped up into the vehicle and smiled in reassurance. "The stables are busy today. Two of Da's prize mares are foaling and the coach is being repaired." She sat atop the upholstered seat and arranged her skirts, glad the chaise's leather bonnet half hid her from Mamie's probing gaze. "I'll take the back road. 'Tis quicker that way." Feeling a twinge of conscience, she confessed, "I wouldn't want to miss lessons with Chloe Turlock."

"Well, you look like a fine lady even if you be bound for Hades itself."

"Oh, Mamie, you should see it. Next to New Hope, River Hill is the most wondrous place in all of Allegheny County." She took up the reins—ribbons, the grooms called them— unable to contain her delight at riding out on so beautiful a day. "I'll be home by suppertime."

Round the stables she went and out a side lane, birdsong bursting all around her. A warm wind tugged at the chin ribbons of her straw hat, and she slowed the horse to a walk, wanting to savor every minute. All dark thoughts seemed to take wing on such a sunny afternoon.

She'd not taken the back road for years. In the early days it had been little more than an Indian trail north, bordered by giant hardwoods and abundant berry vines. Seldom used, it seemed safer than the main thoroughfares. Her brothers needn't worry, nor Mamie.

Reaching down, she felt beneath the seat for her basket, her anticipation of planting a garden making the miles fade to mere inches. Chloe's enthusiasm had surprised her—the prospect of digging in the dirt garnered as much interest as fishing. Contrary to what she'd expected, Chloe threw herself wholeheartedly into anything Ellie suggested. Even Jack seemed surprised.

Her pulse quickened as River Hill's gate loomed in the distance. How different than the dread she'd felt at first, when she'd gone to honor Chloe's request and Jack had turned her away. Unconventional, unpredictable Jack. She flicked the ribbons harder as if to outrun any further thought of him, sliding slightly on the seat as she took a bend in the road too quickly.

Here the trees grew so close the way was dark as a tunnel. Shadows loomed everywhere she looked. Her gaze fixed on a break in the trees just ahead where light again limned the road. The bay was acting strangely skittish, slowing down slightly, ears flickering nervously. Ellie ignored the shiver of fear that skimmed over her till the chaise shuddered to a sudden halt . . .

Before a wall of men.

Bullwhips, ropes, and handcuffs were lashed to half a dozen saddles, the horses restless, the dust roiling. She blinked against the grit of gray, and the reins grew slack in her gloved hands.

If ill will could be felt, she felt it—a cold malevolence like icy fingers on warm skin.

Three men were on horses, three on foot. All were masked. In seconds a hard hand clutched her arm, propelling her out of her seat. She heard the jarring tear of fabric as it caught on some trappings. Her skirt? The men circled round, tightening like a noose. Though her eyes were everywhere at once, her breath came in short, desperate bursts, her voice not at all.

"Well, Miss Ballantyne, I've a mind to hold you for ransom. But since your pa ain't here to pay, we're after other things."

She stood, limbs like wax, as the vehicle was searched, her sewing basket flung open, seeds scattered, the pistol confiscated. A sudden slashing sent her shaking. Were they knifing the bonnet of the carriage to ribbons? The poor bay was straining against the harness, clearly as terrified as she.

"Stop!" The word burst out of her but was drowned out by their laughter as they held up a dainty handkerchief meant for Chloe.

Another man drew near, dwarfing her with his largeness. "Let me have a look."

The dark eyes slanting down at her were full of some darkness she couldn't name. With one deft move he jerked her hat free and sent it into a ditch before taking her roughly by the chin.

"God forbid, but you're ever' bit as pretty as I've been told." His other hand was in her hair, scattering its pins. At his touch she felt soiled, nearly nauseous.

"Please—stop!" Jerking away, she tripped over the boots of one man only to be righted by another. Ensnared again. They were laughing harder, the carriage in tatters, passing her from hand to hand in an endless circle, groping at her skirts, her tumbled hair, her gloves.

"Leave her be." The lone man left on horseback spoke, angling his head to the east. Without another word, he rode off in the direction she'd come, his henchmen following.

Pulling in one ragged breath, then two, Ellie didn't think she'd make it one step farther. Her heart drew her to home, but she couldn't go back that way lest she meet up with the men again. Her only recourse was forward. Fixing her gaze on River Hill's distant gates, she tried to calm the bay before climbing shakily into the battered chaise, hoping Jack would be away, trying to summon words for Chloe when she saw her.

The crunch of wheels atop the cobbled courtyard seemed to shout her arrival—as did the decrepit condition of her vehicle. A stable hand rushed to assist her, his shocked expression underscoring her predicament. Ellie's heart sank further when Chloe came running from the garden, Ben trailing. At the sight of her, Chloe's mouth formed a perfect O. White-faced, she wheeled toward the house, Jack's name on her lips.

Standing in the sunlight as a great many men gathered to examine the chaise, Ellie put trembling hands to her hair, trying to draw the length into a knot only to realize she couldn't. Nary a hairpin.

"You all right, Miz Ballantyne?" To her left was an elderly black man she'd never before seen, concern deepening the grooves in his solemn face.

She managed a nod, unable to force a reply past her parched throat. Spots began to dance before her eyes, stealing away her vision. Her skin felt warm to the point of fever, her stomach at sea.

Oh, for a shaded eave . . . a sip of water.

She tried to anchor her faltering gaze to an approaching figure, to little avail. Aside from the purposeful stride, she could barely make out who it was. Taking a few tentative steps toward the tall shadow, she collapsed at Jack Turlock's feet.

16

He felt now that he was not simply close to her but that he did not know where he ended and she began.

LEO TOLSTOY

At Chloe's cry, Jack shot upright, almost overturning a bottle of ink. He'd been writing out the notice of sale for River Hill, carefully considering the terms, wanting no distractions. Pushing away from his desk, he left his study and cleared the hall in long strides, the alarm in her tone raking his every nerve. She rounded the corner to the foyer just as he did, her eyes alive with panic.

"Miss Ellie—she's—"

Ellie? Alarm drenched him at the mere mention of her name. Brushing past Chloe, he strode through the open front door, assessing everything in a heartbeat. The battered chaise. A passel of helpless stable hands. Dust and sunlight. And Ellie standing forlornly on the cobbles, hatless, her hair falling like a sooty curtain to her waist, her body trembling beneath a disheveled blue dress.

165

His voice rang out harshly as he cleared the steps. "Take the carriage to the coach house and turn the horse to pasture!" Used to his demands, the help scattered, sparing him their gawking.

"Ellie . . ." He held out a hand as he walked toward her, but it seemed she couldn't see him, couldn't focus. Her eyes were strangely blank, her cheeks like fire.

"Jack . . . ?" She seemed to melt before his eyes, swaying before he could reach her, and fell to the ground at his feet.

"Send for Dr. Brunot!" He shouted it, so panicked himself it seemed he shook when he gathered her up in his arms. He was barely aware of Chloe on his heels, crying and asking frantic questions till Mrs. Malarkey led her away.

He carried Ellie into the house, across the foyer into the blue room, and gently laid her on a sofa covered with an enormous dust cloth. Dirt smudged one of her cheeks, and he spied a dangling button on her bodice, a tear in her skirt. The sight shattered what little remained of his calm. He felt a wild, thundering rush of something he couldn't name. She'd clearly been hurt. Manhandled. Assaulted?

God, no. God, help.

Her eyes slowly opened. "Where am I?"

His voice sounded strangled. "In the blue room. The front parlor."

"I-I need to go home." She struggled to sit up, palms flat against the sofa.

He knelt in front of her, taking her gloved hands in his. "Ellie, I can't let you leave till you tell me what's happened."

Instead of answering, she wilted against him, her face nestled against the curve of his neck. This close he could feel the tick of her heart against his own racing pulse. She seemed so fragile . . . like lace or new snow. And the scent of her was like nothing he'd ever known. It was all too easy to cradle her, solace her. "You're safe now. Dr. Brunot is coming."

She drew back a bit. "I'm not hurt. Just frightened. Please—send for Ansel."

Ansel. Not Peyton. Why, he wondered?

"Ellie, talk to me." His mouth was near her ear, his face half buried in the glossy length of her hair. He shut his eyes, overcome. Ashamed of his desire when she was in need of comfort, protection. "Tell me what happened."

She shuddered. "Some men—they stopped me on my way here."

"Do you know them?"

"No . . . they were all masked. I-I can't remember what they said. They'd been drinking—I could smell spirits. One of them knew my name."

He swallowed hard, all but choking on the question, "Did they . . . hurt you?"

"Only the chaise. They seemed to be searching for something." She raised her head, regret in her gaze. "I shouldn't have come alone."

"Aye, but what's done is done." His relief was short-lived as fury gained the upper hand, white-hot and unrelenting. He was far more at home with this than any fine feeling, only too glad to let his yearning ebb. "Stay here till Dr. Brunot and Ansel come."

She nodded absently, sitting back on the sofa. The blue room, unused for a quarter of a century or better, was dark, and he went to get a light. Dust cloths covered the finely crafted Chippendale furnishings, hiding their graceful lines and rococo ornamentation, the damask drapes and shutters drawn. He returned with a candelabra, glad the room was cool, if stale. Pulling on an antique bell cord, he summoned Mrs. Malarkey and asked for tea, lingering on Ellie as she looked about the once grand room.

"What is that hiding in the corner?" she asked quietly.

Glad to distract her, he glanced at the musical instrument the judge had been so fond of. "The first armonica west of the mountains."

"A glass harp? Dr. Franklin's invention?" Her haunted expression now shone with such delight it almost seemed the wretched afternoon had never happened. "Do you . . . play anything, Jack?"

"Cards," he murmured, taking a chair across from her and trying to keep his eye on the musical novelty.

She smiled slightly, bemusedly, drawing his attention back to her again. Candlelight was gilding her hair as it fell in waves to her waist, turning her so fetching he felt his throat tighten. He'd never seen her with her hair down. He'd only imagined it . . . and had fallen fall short of the mark. "Do you . . ." he asked, more polite than he'd ever been, "play an instrument?"

"Only the harp."

Only. Like the angel she was. Like the angelic mural gracing the stairwell at Broad Oak, the only bit of heaven in an otherwise miserable house. "I've never heard the harp," he admitted.

Her surprise was plain. "Never?"

"There's precious little chamber music in gin rooms, Ellie."

"Oh, Jack . . ."

He wasn't sure what dismayed her more, mentioning gin rooms or his complete ignorance of music. He wasn't even sure how to operate the armonica, if time and neglect hadn't stilled it forever. Tearing his attention from her, he looked toward the door and spied Chloe peering through a crack. Before he could motion her in, the door clicked closed.

Thankfully, Mrs. Malarkey soon served tea, eyes round as carriage wheels at Ellie's tumbled appearance. He half expected her to bring hairpins next, but she left as quickly as her arthritic legs would allow, leaving the door open wide in her wake as if to rebuke them for being alone.

As Ellie sipped her tea, he excused himself and sent word to Ansel, wishing Dr. Brunot would hurry. He had important business at Broad Oak and was determined to finish it before dusk.

Ansel rode in within the hour, his expression fraught with anxiety as he bypassed the stables and dismounted in front of River Hill's front veranda. Jack met him there, realizing he'd been a bit too terse in his note, wishing he'd gone to fetch Ansel himself. He'd not spoken with Ellie's youngest brother in years, only seen him along the levee at a distance or in passing on the road. Unlike Peyton, who ignored him, Ansel always nodded and gave a greeting. But he had none for Jack now and looked absolutely perplexed at finding Ellie at River Hill.

"She's all right," Jack said, leading him into the house. "There was some trouble on the road—highwaymen, maybe. They ruined the hood of her carriage, but she's unharmed."

"So she came here?"

The confusion on his face set Jack's heart to pounding. This, he realized, was the end for Ellie and Chloe. Obviously Ansel didn't know of their arrangement. And didn't approve. Why hadn't she told him? The answer came, and there was no shrugging it off.

Because Ellie was ashamed of their tie.

The certainty left him slightly sick. It was just as he'd told Chloe in the garden. A Ballantyne would never consort with a Turlock unless it was some sort of mercy mission. And Ansel's shocked expression was confirming it now.

Jack stopped just shy of the blue room. "Dr. Brunot is on his way. I've some business elsewhere. If you need a coach, an escort to return you home—"

"Nay," Ansel replied, going in to Ellie and shutting the parlor door.

Jack galloped down the back road linking New Hope and River Hill like a man possessed, his stallion raising clouds of dust that swirled like smoke to his thighs. The sight of the fracas was easy enough to find. Signs of several horses lingered in the dirt, as well as Ellie's carriage tracks. Their wayward trail indicated she'd nearly been run off the road.

His fury spiked at the sight of a sewing basket discarded in a ditch amidst scattered garden seed. She'd obviously been too frightened to retrieve what was left of it. His worry deepened. Were these random thugs . . . highwaymen? Or slave catchers and bounty hunters? They'd left no evidence as to their identity, none that he could discern after a thorough going-over of the sight.

He picked up Ellie's basket, eyes drawn to her discarded hat in a near ditch, the fine fabric and flowers battered beyond repair. He secreted both in the hollow of an oak to retrieve for her on his way home. For now he was intent on Broad Oak, wretched mission that it was.

As usual, he found Wade supervising the steaming mash tubs, with Josiah Kilgore inside the main distilling room. Glasses in hand, they downed the contents at Jack's approach and turned toward him with little trace of welcome.

"Join us for a little pre-supper libation, Jack?" Already half inebriated, Kilgore gestured to a tapped barrel.

Wade was regarding Jack with mild amusement—maybe even a touch of scorn. Jack preferred gin, cheap and plentiful, a betrayal of the Turlock name and trade. It had been a source of dissension for years.

Jack shook his head and sent Kilgore on his way with a

look. Thoughts full of Ellie, he motioned Wade beyond the hearing of numerous slaves. His voice, when it finally came, was so low it belied the storm inside him. "What's happening with the bounty hunters?"

Wade regarded him coldly. "What bounty hunters?"

"You led me to believe you'd called off the search."

Heat threaded the blue-gray eyes. "No, Jack, *you* did when you pinned a McTavish to the wall."

"Last time I was here, standing by the new still, you said you'd not enforce the bounty if it gained you the shipping deal with Peyton Ballantyne."

Wade shrugged, turning surly and evasive, a habit Jack hated. No matter what was said, he couldn't trust his brother—and never turned his back to him. Wade bent nearer the barrel to refill his glass, his smile in place when he straightened. "I've not yet sealed the deal, so—"

Muttering a curse, Jack seized his shirtfront and shoved him against the nearest wall. The glass Wade held clattered to the wooden floor, sloshing whiskey onto Jack's boots. Jack jerked the pistol from his waistband and pressed it against his brother's temple. "I want proof that the bounty is void by tonight. And I need to know what the McTavishes were doing around one o'clock this afternoon."

"Careful, Jack." Wade tried to shake him off, but Jack pressed the pistol nearer till he stilled.

"By tonight," he repeated. "And if I find you lied—"

"Having a disagreement, boys?" Their father's sturdy silhouette filled the nearest doorway, his voice low and deep. It was the same quiet, measured tone that warned Henry's mood was growing dangerous. "Put away your pistol, Jack. Surely there's no call for that."

The irony of the words shattered Jack's focus.

Surely there's no call . . .

Yet Henry Turlock had shot a lawman in the back before his very eyes when Jack was just a boy. Over whiskey and an unpaid debt. No one but the two of them knew where the sheriff was buried. His father had threatened to kill Jack if he told.

Slowly Jack lowered the pistol, letting it go slack in his hand, though his gaze remained locked with Wade's, underscoring his words. Would he kill a man to ensure Ellie's safety? Aye. His own brother? Aye. The violent footprints his father had made were all too easy to follow.

"Ansel, please, I didn't mean to deceive. I was only trying to help school Chloe." Ellie's plea fell flat in the stuffy confines of the Turlock coach as its antique frame bumped and swayed over the main road to New Hope. Though it was a decidedly neglected conveyance, much like the rest of River Hill, she was thankful Jack had lent it to them. The chaise would remain behind for now till Ansel arranged for repairs.

Across from her, her brother's usual calm was decidedly ruffled. Rarely was Ansel angry, but today she'd dealt him a double blow. She'd had no escort. And she was consorting with the enemy. Though he had never maligned the Turlocks to her hearing, his silence was just as damning. He saw them for what they were—poisonous distillers and slave owners in dire need of God's saving grace, and having none of it.

He leaned back against the upholstered seat, his blue eyes grieved. "El, I received word you'd met with trouble on the back road, something that might have been avoided if you'd had an escort. Then I ride to River Hill to find you looking quite at home in Jack Turlock's parlor—"

"It's not what it seems. I go there for Chloe. For lessons." Even as she spoke the words, she felt warm as a cup of tea—

and more than a tad blameworthy. "She's like any other girl under my tutelage."

"How long has this gone on?"

"More than a month . . ." She cringed at the surprise in his eyes. "I-I've said little, knowing Andra wouldn't be pleased—"

"Not only Andra. Our saintly mother might make peace with your mission, but the rest of us see it for what it is— foolish, dangerous. This afternoon, riding unescorted, you could have been . . ." He left off, delivering the dreaded ulti-matum. "You can't return to River Hill."

Ellie clenched her hands in her lap, thinking of Chloe's frightened face as they'd ridden away. She'd appeared in an upstairs window, likely banished there by Jack, who'd disap-peared once Ansel arrived. Ellie had wanted to say goodbye, reassure Chloe all was well, but there'd been no time. The thought of not seeing her again held a wrench she'd not an-ticipated.

"Please don't say anything to anyone about the trouble," Ellie entreated, thinking how caustic Peyton could be.

"I won't, but you will." Ansel's voice, in his dismay, held a hint of Scots, so like their father's. "The *Elinor* docked an hour ago. Da and Mama have disembarked and are on their way home to New Hope."

As she brushed and repinned her hair, Ellie's fingers trem-bled with excitement—and trepidation. Of all the days for her parents to return! The mirror in her room cast back a pale face and a slight bruise on her chin, a telling reminder of the frightening afternoon. She would tell her father and mother the truth—but not on the day of their homecoming. Thankfully, the ruined chaise was hidden away at River Hill, and the Turlock coach that returned them home had ridden out of sight. The ugly bruise she could do little about. She feared it was something her keen-eyed father wouldn't miss.

She hid her torn dress in the clothespress, left her bedchamber, and hurried to the third-floor window of the landing, taking in the expansive view. The Allegheny glided by, a mesmerizing blue, the road alongside bearing a passing dray and a few riders on horseback. No Ballantyne coach or baggage wagon stirred the summer dust just yet.

By now Andra would have had the house in a spin, issuing last-minute orders, airing their parents' rooms, reviewing the dinner menu, sending the staff for fresh flowers. Thinking it, Ellie felt mired in inadequacy. Andra wasn't here but in York. She herself had been home mere minutes, feeling chastised as a child by Ansel in the coach. The household was utterly unprepared. She didn't even know where the maids were.

As she tread the staircase to the foyer below, Mari and Gwyn sped past, arms full of flowers. Mama loved her garden, and thankfully, despite the storm, it had survived, even thrived. Truly, the lilies had never seemed so fragrant, the late June roses so deep a pink. Ellie caught their perfume as they went by and breathed a prayer of thanks.

Ansel came down the stairs, expression still tense. "I wouldn't say anything about this afternoon, El. Save it for later. We've enough on our hands explaining Andra's absence . . . among other things."

He was thinking of Peyton, she knew. Each of them had a story to tell. Of jail time and York and being accosted on a back road. Ellie was ashamed that so much had transpired in her parents' absence. It made them all seem so . . . inadequate. Likely her parents would never go traveling again.

Taking a bracing breath, she stood on the wide front veranda, fighting for poise when she felt like pacing, unwelcome images springing to mind. The beguiling blue parlor. The antique armonica. The moment Jack's concern for her had melted his unflappable reserve and allowed her a glimpse into his heart. Strangely, it was these impressions that were uppermost, not the terror of what had happened along the back road.

"Here they come," Ansel said.

Ellie focused, done with daydreaming, her whole world righting again. Shoulder to shoulder, she and her brother followed the dusty path of the largest Ballantyne coach with expectant eyes, its journey weighted with luggage, the big wheels turning impossibly slow.

Despite everything that had happened, she felt an unbridled happiness take hold. It seemed she was a child again, awaiting her handsome father after some trip, shivering with delight at the very thought of what he might bring her. A wax doll. A miniature tea set. Some frippery from a far port. Only now she was nearly one and twenty. And he wasn't even aware she was waiting.

The servants were assembling—maids, stable hands, the gardener, and Mamie—though they remained on the porch behind Ellie and Ansel. Emotions running high, Ellie wished for a more private homecoming, though Mama always liked to include everyone.

The coachman began to slow the horses as they rounded the circular drive, keeping the summer dust to a minimum. When the vehicle shuddered to a halt, the finely painted door swung open with the aid of a groom, and everyone seemed to hold a collective breath.

The first to alight, Eden Lee Ballantyne fastened her warm gaze on Ellie, unabashed surprise and pleasure in their depths. Ellie had almost forgotten how lovely her mother was. She had a timeless beauty that never seemed to ebb, though her fiery hair at midcentury had faded to auburn.

"Daughter, you've come home—all the way from Philadelphia!" There was an undeniable question in the welcome as Ansel helped her down. She hugged them both but clung to Ellie the longest. "Well, let me look at you . . . You're every bit the rose I remember. But where's Andra?"

"Andra is away—" Ellie began.

"We've much to tell you," Ansel said, turning to their father next. "I suppose you saw Peyton at the levee."

"Aye." Silas Ballantyne cast a formidable shadow in the glare of sunlight. He squinted as he looked toward Ellie, his tanned face creasing in a smile. "But he said naught about Ellie being home."

Slipping free of her mother's embrace, Ellie found herself locked in her father's hard arms till all the breath left her lungs. "I'd hoped to surprise you—for your birthday."

"Surprise me? That you've done in spades."

"I came home in April, during the storm," she said in a little rush, "but safely."

Ansel shot a wary glance her way as if he feared she'd mention Jack. But she simply smiled up at her father, determined to steer clear of such foundering matters. "You and Mama look wonderful, rested, despite all the merriment in New Orleans."

He clasped her shoulders with gloved hands, jade eyes roaming over her as if he couldn't quite believe it was she. "And you? Have you had enough of Philadelphia? Are you quite finished?"

She bit her lip, moved by the emotion in his lined face. "Madame Moreau might say otherwise, but I believe I am."

When he brought her close again, she tried to stem her emotions, but her relief at having him home was so great and her ordeal of the afternoon was so harrowing, she rested her cheek against the lapel of his fine broadcloth coat and cried.

"Is *oniething* the matter, Daughter? Or are you just glad to have us *hame*?"

His tender Scots set her at ease. "Both," she whispered, not wanting to alarm him. "I'll tell you all about it soon."

She stepped back when Mamie's voice sounded, calling for them to come inside. She had a tea tray set for Mama, some flip for Father. The evening promised to be very late indeed.

17

He who bestows his goods upon the poor shall have as much again, and ten times more.

JOHN BUNYAN

The day, Jack mused, seemed to have a touch of eternity in it. Since Ellie had met with trouble that afternoon, time seemed to drag with little to fill the long hours but dark thoughts. Returning to his study after confronting Wade at Broad Oak, he sat at his desk, his emotions in a snarl, unsettled as the Monongahela at flood stage. It was all he could do to scrawl empty words across the paper before him, trying to ignore the fierce knot in his gut.

> *The land, twelve hundred acres, is very good, drained and ditched. The house, built in the former century, is sound, the dependencies made of Fort Pitt brick . . .*

If this was the proper course of action, why did his soul sink lower with every word?

Vexatio dat intellectum. Vexation sharpens the intellect.

Nay, he thought, pushing away from the desk. A little vexation, perhaps, not a boatload. Although Dr. Brunot had come and assured him Ellie had only been frightened and roughly handled, it failed to ease him. His ensuing confrontation with Wade had resulted in frustration and few answers. Chloe was now sulking and morose, likely realizing Ellie wouldn't be back. Even Mrs. Malarkey was keeping to her room. And the battered chaise remained in River Hill's coach house, an ever-present reminder of all the trouble.

At candlelight, he left his office, the gloom of evening matching his mood. Sweat slicked his brow, as the day had been the warmest thus far, promising a feverish summer. Undressing by the riverbank, he left his clothes atop a rhododendron bush and dove into the cold current, wishing the water could wash away his turmoil. The far bank seemed endless, but he finally reached it, spent and nearly sick, lungs seared from lack of air. He'd not eaten, he remembered, since breakfast.

Still winded, he returned to the opposite shore, where he shook off and dressed, his gaze drawn to the ground beyond his boots. Sometimes he sighted bear, cougar, and other animal signs in the tangle of reeds and underbrush, but these . . . These were human footprints, each distinct as bare feet met river sand, all leading to one place.

The forgotten tunnel.

In his grandfather's day, when hospitality was at its peak, before Jack's mother had disgraced herself by running off with a Turlock, the tunnel had been built to hasten supplies from boat to house in all kinds of weather. Busy as he'd been elsewhere, he'd never used it, letting the vegetation choke the entrance, the dock and moorings fall into disrepair.

Curious, he followed the trail, finding the overgrowth slightly disturbed, as if the trespassers were being careful . . .

wary. Alarm scissored inside him, and his right hand rested on the pistol at his waist. Shoving aside a mulberry branch, he ducked low and stepped inside the tunnel's entrance.

Smoke stung his senses, and he heard the drip of water from moss-covered bricks taken from Fort Pitt the century before. Smoke, aye . . . an endless dripping . . . a distressed cry. The latter sent the hair on his neck bristling. He wanted it to be an animal, but there was no mistake. He'd heard the sound of newborns wailing in the servants' quarters at Broad Oak for years.

"Who's there?" His voice was thunderous, hurling through the tunnel and sounding just like his father's.

Silence.

He sprinted back to the house, taking a different route so he wouldn't be seen, and came into the keeping room that led to the brick-lined cellar and the tunnel's other entrance. Taking up a lantern, he fumbled with flint and tinder till it flashed before jerking open the heavy door closed for a decade or better. The resulting groan threatened his resolve, but he shrugged aside his misgivings and plunged ahead through spiderwebbing and dank darkness.

"Please, sir—don't shoot!"

Lantern held high, he stood over them, a ragged, frightened knot of slumped shoulders and bare backs etched perma-nently with a horse whip, a dozen terrified eyes turned his way. A woman's sobs tore at him, but it was the babe's crying that rent his heart.

Jack took in the young mother's tear-wet face, saw the newborn she clutched as if fearing he would grab hold and fling it away from her. Bloodied rags lay in a heap about her, and her thin dress was little better. Was she hemorrhaging?

"We be gone soon, sir," one man said. "We mean no harm. Just lookin' for a place called Hope."

New Hope?

The Ballantynes were deeply involved then. Jack leaned into the wall, eyes on the faint remains of a fire they'd made. The smell of river water overrode the odor of old bricks, even smoke. Indecision weighted him. He could simply wait till dark, send them a few miles more to Ballantyne land and be done with it. "Come with me. I won't cause trouble for you if you'll cooperate."

At that, a muscular man lumbered to his feet, a younger man after him. Out of the shadows came another woman. Blast! How many?

Someone moved to pick up the new mother, another the child. Turning, Jack led the way back through the tunnel to the keeping room, the events of a too-long day overtaking him. Above ground, he summoned Mrs. Malarkey, who surveyed the tattered company with such abhorrence it seemed she was seeing ghosts. In a heartbeat he recalled her Southern, proslavery roots.

"Ready the empty cottage nearest the house. My father's transferred these slaves downriver to me." The lie was strangely bitter, but he pressed on. "And tell Solomon I want Dr. Brunot sent for . . . again."

Sated from Mamie's feast of chicken fricassee followed by raspberry flummery, Ellie sat with Mama on the back veranda till she went upstairs to bed. A night wind was coming off the river, ruffling the edges of Ellie's muslin dress and spreading the scent of honeysuckle to the far corners. An occasional insect flitted about but was hardly noticed, quickly banished with the swish of a fan.

Table talk had been light at supper, in keeping with the spirit of thankfulness that graced every gathering. The Scots meals of his youth had been merry if meager, her father always said, and he'd not ruin fine fare with unpalatable conversation. Weighty matters always waited till later, often discussed behind closed doors. Still, Ellie's thoughts wove about in a decidedly unmerry manner, and she wondered if Peyton would tell of his time in jail or Ansel of the bounty hunters. As it was, Ellie couldn't dismiss the shocked look on Mama's face when she'd first set foot in the house and learned Andra had gone east.

"To York? Is my mother ill again?"

Ellie hoped Ansel would give a soft answer, but Peyton spoke first, ever brusque. "Ill, aye. Perhaps dying. Last month a letter came from your sister Elspeth."

Her parents exchanged a glance.

"The post is on Andra's desk," Ellie said softly, starting up the stairs to retrieve it.

The foyer was all too quiet when she returned. Mama took the letter, expression laden with alarm.

Da fixed them all with a solemn eye. "When did your sister leave for York?"

"Early this month, soon after she received the post." Ansel rubbed his jaw, where a day's growth of beard glinted. "There was no dissuading her. She promised to send word once she arrived, but we've not yet heard."

Mama finished reading the letter and passed it to their father, who simply pocketed it. No more was said, the conversation turning to the storm and repairs both at home and in town. As the night lengthened and a late supper was served, Ellie fought to stay awake, waiting till Mama was abed and her brothers had left the study to take her turn. Despite the late hour, the study door was ajar in invitation.

She stood on the threshold, drinking in the sight of the man her small world revolved around. He glanced up from his desk, a smile softening his intensity in the glow of candlelight. "You're a patient lass to wait so long."

Relieved, she took a stool nearest him, the embroidered top fashioned by Mama's own hand. When little, she'd twirled upon it till she grew dizzy, but tonight she sat stone still, hands folded in her lap. If confession was good for the soul, she was anxious to end the tumultuous day and bare her heart. "Did Ansel tell you . . . anything?"

"About you?" Their eyes met, his questioning. "Nae."

"Then I'd best start from the beginning." Not one to mince words with her plain-speaking father, she came straight to the point. "I left Philadelphia because the Matrimonial Society was hounding me."

His mouth quirked in a wry grin. "You're of an age to be hounded, aye?"

She nearly smiled. "I suppose I am." In hindsight, the society didn't seem so bad. Perhaps they'd simply had a mission. "On the way home the weather overtook me, and I sought refuge at Widow Meyer's tavern."

"A tavern." The words were threaded with surprise. "Where was your maid?"

Where, indeed. "Rose eloped after I released her from her indenture document. She wanted to marry a tradesman she'd met in the city. I wanted to come home."

He nodded thoughtfully, never taking his eyes off her.

"There, along the turnpike, I met up with Jack Turlock." Her gaze fell to the paperwork atop the broad desk, all awaiting his signature or perusal. She couldn't bear the displeasure she feared she'd find in his face. "A storm had swept through and a great many people were stranded. He was clearing the road. He brought me home as soon as it was safe to do so." She met his eyes again, thinking there'd been nothing safe about it. They'd forged on despite a second storm, come what may, in typical Turlock fashion. "I thought that was the end to the matter, but . . ."

"But . . ." His expression held a flash of amused exasperation. "The Turlocks have a way of continually cropping up."

"Truly. Within days I found there was little for me to do here at home, as Andra is so . . . competent." *Bossy*, she refrained from saying. "So I posted an advertisement for a day school. Soon I had a few young ladies signed on for dancing and French and needlework." She rattled off the names of prominent Pittsburghers her father knew, saving Chloe for the last. "She came here and nearly begged me to school her. I-I didn't have the heart to refuse her, though Ja—Mr. Turlock turned me down."

"Why would he?"

"He cautioned me against taking her, saying it would spoil what I'd set out to do and I'd likely lose my other students. Chloe is living at River Hill, you see." She paused, still puzzled by Jack's sudden reversal. "Then he changed his mind and allowed the lessons after all. Chloe is certainly in need of a feminine touch."

"You're fond of her, I take it."

"More than fond. She needs me, or seems to, though I sometimes think we'll accomplish little."

"You hold lessons at the girls' homes?"

"Aside from a weekly dancing lesson here, yes. Till today it's never been a worry. I've always had an escort. But this afternoon, the stables were busy and I decided to take the chaise myself. River Hill isn't far along the back road, as you know . . ." At the admission, all the levity was chased from his expression. She forged on, surprised at the chill of memory. "As I was riding to meet Chloe, some men stopped me and searched the carriage. I don't know what they wanted, but they damaged the chaise's hood. It's still at River Hill. They even took the pistol Peyton gave me from your gun case—"

"Did they hurt you?"

"They frightened me, but little else."

"I wondered at the bruise on your chin." He leaned nearer, his callused fingers grazing her cheek. Apprehension and anger were etched around his eyes, marring his beloved face. "You've ne'er seen these men before?"

"They were all masked. No voice was familiar to me, though one knew my name." She covered his large hand with her own as it cupped her cheek. "Once they rode on, I made it to River Hill. When I arrived, Jack Turlock sent for Dr. Brunot and Ansel." Tears stung her eyes at his obvious disquiet. "I'm sorry, Da. I'll not ride out alone again."

"Nae, we'll keep you here at home for a time. Your mother has need of you, especially with your sister in York. I want you near at hand." His eyes glittered as his hand fell away. "I have a confession of my own. Things are not as they were when you left for finishing school four years ago." Studying her, he leaned back in his chair. "By now you must know of the situation in the attic."

She nodded, thinking how empty it was without Adam and Ulie and the baby.

"It's likely those men who waylaid you are professional bounty hunters. Now that summer is here, more runaways will come, as will slave catchers and their ilk."

"How is it the one man knew my name?"

"They ken the Ballantyne name and suspect New Hope is a safe haven. I don't want to trouble you with the details. Just help as you can when the attic is full, and say nothing to anyone outside these walls. For now bid me good night. You're in need of some sleep to put the roses back in your cheeks."

He started to say more then stood, bringing her to her feet

and enclosing her in his hard arms. For a few seconds she was struck with the power of his presence, the unspoken feeling between them. His thankfulness to be home, to find her safe, was profound, even palpable. As was hers.

The cupola remained dark that night.

18

The more we knew of freedom the more we desired it.

AUSTIN STEWARD, FORMER SLAVE

"Miss Ellie won't be teaching for a fortnight but will remain at home." Chloe thrust a piece of paper Jack's way, pleasure and worry mingling on her flushed face. "Do you think she'll ever come back here?"

"Nay." He took the note, thinking how every elegant slant and dip of Ellie's pen was so like her. "Her mother and father have just returned from New Orleans. They likely want an end to her teaching."

Though he hadn't seen the steamer's arrival himself, word of Silas and Eden's homecoming had spread through Pittsburgh like the fire of 1812. The *Elinor* had docked, and in the darkest alleys and gin rooms, the rumor was that she'd carried a dozen slaves nearer freedom, a notable feat given that at every landfall, steamboats were searched for stowaways. The fugitives had since been spirited north to sympathetic Quaker settlements or hidden among Pittsburgh's free black population, or so he'd heard.

Chloe's expression darkened and grew desperate. "Are you going to bribe them to let Miss Ellie come back here by fixing their chaise?"

"The Ballantynes are immune to bribes," he said, passing back the paper. "I'm having it repaired, but not for the reason you think."

Chloe pocketed the paper, looking decidedly more disheveled in Ellie's absence. "Could it be because you find her pretty—or want to kiss her?"

"Chloe Isabel . . ." The words were more growl. He inclined his head toward the study door, her signal to exit. "I've no time to talk, nor do you. Where are the books she gave you? Have you even opened them?"

She nodded, trying to look dutiful but failing. "She asked me to read a chapter of Scripture every day. You see, there are thirty-one chapters of Proverbs in the Bible and thirty-one days in most months—"

"Aye," he said, in no mood for her babbling. "You'd best get started then."

"Miss Ellie was hoping you might supervise . . . read them with me. See? It says so right here." She dug out the paper again and tried to pass it back to him, but he waved it away.

"I've other matters to take care of."

"I suppose you do." Her chin jutted stubbornly, reminding him of Wade, smoky eyes narrowing to suspicious slits. "We have some slaves here you claim are Pa's, but I've never seen them before in my life."

His jaw tensed. "That's none of your business."

"Well? Are you going to send them back across the river and collect the bounty?"

When he hesitated, she looked hard at him, shock sprawled across her face. "You're not going to . . . *help them*?"

Refusing to answer, he glanced out the window he'd left open to better see the front drive.

"Jack! You well know what the overseer does at Broad Oak when he thinks a slave is about to run. Even Pa says everyone who helps them should be chained and whipped right along with them. You could be arrested for Negro stealing—which means you'd be hung!"

His chair came down with a thud. "All the more reason to keep your mouth shut." Shooting to his feet, he circled the desk and took her by the elbow, intent on the hall. "Here's a proverb to chew on: 'He that keepeth his mouth keepeth his life.'"

"Dash, Jack! Do you always have an answer for everything?"

He slammed the door and locked it after her, running an agitated hand through his hair. If he ever felt in need of a spree at Teague's, it was now. Uncertainty gnawed a deep hole in him, and his usual decisiveness turned to mush. His every instinct told him to move the fugitives to the attic, as having them on River Row was too risky. Yet Mrs. Malarkey was sure to become suspicious should he do so.

He remembered there was a secret stair, seldom used, accessed by a paneled door in the back wall of the second-floor landing. If worse came to worst, he could hide them there. How did Ellie's family do such clandestine work? With so much at stake? Though sound reason told him to despise the risks they took, he felt a surge of admiration instead.

Looking toward the window again, he contemplated a threat far worse than Mrs. Malarkey. Maybe he should shut River Hill's gate, though doing so seemed like a signpost advertising guilt.

He whirled at the sound of hoofbeats, a high whinny. Dr. Brunot? He was expected this afternoon, and it was nearing one o'clock. Jack hoped the couple and their newborn could go with him in his carriage yet sensed the young mother was still too weak to move. While they remained at River Hill, he felt an impending sense of doom. His trepidation deepened when he heard Chloe call out a name in confirmation.

Wade.

He'd sooner deal with bounty hunters.

He left his study and tried to strike an indifferent pose as he stepped onto the veranda. Chloe waited on the steps, eyeing him ominously as Wade tied his horse to the hitching post a stone's throw away. He swallowed down an admonishment for her to say nothing, nearly choking on the dust Wade had raised. If Dr. Brunot rode up next, what would he say? Sweat trickled down his back, more from his own turmoil than the heat, turning him cross as a bear.

"You look like Ma on a bad day," Wade quipped when Jack gave no greeting, stepping round him and entering the foyer. "The least you could do is offer me a drink."

"There's plenty of water west of the house."

Chuckling humorlessly, Wade began walking down the hall toward the study. "River water isn't what I'm after." Stopping at the liquor chest, he bent down and extracted the cologne Chloe had tried to ply Jack with. "Number Six? Isn't that what the dandies at the gentleman's club wear?" Clearly disgusted, he traded it for a bottle and glass.

Jack followed him into the study, shutting the door a bit too forcefully. "What do you want?"

"A drink first." He downed the liquid in two gulps before facing Jack across the cluttered expanse of desk. "Pa and I have a plan."

Jack felt a clutch of concern. The words, all too familiar, usually heralded some nefarious scheme, and he had no wish to become embroiled in any more than he was.

"But first a bit of good news." Taking a seat, Wade propped his boots on a low table. "We finally shipped two hundred barrels of Turlock whiskey, disguised as molasses, on a Ballantyne steamer all the way to Louisville. All with Peyton Ballantyne's approval. Before his daddy came home."

The smugness of Wade's expression rubbed Jack raw. "You'll not get away with such now that Silas is back."

Wade shrugged and refilled his glass. "The whiskey hardly matters, Jack. It's more the dent in the Ballantyne armor. Peyton was most obliging, given he pocketed a hefty sum."

Jack hid his surprise. "So what's the plan?"

"Pa's thinking of blending whiskey—"

"Rectifying?"

"Call it what you like. All that's required is combining small amounts of genuine rye with large quantities of cull spirits and labeling it as premium grade for a hefty profit. How does that sound?"

"Like thievery."

"Exactly. We're also considering using new instead of aged barrels for some of our own rye. The sutlers and Indians in Missouri territory won't know the difference. Besides, you'll have a hard time finding a cooper to turn out charred oak once you go west."

Jack furrowed his brow, knowing that to argue would prolong Wade's visit, and every minute he tarried spelled disaster. "Are you on your way to Broad Oak or town?"

"Town."

"Then stop and see Benedick Kimber at the warehouse and put in an order for bottles. He needs notice today."

"You aren't coming?" Surprise washed Wade's face, and his tone turned accusatory. "Janey told me you've not been at Teague's for weeks."

"So?"

"Blast, Jack! You're rarely pleasant, but today you're about as cordial as a river snake."

Jack moved toward the door to hasten him out, then felt his color drain by degrees at the high-pitched wail of a newborn. Clear as crystal. Why hadn't he thought to shut the window?

Wade lifted the bottle and made a show of pouring another shot. "One more swallow and I'll be on my way." He took Jack in over the edge of the glass. "You look in need of a drink yourself." He passed him the whiskey bottle, a clear challenge in his gaze.

Sensing Wade wouldn't leave till he complied, Jack took a short swig. The pit of his stomach caught fire when he swallowed. Tannin and vanilla lingered on his tongue, and he could taste the char of oak. The baby's cries trilled higher. Did Wade not hear?

Dear God . . . silence the child.

The wailing stopped. Relief raced over him like rain. Setting the bottle down, he took a slow breath as he and Wade left the study.

On the veranda, Wade hesitated, his gaze restless, roaming. "Is it true what I heard about the youngest Ballantyne daughter? Some trouble on the back road between here and New Hope?"

The very mention turned Jack chill. The McTavishes had denied any wrongdoing, claiming the bounty was null and void. Only Jack didn't believe them. He could only imagine what Wade would do if he knew the Ballantynes were sheltering Broad Oak's slaves. "What about it?"

"Is Elinor Ballantyne the reason you nailed McTavish to a wall in town? And pulled a pistol on me?"

Jack swallowed hard. "No woman should be a part of this."

Wade turned the full force of his gaze on Jack. "What do you mean by 'this'?"

"I don't know," Jack replied, turning away. "But I intend to find out."

Shaken by Wade's unexpected visit, Jack crossed the cobblestones, bypassing the stables to reach River Row. The one cottage he sought, the last of a dozen, had once been whitewashed, the trim a pleasing green. Now the roof and a corner of the porch were crumbling and choked with ivy, something he'd have to remedy prior to posting the sale. He'd hired a carpenter to mend the summer kitchen and springhouse, both storm damaged, and work was under way. River Row would be next.

The garden he could do little about. It was a green, weedy mess, all but the west corner where Ellie and Chloe had readied to plant. Shrugging off the hollowness he felt when he looked at it, he stepped onto the rickety porch and knocked on a worn door.

Silence.

Realizing a runaway wouldn't answer, Jack cracked it open to find anxious eyes staring back at him. He started to say something to put the man at ease, then realized he didn't even know his name. On a bed in the far corner lay the woman and baby, asleep. The rest of the runaways had been moved by Brunot, taken to yet another hiding place.

Letting himself in, Jack took a crude chair by the door. The whine of mosquitoes rose in the heat, and he batted one away before it landed. "Dr. Brunot should be here soon." Though his throat felt dry as sand, he inclined his head toward the bed and asked, "How is she?"

"Some better, master—"

"You don't have to call me that."

The man nodded but still seemed wary. "I forget myself.

Trouble is . . ." He darted a glance about the small room as if trying to get his bearings. "I don't even know where we be."

"You're in Pennsylvania, a supposedly free state. I don't own slaves. I simply lease land to tenants."

"I saw another black man here, and a boy."

"The old man, Solomon, was my grandfather's valet years ago. But he's now free. The boy belongs to someone downriver." Warmth crept into his face. He was reluctant to say it was his own family who owned Ben, shame gaining the upper hand. "Care to tell me your name?"

The man's gaze fell to his bare feet. "My name—my master in Maryland, he called me Jarm."

"Well, Jarm. You're safe for the moment. But we have to think about getting you moved."

He nodded obligingly, eyes returning to the woman on the bed. "We didn't mean to come here. We be searchin' for another place. Heard about a true-hearted man by the name of Ballantyne."

Jack felt buffeted by yet another confirmation that Ellie's family was so deeply involved. "The Ballantynes are farther downriver." The words came slowly as he struggled to remember all that the doctor had told him about the transfer. "When you're able, Dr. Brunot wants you to travel north in a market wagon some fifteen miles or so to a Quaker settlement like your friends did. It's safer there."

Though he spoke calmly, Jack felt his own heart trip at the task. For a lone man on the run, the prospect of freedom was daunting. To flee with a wife and child in tow was madness—or a sort of harrowing heroism the likes of which Jack had never seen. These people, he realized with fresh angst, had little but the rags on their backs.

"I'll do what I can to help you and . . ." Jack cast a look at the bed.

"Cherry's my wife. We ain't decided what to call the baby yet."

Jack hoped the overwhelming futility he felt didn't show on his face. Concern for others, risk for their welfare, took his thoughts places he didn't want to go.

"I'm obliged to you, Mister . . ."

"Jack."

He tried to think of something reassuring to say, but expressing sympathy was like a foreign language to him. He'd been raised with slaves, had thought little of their plight. Most of the white men he rubbed shoulders with had prejudices as deep as his family's own. There were those who appeared sympathetic to slaves but were anti-abolitionists in disguise, and they crawled all over Pittsburgh like river rats.

"Why—" Jack swallowed, seeing an upraised scar along Jarm's thin neck just below the jawline. "What made you leave Maryland?"

The woman on the bed turned over, and the baby gave a little cry. Jarm's eyes grew damp. "The master—he was going to sell Cherry."

Sell a woman. Sell a soul.

Jarm's grief was palpable. It wasn't his own mistreatment that had made him run, but hers. Jack shifted uncomfortably in his chair. Who had told him slaves couldn't think? Couldn't feel?

His father.

The silence turned thick with undisguised misery. Jack looked at his own boots and drew in a lungful of hot, sweat-stained air. When Jarm was about to lose what he'd cared about most, he'd run. Jack couldn't fathom it till his mind filled with Ellie. It was the only comparison he could muster. He'd been livid when she'd been accosted along the road. He'd wanted to kill the man who'd simply bruised her chin.

195

What if he never again caught sight of Ellie, head bent over a book? Never felt the warmth of her smile? Never resolved the unspoken questions in her eyes, that half-hopeful, half-wistful way she always seemed to regard him?

"I understand," Jack said, pulling himself to his feet and going out.

Dr. Brunot came again at dusk. Though only a few days had passed since the runaways' arrival, Jack was becoming increasingly uneasy with Jarm and Cherry's presence. Chloe and Ben looked continually toward River Row, clearly intrigued, though Jarm was careful to come out of the cottage only at night. Luckily, Mrs. Malarkey seemed to forget all about them, though Sol had raided the kitchen oft enough to bring the fugitives food and drink and raise her suspicions.

Jack had warned Chloe and Ben more than once to say nothing, yet his sister had always been glib as a spring freshet. He could hardly wait to extricate himself from the whole affair and quietly return to his crops and ledgers. Always near at hand, Sol had readied a wagon for the fugitives' departure, the bed filled with grain sacks. All that remained was for Brunot to provide the details.

Finally, in the humid, firefly-ridden twilight, plans were laid for Jarm and Cherry's leave-taking. Seated inside the cottage, Jarm sat hunch-shouldered between Jack and the doctor around a crude table, all alert to the slightest sound. The baying of hounds. The nickering of horses. Any sudden commotion.

Brunot's aging features held a wariness and weariness that troubled Jack, though the doctor smoked his pipe nonchalantly as he examined the map spread before them, the rich-smelling smoke spiraling round their bent heads. "You'll leave before first light along the old Warrior's Trace." He spoke slowly, as if careful not to overwhelm the understandably skittish Jarm. "It's best to take a market wagon, as Cherry is still too weak to walk the distance. If you're stopped, produce the pass I gave you and say as little as possible. You're simply moving grain to the Quakers at Harmony Grove."

Jarm nodded. "We're to keep north, follow the North Star."

Dr. Brunot leaned nearer the map. "You have sturdy shoes, clothes, and pocket money. Enough food to see you there. The Quaker you're looking for is John Hogue. The miller who provided you with the grain is Abel Simons."

"John Hogue," Jarm repeated, his voice sounding undeniably haggard, as if the journey was fifteen hundred miles instead of fifteen. "And Abel Simons."

Sensing his fear, Jack removed a small pistol from his belt and placed it on the table. "Hide this under the wagon seat. It's primed and loaded."

The gnarled, ebony hands picked up the gun hesitantly, making Jack realize Jarm had never used one. Jarm set it down as if bitten when Dr. Brunot said, "Giving a Negro a gun is a crime, Jack. You could be jailed, even executed, if found out."

"So be it." Jack reached for the pistol and fitted it to Jarm's hand, showing him how to aim and pull the trigger and reload, then passed him a small bullet bag when he was able to handle the gun with more ease. "Use it only as a last resort."

Brown eyes met gray, and for once Jarm didn't look away.

"That's right," Jack reiterated firmly. "Be bold. Act free. Look people in the eye. Give them no reason to suspect you're anything but your own man."

"Wise advice," Dr. Brunot murmured, leaning over to dump the ashes from his pipe into the cold hearth. "Now if you'll excuse me, I need to return home. After a stillbirth and a catarrh, it's been a long day."

There was a brief pause as Cherry rose from the bed to thank them, tears in her eyes. Jack felt his throat knot at the sight of her, rail thin, clutching her newborn, a smile on her lips though her ordeal was far from over.

Dr. Brunot motioned them all nearer. "I never part with anyone till the journey is covered in prayer." Putting his pipe in his breast pocket, he clamped a firm hand on Jarm's shoulder and gently took Cherry's elbow. Never having prayed, nor been with people who did, Jack kept his eyes open, though he did lower his head as the doctor began.

"Almighty Father, you created all men equal, and for that liberty we give you heartfelt thanks. Jarm's and Cherry's lives—and that of their child—are in Your faithful hands. Guide them safely to Harmony Grove and on to freedom. For this we plead Your everlasting mercy."

Their combined "Amens" assured Jack that he was the only spiritual imposter in the group. He stepped onto the porch into welcome darkness with an embarrassment he'd not felt since boyhood.

Dr. Brunot's tone lightened as he drew the door shut. "Did you hear that, Jack? They've named the baby after you. It's a boy, if you didn't know."

"They'd have been better off naming him after you."

"What? Theophilus?" Brunot chuckled. "I've often thanked the Lord it was shortened to Theo. I still don't know what my dear mother had in mind."

Jack managed a smile. "It's no shame to be named after a Roman official. Or a New Testament saint."

Brunot's eyebrows peaked. "Your grandfather the judge schooled you well."

"He tried." The pride he felt in Hugh O'Hara was overshadowed by the memory of his paternal grandfather, who had been killed in a brawl. Though Jack had only been a boy at the time, the scandal had rocked Allegheny County, the memory still vivid. No doubt the doctor remembered it too.

"Besides," Brunot said, unhitching his horse, "you're Jarm and Cherry's first taste of freedom. They'll not soon forget it."

Jack checked a sigh, kicking at a stone near the toe of his boot as the doctor rode off into the night. So the baby was to be called Jack. The honor brought more regret than pleasure.

What was in a name? What did it matter?

Depending on whether you were a Ballantyne or a Turlock . . . everything.

19

Love and a cough cannot be hid.
ENGLISH PROVERB

Spending days in the garden with Mama, peaceful and joyous though they were, reminded Ellie of Chloe and their shared anticipation of turning a corner of River Hill's garden glorious again. Sadly, Ellie tucked that wish away. At her parents' prompting, she'd written notes to her students, telling them she'd not be teaching for a fortnight. What transpired next remained to be seen, but she prayed she could continue, even if it meant being escorted everywhere, almost under guard. She'd not use the back road again. Its shady lane had assumed nightmarish proportions.

"Your students will understand, Ellie," Mama reassured her. "We've just returned from a long trip. There are things to be done . . . planned."

The last word was not lost on Ellie. She contemplated her mother, who was busy snipping dozens of tiny rosebuds with small pruners and filling a willow basket dangling from one arm. In years past they'd spent countless hours together in just this way, making sachet and rose soap and lavender water for the household.

"Your birthday will soon be here." Looking over her shoulder, Mama regarded Ellie with a mix of wonder and affection. "I well recall the day you were born, every detail. Your father planted this climbing rose that very morning, sure you'd be a girl. It's hard to believe both you and these blossoms are of age."

Ellie smiled, looking over voluminous beds of hollyhocks and peonies. "Do we have enough flowers for sachet?"

"We're in need of lavender next." Starting down a bricked path, Ellie trailing, Mama surveyed the fragrant purple spikes. "The French variety is preferable to the English, as it holds its fragrance and color far longer. I thought you might take some sachet to your girls in the day school . . . Chloe in particular."

The mention seemed to invite conversation, but Ellie's mouth went dry. So Da had told her of the Turlock connection. Did Mama know about the incident on the back road too?

"The girls could line their petticoats with lavender like I used to." Mama knelt by a vigorous patch of English munstead. "I had a modest garden growing up in York." *Snip. Snip.* The purple spires waved and fell. "And I lived near an estate with a lovely formal garden called Hope Rising."

"Hope Rising?" Ellie's curiosity peaked. "'Tis an unusual name."

Mama sat back on her heels, her full skirts in a swirl about her. "I can't remember why it was called that. I only remember the people there." Her flushed features, so lightly lined, took on a rare wistfulness. "'Twas long ago—like a dream, really."

"It seems strange to think of Andra in York."

"I wonder if I shouldn't be there too. But your father is against it, and he's far wiser than I. My every emotion often clouds matters." Her smile resurfaced. "Besides, I'd much rather deal with what's before me." She set her clippers aside and tugged off her gloves. "And the birthday ball that begs planning for my daughter."

"A ball?"

"Yes, we'll need to make up the guest list, send invitations, decide on a menu for the midnight supper. 'Tis not every day a girl turns one and twenty."

A birthday ball? Though a delightful prospect, the event had ominous overtones.

Rather the ball-to-wed-me-off.

Ellie tried to summon some excitement as Mama shared the details. "There's a new French seamstress on Market Street, fresh from Paris. She's gifted with a needle and privy to the very latest fashions. I'm sure the three of us can come up with something suitable. Beautiful."

This sparked some interest. Ellie dearly loved a new gown. Mama had made most of her clothes till she turned twelve, and a few favorites still lingered in old chests. Her current wardrobe was a bit stale, if sufficient. "Whom all shall we invite?"

"Whomever you like—and then some," Mama replied, meaning the obligatory crowd. "You'll have at least one willing partner, or so Mina tells me."

"Oh?" Ellie mused, looking up from the lavender basket.

"I daresay I don't have to name him." With a fleeting smile, Mama turned toward a bed of woolly betony, leaving Ellie to her conflicted feelings.

Oh, Daniel, it's been so long. Will I even recognize you when you return?

Madame de Rocher's shop was on Market Street, by far the busiest thoroughfare in Pittsburgh, and was directly across from her competitor, Miss Rachel Endicott. The latter, bedecked in a Turkey Red gown that could hardly be missed, was standing in her open doorway as the Ballantyne coach pulled along the curb, something that didn't escape Ellie's—or Mama's—notice.

"We'll order your gown from Madame de Rocher and then meet with Miss Endicott for all your accessories," Mama told her as a groom helped them down.

Ellie felt a rush of thankfulness. It was no secret the two dressmakers didn't get along. While some Pittsburghers enjoyed the drama of their rivalry as they sought to outdo the other in the quality of goods or window dressing, Mama, ever the peacemaker, sought to build a bridge in her own small way.

Ellie's gaze rose to the large bay window of the newly refurbished shop, excitement rising. The day was sultry, sharpening her appreciation for the East Indian chintz gowns on display, all in brilliant, polished hues. There would be no Spitalfields silk for a July ball, though it was what Andra preferred for her December birthday, straight from Bond Street in London. She found Pittsburgh dressmakers too rustic, she said, and Da allowed her the extravagance.

A bell jingled as they entered the shop, bringing Madame from behind the counter, hands full of the latest fashion plates in *Magasin des Modes*. Clearly she was expecting them. *"Accueillex, les belles dames!"*

When Mama hesitated, Ellie answered with a smile, *"Bonjour*, we are indeed glad to be here."

Clearly delighted, Madame seated them at a small corner table, chatting in a charming mix of French and English as she spread the fashion plates before them. Ellie took a last look about, breathing in the heady scent of honeysuckle and lily of the valley that perfumed an enormous collection of soaps displayed in a glass case nearby. A far cry from the foul odors of the tanyards and levee.

Two shop girls waited on other customers, displaying lengths of lace and delicate handkerchiefs, ever accommodating. Ellie had a hard time keeping her mind on matters at hand with so tempting an array of luxury goods surrounding them, far more enticing than the more practical merchandise sold at the Ballantyne mercantile.

"We must, of course, take your measurements," Madame was saying, eyeing Ellie discreetly.

"I have in mind a modest gown." Mama held up some embroidered gauze to the light. "Nothing so sheer that you can see right through . . ."

Perusing the fashion plates, Ellie wondered if Chloe was wearing her town-made clothes or had resumed going barefoot in breeches. A week had passed since she'd left River Hill. Why did it seem far longer? She'd heard her father and Ansel discussing the battered chaise and wondered when they'd bring it home.

Madame held up a colorful plate. "Here is a fashion-forward gown with a diaphanous overskirt, perfect for certain dance moves such as the *pas d'été*."

Ellie studied the design, smiling absently, her mind on the guest list instead. Just that morning she'd returned over one hundred names to Mama . . .

After putting Chloe and Jack at the very top.

Her next breath came up short as she realized her blunder. Mama now had the list and was going to discuss it with her father. Though Mama might not see it for what it was, Da missed nothing. At least where Ellie was concerned.

"Ellie, how does this sound?" Mama's dulcet voice returned her to the present. "A fitted bodice and wide waistband with a full skirt and overskirt of net, in a soft mint or this delicate shade of coral."

"Coral," Ellie said without thought, fingering the proffered fabric.

Madame beamed as if she'd chosen correctly and summoned a shop girl. In moments the fashion plates disappeared and the table was beautifully laid out for tea. Ellie sat in pained silence, wishing back the guest list, ruing her foolishness. But the image of Jack and Chloe's names in bold black ink was scrawled across her thoughts as plainly as the chocolate bonbons nested in ruffled paper now being placed upon the linen tablecloth. Why hadn't she tucked their names in the middle of the list or saved them till the last?

But she'd done nothing wrong, truly. She'd simply behaved foolishly. And revealed the state of her heart with the stroke of a pen.

In the days following, Ellie stayed busy helping Mama as needed, playing her harp and plying her needle in a particularly frustrating attempt at whitework embroidery in spare moments. She found herself missing Adam and Ulie and the baby, praying for their safety. Chloe and the day school seemed distant as a dream. Life slowly resumed its regular rhythms. Feathers stopped his plucking and resumed his singing. They even received a disappointingly terse letter from Andra.

Arrived safely in York.

Mama sighed but said nothing when she read the post, then promptly turned her attention to other matters. The coming ball was scheduled for the last of July, to be crowned with a midnight celebratory supper and dancing till dawn. Even now the rooms were being readied and extra help hired, Mari and Gwyn nearly taking up residence in the formal dining room and third-floor ballroom.

The invitations were being engraved at the printers, and

not one word had been said about the names crowning the guest list. Thinking of it left Ellie slightly sick. Would they be stricken, written off? Or sent with the hope of being refused? If Andra was home and had her way, they would be. No Turlock, to her knowledge, had ever set foot inside New Hope save Chloe when she'd come begging to be taught. Jack, she remembered all too vividly, had stopped just shy of the veranda on that stormy April day when he'd returned her home. Andra had seen to that.

A fortnight had passed, and nothing more was said about resuming her teaching. Impatience frayed her every nerve, as did the summer's mounting heat. Despite the feverish temperatures, she ventured beyond the coolness of the house, intent on a walk. Leaving out the back door, she donned a straw hat and meandered down the bricked path to the coach house. There the stable hands gave nods of greeting and resumed their work. All manner of vehicles met her eyes as she passed through—phaeton, cutter, coach—but the chaise stall remained empty.

She set off beneath a half-cast sky, clouds tumbling across the expanse of endless blue. A vast meadow stretched before her, dotted with black merino and Leicester longwool sheep, the shaggy briards her father preferred moving amidst the flocks.

When she was small, they'd had a briard pup who'd thought her a lamb, herding her this way and that when she toddled about, and barking and trying to right her when she fell, much to everyone's amusement. Da had always rescued her and carried her on his shoulders back then, tending his sheep as he'd done as a boy in Scotland.

She found him in a far meadow standing with his farm manager and a few tenant lads who minded the flock. His handsome features were seasoned by the sun, the set of his shoulders and line of his back as straight as the younger men alongside him. In the stark light of day, the edges of his russet hair were silvered, a detail that till now had escaped her notice. She felt a hitch of sadness at the passing of time.

Oh, Da, I've been away far too long.

She moved across the cropped grass in his direction, pausing to pick some milkweed, wishing she was little again and could run to him and feel the exhilaration of old, when he'd swing her up on his wide shoulders.

Why did he keep mostly to home when endless business awaited in town? No doubt the trouble she'd encountered had left him deeply shaken. And she was to blame . . .

When he swung round to face her, his eyes lit with such delight her melancholy vanished. "For a wee bit I took you for your mother, come to call me home."

She smiled up at him beneath the brim of her wide straw hat, savoring the unintended compliment. "I was remembering when you used to carry me on your shoulders across this very meadow—and our old sheepdog would accompany us."

"*Och*, Sebastian! Those were the days." He linked arms with her. "I'd gladly turn the clock back if I could. Or move it forward."

"Forward?"

"To tote my grandbairns round." With a sly wink, he helped her across a low stone fence, righting her when she stumbled.

"Speaking of grandbairns . . ." She looked down at the petals in her hands, heat touching her cheeks. "I'd hoped you and Mama would have a few by now."

"In time, mayhap," he said matter-of-factly. "Some matters you have little control over. Love is one of them."

She sensed his disappointment, and it matched her own. Was that why Mama spent so many hours at the orphan home in town? Had she given up on Peyton and Andra entirely? Even Ansel?

He eyed her with a telling intensity. "I ken you didn't come all this way on so *sweltrie* a day to talk bairns and weddings."

"I thought a walk might do me good. I'm feeling . . ." She softened the Scots word with a smile. "*Pernickitie*."

"You want to return to teaching."

She nodded, relieved to have it confessed. "I can still be of help at home in the mornings. And Andra should soon be back."

"Very well." He picked up a stone and skimmed it across the surface of a small pond they skirted. "There's a vacant building on Race Street. Small and respectable. Or you can take the room over the confectionery near the boatyard. It has plenty of light, a sound floor for dancing lessons. Either place should suffice for a day school."

"Truly?" 'Twas more than she'd hoped for. Casting aside her flowers, she threw her arms around him, too moved to speak.

He held her close. "We can go in this afternoon and look around. Take stock of what you'll need."

"I'll ask Mama to come too." Her delight reached so deep she couldn't stop smiling. "Opening the school in town will be far easier than taking all my teaching supplies from place to place. And since all but one student lives in Pittsburgh," she said, thinking of Chloe, "'twill be no trouble for them."

They were heading the other direction now, toward the house. He was regarding her in that bemused way he had, as if trying to reconcile the little girl she'd once been with the grown creature who stood before him. She sensed he might even be thinking of Andra, who, with typical Scots stoicism, never gave way to such a frivolous emotional display.

Suddenly beset with misgivings, she pulled her hat free and

used the brim to fan her flushed face. "Sometimes I feel I've rushed headlong into the day school with little thought or prayer. What is it you want for me? You and Mama?"

"We want you to follow the Almighty's leading. Talk about what's in your head and heart, just as you are now. A day school is a worthy endeavor. But your mother and I hope that someday you'll want to settle down and know the joys we've had. 'Tis heaven's best gift, ye ken. Leaving a legacy of family. Faith."

Was he thinking of the Camerons? She ventured carefully, "Is it true what Mina said? Did Daniel come to you . . . ask about me?"

"He did."

"And . . . ?" She stopped walking, on her tiptoes inwardly.

"It wasn't what I'd hoped for."

She met his eyes in question. "Did he not ask for my hand?"

"Aye. But not your heart."

The regret in his eyes bruised her. He had such high hopes, wanted her to make a good match. Daniel had always seemed a fine choice. But now . . . They resumed walking, his words of minutes before returning with sudden poignancy.

Some matters you have little control over. Love is one of them.

She felt a flicker of insight. *Oh, Da, you are right. You cannot make someone love you . . . nor can you predict who you'll lose your heart to.*

"Once I nearly wed a lass I did not love to gain a fortune faster than I did." His voice was low and reflective. "But God Almighty intervened."

She darted a look at him. Did he mean Jack and Chloe's mother? Her heart tugged at life's twists and turns, how entire futures sometimes hinged on the most unpredictable, unlikely things.

They were nearing the rear veranda now, and Ellie's gaze settled on Mama sewing at one end of the wide porch. She was humming a hymn, unaware of their approach, pleasantly lost in her task. Everything about her bespoke grace . . . peace. She was the essence of a woman well loved.

Oh, Lord, please let me be like Mama.

Chloe held the ivory invitation in a hand soiled from digging worms, and her fingers seemed to shake. From excitement, Jack guessed.

"Look, Jack, your name is on it too! The Ballantynes are having a ball later this month—and we're invited." She dropped the elegantly sealed paper on his desk and leaned down to blow away the dirt, but the stubborn smudge remained. "Dash!"

He scanned the invitation, every engraved word fueling surprise—and fresh misery. Something was obviously afoot with the Ballantynes. Some pending announcement or celebration. Pushing his spectacles atop his head, he rubbed the bridge of his nose. "Invited and welcomed are two different things."

Chloe stared at him in consternation. "What do you mean?"

Feigning indifference, he returned to the notice of sale he'd almost finished. "We're not going."

"What?" Her protest was a strangled wail. Dirty hands forgotten, Chloe snatched up the summons from New Hope and held it to her heart, as pitiful a ploy as he'd ever seen. "I just have to see Miss Ellie again, Jack!"

"I'll be heavy into the harvest come then, as will you. Everyone at River Hill is needed for the work, even Sol and Ben. No one is exempt." He needn't remind her that they, along with the tenants, were in the fields before dawn and often worked by moonlight to bring the harvest in. The prospect of a dance filled him with dread, the gleaning with elation. He would extract the thought of Ellie from his mind with the sweat of his brow and every swing of his scythe if it was the last thing he did.

"But Jack!" Her lower lip trembled. "One ball?"

Immune to her antics, he signed a document and moved on to the ledgers. "Another word and I'll send you back to Broad Oak."

She threw the invitation down and fled, slamming the study door behind her. Glad to be alone, he reached into his breast pocket and withdrew a letter, delivered that morning and addressed solely to him. For a moment he fought returning it to his pocket, sure Ellie had penned her goodbye, severing their tie.

Studying the familiar writing, he wanted to groan. How was it that the mere slant of her pen turned him inside out? He could no longer deny he missed her. Her lemon-lavender scent. The graceful way she moved across a room. The wistful way she regarded him. He even craved the sound of her voice.

With a sigh, he broke the indigo seal with a swipe of his thumb.

Dear Jack . . .

He leaned back in his chair, softening at her lack of formality. No "Mr. Turlock," at least.

I'll soon be opening a day school in Pittsburgh above the confectionery at the corner of First and Water Streets.

So her father could keep a close eye on her? After the trouble on the road, he wasn't surprised.

My wish is for Chloe to continue lessons two afternoons a week if agreeable to you both.

211

Two afternoons? He set his jaw against the elation he felt. It was time for Chloe to put her matchmaking plans to bed.

I've missed your sister and hope she's missed
our time together too.

His resolve thawed. He'd have to be made of ice to refuse her.

Fondly, Ellie.

Fondly. He felt a hitch of regret. He supposed that to expect *Love* was asking far too much.

20

I love thee, I love but thee
With a love that shall not die
Till the sun grows cold
And the stars grow old.
WILLIAM SHAKESPEARE

Ellie pulled off her gloves and stood in the middle of her second-floor schoolroom. The polished maple floor was pleasing, the furnishings mismatched but adequate. Most delightful of all was the smell—not beeswax and books, but the overwhelming aroma of delicacies wafting up from the confectionery just below.

Marzipan and lemon custard and candied orange peel stormed her senses, begging her to hurry downstairs and shun her books and grow thick-waisted before her time. She took a deep breath, feeling the pinch of her stays. She'd already eaten two lemon tarts since resuming teaching yesterday. Perhaps it would have been wiser to occupy the vacant building on Race Street . . .

She moved to the south-facing windows, admiring the

expansive view of the Monongahela waterfront. If she tarried long enough, she was sure to see Da or her brothers going from office to mercantile to warehouse. The *Elinor* was docked like a queen amidst the less regal packets, its giant paddlewheel idle in the swift current. She felt a sense of contentment despite the levee's endless scuttle and the pungent swirl of pitch and brine. 'Twas the landscape she'd been born and bred to. It seemed right to be near her family.

Opening a window, she was thankful the July wind was leeward, gently stirring the petals of the lilies one of her students had brought her. Beside it was a wicker basket filled with Mamie's finest. Biscuits layered with ham. A small wheel of cheddar cheese. Sugared almonds. Berry tarts. Jars of lemonade. And her father's midday meal. She'd asked Mamie to pack extra, hoping to take a picnic to the point, just her and Chloe.

Ansel had ridden in with her at noon, well ahead of her one o'clock lesson, before going to the boatyard. As the clock ticked nearer to the appointed time, her spirits began to sag. Jack hadn't responded to the note she'd sent to River Hill saying she was resuming teaching. In light of his painful silence, the day school did seem silly, a frivolous means for a privileged girl to fill her hours, just as Andra said. Her time seemed better spent in the attic, which was now occupied again since the cupola had been lit.

If Chloe didn't come, she'd tote the basket across the street and take the midday meal with her father, then wander up the street to the orphan home and find Mama. She reached for her bonnet and began tying the chin ribbons, trying to ignore the disappointment carving a hole inside her. Her fingers stilled at a sudden sound on the stair.

Such a *clomp, clomp, clomp* could only be Chloe. Her hopes soared along with every ungracious step. She tried

214

hiding her glee, but her rush to the door revealed everything, as did her breathless words when she flung it open. "I didn't see you on the street."

Chloe stared back at her, clearly exasperated. "Jack brought me down the back alley. *Sidesaddle.*"

The word was spat out with such disgust Ellie laughed. "A young lady should always ride so, especially about town." Her gaze slid from Chloe to Jack as he came to an abrupt halt on the landing behind her.

Beneath his shock of sunny hair, his gaze was tremendously stormy. She groped for something more to say and came up woefully short.

Fortunately, Chloe flew past, pronouncing the room a wonder. "Oh, it smells heavenly! Whoever would have thought you'd be over a sweet shop? You even have our sewing by the windows so I can better see my stitches."

Ellie turned back to Jack. "Won't you come in?"

"Nay, I have business elsewhere." He broke their gaze to watch Chloe as she wandered about the room. "I'll be back at four o'clock."

"Four is fine, plenty of time to finish our lessons." She hesitated, wanting to keep him longer, though he was clearly ready to leave. "Thank you for bringing her."

"I'd get little peace otherwise." His expression remained cold, distant, denying her the spark of warmth she craved. "We're good till autumn. After that she returns to Broad Oak."

Her gladness at seeing them shattered. Did Chloe know? She sensed there was far more to his terse words, but now wasn't the time or place to delve deeper.

"Till autumn." She stated their new terms, trying to keep the dismay from her tone.

With a nod, he turned and started down the stair, erasing

the memory that he'd ever been tender with her in River Hill's dusty parlor. Had she only imagined it, then?

She turned back to Chloe, forcing a smile. "It's such a pretty day, not too warm. I thought we'd have a picnic at the point."

"Down by old Fort Pitt?"

Ellie nodded. "The King's Garden, or what's remaining."

Chloe was poking around the basket now, her delight contagious. "Is all this food for us?"

"Some is for my father. We'll stop by the boatyard on our way."

Her eyes rounded. "I've never met Silas Ballantyne, only seen him."

"Come along then. It's getting late, and I need to have something to show for our afternoon besides stuffing ourselves. We'll have some sewing for dessert."

Chloe made a face. "Marzipan sounds better."

Till autumn. A bittersweet sense of urgency spurred Ellie on as she held out her hand. Chloe took it, catching up the basket with her other. Pleasure softened the solemn slant to her features. Had she never been on a picnic? Ellie felt a tug of sympathy for her—and Jack. He'd likely never been on one either.

The front door to Ballantyne Boatworks swept shut in their wake, heralding their arrival by the ringing of a bell. Ellie smiled at her father as he pulled himself to his full height and faced them, coming out from behind his desk. "Miss Chloe Turlock, I presume."

Chloe eyed Ellie fiercely and hissed, "Am I supposed to curtsy?"

"Not necessary for an old Scotsman," he said with a smile, sparing Ellie an answer.

Ansel eyed them with amusement before returning to the plans spread upon the drafting table by a window. All was still, expectant. Ellie hoped Chloe wouldn't misspeak, but there was no guarantee . . .

Chloe roamed the cluttered office with curious eyes before alighting on Da once more.

"So you're the man my mother almost married."

"Chloe!" Ellie's tone was far more forceful than she intended, but her father simply chuckled. Ansel winked at her, obviously enjoying her disquiet, while Chloe studied Da without apology.

"If I had done so, neither you nor my daughter would be standing here," he returned with his usual aplomb. "So all's well that ends well, aye?"

With a smile, Chloe showed him the basket. "I didn't eat your dinner, though I had a mind to."

Ellie took the wicker container and began unpacking items, laying them atop her father's desk. "We're going to have a picnic at the point," she announced, anxious to be on their way. "Mamie has packed a feast for us all."

Behind them, Chloe moved to a window, clearly awed at her view of the crowded levee. "I've never ridden on a steamer."

"Nor has Ellie," Da replied, coming to stand beside her. "They're a wee bit dangerous. When you're older, they'll likely be less so."

"It must be grand to have a boat named after you." She regarded him openly, her chin firming in calculation. "If you build another, perhaps you can call it *Chloe Isabel*."

He smiled down at her. "Mayhap I will."

Ellie intervened, glancing at the wall clock. "Come along, Chloe. Ja—your brother will be back for you this afternoon, and we don't want to keep him waiting."

"Oh, you needn't worry about Jack. He'll just go up the alley to one of the gin roo—"

Ellie stepped on her toe to silence her. "Goodbye, Da, Ansel." She didn't listen for their reply, just swept Chloe outside among roustabouts as plain-speaking as she.

Linking arms, they headed west along the Monongahela toward the point. Lombardy poplars and weeping willows softened the street's rough edges and provided welcome shade as carriages and wagons lumbered past.

"Your father's handsome, even if he is an antique," Chloe exclaimed.

Caught between a sigh and a chuckle, Ellie fixed her attention on a street marker denoting the latest flood stage of the river.

"Do you think Jack . . ." Chloe gave her a sidelong glance. "Handsome?"

The question wrenched her. Truly, today Chloe was at her candid best. "Yes," she admitted reluctantly, wishing an end to the matter.

A look of near triumph graced Chloe's face. "You're always honest with me, Miss Ellie. You never tell a lie. Lies are wicked things, Sally says."

"Sally?"

"Ben's granny. She's our cook at Broad Oak."

"'Tis always best to be truthful but never hurtful," Ellie told her. "There are ways of saying things, sparing people's feelings. We're to speak the truth in love."

Chloe's expression grew shadowed. "Then I need to tell you the truth about Jack."

Ellie kept on walking as her mind began a precarious whirl. Was Jack ill, in some trouble? Why did she always feel so raw at the mere mention of him?

Sidestepping a mound of horse droppings, Chloe looked

as if the confession might choke her. "The truth is Jack never wanted you at River Hill. I lied and said he did. I-I didn't even want you to teach me at first. I just wanted you and Jack . . ."

Ellie's steps slowed, her disbelieving gaze resting on Chloe. "You mean he never agreed to our time together? But in the note you wrote—"

"I made it all up after he told me no." Her expressive eyes were a wash of gray. "I hoped—if you came to River Hill—he might fall in love with you."

Ellie resumed walking, face aflame. She felt a breathless bewilderment at such scheming. Did Jack know Chloe's true intent? She prayed not.

Chloe's voice dwindled to a thread of misery. "Jack told me a Ballantyne would never settle for a Turlock."

Had he? *Oh, Jack . . .*

"I-I just want him to be happy—to have someone who'll be good to him and love him. Someone like you."

Intent on some trees on the Allegheny side of the river, Ellie headed for an iron bench in their shade, the picnic forgotten. Chloe was crying now, not in the sly, manipulative way she sometimes did, but openly, drawing notice from the near street.

Gently, Ellie drew her down on the bench and put an arm around her slumped shoulders. "Your motives were good. But your methods were lacking." It was something her father sometimes said, though she'd never felt the truth of it so keenly till now.

"Th-there's m-more," Chloe stuttered.

"More?"

"Jack's leaving . . . selling River Hill. I-I found some papers on his desk. Come the next fall run—"

"The fall run?"

"The whiskey-making come September. When that's done,

he's going downriver. He plans to open a distillery in Missouri—do business with Indians and traders and frontiersmen." Chloe was crying again, sending Ellie searching for a handkerchief. "But it's wild and dangerous in the West, Wade says. I-I'm afraid he'll never come back." She fisted the hankie, regret in her gaze. "Don't tell Jack I told you. He'll be angry that I was snooping through his papers and talking."

Once again, Ellie felt the ground cut from under her. "I won't say a word, Chloe. 'Tis none of my business, truly."

In hindsight, Jack's terse words an hour before took on new meaning. *We're good till autumn. After that she returns to Broad Oak.*

But Broad Oak was not home, not safety or peace. Chloe had no wish to return there, and Jack was obviously more than willing to leave it all behind.

Chloe's small hand snuck into her own. "I thought—hoped—we could live at River Hill and be a family, just the three of us."

The plea was so heartfelt Ellie's own eyes grew damp. With every breathless word, Chloe was revealing the depths of her discontent—and Jack's. Ellie felt privy to a great many things—family secrets and futile desires that were far beyond her ken.

"Have you ever prayed about this, Chloe? Poured out your heart to God like you are with me?" The sorrowful shake of her fair head confirmed Ellie's suspicions. "Jack won't always be here, nor will I. But God never leaves you—and always listens." She hesitated, wishing for more than words, wanting the vulnerable Chloe to have something tangible to hold on to. "I'm sad about River Hill too. I'd like to see it restored to its former grandeur, the garden especially."

"You'd have to become its mistress. Marry Jack."

Ellie looked away. The prospect unfurled like a flower,

alluring and sweet. She discarded it as quickly as it came. "Jack hasn't asked me, and I . . . I couldn't even if he did."

Chloe lifted her head. "Because Ballantynes are better than Turlocks?"

"No." She'd put that notion to rest once and for all. "Because we're two very different people." Seeing Chloe's confusion, she sought a sound explanation. "We value different things, Jack and I. He's fond of travel. I like being home. My passion is music. Jack prefers . . . "

"Gin rooms," Chloe finished.

Ellie sighed. "Not only that. My family—they're believers, Presbyterians . . ."

"And mine aren't anything." The hopelessness in her tone struck Ellie hard. "No one prays or goes to church. The only time they mention God is to take His name in vain. Another vile thing, Sally says."

"You can change that," Ellie said softly.

Chloe let out a breath, looking older than her years. "Show us how, Miss Ellie. We don't know where to start, Jack and I. We Turlocks tend to make a mess of things. If you married him and came to live at River Hill—"

"Jack doesn't love me, Chloe. He—"

"He does care for you." Her damp eyes flashed. "He might even love you. I've watched the way he looks at you. He even keeps your notes—letters—in his breast pocket. And he reads the books you mean for me, every one."

Ellie tried to mask her doubt. "Truly?"

"Cross my heart." She touched her chest. "I won't lie to you again—or Jack."

Appetite gone, Ellie began unpacking the basket, hands stilling at Chloe's next words.

"I might as well tell you all the rest too. Ben hears the gossip at Broad Oak when he visits." She'd dried her tears, but her lip still trembled. "Rumor is Jack even threatened some bounty hunters—and Wade—over you."

A chill crept over Ellie despite the day's heat. Were bounty hunters the men who had stopped her on the road? Was Wade involved in some way? Despite her fears, why did she warm to the thought of Jack leaping to her defense, if indeed he had?

Shaken, she placed a biscuit in Chloe's open, entreating hand, wanting to give her far more. Ellie bowed her head, uttering a prayer as much for herself as for Chloe and Jack, her heart unbearably sore.

Lord, please fill our needy souls.

21

I have grown to love secrecy.
OSCAR WILDE

The days leading to the ball ticked by with agonizing slowness. Ellie's gown hung in her bedchamber, so lovely her heart ached inexplicably when she looked at it. Madame had fussed over the final fitting, insisting her rival, Miss Endicott, redye Ellie's slippers to better match the gown's exquisite coral hue—or order new shoes altogether. A mother-of-pearl fan rested in a case atop her dressing table beside pristine white gloves. There'd even been whisperings about a set of pearls, a birthday gift from her parents.

Despite all the finery and fuss, Ellie's thoughts strayed repeatedly from the coming event, clinging stubbornly to Chloe's startling revelation at the point. Chloe's words seemed pinned to her heart, sore and painful as a wound. She couldn't quite shake the humiliation she felt over being at River Hill unwanted, uninvited. Chloe's duplicity stung, but Ellie understood her motives.

Though she dreaded seeing Jack again, she continued to

wait at the window on the days of Chloe's lessons, a fading hope in her breast, wishing he'd appear. But he simply sent Ben to bring Chloe and fetch her home, lending far less weight to what she'd shared.

He does care for you. He might even love you.

Impossible. Chloe had simply been woolgathering. Jack would soon go west. River Hill would be sold. Chloe would return to Broad Oak. Daniel would propose. Ellie felt the certainty to her bones. Thankfully, she had only to look toward the attic to regain a sense of what really mattered.

"Ellie, I need your help upstairs today." Mama prefaced the request with a smile, despite Gwyn being ill from a fever and the ball drawing near and another fugitive having come at dawn. "'Tis name day. Dr. Brunot will be coming soon."

Ellie gladly swept up the stairs to the attic, where dormer windows were open wide to relieve the summer's heat. She gathered slates and pencils from a small corner chest and took a seat as the group gathered in a tight circle, Mama at their heart. Despite the swell of sweat and anxiety that seemed ever palpable, Ellie always found their time together rewarding—and a blessed distraction.

Mama's voice was clear and calm, never giving way to the pressures and worries beyond the attic rafters. "You'll soon be leaving New Hope and your old ways behind. Our Quaker friends in the north would like for you to come with new names of your own choosing."

"We used to the name game, Mistress Eden. We don't even own our African names," a woman said. "Those we had was stolen away right along with us."

"And I'm sorry for that," Mama replied. "Hopefully you'll need not change names ever again. The reason for doing so now is to protect you from the past, from those who knew you as slaves. These new names will help you gain freedom."

"I always wanted to be called Paul," one man told them. "It was the name of a whole-souled man in Kentucky who preached to us slaves in secret."

"I'm sure he'd be pleased," Mama said with a smile. "Plus it's one you're likely to remember."

Looking down at her slate, Ellie printed the name in large block letters and passed it round the circle.

"I'll take Rachel," the woman beside Ellie said. "It's a good Bible name."

Ellie marveled that Mama almost made a game of it, having them practice their chosen names till they were comfortable as a well-worn garment, mixing up the slates and having everyone remember who they were with a great deal of high-spirited merriment. Next the women stitched their new initials in their dress hems and the collars of the linen shirts Mama had sewn for the men. They wouldn't leave till their new identities were firmly in place. Even then some didn't want to go.

"Can you make a place for me at New Hope?" The question, asked again and again, never failed to stir Ellie's spirit. "I can work in the house or the fields, whatever you need."

"You're always welcome here," she'd often heard Mama say, "but 'tis too close to the river to tarry."

As if to anchor them all, her father held family devotions in the evenings after supper. A maid was posted at both front and back doors in case of trouble, and only then did the attic empty in lieu of the cooler, shuttered parlor. There Da chose "freedom passages," as he called them—the stories of Moses leading the Israelites from Egypt and Joseph fleeing bondage to rise to power. No one was caught napping, wooed as they were by his rich Scots speech as he stood before the cold hearth.

"Da should have been a preacher," Peyton murmured as

he sat beside Ellie on a sofa. "You know what they say of Scottish sons. The firstborn is laird and heir. The second is the military's and the third the pulpit's."

"God had but one Son and made a minister of Him," she said softly. "I daresay the rest is second best."

He gave her a wry glance. "I'd rather be laird and heir."

The pride in his tone gave her pause. Peyton had all of their father's business sense but none of his humility. Not even a stint in jail had dinted what Ellie feared was arrogance. Across from them sat Ansel, as different from Peyton as she was from Andra. She studied him in the flickering candlelight, grieved by the cheerless slant of his features that bespoke a burden.

With the coming harvest, the gristmill would operate almost continuously, requiring all of Ansel's time. How he'd transport fugitives was a mystery. And Peyton? While the enslaved in their care were running from danger, he seemed to be running headlong toward it, or so she feared. Rumor was that he was still seen in the company of Wade Turlock in town.

Devotions done, Ellie lingered in the parlor as the fugitives padded upstairs on quiet feet and her father and brothers crossed to the study. Mari drew the cover over Feathers's cage, shuttering his late-night song before disappearing to snuff the candles in the adjoining room.

"'Tis too hot to sleep," Mama told her. "Why don't we go onto the back porch till it cools down?"

Relieved, Ellie nodded, having no desire to retire to her room, where thoughts of Jack crowded in, unrelenting as the summer heat. They took seats amidst the glow of fireflies, the low cadence of Da's and Peyton's voices drifting through an open window. Other than that, all was still save the haunting call of a mockingbird.

"What a peaceful night." Mama looked skyward at the moon. "Full and silver-bright. Perfect for the harvest."

Ellie's gaze flickered east toward River Hill's unseen fields. 'Twas all too easy to imagine Jack swinging a scythe in the moonlight. Better to ponder the reality of the coming autumn with its corn stubble and spent fields . . . and winter's rivers locked fast with ice, barring his way back to them.

Eyes damp, she bit her lip, stunned by the ferocity of her feelings. Since Chloe had told her Jack was leaving, selling River Hill, she'd longed to confide in someone, but pouring out her heart to her parents would only make matters more complicated. She'd caused the household worry enough with her waywardness on the road. She wouldn't add to it with her distress over Jack and Chloe too.

To her relief, Mama began to talk of more mundane matters. "Your birthday ball is but a fortnight away."

"I suppose most everyone is coming."

"Most, yes." Mama's fan stirred the air around them. "A few will be traveling and have sent their regrets. Not everyone has responded yet."

Nor will they, Ellie didn't say, thinking again of River Hill. "My gown fits perfectly. I don't think I'll need another fitting."

"I'm afraid you might." Mama turned to her, profile pensive. "Lately you hardly seem to eat a bite."

Ellie shifted uncomfortably in her chair, wishing she could brush aside any concerns like yesterday's tea crumbs. "I'm afraid the heat has stolen my appetite."

"Only the heat, Ellie?" Mama's gaze didn't waver. "We're concerned the incident on the road might have upset you more than you let on."

Not the incident on the road, Mama, but what happened afterward, in Jack Turlock's parlor.

Ellie looked to her lap. Jack's closeness and concern had upended her in ways she couldn't fathom or forget. He'd been so tender with her. As if he truly cared for her, like

Chloe said. But she could hardly speak of that. "'Tis not the past—the incident on the road—so much as the future. There are so many possibilities before me at one and twenty. Anything might happen. I could be married and a mother by next July."

"That's certainly how it was for me." Mama's soft voice caught in a throaty chuckle. "I came face-to-face with your father in River Hill's ballroom one summer, wed him soon after, and bore Peyton nine months later."

"You knew Da was yours from the first—and you were his."

"Yes, we knew, but circumstances conspired against us. Thankfully, love and the Lord Himself often make a way when there seems to be none."

The gentle words struck Ellie hard. True for some, perhaps, but not for her. Nor Jack.

"I'll never forget the beauty of that ballroom," Mama said. "All the candlelight shimmering off gowns and greatcoats. The music and dancing. Once, River Hill was the jewel of Allegheny County."

Once. Ellie roamed the many rooms in memory, all but Jack's, though Chloe had offered to show her that too. "It's still beautiful, though neglected. Sometimes when I was there, it was hard to keep my mind on lessons. I'd look around and imagine all the pleasure to be had in turning it lovely again, especially the garden."

"It's been forgotten, then. Overgrown."

"Sadly, yes. Chloe and I were hoping to bring a corner to life on the south side, where there's a charming dripping cistern. It overlooks the river . . ." She left off, letting go of the dream like the scattered garden seed on the back road.

"You share your father's fondness for the place. He once spent many pleasant hours there." She rested her fan in her lap. "Every house, to be a true home, needs a mistress. River

Hill has been without one for fifty years or better. Perhaps Mr. Turlock will settle down and make it grand again."

"I doubt that will ever happen. He's—" Ellie changed course lest she betray what Chloe had confided about the sale. "He's a very busy man. His interests lie elsewhere. Though I wish he would settle down, if only for Chloe's sake."

"You're very fond of her."

"I worry about what will become of her." A breeze stirred the loose tendrils about her flushed face, and she turned in its direction. "Like you, my every emotion seems to cloud matters. I wish I had more of the Ballantyne steel."

"Oh, 'tis there but buried deep."

Was it? Then why did she feel so tossed about, her thoughts and emotions in a perpetual tangle? Feigning calm, she kissed Mama's smooth cheek. "I'd best go to bed . . . say my prayers. And I promise to eat a hearty breakfast on the morrow."

Mama gave no answer, just squeezed her hand in a wordless good night.

22

On matters of fashion, swim with
the current, on matters of principle,
stand like a rock.

THOMAS JEFFERSON

As thunder rumbled like whiskey wagons overhead, Jack ducked into the glass-fronted shop after studying the bold sign emblazoned with gilded scissors and a spool of blue thread.

WILLIAM DAVENPORT, TAILOR.

The spacious room was empty, and he nearly sighed with relief. He couldn't spare a day in town with the harvest under way, yet here he was, sweating and harried, his temper as sharp as the scissors on a near table. Davenport emerged from a back room, waddling more than walking, his portly frame encased in black. His eyes flared with surprise when Jack shut the door and walked toward him. Drawing up short behind a worn wooden cutting table, he gave a wary greeting. "Mr. Turlock, sir."

"No need for formalities. Just call me Jack."

"Well . . . Jack. What brings you to High Street?"

"I'm in need of a suit of clothes, and I hear you work quickly."

The tailor cleared his throat, looking only slightly less nervous. "How quickly?"

"A fortnight."

"Is this to be a formal occasion?"

"Regrettably." Jack flinched as the man circled him appraisingly, removed the tape dangling about his thick neck, and pulled it tight about Jack's waist. His balding pate shone in the dim light as he bent to measure a leg next, leaving Jack free to look about the tidy room.

Clothing hung from wall pegs in various stages of construction or repair—pants, shirts, greatcoats, and more. Beneath shelves stuffed with fabric stood an enormous sewing chest with manifold drawers. His gaze stopped circling, fastening on an elongated looking glass. The large mirror reflected a somewhat shocking image back to him. Tall. Slim. Straight. Dark as an Indian and maybe mistaken for one, but for his hair.

The tailor straightened. "I have the finest broadcloth in bottle-green or midnight-blue, and cut-steel buttons for suits. Do you prefer breeches or trousers?"

"Trousers."

"Then you shall have a fine cutaway coat."

Jack had no clue as to the details. He simply nodded glumly. If this is what it took to make a gentleman, he'd gladly go west and don buckskins.

"And the color?" The tailor's clipped British accent was unrelenting.

"Color? Um . . . midnight-blue, I think you called it."

The bald head bobbed in satisfaction as the tailor applied the tape to Jack's shoulders. Jack bristled at the familiarity.

How in blazes did Davenport remember all the figures? "Shouldn't you be writing this down?"

There was a derisive snort. "Mr. Tur—Jack, when you've kept shop as long as I have, there's no need for such a crutch. Besides, your measurements are uncommon enough to be memorable. Now if you'll kindly turn round."

Jack did as he bid, enduring more taping. All for Chloe's benefit. He'd read the misery in her eyes when she'd found the Ballantynes' invitation crumpled in the study's cold hearth, and it moved him more than any tirade ever could. He kept forgetting, despite her fierce demeanor, that she was still half girl. On more than one occasion of late, he'd found her upstairs playing with their mother's old dolls, reminding him he needed to tread more carefully.

"All right, we'll go," he'd finally told her, his every word forced as he watched her press the wrinkles from the invitation with an agitated hand.

She looked up, lashes glistening with tears, reminding him of when she'd barely come up to his knee, all rolls and dimples, and he hadn't been able to say no to her. "Promise?"

"Aye, but not a word to Ellie, understand? This is a . . . surprise." A farce was more like it. He'd ignored the *répondez s'il vous plaît* at the invitation's bottom, as he wanted to be able to back out at the last moment if his misgivings gained the upper hand. He feared they would.

"We'll have to learn to dance, Jack. Otherwise we'll both be outcasts."

He shook his head. "No dancing. Period."

Flashing him a determined glare, she disappeared upstairs and returned with a thin, dog-eared book. "It's Playford's *The English Dancing Master*. I found it in Ma's old desk."

"So?"

"Don't you see? We'll be able to memorize the steps to a

few country dances, at least. But," she said pointedly, "we'll have to have a fiddler like Ellie does for the dancing lessons you've denied me."

"*Touché,*" he said, seizing on one of the few French words he knew.

Now, having agreed to it, he felt disbelief take hold. He'd hired not only a fiddler but a dancing master, both due this very afternoon. Guilt had snagged him, he guessed. He'd yet to tell Chloe he was selling River Hill and returning her to Broad Oak. Given that, he owed her a grand finish. The Ballantyne ball should suffice.

Davenport's fumbling returned him to the present. "Have you never been to a tailor, Mr. Tur—Jack?"

"Never." *And I'll not make the same mistake twice.*

As he'd grown up, his clothes had been made by Broad Oak slaves or ordered from Philadelphia by his mother for special occasions, none of them memorable. She'd shunned Pittsburgh's shops, calling them countrified. And he, hating civility and fuss, had simply worn the clothes left in his grandfather's wardrobe since his passing.

At last Davenport ambled over to a near shelf, where he selected a length of rich blue fabric. "Is the color and nap to your satisfaction?"

Reaching out a callused hand, Jack found the broadcloth soft as felt. "Aye, but if you dare give me the look of a dandy . . ."

"Say no more. I know how a man of your station and reputation should look. The suit shall be done a week from Wednesday."

As the fiddle music ended, Jack uttered an oath and collapsed in the nearest chair. Chloe, far less perplexed, simply succumbed to a fit of giggles atop the ballroom floor.

"Dancing be hanged! I'd rather swing a scythe any day."
Wiping his brow with a rolled-back sleeve, he glanced out an
open window toward fields he couldn't see. His astonished farm
manager had come to the door half an hour before, interrupting
a rousing reel to report finding rust among the winter wheat.

Jack dismissed him with a shrug and a promise to ride
out and investigate before dusk . . . if the lesson ever ended.
Baffled by a great many intricate steps and trilling notes, he
ached to be out-of-doors amidst windrows of grain, fatigued
in the old familiar way, not laid low by silly maneuvers in a
dusty ballroom.

Thunder growled, but it was a distant rumble, a threat
he hoped would soon dissipate. Hay-making waited on the
morrow, and dry weather was needed—as was he.

"Blast, Jack!" Chloe was on her feet, arms crossed. "You
tripped me midstep on that last country dance and almost
sent me sailing out a window!"

He exhaled, tugging at his banded collar in a bid for air.

"You'd best not do the same with Miss Ellie the night of
the ball."

Ignoring her, he studied the finely paneled walls and
wondered if New Hope's ballroom resembled River Hill's.
The dog ears of the three French doors facing the river were
trimmed with mahogany rosettes, the elegant plasterwork
ceiling a rich ivory bearing the O'Hara crest. He was Irish
to the bone on both sides, though the Turlocks were of less
impressive pedigree than the landed O'Haras.

This was the very room where Ellie's father had shifted
his allegiance from Isabel O'Hara to Eden Lee so many years
before. Jack had never understood it till he'd succumbed to
their daughter in the shadows of the blue room, frantic and
half sick with alarm at what had befallen her along the back
road. If Eden Lee had half the charm of the lovely Ellie . . .

"Jack, are you listening?"

He lowered his gaze to take Chloe in, thirsty for some switchel, and pushed up from his chair. "Nay."

Her flushed face turned entreating. "You simply need to memorize the steps. Remember what Master Playford said— very nippy, keep the turns tight, always be aware of other dancers. And if you go wrong, recover!"

He left the room grumbling.

The following day, Jack could see Chloe and Ben at the edge of the half-mown field. Concern crowded in, but he didn't want to break the rhythm of the eight-man team he was aligned with, so he kept on moving. Chloe was supposed to be at her lessons, reading the books Ellie had left her, though he knew the hum of the harvest was as tempting to her as it was him.

Rain was in the air, its heaviness mingling with his own sweat, turning the day sultry, his shirt damp. Low-hanging charcoal clouds pressed in, threatening to burst. Studying the sky, he picked up his pace. Hay making was akin to dancing, he decided, requiring grace and careful execution, staying in careful step with one's fellow mowers, every swipe of the blade laying the grass low in neat windrows.

If only he could perform as flawlessly in New Hope's ballroom.

They'd been at work since first light, and it was now the nooning. Half a dozen tenants' wives stood waiting at the fringes of the field, bearing baskets of food and small kegs of switchel spiked with cider. On harvest days the midday meal of meat, molasses bread, cheese, and watermelon was a feast, indulged for a full hour before the men began cradling again.

When the scythes finally slowed to a stop, Chloe made a

beeline toward Jack, Ben in tow. Unfolding a square of linen, she revealed a loaf reddened and studded with raisins. "Mrs. Malarkey sent you some watermelon cake."

A staple of the harvest meal. Jack wagered every basket contained it.

He lowered himself onto the shaded grass of a solitary oak, slightly apart from his tenants, eyeing Ben as he tugged the leather strap of the switchel keg off his shoulder.

"Want some?" Jack asked, gesturing to the cake.

"I'll give you a shilling if you can swallow it," Chloe dared Ben, grimacing at the crusty piece.

Jack chuckled and reached into the basket she'd brought. Mrs. Malarkey hadn't ruined the meat and cheese, at least, though the hearty bread she'd packed looked as dry and leathery as the cake.

Chloe looked heavenward as a slice of lightning rent the landscape. "You'd best be building some haystacks right quick. With a good many thatched roofs."

"You'd best go back to the house," Jack growled as thunder rumbled. Chloe and Ben exchanged glances, the worried cast of their features a clear sign all was not well. Ben scooted closer to Jack, his voice a mere whisper. "This mornin' we was fishin' and heard some voices."

Chloe leaned in from the other side, her small shoulder snug against Jack's hard arm. "There are people in the tunnel talking real low, Jack. Maybe runaways. There's even a raft hidden in the reeds."

He swallowed hard, eyes on the lightning-lit sky. "You tell anyone?"

"Nobody," Ben said. "But Sol knows. He was with us."

"Fishing, you mean?"

"Yep, he caught a big ol' catfish. Said he was gonna cook it and give it to them hungry souls."

Jack took a bite of bread, chewing thoughtfully. "Well, let Sol do his good deed, but stay out of it. The trespassers will likely move on."

The look Chloe gave him implied doubt. "Trespassers? I think they're escaped slaves, same as last time—"

He shushed her with a look. "Best get back to the house." He didn't want Jarm and Cherry mentioned. They'd made it safely to Harmony Grove, and he'd deemed it the end of the matter. "If you see Sol, tell him I want him in my study after dark."

He had few qualms about his grandfather's former man-servant, trustworthy as he was, but he wanted to determine Sol's part in the sudden slave activity and discourage it if he could. One bout of helping fugitives was enough. He'd not be entangled twice. Taking a long swig of switchel, he leaned back against the tree.

Chloe's face darkened. "But what if someone in the tunnel is sick or hurt—"

His jaw hardened. "Get back to the house. *Now.*" He stopped short of threatening to send her back to Broad Oak. That would happen soon enough, and the very thought grieved him.

Nodding, she took Ben's hand and started through the tall grass with bare feet, more child than young lady under the tutelage of Ellie Ballantyne.

Jack watched them go, mulling the situation. If he didn't intervene but simply left the runaways—if that was what they were—alone, they'd likely move on. He didn't begrudge them the use of the tunnel or his land if they just passed through. To New Hope or the Quaker settlements sympathetic to their cause. He had enough on his plate without turning abolitionist.

Toward dusk the last of the light leeched from the fields and the mowers slowed, thankful the threat of rain had passed. Bidding the tenants farewell, Jack stood and surveyed the toppled grass to be ricked on the morrow. Endless acres. Spent and thirsty, he caught up the switchel keg and uncorked it with his teeth, spitting the plug into the weeds at his feet.

As the last of the liquid trickled down his throat, his thoughts began to run rampant, consumed with Ellie and dance steps and meeting Sol after dark. He simply wanted a quiet corner. Some peace. But when he shouldered the keg and turned toward River Hill, all thoughts of rest vanished. There, across the cropped meadow, was a lone shadow. Tall. Still. Distinct.

Silas Ballantyne.

He felt biting surprise—and a shiver of fear.

Ellie.

Was she all right? The question cut through him like a scythe. Since she'd been waylaid the month before, the dread of it happening again fettered him night and day.

It seemed an eternity before he crossed to where Silas waited in the firefly-studded dusk. This close he could see no sign of tension in Silas's face. Just the same clarity of countenance he'd observed before—an inner strength that led to an outward calm. He'd often coveted that look. Likely the eternal struggle in his soul showed on his face . . .

"A fine harvest, Jack."

"Fine, indeed," he replied, suddenly aware of how disheveled he looked—grass-flecked and sweat-stained and reeking of switchel. This was how he'd feel at New Hope at month's end, surely. Flummoxed. Out of his element. An outcast. Yet there was no censure in Silas's eyes or demeanor.

He simply smiled and said, "Patience and persistence conquer all, aye?"

Jack shook his outstretched hand with a firmness he was far from feeling. "I've always been at home swinging a scythe."

"It shows."

The terse words were tinged with appreciation, or so he imagined. Just how long had Ellie's father stood watching him work? And why? Silas hadn't set foot at River Hill since Jack's grandfather's passing. The memory was always melancholy, and he had no wish to revisit it now.

Anxiety turned him blunt. "I doubt you're here to talk about the harvest."

With a slight nod, Silas turned toward River Hill. "I wanted to thank you, reimburse you, for repairing the chaise and returning it to New Hope."

Jack fell into step beside him. "No repayment needed. It was the least I could do for El—you." The near slip of her name lent to his loose ends, and he felt sweat bead his brow. No doubt the lapse was noticed. Desperate for firmer footing, he returned to the matter at hand. "There's been no more trouble, I hope."

"Nae." Silas was looking toward the horizon as the sun smudged the western sky a fiery red. "I've come about another matter. The sale of River Hill."

Jack tensed, his surprise plain. "I've not yet posted the sale."

"Some things need no advertisement," Silas replied.

"Are you . . . interested?" The question came through clenched teeth, revealing his reluctance. He looked down at the ground, wondering who had let the matter slip. Wade? Chloe? His father? Someone at Broad Oak, more than likely. He supposed it didn't matter. He now had a buyer and hadn't even had to advertise.

"I'm torn between trying to talk you out of it and making you an offer."

Jack met his unnervingly direct gaze. "Talk me out of it?"

"'Twould be selling your birthright, your inheritance—a mistake I once made myself years ago."

Had he? Such a blunder seemed beyond a Ballantyne. Jack slowed his steps, forgetting his fatigue, curiosity gaining the upper hand.

"When you're young, your judgment is often clouded," Silas told him. "You make decisions better left to time and experience. I cannot turn the clock back on what was done, but I can urge caution for someone else."

Jack's hand tightened on the scythe's smooth handle. "My grandfather meant this land for me. But there comes a time when one opportunity needs to be set aside for another or be lost altogether."

"You have other plans, then. Besides settling down here and raising a family."

"I've no plans to settle down," Jack said with vehemence, leaving little doubt about the matter. Ellie flashed to mind and he blocked the image, though it was getting harder and harder to do so. "My future lies elsewhere."

"You're certain of the sale."

Jack gave a decisive nod. "Aye."

Still, Silas showed no pleasure. "I've always had an attachment to this place. Your grandfather and I—" He broke off, emotion weighting his voice. "It goes without saying I have a history here. 'Twould grieve me to see the property pass into the wrong hands."

The possibility, coupled with the mention of Hugh O'Hara, left Jack's eyes stinging and damp. What would his mother say to this? There was no question that she'd try to block the sale if she knew it involved a Ballantyne. Only he didn't plan to tell her about it beforehand.

Silas had obviously given the matter much thought. "I'll

gladly purchase River Hill for whatever it is you're asking
. . . as a wedding gift for my daughter."

Jack stopped walking, his heart tripping on the last words
he'd expected to hear.

A *wedding gift*.

Not for Andra. *Ellie*. He felt all the breath had been
knocked out of him. Speechless, he couldn't even summon
an "aye" to the sale.

Silas resumed walking. "When you're ready to discuss the
terms, I'll be waiting."

They were nearing the stables, where a big bay horse was
tethered to a hitch rail. Without another word, Silas loosened
the reins and swung himself into the saddle, turning down
the long drive toward home. Jack watched him go, unable
to shake the certainty they hadn't been discussing the sale
of River Hill but Ellie.

Ellie and the future and Jack's own intentions.

23

*Life often presents us with a choice
of evils rather than of goods.*

CHARLES CALEB COLTON

Lightning flashed River Hill's way, making Ellie second-guess
her walk. But the sky above New Hope was clear and blue
as a robin's egg, and the letter she'd just received seemed to
burn a hole in her pocket, spurring her on. Now, at three
o'clock, the big house was empty, the only sounds coming
from the summer kitchen, where Mamie banged crockery in
preparation for supper, and from the stables, where horses
nickered and grooms cajoled as Ellie quietly walked past.

The attic was empty, the latest fugitives whisked away the
previous night by Ansel instead of Dr. Brunot. He'd passed
her on the stairs beforehand, disguised as a common laborer
in brogans and homespun, giving her a slight smile. She'd
watched from the landing window as a wagon full of grain,
disguising fugitives, was driven to an unknown destination
under half-filled burlap bags and the cover of darkness.

Lord, please hide them in their going and bring Ansel home.
Something bittersweet swept through Ellie as the night

swallowed them from view. What would become of all these people who'd shared her home and heart? They were headed to a place called freedom, yet neither she nor they knew if they'd ever get there.

Now, even with the sun on her shoulders, the brilliant rays skimming off the wide brim of her bonnet, she felt a thread of fear. The meadow was open, sheep grazing by a pond, the briards herding, a shepherd lad or two dotting the landscape. Green pastures and still waters. Why, then, did she feel uneasy? The day was ordinary in every way. Mama was in town at the orphan home. Father and Peyton were at the boatyard and mercantile . . .

And Andra had sent a letter.

She wasn't coming home yet, she'd penned. The Lees had been most welcoming, namely Aunt Elspeth and Uncle Thomas, who manned the blacksmith shop along with his wife, Felicity. Grandmother Lee had rallied at Andra's appearing, thinking she was Mama. 'Twas an easy mistake. Andra was Mama's twin physically but for her fair hair. Only she didn't *act* like Mama. That was Ellie's inheritance, something Andra claimed made her a favorite. "'Tis no secret you're the jewel of Da's heart," she'd said. But Ellie always dismissed the notion. Their father was simply too fair-minded to play favorites.

The Ballantyne mill stood alongside Rogue Creek, fed by a large pond upstream on Cameron land. Inside the cavernous building, water poured over a huge mill wheel that operated alongside gears designed the century before for grinding grain. Climbing up the grassy bank to the nearest stone wall, Ellie sought a small door, expecting Ansel to be at work within after his long night.

As the hinges groaned, she shuddered and shrank back. The place had always frightened more than fascinated her with its shadows and mist. Stepping inside, she let her eyes adjust to the dimness, making sense of ladders and sacks and barrels, a scattering of grain upon the wooden floor.

The mill was like any other save the small room in back of the waterwheel, where fugitives could hide undetected when the wheel was in motion. She wanted to call out Ansel's name but knew she'd never be heard above the din of rushing water.

A sudden shadow sent her spinning round.

"El, you all right?" Ansel loomed over her, bringing sudden relief. She rarely came here and sensed his surprise.

"I just wanted to . . ." Her voice was a near shout over the fall of water. "Talk."

He nodded and disappeared for a few moments. She heard the slowing of the wheel and the gentling of water.

"You've come at a good time. I'm done for the day." He drew the door shut behind them, and they passed out into light and fresh air. "All the tenants delivered their loads at first light."

"I wish I could be of more help."

"What? Grinding grain and smuggling slaves?" He winked at her, dispelling her worry. "I'd rather you manage your day school and play your harp and prepare for the ball."

She smiled at his teasing. "Speaking of balls, Mama has asked for a duet after supper that evening, before the dancing resumes." Sensing his reluctance, she said gently, "Consider it a birthday present to me."

"A present, aye." He helped her down the steep bank to level ground, giving a last look at the silent mill. "What do you have in mind?"

"A sonata, perhaps."

"Then we'll have to tune your harp lower than concert pitch if we're to keep from breaking any more of your strings."

"I'm sure any key you choose will be fine. You'll not even have to practice much and 'twill still sound divine."

"You flatter me. How many days is it now?"

"Only eight." She felt a tremor of trepidation thinking of all they had yet to do. "The fuss will soon be over."

"Fuss, indeed. Dining on oysters and dancing till dawn? Whose idea was this anyway?" His blue eyes swung back to her, questioning. "You're not going to make some announcement that night? Proclaim a betrothal I don't know about?"

"I might ask you that same question."

He frowned, kicking at a rock in the grass, and she wondered if he might be thinking of Mina.

She said quietly, "I think everyone expects—hopes—the ball will be the turning point for me and Daniel."

"How long since you've seen him?"

"Two years."

"Do you want a future with him, El?"

She shrugged lightly. "I used to think so. And then I saw how happy Rose was with her Matthew. Nothing was arranged or expected. It just happened . . . naturally."

Like . . . Jack.

Her feelings for him, so new and sweet, rose up and turned her breathless. She didn't know how to stop whatever it was that had started. If he wasn't a Turlock . . . If they weren't unequally yoked . . .

"I've ne'er been the romantic sort, I'm afraid," Ansel told her. "Either that or I've little time to think of such things."

"Well, someone has to!" she said in a rush, exasperation gaining the upper hand. "And it shan't only be me."

Chuckling ruefully, he thrust his hands into his pockets. "My guess is that Peyton and Andra will be the old man and old maid. The Ballantyne legacy depends on us."

"So what are we waiting for?"

"You tell me."

She hesitated, bending low to pluck a lone daisy. She felt a stab of embarrassment at sharing her romantic heart, though Ansel, unlike Peyton, wouldn't laugh if she did. "I'm waiting for someone I care so soul-deep about that being apart is anguish."

"Some grand passion, aye?"

"Is that asking too much?"

"I don't know, El. Mayhap friendship, mutual respect, are the best footing. Feelings can be fickle. Fleeting."

"But what of Mama and Da? I've never witnessed such devotion."

He nodded, more solemn than she'd ever seen him. "Theirs was a love forged amidst hardship and absence and a great many things you know little about. Such a bond comes along rarely, if at all. We can't expect the same."

Her heart sank at his practical words. "Then why, given that dismal pronouncement, don't I simply marry Daniel and you marry Mina?"

"Why?" He gave her a slow grin as if she'd caught him in a conundrum. "Because it's not that simple."

Reaching into her pocket, she fingered the post. "I didn't come out here to bother you about matrimony. I've a letter from Andra."

Passing him the paper, she awaited his reaction. He slowed his steps as he read, glancing up occasionally to navigate the grass. "So she's to stay on in York, till Grandma Lee has recovered or passes away. And when she returns . . . what? She's bringing someone with her?"

"She's asked me not to say a word but ready one of the guest rooms in secret. She wants it to be a surprise." She looked at him entreatingly. "But what if the surprise isn't a welcome one?"

"It may not be." Concern skimmed his features. "It's a bit risky having anyone stay at New Hope with fugitives coming and going."

"Which makes me want to forewarn Mama."

"Even if we were to write and caution Andra, she'd do what she wanted anyway." He refolded the post. "I'd give this to Da. He's the only one who's ever been able to reckon with Andra."

She nodded, gaze drifting to the climbing roses spilling over the garden wall like a pink waterfall. "A moment ago you said something . . ." She paused, unsure if she should ask. "That I know so little about Mama and Da's past—their love affair."

"Aye, but it's their story to tell, El, not mine." He gentled his tone when he said it, as if to soften his stance. "Let's go practice that music you mentioned and forget about all this York business. And pray Andra and her guest don't arrive the eve of the ball."

The door to the study yawned open, as if her father was expecting her. Ellie slipped inside, marveling that the scent of leather, books, and bergamot was as timeworn as her surroundings. Everything bespoke security and comfort and peace, the very things that had eluded her of late. A lone candelabrum flickered across a Gaelic Bible open on the large desk, gilding a worn page. One glance about the large room told her he'd stepped out.

"Ellie." The door clicked closed, and she turned toward him, warmed by the welcome in his voice. "I had to mind the light."

She nodded, wondering if, come morning, the attic would be full again. Taking the stool near his desk, she watched as he opened a box, withdrew his favorite pipe, and packed it full of tobacco crumbles. He glanced up at her before he lit the bowl. "D'ye mind?"

"Nae, I find it *cantie* enough," she replied, lapsing into the little Scots she knew.

He grinned, so boyish it seemed he was rewarding her with a rare glimpse of the lad he'd been. "More *cantie* than *ugsome*?"

She nodded. Drawing her feet up on the stool's edge, she wrapped her arms around her legs and the voluminous folds of her linen skirt, feeling like a little girl again. "I wish I could speak Gaelic like you."

"'Tis ne'er too late to learn." He drew hard on his pipe and leaned back in his chair, studying her through skirls of smoke. "I've been thinking hard of Scotlain. The Highlands. Mayhap I'll go home again."

She felt a little start. Home wasn't here, then, but the place of his birth. The realization left her slightly misty-eyed. Sometimes her beloved father seemed a mystery. The past—Scotland, his life before Pittsburgh—seemed to belong to someone else, a stranger. Growing up in the cocoon of New Hope, she'd not thought to ask many questions. Till now the world seemed to begin and end at its gates.

"Mayhap I'll go with you," she ventured.

He looked hard at her as if weighing her response. "'Tis a hard crossing. Eight weeks in a wooden tub with no guarantee you'll ever get there."

"You did it once."

"I was in good company. 'Twas the eve of the Revolution. Scots were coming to the colonies in droves."

"Why Scotland after so long?"

"I've kin there—a nephew." Seeing her confusion, he added, "My sister Naomi's son."

"I have a Scottish cousin?" She couldn't hide her surprise. All of a sudden he seemed to have as many family secrets as Mama.

"He lives on the duke of Atholl's estate and is a relative of the Murray clan. The Ballantynes were tenants long ago. You ken my father—your grandfather—was fiddler and composer to the duke." His gaze fixed on some distant point beyond the study windows before returning to her. "But I've no wish to dredge up the past. I'd rather talk about you."

"Me?" She felt a little start, nearly forgetting the letter in her pocket.

"You're rarely awake this time of night. You and your mother keep early hours."

"I'm glad Mama's abed." She glanced toward the empty desk across the carpeted floor, thinking how disturbed Mama would be if she knew of the post. "There's something I need to show you." Reluctant, she passed him Andra's letter, wishing she had something else to share instead.

Setting his pipe aside, he read it thoughtfully, passing a hand over his eyes and murmuring in Gaelic when done. Oh, that she understood more of his native tongue!

"When did you receive this?"

"Just yesterday. I showed it to Ansel and he told me to come to you."

"A wise decision." She detected a bite of disapproval in his tone, though he never spoke disparagingly of any of his children. "Andra's willfulness often gets in the way of her reason."

She gave a little sigh. "She'll be vexed that I told you."

He pocketed the letter. "I'd be more vexed if you did not."

"Who do you think might be coming from York?"

He took up his smoking pipe again but looked as if he'd lost all pleasure in it. "It can be none other than Elspeth, your mother's half sister."

"Half?" Shock pinched her. "But I thought—"

"They did not share the same father."

"Mama's father was not a blacksmith?"

"Nae, he was landed gentry—one of Philadelphia's benefactors and the laird of York County."

"But . . ." She stared at him as all the implications came crashing down, tumbling her every assumption.

"There's good reason you've not met your mother's sister. When they were young, your mother and Elspeth were at odds. Elspeth was . . ." He hesitated, clearly flummoxed. "I have no words for it. I doubt she'd be any different today, unless God Himself has got hold of her. Once, when your mother and I were newly wedded, she came here. Your mother was expecting Peyton. I sensed Elspeth would make trouble as she was wont to do, so I sent her packing."

"She's not been back since?"

"Nae. But I expect she's on her way. As I said before, you were wise to give me the letter." He drew on his pipe again, drawing a close to the unsettling conversation. "Now, who are you going to partner with at the ball?"

The ball. She'd almost forgotten Madame was coming in the morning for a final fitting.

"Your auld father should have the first dance, ye ken."

"You'll always be first, Da."

His keen gaze held hers and sent her flushing. "Till your beloved woos and wins you, aye?"

Your beloved.

All at once Jack, the guest list, her wayward emotions, came rushing back with his simple, guileless words. She was glad the dimness hid her high color and he couldn't sense the sudden pulsing of her heart.

Jack. Her beloved.

Oh, Da, if you only knew . . .

But something told her he did.

24

No man is a hero to his valet.
ENGLISH PROVERB

He was hopeless, Jack decided, at English country dances. His mind ran in straight lines, so at odds with the intricate steps and required turns. He had better luck with the waltz, still seen as scandalous in many circles but coming into fashion, so the dancing master said. Jack felt a measure of relief, then wondered if the waltz would be allowed at New Hope's gala.

Monsieur Boucher applauded his efforts then shrugged. "My advice, Monsieur Turlock, is to hug the wall till the waltz begins. The Scotch reel and mazurka are simply too complicated for a man of your experience. But the waltz—ah!" Boucher winked at Chloe as the music began again. "Within its close embrace, your brother may shine."

Jack doubted it. He didn't plan on dancing but would hug the wall, as Boucher so succinctly put it, the whole night through. This was all for Chloe's sake anyway. He was simply acting as her escort. Come what may, he planned to get through the evening with gritted teeth, alert to an escape as soon as possible.

"Like my dress, Jack?" Chloe was pirouetting before him in a swirl of lace and lilac silk, gotten on her recent trip to the seamstress with Mrs. Malarkey.

"Aye," he said quietly, thoughts trailing to what Ellie would be wearing. It was her ball, after all. An occasion to announce her engagement, he felt certain. Silas Ballantyne's terse words of days before returned in force.

I'll gladly purchase River Hill for whatever it is you're asking . . . as a wedding gift for my daughter.

The unexpected words had broadsided him like a wayward skiff, and he'd yet to shake off his surprise. Who had won Ellie's tender heart? In hindsight he wished he'd asked outright, but he'd felt tongue-tied as a boy, unworthy of so intimate a question.

Standing with Silas at the edge of the field, he'd been cast back to their last meeting—to the swearing and retching and stench of the jail, and the startling sight of Silas's tall shadow moving among the iron bars. It had been anything but a holy moment. It had been hell. Yet Silas had talked to him. Given him a Bible. Prayed for him.

"Jack, I found some old pearls in Ma's jewelry box. Mind if I wear them to the ball?"

Chloe pulled him back to the present, pirouetting again. He gave an absent nod and left the ballroom, returning to his study as Mrs. Malarkey saw the fiddler and dancing master out. Wanting to be alone, he cast a last glance at his sister now taking the stairs two at a time to her room.

Try as he might, he couldn't decide on a worthy suitor. Was it an Ormsby? A Denny or Neville? Maybe a Herron? Taking a *Pittsburgh Directory* from a bookcase, he scanned the ranks of prominent citizens, all from founding families, finding himself on the list below his father and Wade. *Whiskey magnates.* At the bottom of the column, adjusted according to assets, were the Camerons. *Farmers and landowners.*

A dim memory kindled.

The Ballantynes and Camerons were close friends and had ever been. Not so the Camerons and Turlocks. Ever since they'd faced off at Rogue's Creek as children, he and Daniel had shared a mutual dislike for each other despite being the same age. Their hostility shadowed him now, along with a disturbing realization.

Daniel was perfect for Ellie. Handsome. Pious. Clever. Temperate. Of good family and reputation. And he was fighting his way to the top just as Silas Ballantyne had done, starting with an apprenticeship at Ballantyne Glassworks, then touring eastern factories before returning to Pittsburgh, the papers said.

It could be no one else.

Taking a chair, Jack tunneled a hand through his hair and fought the recurring wish that he was someone other than who he was. Someone respectable. Sought after. Then Ellie could be his. He'd not have to let go of River Hill. Together they could settle down and have a family. The sale of his estate was made more poignant knowing Ellie would find the happiness here that had eluded him.

With a man he hated.

A soft tap at the door ended his musings, and he thrust the directory into a drawer. Solomon entered at his call, hat in his gnarled hands, ebony face shining. "Mornin', sir."

"Morning, Sol," he replied, struck by the man's perpetual good humor.

"I'm about to run those errands of yours in town. Ten o' the clock. But I remembered you wanted to see me first."

"You're always on time, though I don't know how you do it minus a watch."

"When you're as old as dirt, you have a clock right here." He tapped on his chest, his grin widening.

Chuckling, Jack gestured to a chair, inviting him to sit. "Any more activity down by the water?"

He took a seat. "Not since I fed them strangers that catfish and directed 'em upriver."

To New Hope, no doubt. He'd let Sol handle everything, not wanting to involve himself or send for Dr. Brunot. The matter was resolved. So why did he feel he'd shoved the burden onto someone else? Though the incident had passed quietly enough, he sensed, now at summer's peak, that more runaways would come. What then?

"I'm thinking of sealing off the tunnel," he said abruptly. "At the river's entrance."

Sol nodded thoughtfully. "Whatever you think best, sir."

"I don't have time to traffic in runaways." Before the words left his mouth, he felt a bite of rebuke. Did Brunot or Ballantyne have time? *Nay.* Dismissing the thought, he returned to the matter he'd wanted to discuss in the first place. "Just so you know . . . River Hill is for sale."

Sol was regarding him intently, his cheerful demeanor dimming.

"I plan on asking the Ballantynes to let you stay on as a condition of the sale, out of respect for the agreement you had with my grandfather."

Sol brightened. "So the Ballantynes are to own this place?"

"A daughter and her future husband, apparently."

"Miz Ellie, I take it?" He gave a low whistle. "That sounds just fine. But what about you, sir?"

Could Sol sense his reluctance? His distress? "I'm going west to Missouri and beyond on my father's business." Suddenly the manservant's future seemed more secure than his own. "I doubt I'll be back."

The dark eyes seemed shadowed now. "When you leavin'?"

"October at the latest. I need to start ahead of the weather. The rivers freeze early west of here, as you know."

"That's a far piece to go. I always hoped—" He seemed flustered before forging on. "Master Hugh hoped you'd settle down and have a family to call your own."

A stitch of guilt added to Jack's misery. "I'm glad he's not here to see it. He had enough heartbreak over my mother."

"Say no more, sir."

"There's another matter . . ." Jack cleared his throat and stood. "I could use your services as valet."

"Valet?"

"For one night, anyway."

A grin pulled at the corners of Sol's mouth. "I ain't so old that I forgot how to tie a cravat. When you be wantin' me?"

"Saturday night. I have to go to New Hope."

His grin broadened. "You *get* to go, you mean."

"Have to or get to, I'm going," Jack replied. "When you're in town today, maybe you can pick up anything you think I might need that night."

"Um . . . like a clothes brush or some hair pomade?"

Jack winced at the thought. "Something like that."

Jack studied himself in the full-length mirror of his bed-chamber, a rare indulgence, and tried not to grimace, feeling the rush of time as the mantel clock ticked against him. Sol, somewhat of a perfectionist, seemed paralyzingly slow as he tied Jack's cravat into a knot that rivaled the one in his throat. Despite the tailor's strangeness, William Davenport had turned out a remarkably handsome suit.

"You look mighty fine, sir," Sol said, standing back to

admire his work. "Your grandfather the judge would be proud. 'Splendid,' he'd say."

Jack merely nodded. He was unspeakably nervous. For a few seconds he eyed the basin beneath his bed, reserved for one of his rare binges. He felt nearly as sick. His heart was galloping about his chest so wildly he had sweat stains beneath the arms of his pristine shirt—and he hadn't yet donned his swallowtail coat or danced a step. Down the hall, Chloe's occasional howls added to his discomfort.

"What the devil is happening next door?"

"Aw, just Miz Malarkey torturin' your poor sister with some curlin' tongs." Sol helped him into his coat and began brushing it free of any lint. "Reminds me of the time the judge and Miss Isabel were turnin' out for a town ball. She made as much noise as Miss Chloe here but come out of it with a shine." He chuckled. "You remember when you was a boy 'bout ten and went with the judge to that reception for the president?"

"Aye," Jack said reluctantly. He'd eaten too much marzipan and gotten sick. "I recollect I threw up on the judge's shoes."

Sol grinned. "Yeah, but you still managed to shake ol' Jefferson's hand."

At the slamming of a door below, Jack almost groaned. He knew it was Wade from all the commotion.

Tucking the clothes brush away, Sol circled Jack. "You expectin' company, sir?"

"None that I know of." He could hear Chloe clashing with her older brother on the landing, giving him what for and sounding like their mother.

"I'll not make you late to your little party. I just want to see Jack." With that, Wade stepped into the room, a look of outright astonishment on his face. "Blast, but you're a dandy!"

"Don't start," Jack warned.

"Where you headed?"

"Out."

"Out?" The surly echo underscored Jack's determination to keep their destination a secret. Wade wasn't above raising a ruckus at New Hope, uninvited or no. Jack went ice-cold at the thought.

He could smell Wade's intoxication from five feet away and sensed there'd be no easy exit. Squaring his shoulders beneath the snug lines of his new coat, he said far more calmly than he felt, "State your business and be quick about it."

But Wade simply collapsed into a chair, legs splayed long enough to trip Sol as he came back into the bedchamber from the dressing room. A silver chain dangled from one ebony hand, glinting in the candlelight. Sol passed the intricately engraved timepiece to Jack, who wasn't quite sure what to do with it.

"For your waistcoat pocket." Sol started across the room with nary a glance at Wade. "Ben's brought the carriage round when you be ready, sir."

"*Sir?*" Wade mocked, watching him go. "That's the most impudent Negro I've ever met." Looking agitated, he stood, tottering a bit. "The judge ruined Sol, giving him free papers like he did, and here's proof. Too big-breeched even to greet me."

Nerves shot, Jack grabbed hold of the back of Wade's shirt, intent on seeing him out. Chloe appeared in the doorway just then, her vexed expression at odds with her pretty dress, her hair a halo of curls. "We can't be late, not to New—" The words died on her lips as she realized her mistake.

Wade's gaze sharpened. "New Hope? What's happening there?"

A hint of desperation crossed Chloe's face as she looked to Jack.

"Nothing that concerns you," Jack said, eyes on Wade. "And whatever you have to say can wait till tomorrow."

"Tomorrow I want you to attend that horse auction in Washington County with me. Maybe do a little betting on a side race." Wade jerked free of Jack's grip and started for the hall. "Guess I'll have to go to Teague's by myself tonight and tell Janey you're stepping out on her. She's suspected as much, the way you've been shunning town."

Chloe opened her mouth—to bicker, no doubt—but Jack silenced her with a look. No sense prolonging Wade's stay with an argument. As it was, the clock struck half past eight, resounding to the far corners as they came down the stairs. The ball had begun and they were now late. As Jack thought it, Wade stumbled and careened into the walnut banister, the only impediment that kept him from falling headlong into the foyer below. Chloe's eyes flared as Jack righted him and steered him straight.

"You know what Ma always says," she hissed. "Wade's going to get himself killed, and then you'll be the master of everything."

Master of everything.

And he wanted none of it.

25

*I am now quite cured of seeking
pleasure in society, be it country or
town. A sensible man ought to
find sufficient company in himself.*

EMILY BRONTË

Ellie stood at the doorway of the ballroom beneath the glitter of countless spermaceti candles. Every window was open to the river, which emitted a blessed evening breeze that buffeted the flame in a merry dance. Roses of every hue spilled from cut glass vases, specially made for the occasion by the glassworks.

Everything was so breathtaking, she wanted to frame it in her heart and head forever. Her excitement was tinged with a bittersweet relief that it would end in a matter of hours. Soon the rich parquet floor would be scuffed by a hundred or more dancers. The punch toasted and drunk. Mamie's fine supper devoured. The flowers wilted in the summer's heat.

For now the musicians were assembling at one end of the long room near her harp and Ansel's violin, a reminder of their midnight duet.

Clad in her coral gown, she felt conspicuous, her French stays cinching her waist impossibly small, her breathing almost nonexistent. Raising a hand, she touched the pearls wending through her hair, twin to the strand circling her throat.

All day she'd teetered between elation and expectation, one thought uppermost.

Would Chloe come? Would Jack? Not once had Chloe made mention of the ball during lessons. Perhaps Jack hadn't shown her the invitation or had thrown it away. His stance on dancing was clear enough. It was foolish to hold on to false hope, yet it bloomed inside her like the most stubborn weed. The duet with Ansel she could manage. Seeing Daniel again after so long was feasible. But navigating the disappointment pooling in her chest was far more daunting.

Oh, Jack, won't you come?

The guests began to arrive along the lantern-lit drive, first a trickle and then a steady stream. Ellie stood with her family at the entrance to the third-floor ballroom as extra staff hired for the occasion showed people upstairs. Her parents looked resplendent in full evening dress, the emeralds about Mama's throat catching the light. Mina had arrived early and was beside Ansel, his charcoal suit and her saffron dress a comely pairing. Peyton stood off to one side, more arrogant than ever in formal attire.

As the crowd swelled, there were a great many names to recall. Being in Philadelphia for four years save Christmas had dulled Ellie's memory. Some people she barely recognized. A stray glance in a gilt-edged mirror told her she scarcely knew herself. When she turned round, she found Daniel Cameron standing before her, in no way resembling the man she remembered.

"Daniel?"

He was as tall as Jack Turlock but leaner, the formal lines of his attire lending a severity to his narrow features, all boyishness gone. But his eyes were the same unusual hue, a pale lichen-green, sweeping her from head to toe with the familiarity of old and shining with new appreciation.

"Elinor?" Not once had he ever called her Ellie. Nor would he answer to anything but Daniel.

Daniel and Elinor Cameron.

He'd teased her about it once years before, saying it sounded rich and right. Now the words returned to her in all their intimacy, making slush of her insides. Or perhaps it was the intensity of his gaze as it slanted over her.

Mina hovered as if sensing her discomfort. "Make haste, dear Daniel! You'd best claim Elinor for a dance before the music begins."

He took her hand, and Ellie was aware of a great many eyes on them. The warm pressure of his fingers was felt through her gloves. When he didn't let go, she sensed she was turning the color of her gown.

"I reserve the last dance—and the one preceding midnight if it's not taken." With that, he claimed her as his supper partner, a coveted feat. "I also have something to discuss when we find a moment alone."

She nodded, keeping her smile in place, as he stepped aside to speak with her parents. When he turned back to her, bending to whisper a compliment in her ear before moving on, she felt the heat of the ballroom like never before.

The receiving line was dwindling now, the hum of a great many voices swelling louder. With all the hubbub, no one could hear the noises on the floor above. How many of their guests would be shocked by the activity in the attic? How many were opposed, perhaps violently so? She wasn't even sure of Daniel's stance . . .

"Are you looking for someone, El?" Ansel was at her elbow, punch cup in hand.

She opened her fan to cool her face, turning her back on the room's entrance. "No," she replied, trying to keep the disappointment from her tone. "Everyone seems to be accounted for."

"All but two," he mused, his gaze fixed on the doorway. "You wouldn't be expecting the Turlocks, by any chance?"

She whirled about, the fabric of her skirts shuddering from the sudden movement. There, filling the doorway, stood Chloe, Jack at her side. In that instant, his hold on her heart tightened, never to let go. The ballroom seemed to grow hushed, her amazement eclipsed by that of a hundred onlookers. She felt Ansel's restraining hand at her elbow as if he sensed she wanted to rush forward and greet them.

Her father was shaking Jack's hand heartily, his expression earnest, welcoming. Mama was speaking with Chloe, making much of her dress. Breathless, Ellie waited her turn. Her hungry gaze fastened on Jack's dress coat—a midnight-blue—and his flawlessly tied cravat. It seemed she couldn't have enough of him in a glance. His hair, usually rumpled and awry, was more sun-shocked than she remembered but tonight was considerably tamed.

At last he stood before her. "Ellie . . ." The cords in his neck tightened. "You look . . ."

She waited for him to finish, her elation starting to ebb. All she could think of was that he hadn't wanted her at River Hill. They'd simply been thrust together through Chloe's scheming. He likely didn't want to be here now.

"Miss Ellie!" Chloe hugged her, dispensing with all propriety, crushing both their dresses in a heartfelt embrace.

They stood in a conspicuous circle, Chloe chattering and masking their momentary awkwardness while a great many guests looked on. Ellie realized with a sinking certainty that this might well be the last time the three of them were together. As it was, she hadn't seen Jack for weeks, preoccupied as he'd been with plans for going west, so Chloe said.

Was this why he braved a ballroom, risked people's staring and murmuring, and stepped far beyond his ken? Because he'd turn his back on it all come autumn?

"You look . . ." he began, locking eyes with her again, "like it's your birthday."

It was as near a compliment as he'd ever given her. She embraced it as if he'd handed her a bouquet of roses, holding the words close, savoring their sweetness. "Thank you," she said softly, "for bringing Chloe."

His smile was tight. "Just don't ask me to dance, Ellie."

She tried not to laugh, finding him as irreverent as ever despite his exquisite attire.

Standing at her side, he scanned the crowded room as if contemplating battle. There was a fiercely palpable tension about him, and she realized it had taken tremendous courage for him to come. He was surrounded by young men all pampered and polished—the pride of Pittsburgh—who'd inherited their fortunes by order of birth, who toasted business deals with Turlock whiskey but despised its namesake. Who were lined up to flaunt their fortunes and woo her if they could.

It *was* a battlefield.

An opening reel was struck, and Ellie was the first on the floor with her father. Jack took Chloe by the elbow and guided her toward the nearest wall. Chairs and loveseats were placed at the room's edges, many occupied by the aged or those declining the dancing. Having never been exposed to much more than tawdry taverns and bawdy fiddlers, he was a bit overwhelmed by the novelty of New Hope's ballroom. Everything was polish, perfection, undercutting what little confidence he'd mustered.

Too tense to sit, fearing his large frame would reduce the fragile chair in front of him to kindling, he hugged the finely papered wall as Monsieur Boucher recommended, Chloe at his side.

"Oh, Jack!" She was beginning to sound more like Ellie. Softer. More ladylike. Less like a Turlock. Her excitement lent a becoming glow to her face as she drank everything in. "Miss Ellie . . . she's so lovely. Are you sure you don't want to dance with her?"

He didn't answer, following Ellie with his eyes as she swirled about the room on impossibly graceful feet. Partnered with her, Silas Ballantyne looked every inch the proud father. Watching them, Chloe seemed almost wistful. He wondered if she was thinking of their own father, cold and distant, rarely sparing a kind word—and never an embrace.

He tried to smile as a black-clad servant served punch. There were no spirits in evidence tonight, not even a glass of champagne, but he wasn't surprised. He'd heard the Ballantynes avoided liquor at all costs.

Another strike against the Turlocks.

As the evening inched forward, Jack spoke with a few of the men, mostly business associates who approached him, as did Dr. Brunot and Ansel. Peyton stayed at the far end of the room with Mina Cameron when he wasn't dancing, and Jack had yet to see Andra. That alone brought some measure of relief. Andra would be appalled by his very presence.

Strangely enough, his suit was comfortable as a second skin, the stock Sol had tied not overly tight. As his gaze swept the crowd warily, he was amused to find several young ladies eyeing him over the edges of their lace-tipped fans. None held the appeal of Ellie. Looking down, he pulled on the silver chain of the watch Sol insisted he bring, raising it out of his pocket a notch to check the time. Ten o'clock. He'd arrived late and still the evening was progressing as if mired in molasses.

"May I have this dance?"

It was Ansel, bowing slightly over Chloe's hand, as a cotillion began. She giggled and managed a curtsy, then followed him onto the gleaming floor. Jack felt a flicker of gratitude, his gaze circling the room a second time. Nowhere did he see Daniel Cameron, though it had been so long he doubted he'd recognize him if he did.

By the time the midnight supper was announced, Jack was too on edge to be hungry, craving the solitude of River Hill instead. Attending a ball and being formal was a bit like having the influenza. He couldn't wait till it was over and dreaded the thought of it happening again.

Somehow, as supper ensued, he managed to down a white soup and some dishes he couldn't name, as well as fruits and vegetables from New Hope's hothouse and gardens, followed by cheeses and nuts. Berry trifle and ice cream ended his misery, and he found himself back in the ballroom as Ellie and Ansel took their places on the dais, the rest of the musicians sitting idly by their instruments. For a moment he grappled with the obvious.

Her harp.

She was seated on an upholstered bench, her left foot upon the harp's pedal near the floor. Countless strings were tightly aligned alongside a fluted column covered with what looked to be gold leaf. At her nod, Ansel raised his violin. Someone near Jack whispered the piece. *Sonata in D Major* by Louis Spohr. The words meant nothing to him.

Her eyes were closed. Was she nervous? Not a sound was heard in the cavernous room. When she leaned her flawless shoulder into the instrument, her fingers poised to play, his breathing thinned to nothingness. Even Chloe stood slightly openmouthed beside him as the music began.

For a few moments his tension ebbed, lost as he was in the movement of her fingers as they teased forth every delicate note, as lithe upon the strings as her feet had been upon the floor while dancing. The richness of the violin wove an equally mesmerizing spell, rising sweetly and then falling silent so that only the harp was heard.

Chloe tilted her face up to his, eyes shimmering in the candlelight. He ignored the catch in his throat and stayed perfectly still, as if moving might shatter his reserve. He'd never heard such music. Ellie played with such . . . feeling. Her heart seemed wedded to every note, inexplicably wrenching his, reviving emotions he hadn't experienced in years.

Wonder. Tenderness. A thirst for finer, deeper things.

The enthusiastic applause braced him, as did Chloe's heartfelt plea. "Jack . . . you all right?"

He didn't answer but looked toward the exit. It was long past midnight now, and he was beyond weary from the harvest and more than a tad lost amidst such refinement. Ellie was leaving the stage now, smiling at Ansel, touching his arm in silent thanks.

And heading straight for Jack.

He took a breath, hopeful she might seek him out, only to be jarred by the sight of Daniel Cameron stepping into her path. Expectation turned to irritation as Daniel took her hand, claiming her for a quadrille. She looked back at him over her shoulder, still smiling, as if to say, "See, Jack, now you can say you've heard the harp."

He turned his attention to a lad not much older than Chloe

who was asking her to dance. Nodding his approval, he made his way to a punch bowl, waiting for the announcement that had yet to be made. He needed to hear the news of Ellie's engagement, no matter how painful, needed to rein in his feelings for her now spiraling out of control. He felt certain her intended was Daniel Cameron, who would be master of River Hill. He wanted to choke thinking it, the punch sour to the taste.

He was having a hard time trying not to watch her, and in a room full of onlookers, particularly meddling Pittsburgh matrons, he felt on dangerous ground. Turning his back to the dancers, he pretended interest in a painting. The landscape reminded him of Scotland, of distilleries locked deep in both highlands and lowlands. He'd gone there with his father years before after a brutal Atlantic crossing, not sure they'd make landfall. The West—Missouri—seemed just as far.

"Have you been to Scotlain, Jack?"

He turned and acknowledged Silas, then fixed his eye on the painting again. "Aye, Glenlossie and Glenkinchie, mostly. The Steins and Haigs."

"The master distillers? 'Tis a long tradition."

"Far longer than ours," he replied, uncomfortable with the subject. In the glare of Silas Ballantyne's success, his livelihood seemed lacking, tarnished by generations of Turlocks with less than sterling reputations.

"Have you ever considered another line of work? Say, iron or a trade?"

His attention swung back to Silas, his surprise plain. "I—nay."

"Mayhap because you've tried little else."

Little but farming and distilling. Because he'd had no choice. Henry Turlock wasn't one to give his sons options. Just orders. Jack sensed Silas knew that, and it lessened the scour of guilt Jack felt.

"I've not given it much thought," he admitted. "There was a time—when my grandfather was alive—that I considered law."

"It's not too late, is it?"

"I suppose that depends on who you ask. My father has threatened to disown me if I do anything but further Turlock whiskey."

"What happens upon the sale of River Hill?"

"I'll move on to Missouri. Establish a distillery in Indian territory." The words rolled out of him, sounding empty, rehearsed. "There's a plan in place to supply trading posts—military garrisons—with spirits. Keep pushing west."

"You'll not be back then."

"Nay." It wasn't a question but he answered it anyway, struck by how forthright Silas was, willing to discuss such things. As if it mattered. As if he cared. As if there might be another, better way.

Once again Jack couldn't shake the certainty that their conversation was more than about business, that at the deepest level it was about Ellie. If he had nerve enough, he'd simply ask Silas outright. If there'd been a trace of liquor in his punch cup, he'd have done so. But tonight, weary and out of his element, he couldn't muster the words.

The coral roses, imprisoned in crystal vases, were wilting as fast as Ellie's spirits. 'Twas three o'clock in the morning—the wee sm' hours, as her father said. A few guests had departed, mostly the elderly and infirm, bidding Ellie a happy birthday or kissing her flushed cheeks. After hours of dancing, her slipper-clad feet were pinched, her smile strained, her voice cracking from too much conversation.

"I'll be back," she murmured to Daniel, who'd not ceased shadowing her the entire evening.

Excusing herself, she slipped downstairs and out onto the back veranda, desperate for a measure of privacy. The lantern-lit stables and driveway were busy, the sultry predawn stillness filled with the nickering of countless horses and all manner of conveyances. But here, in back of the house, all was still save the summer kitchen and icehouses and a lone figure making his way to the necessary.

Passing into the garden, she tried to savor the stillness, but her rising turmoil stole it away. Jack was still upstairs but out of her reach, tonight and always. Nothing could bridge the chasm that separated them. He was clearly uncomfortable in her world—with the dancing, the formality, the social niceties. And somehow, without him, her privileged life failed to have the appeal it once did.

Closing her eyes, she heard a reel end and a waltz begin, the sound drifting down from the third-floor windows.

"Ellie."

A touch to her back along a row of tiny buttons sent her spinning round. Jack looked down at her, features shadowed. "I wanted to say goodbye."

Something stirred in her, sad and wistful. "Where's Chloe?"

"Waiting in the coach."

She tried to smile. "Thank you for coming."

He looked away and then back at her as if wanting to say more. Weighing his words. Discarding them. There seemed so much that was unspoken between them. She longed to tell him she knew about his leaving, selling River Hill. But the truth stayed locked in her heart, sore and silent.

"Ellie, I'm not very good at this." Slowly he reached out and placed his hands on the soft slope of her shoulders. "But since it's your birthday . . ."

She waited, breath held. Her whole world seemed to hinge on his next words.

"One dance," he said gently.

Something melted inside her. Like a woman drowning, she reached for him, admissible for the waltz, though her thoughts were far from dancing. She wanted to fall headlong into his arms, feel the scrape of his whiskers against her flushed cheek, breathe in the very essence of him.

Become his.

"Elinor, is that you?"

They drew back, the tender moment lost. Daniel loomed by the garden gate. Lights from the house revealed his blatant displeasure. He stepped onto the brick pathway as if to come between them.

"Are you all right, Elinor? Any trouble here?"

There was a painful pause. For a moment Ellie feared Jack, given the intrusion, might lash out. But he simply turned away without a word, leaving through the gate Daniel had left open.

"Isn't that a Turlock?"

The contempt in his tone sent her reeling. "Yes, that's Jack Turlock. You might have greeted him, made introductions. He was simply saying goodbye—"

"Out here? In the dark?"

She knotted her hands. What was innocent now seemed tawdry. "'Tis not what you think. His sister is my pupil. He's a friend—"

"Friend? Come now, Elinor. Everyone knows his reputation—"

"His family's reputation, perhaps. You misjudge Jack."

"*Jack*, is it?"

"What of it? I call you Daniel." She stood her ground, voice fraying with fury and fatigue. "You—he—*we've* been acquainted for years, ever since childhood. Calling either of you 'mister' seems ridiculous, at least in private."

"You can't possibly feel the same level of familiarity for

270

the both of us. Equating a Cameron with a Turlock?" He came closer and she took a step back. "I hate to say it, but you seem testy as Andra tonight."

The barb stung, though there was truth in it. She managed a brittle reply. "If you'll excuse me, I need to return to my guests."

Relief washed through her when soon he and Mina took their leave without his claiming the last dance. Whatever Daniel Cameron had to tell her could wait.

Forever, if needs be.

26

*Let men tremble to win the hand of
woman,
Unless they win along with it the
utmost passion of her heart!*

NATHANIEL HAWTHORNE

Dawn lit the eastern rim of the horizon, promising another clear, if sultry, summer day. Ansel moved through the house, having just left the attic. Ellie and Peyton were abed, the staff resting before the house was set to rights again. The last guest had departed and all yawned empty, the only sound coming from the immense case clock chiming six in the foyer—and muted voices in his father's study. Thinking a guest remained to discuss some business matter, Ansel looked through the open doorway and found his parents at the bank of windows facing the sunrise.

For five and twenty years he'd come upon this scene—his mother standing in front of his father, her back to him, his arms wrapped around her and his chin resting atop her head as they looked out the sparkling glass. Still in formal dress, they seemed oblivious to everything but each other.

His mother's quiet voice held a lament. "She's in love with him. As in love with him as I was with you at first."

"Was?" His father's brogue thickened playfully. "D'ye mean to tell me ye love me nae longer?"

A slight smile. "Hush. I love you even more."

He kissed the russet curls at the back of her head, his mouth near her ear. "You fear he's Turlock to the bone and will break her heart."

"Yes . . . ours too."

"He well may, though he told me in good faith that he's leaving."

"Leaving?"

"Aye. Selling River Hill. Going west to Missouri come autumn."

"Does Ellie know?"

"She's made no mention of it to me."

"You don't think—" She turned round to face him, her lovely face haunted. "You don't think she'd go with him? Elope?"

"Nae. I ken Ellie doesn't even realize she loves him—or he her."

"Love her?" There was a breathless pause. "Oh, Silas, 'tis not love I fear but—"

"I ken your thoughts. You're remembering your own misfortune at the hands of a rogue." He took her in his arms again. "Try to set your mind at ease. Jack Turlock is more like his grandfather the judge than his own father. True, there were years past when he went awry, as many a lad does. But he has more mettle than his brother and none of Henry's ruthlessness. You forget he was reared mostly at River Hill."

"Yes, but . . ."

"Last night he was careful with Ellie, respectful of her. Not once did he ask her to dance. Surely that speaks to his self-restraint."

Ansel marveled at the conclusions his father was drawing yet couldn't refute them. He'd observed the same yet had seen Ellie and Jack alone in the garden together and remained unsure of what to make of it.

His mother was clearly at sea with the subject. "Still, I fear . . ." She seemed too awash in dismay to continue.

"I've sensed no *collieshangie* when I've talked with him. The man certainly knows the measure of hard work." A slight smile softened his seriousness. "*Och*, if you could see him lay low a field of grain."

She laid her head upon his shoulder. "If it was Andra, I'd not worry. Andra would be more than a match for any Turlock. But Ellie . . ."

"Ellie is your lamb."

"And the jewel of your heart."

"Aye, and since the day she was born we've asked heaven to guide and protect her. We have to trust the Almighty to do just that."

She nodded. "And while we've prayed for Ellie her whole life, I've often neglected to pray for Jack or any of the Turlocks, all but Chloe. I suppose . . ." She hesitated as if grieved by the admission. "I suppose I've seen them as a lost cause."

"They've oft been in my thoughts and prayers, especially the boys, ever since they were small and wrangling at the creek. Mayhap we need to renew our petitions with a vengeance." His expression when he looked down at her was reassuring, if careworn. "For now our Ellie is safe in her bed and has lived to be one and twenty. 'Tis enough."

"Perhaps. Yet I long for the day when she's settled and we have grandchildren running about . . ."

Ansel moved away, knowing his mother's wish was for more than Ellie. It seemed everyone was awaiting news of his own engagement and was now nursing dashed hopes he'd not announced it at the ball. He'd read the expectation in Mina's expression and seen it ebb as the night wore on. Not wanting to hurt her, resigned to the fact he needed to wed, he'd nearly stood during the midnight supper to formalize the engagement, but his resolve had vanished.

Regret now seemed to follow him down the hall to the music room. He opened the violin case resting on a corner table, wishing it was the lost Guarneri instead. There was no worry about disturbing anyone's asleep, not with walls two feet thick. When the house was built, his father had replicated Blair Castle in Scotland and created a sound barrier that couldn't be breached.

How many nights had he spent here after everyone was abed, confident he couldn't be heard? Forgetting the time? It was his own fault he couldn't concentrate at the boatyard or anywhere else with the hours he kept. Between running fugitives and seeking solace in his music, he led a strange double life.

"I'm sorry, Elinor. The hour was late, my temper was short."
You should be apologizing to Jack Turlock.
The thought remained unspoken, though Ellie meant it with all her heart. She was seated beside Daniel on the garden bench in the shade of a giant willow, a bed of blue Michaelmas daisies at their feet, her thoughts far from forgiveness and making amends this morning.

A stone's throw away was a sparkling fountain similar to River Hill's, though New Hope's masonry wasn't chipped, nor the pool dry. Ellie was again reminded, unwillingly, of Jack. She'd thought of little else since the ball's end. And now this . . .

In her lap lay two letters. From parents withdrawing their daughters from lessons on account of her Turlock connections.

They hadn't penned as much, of course, just politely declined further schooling, but Ellie had read their reasons between each and every line. She felt numb. Shocked. Even though Jack had warned her weeks ago it might happen.

"You're forgiven, Daniel," she said absently. "Let's not speak of it again."

He nodded, plucking a daisy and handing it to her. She took it, uncovering the letters in her lap.

He glanced down at them. "Is that news from Andra?"

"No . . . friends." The irony was bitter. She'd thought them friends. Fair-weather friends they'd proved to be. She didn't want Daniel to know lest it affirm his low opinion of Jack.

"I'd meant to talk to you at the ball, tell you I have a few days more of helping my father at the farm before I begin at the glassworks. I was hoping we might have a look at that untilled acreage to the south."

She fixed her gaze on the splashing fountain, reluctant to meet his eyes. "The land that borders New Hope?" She knew it well enough, lovely as it was. Mina had told her he meant to have a house there.

"It's a good site, newly cleared with a creek running through. I'm trying to decide whether to build in stone or brick."

She stayed silent lest she encourage him.

"Your father has recommended a good carpenter."

Oh, Da.

"I thought you might look at the plans with me beforehand or ride over and see how the foundation is coming."

She checked a sigh. Was he asking her to marry him or help build his house? Why was it that she was smitten with a man who didn't want her, while the man who did went about it with hammer and nails, not kisses and compliments?

"I've spoken with your father."

Who said you asked for my hand, not my heart.

She looked at him, saw the blighted hope in his eyes, and willed herself to respond. He *did* care for her. Just not in the way she'd imagined. "I'm honored, Daniel."

"I've never been good at expressing my feelings, but by now my intentions should be plain." He reached for her hand. "We've grown up knowing each other, Elinor. There's always been a sort of unspoken agreement about the future between us. It's no secret I want to have a life with you . . . marry you. With your father's approval. But he's not yet given his blessing. I suppose he's waiting for me to prove myself further, become more established at the glassworks."

Inwardly she wilted. Somehow he'd missed the root of her father's reluctance. Da wasn't concerned about business prospects or patents. He merely wanted to know Daniel loved her.

"There's plenty of time yet, isn't there?" she asked softly. "I've only just come home . . ."

His fingers tightened about her own. "Yes, you've just come home. And everyone is now aware of that fact. I watched no less than a dozen men vying for your attentions at the ball, all of whom would leap at the chance to wed you if you'd simply look their way." The jut of his jaw underscored his determination. "Do you honestly think I'm going to stand by and let someone else cut in front of me?"

He meant Jack, of course. The vehemence in his tone left little doubt.

"You flatter me. I-I don't remember being the center of so much attention."

"Then you're blind, Elinor. Or naive."

"I wonder just *who* all the men you speak of want to wed?" She felt the same needling exasperation she'd felt when being pursued by the Matrimonial Society, her dowry on display. "Me? Or my fortune?"

"You needn't worry overlong about that." He gave a

knowing chuckle. "Some might be smitten with such matters at first. But you have your own charms aplenty."

She could feel his eyes on her, tracing her features before falling to the loose lines of her gown. Her gaze remained locked on her lap, on the disturbing letters, awkwardness gaining the upper hand. "I need time to ponder it all . . . to consider things prayerfully."

Paying no heed to her words, he pulled her toward him in a firm embrace, kissing her full on the mouth.

"Daniel, I—please—" Stunned, she gave a push to his shirtfront, revealing her distaste.

"There she is!" The strident voice, oddly unfamiliar after so long an absence, held a trill of excitement. For once Ellie thrilled to the sound of Andra. "Elinor, come and meet your aunt Elspeth!"

Clearly irritated at the interruption, Daniel stood abruptly and she followed, stepping from the shade into bright sunlight. Andra was coming toward them, a voluptuous figure trailing behind. The stranger looked to the right and left as if taking in every inch of the lovely garden.

Surprise stole Ellie's tongue. Her lack of a bonnet left her squinting in the light when she so wanted an unhindered look at her unknown aunt. She tried to speak, but the memory of her father's terse words chased the slightest syllable away. What had he said?

Elspeth . . . I have no words for it.

"Is no one home?" Andra's tone held a hint of exasperation. "I suppose Mama is at the orphan home and Peyton and Ansel are in town. I spoke with Da briefly at the boatyard before coming here."

"Oh?" Ellie mulled what might have been said about Elspeth's arrival. She embraced Andra, unsure if she should hug Elspeth as well.

"You must be Elinor." The voice was cordial and far more sonorous than Mama's, suggesting strength of will to match.

"Hello . . . Aunt." Ellie rocked back slightly on her heels as if buffeted by her misassumptions. This wasn't the dour, sour spinster she'd suspected.

"I'm Daniel Cameron, a neighbor." Beside her, Daniel gave a little bow.

"Oh, don't be coy," Andra chided, taking in the spot where they'd been sitting. "Daniel is more family than neighbor, or soon will be." Her keen gaze returned to Ellie. "So, sister, how was your birthday? The ball?"

"You were missed," Ellie said, managing an awkward smile, thinking of all Mama had had to handle in Andra's absence. "Ansel and I managed not to mangle a duet, and Daniel kept me dancing through the wee small hours."

"Well, we'd hoped to arrive in time for the festivities, but things in York took a turn . . ." Andra linked arms with Elspeth, her voice trailing off in sympathy.

"How is Grandmother Lee?" Ellie asked hesitantly.

"Buried the twelfth of July," Elspeth replied with unnerving calm.

"Oh," Ellie and Daniel said in tandem. "So sorry."

Neither Andra nor Elspeth wore black. Elspeth, clad in gray, had on the loveliest hat Ellie had ever seen—a rich peacock-blue with a pluming feather, as if in outright defiance of death.

Elspeth took out a handkerchief and dabbed at a dry eye, or so Ellie imagined. "We didn't want to come to Pittsburgh in mourning. Besides, black is such a ghastly color. What happened in York must stay in York."

Ellie schooled her surprise. What could she possibly say to this? Thankfully, Daniel said it for her. "How long will you be in Pittsburgh?"

"I'm unsure," Elspeth replied, fingering her beaded reticule. "It all depends on my welcome."

Andra's smile was decidedly stiff. "Da has made arrangements for Elspeth to stay at a hotel in town."

"The colonel's establishment on Wood Street?" Daniel asked.

At Andra's nod, Ellie felt a keen relief. So Da had taken care of the matter after all. Quietly. Discreetly. Though not to Andra's satisfaction, nor Elspeth's, obviously. But the combination of fugitives in the attic and an aunt who couldn't be trusted was hazardous indeed.

"I'll ask Mamie for refreshments," Ellie said, gesturing to the back veranda and inviting them to sit. "The raspberries are still bearing and make wonderful ice."

"Ah, that sounds welcome on such a *sweltrie* day." Andra began tugging off her gloves. "After that, we shall take the chaise into Pittsburgh and get Elspeth settled."

"I'll ride in with you, as I've a meeting at the glassworks," Daniel volunteered, making Ellie wonder if he was part of some prearranged plan.

"The glassworks?" Andra's interest heightened. "What of this patent I keep hearing about?"

Ellie turned toward the summer kitchen, her mind more on Elspeth than refreshments. This new aunt bore no resemblance to Mama in the slightest, perhaps because they were but half sisters. Elspeth's father had been a common blacksmith while Mama's was . . . what had Da said? Landed gentry? The laird of York County? How had that happened?

She sensed Andra couldn't wait to tell the rest of the story.

27

It is wise to disclose what cannot be concealed.

FRIEDRICH SCHILLER

Ellie sat at her dressing table and pulled a brush through her unbound hair, wincing as its tight bristles caught in a tangle. Working it free, she set the brush down, her customary one hundred strokes forgotten. She noted the tea Mari had left for her on the tilt-top table while listening for the telltale clamor of horse and carriage.

Since Andra and Elspeth had arrived that afternoon, New Hope seemed to hold its breath in anticipation. Andra hadn't yet returned from town, nor had Da or Peyton. Only Mama had come home with Ansel, seeming slightly preoccupied, though she'd greeted Ellie warmly.

Supper had been a small affair with just the three of them at table, and then Mama and Ansel had disappeared to the attic. One of the fugitives was ill. River fever, Ansel said, confining Ellie below stairs. The cupola wouldn't shine again till the malady was dealt with.

Ellie glanced at the dark windowpanes, wondering if any runaways were across the river, watching their backs, breathlessly awaiting the light. With such matters as life and death, freedom and slavery at play all around her, her personal concerns seemed very small. She simply had to deal with disgruntled parents and withdrawn daughters. An unknown future. Daniel.

Jack.

Leaning toward the candelabra flickering on the dressing table, she expelled a breath, as if it could extinguish the image smoldering in her mind just as readily. But one candle stayed fast, mocking her. There was simply no forgetting their last encounter the night of the ball. She'd not quite recovered from the shock of his presence. His exquisite attire. Their near moonlit waltz.

Oh, Jack, you are full of contradictions.

The loud rap at her door pulled her from her reverie, and she scrambled to kindle the other candles again.

"Elinor, are you abed?"

The door cracked open. Ellie feared Andra's wide-eyed countenance spelled a late night.

"Come in."

Taking a chair, Andra sat toying with the hat she'd just pulled from her head. Two hatpins remained at odd angles near her brow, highlighting her discomfiture. She looked chastised as a schoolgirl. "Da just brought me home from town, after I finished settling Elspeth at the hotel." Her voice was quiet, without its exuberant edge. "On the ride home in the carriage—well, I've never seen Da so . . . *birsie.*" She spat out the Scots word as if it soured her tongue. "He actually called me *heidie!*"

Headstrong? And she was surprised?

"He raised his voice to me—'*haud yer wheest,*' he said!"

Hold your tongue. "Well, did you?" Ellie asked.

Andra's red-rimmed eyes glistened in the candlelight. Had she been crying? "I was simply offering him an explanation as to why I'd brought Aunt Elspeth here. But he—he—" She left off, flinging the hat onto a near ottoman. "Tis partly his and Mama's fault this happened. Had I known their history in York, I wouldn't have done so. Not once did they mention Elspeth was but a half sister—and a wayward one at that!"

"They would have if they'd not been in New Orleans when the letter came." Ellie took a sip of lukewarm tea. "It's rather risky having anyone at New Hope, even a relative, given we have fugitives coming and going."

"Those were Da's words exactly. But what's done is done. Elspeth is here, and now we know the details about Mama's past. 'Tis not a pretty tale."

"About Mama's birth, you mean?"

"That's not the half of it." She reached up and pulled the errant hatpins free. "There was a fire, a baby died, years ago in York County. Elspeth was suspected." At Ellie's frown, she sighed. "Of course Elspeth made no mention of such to me, just said how she longed to see Mama again."

"Da told you everything, then?"

She nodded, smoothing a pleat of her gown. "The trouble happened so long ago. Perhaps she's changed. I find her quite entertaining, if unconventional, her shunning mourning and all that."

And all that.

Ellie feared there was far more to be reckoned with. "Does Mama know about Grandmother Lee?"

Andra glanced toward the closed door. "Da's going up to tell her now. I can just imagine what he'll say. There's simply no way to soften the news. 'Your mother has died, and the half sister you hoped never to see again is here . . .'" Looking up, she spied Ellie's half-finished cup of tea. "I have a fierce headache. Do you mind?"

Ellie pushed the cup her way. "Perhaps you need some headache powders. Dr. Brunot is coming."

"Dr. Brunot? Why?"

"There are two new fugitives in the attic. One of them has river fever."

Her face paled. "Oh, would that I had stayed in York! First Da's set-down and now this. "

Seldom had Ellie seen Andra so upset. Feeling a burst of sympathy, she sought to distract her. "I'm sorry you missed the ball. The dancing was wonderful, as was Mamie's midnight supper. Several gentlemen asked about you."

Cool green eyes surveyed Ellie over the rim of the cup.

"But I'll only mention one—the young widower Alec Duncan." The memory of the handsome, bookish lawyer made Ellie smile—and Andra flush. Her dear sister wasn't as chary of romance as she feigned. Not with numerous copies of a romantic serial hidden beneath her bed, like *The Pirate's Treason* and *The Count's Secret*. "I told him you'd soon be back."

Andra gave a fierce shake of her head. "I'd much rather talk about you and Daniel. Find out what the two of you were doing sitting so close on the garden bench earlier today. For a moment I thought I'd stumbled upon a proposal."

"We can hardly think of proposals or weddings with Mama in mourning."

"Oh?" The empty cup rattled in its saucer when Andra set it down. "I thought you might announce your betrothal at the ball."

Taking up the length of her hair, Ellie began braiding it as she always did before bed, a subtle reminder of the late hour. "I'm no nearer marrying Daniel Cameron than you are becoming Mrs. Alec Duncan."

Andra's gaze narrowed. "There's someone else, then."

"No one," Ellie said, tying off the braid's end tightly with a small ribbon and wishing she could do the same with her ungovernable thoughts.

No one permissible, conventional, or nameable.

Just Gentleman Jack.

The old house at the noon hour was unusually quiet. Chloe had left for lessons in town with Ellie, Mrs. Malarkey accompanying her, as it was market day. In the windless, early August heat, the cicadas shrilled beyond the open study windows as Jack perused the newly inked will atop his desk. In it he'd left everything to Chloe, including River Hill. When it dried, he'd secure it in the safe hidden behind the false bookcase next to the hearth.

In the hours following the Ballantyne ball, the idea had come to him to get his affairs in order. He'd lain awake in the heat of his bedroom, his blood warming at the barest thought of Ellie soon to be another man's bride. The idea of her living and loving beneath this very roof should the sale of River Hill become final was so unsettling that he'd come downstairs, unable to sleep.

Silas Ballantyne had been right. Jack couldn't part with River Hill. The only legacy he had was the one he'd inherited. Since he had no heirs, it seemed only right the estate go to Chloe. Knowing how dangerous the West was, he'd drawn up a will, crafting a second copy for his attorney. He'd already arranged passage on a keelboat to the confluence of the Mississippi and Ohio Rivers, where he'd then go north to St. Louis with the whiskey shipment. Farther upriver were the garrison and sutlers and soldiers anticipating his coming—or rather his cargo. The details blurred after that.

He removed his spectacles and dropped them on the desk, then tread down the hall to the kitchen, where he spied a cold coffeepot sitting in the ashes of a cavernous hearth. Straddling a stool, he reached for a poker, hoping for a red ember or two, but nothing sprang to life beneath his hand. Cold coffee it was. Rummaging through a cupboard didn't gain the mug he sought, so he opened another sideboard filled with River Hill's best china. The pattern, a deep delft-blue with floral embellishments, reminded him of Ellie.

The Spode cup seemed fragile in his hand, much as she had felt in his arms the afternoon she'd fainted, the day he realized the feelings at war inside him were more enduring than lusty and fleeting. The night of the ball, he'd ached to hold her, savor her softness and exquisite scent, using the waltz as an excuse. But for Daniel Cameron he would have had that dance.

Instead he was left with a handful of memories. Ellie reading. Ellie fishing. Ellie and Chloe laughing girlishly. Ellie regarding him in that winsome way that made him want to be better than he was. No matter where he roamed, she'd continue to warm him—and haunt him—the rest of his days. Remind him of all he had lost. Drive him wild with desire.

If she knew, Chloe would be beside herself with glee.

Ellie, what have you done to me?

Elspeth Lee had not donned mourning garb, but Eden Lee Ballantyne did. Clad in black, Mama came down for breakfast the next morning looking wan, her hair caught back in a chignon at the nape of her neck without the slightest touch of ribbon or lace to soften its severity.

"Just tea, please," she said to Mamie, who duly brought a steaming pot. Sunlight shimmered on china and crystal, casting Mama in a warm puddle of light, calling out lines of sleeplessness and sorrow.

Ellie's heart clenched. She sensed Mama was mourning Elspeth's visit as much as her mother's passing. "I'm sorry about Grandmother Lee, Mama."

Mama nodded, eyes damp. "I wish I could have seen her a final time."

At the far end of the table, Peyton lowered his newspaper. "At least we didn't receive word of her passing before the ball. It would have been canceled and all that preparation wasted."

Andra glowered at him. "Well, I'm glad to know I did something right by delaying our coming." She softened somewhat when she looked at their mother. "Should we wear mourning, Mama?"

"I see no need to. My mother was a stranger to you, though I wished otherwise." She looked about the table, lingering longest on Ellie. "I didn't want to burden you with the past, but it seems the past has caught up with us."

Peyton set aside his paper and glanced at his watch. "What's to be done with Elspeth?"

Ellie felt a flicker of irritation. Sometimes Peyton's plain-speaking bordered on harshness. If Da were present, he wouldn't be so *fash* . . .

"I don't know what's to be done," Mama replied candidly. "But I'll begin by telling you the truth. Perhaps then you can make sense of Elspeth's coming—and our concerns about having her here."

"But Mama, might another time be better?" Andra looked decidedly uncomfortable, as if the blame for all the trouble sat squarely on her shoulders. "You're clearly upset—"

"Upset, yes, but trusting that God has all in hand. Besides, it's time to tell you." Her gaze came to rest on a far window, and she seemed to struggle with where to begin. "You know I grew up believing I was the daughter of a blacksmith. What I didn't realize is that my mother had long been in love with the largest landowner in York County, a man she'd been forbidden to marry. She bore his child—me—while married and a mother to Elspeth." She paused, and everyone waited, locked in silence. "I had an especially close relationship with the Greathouse daughters, who lived down the lane at the family estate, Hope Rising."

"Greathouse?" Peyton leaned forward. "Are you telling us you're a Greathouse, as in the Philadelphia Greathouses?"

"Only by half. An illegitimate daughter hardly qualifies, though I did arrive in Philadelphia on account of them."

"So you learned of your parentage later?" Ansel's question was quiet, so at odds with Peyton's gruffness.

At Mama's nod, Andra asked, "What has this to do with Elspeth?"

"Elspeth and I were never close, despite our nearness in age. She seemed to resent my relationship with the Greathouses, and in hindsight I don't blame her. Perhaps she knew the true nature of things and saw through their preferential treatment. Later, like our mother, Elspeth came of age and had a child by the Greathouse heir."

"'Tis common enough," Peyton murmured, "though it seems odd happening twice in the same family."

Mama continued, clearly reluctant. "We named him Jon and kept his parentage a secret."

"Jon?" Andra interjected. "Was that the baby who died?"

"Jon was just shy of his first birthday." Mama's voice faltered, the old memory still wounding. "I found him in his cradle one afternoon . . ."

Ellie's gaze strayed to the doorway. No one else seemed to realize Da stood there, concern darkening his face.

"Was he ill?" 'Twas Andra again, drawing Mama out, determined to have answers.

"He didn't seem to be. Other things had happened, all unexplained. There was a fire shortly beforehand. No one knew the cause of that either. But I feared it was Elspeth."

"Why would she do such unspeakable things?"

At Andra's probing, Ellie wanted to put up a hand to spare Mama from answering, when her father's voice sounded behind them.

"Because Elspeth fancied herself in love with me and would stop at nothing to have her way."

The ensuing silence was so heavy, Ellie felt the weight of the past overshadow them like a burial cloth. Tears glistened on Mama's cheeks as she turned her face toward the doorway. "I've often hoped—prayed—over the years that Elspeth has changed, but I don't know that she has."

"She's never married? Lived apart from your mother?" Peyton pulled himself to his feet to join his father at the door.

"Not that I know of." Mama stood as well, her tea mostly untouched. "Enough of the past. 'Tis time I return to the attic. Our patient's fever, I'm thankful to say, has broken, and he was able to take some broth in the night."

All seemed to breathe easier at this. Andra followed at Mama's bidding, leaving Ellie and Ansel alone at table. Peyton and Da soon left for the levee, making the morning more ordinary. Ellie heard the crunch of gravel beneath the departing horses' hooves.

"Perhaps I should go into town," she said, trying to be cheerful. "Have tea at Mistress Prim's or shop for some music at the Sign of the Harp."

Ansel leaned back in his chair and began tying his cravat. "I thought you had lessons."

She toyed with her teacup, still struggling with the turn

of events. "Two of the girls' parents have sent their regrets. Something about unsavory connections."

His expression registered surprise—and understanding. "I'm sorry, El."

"No matter. I'm sure there's something to be done here to fill those hours." Setting aside her napkin, she started to leave, but he reached out and shut the door, hemming her in. "I ken there's more on your mind than the day school."

She almost smiled, thinking how like their father he sounded.

"Something is afoot, aye?"

Biting her lip, she confessed, "I don't know what to make of Jack Turlock."

"A man can't be all bad who takes pains with his little sister."

"The same could be said of you," she replied.

He chuckled then grew serious. "Some shun the Turlocks on account of their reputation. A few court them for their fortune. Jack is something of a riddle. He's not quite with his clan but not quite against them."

She looked down at her knotted hands. "I never meant to become involved so . . . deeply." Now *that* was tantamount to confessing her feelings.

"Is Jack in love with you, El?"

Her head came up. "Jack? He never wanted me at River Hill to begin with."

"Mayhap at first." His eyes held hers. "The Jack Turlock at the ball made quite a different impression. But I can't read the man's mind, so the better question is—what are your feelings for him?"

"I—it doesn't matter." Her gaze faltered and returned to her lap. "He's leaving come autumn. Selling River Hill."

"There's little doubt how you feel about that."

She kept her tone steady. "Not long ago you told me feelings are often fickle, that matters of the heart can't always be trusted. So I've decided to let my head rule . . ."

Her voice tapered off as she thought of all the coming year offered if she married Daniel. A husband. A home. A baby, Lord willing. The latter filled her with joy yet shook her to the core. If she couldn't tolerate Daniel's kiss, how would she bear his repeated embrace? Yet she would give her parents the gift of a grandson or granddaughter. Accept the life that was waiting.

Jack's own future was in place. The West would make him a hard man, harder than he was—more like his father. She'd seen frontiersmen on the levee, trading in the mercantile, manning flatboats and keelboats and other vessels, smothered in buckskin and feathers and all manner of weapons. The West was a wild place, sure to snuff out the little bit of light she'd sensed in Jack's soul, that tiny flicker of hope she'd held on to for his faith, his future. Jack's path was plain. As was hers.

"I've decided to consider Daniel's proposal," she said. "He wants me to ride over and see the house site he has in mind. Of course we can't marry till Mama's mourning ends, sometime in January."

There was an uneasy, prolonged silence. "El . . . don't."

Ansel's voice reached out to her, but he was little more than a blur of broadcloth now, his words so low she was tempted to discard them. Getting up, she opened the door and fled to the chapel.

28

For of all sad words of tongue and
pen, the saddest are these:
"It might have been!"

JOHN GREENLEAF WHITTIER

The confectionery, hot as Hades in the blaze of late August, continued to turn out an infinite variety of sweets that perfumed Ellie's classroom and ensnared passersby on Water Street. Marzipan. Ladyfingers. Sugar plums. Gingerbread. Ellie inhaled the tempting aroma as she unlocked her classroom door ahead of lessons, glad to be alone. The awkwardness she'd felt during the family meeting with Elspeth minutes before hadn't faded. Never had Ellie seen Mama so silent or Da so steely.

"You're welcome here so long as your behavior warrants a welcome." Her father sat in the hotel's parlor, locking eyes with her lovely aunt, tone quiet but intense. "As I told you thirty years ago, if there's any harm done my family while you're in Pittsburgh, any loss to my property or business, I won't bother bringing you before the Allegheny Court. You'll answer to me."

Elspeth's gaze faltered. "Come now, Silas, those thirty years might have wrought changes you know nothing about." She took out a costly-looking ebony fan and waved it back and forth with a gloved hand. "I'm no fool, whatever you think of me. And I didn't come here intending you or your family harm."

Looking on, Ellie felt a burst of sympathy for her aunt. She wanted to believe Elspeth, but her aunt's response had sallied forth all too easily, as if she'd anticipated such an encounter and had prepared a pretty speech. She'd certainly dressed prettily. Clad in a sheer sapphire gown with black embellishments, she looked more a lady of the manor than a York smithy. Ellie found this cause for worry.

Seated beside Elspeth, Peyton spoke more kindly than she had ever heard him. "I'll be glad to show our aunt about the city and keep her duly entertained when I'm not at the mercantile."

Elspeth gave him a small, appreciative smile. "I promise I'll be of little trouble."

"I can come into Pittsburgh whenever you're in need of company," Andra reassured her. "With Ellie home, I have more leisure time than I used to. And I dearly love to shop."

Ansel maintained a thoughtful silence, and as much as Ellie wanted to be of help, any offer of hospitality seemed out of place. She had only to look at Mama and be struck dumb. Seated beside Da, their mother kept her eyes on her lap, her gloved hands interlaced, a study of serenity. But Ellie sensed the roiling turmoil beneath—the hurts and losses of years past, buried deep but never forgotten.

Now, recalling every syllable of that painful exchange, she wished Da had confronted Elspeth in private. But perhaps a more public, memorable meeting was needed. It had certainly put Ellie on guard.

The afternoon wore on within the secure confines of her classroom as she and her students sewed by the open windows. Four o'clock found her intent on a particularly challenging piece of French embroidery while her students chattered and made ready to leave.

"Miles Davies is coming to collect me." Alice Denny began folding up her handwork, giving a quick glance outside. "'Tis my favorite part of the week, as he always insists we go below for a confection before he takes me home."

Ellie glanced up with a smile. "I think the sweet shop is a bigger draw than my day school. There are only four of you now. I'm considering stopping lessons this winter and resuming in spring."

"Oh, you mustn't stop!" Ruth said. All three girls turned toward Ellie, faces lit with alarm. "Winters here are dreadfully dull, and only Alice has a suitor. Whatever will we do with all our time?"

"Whatever, indeed!" Alice stood and put on her bonnet, tying the chin ribbons firmly in place. "I saw you dancing with Jonathan Stiles more than once at the Ballantyne ball. That must mean something."

"Something? He's a friend of my brother's and was simply doing him a favor."

"You're very young," Davina added with the mature condescension of a seventeen-year-old. "At fifteen I had my head more full of books than boys."

"Well, I'll soon be sixteen," Ruth replied with a lift of her chin. "And I must say Mr. Davies is much more entertaining than any book I've ever read. Besides, he's going to inherit his father's ironworks, which Papa says is a worthy accomplishment."

"Ironworks, indeed! I don't give a fig about his occupation, and I doubt you do either." A mischievous light shone in Alice's eyes. "The important question to ask about any man is . . . has he kissed you?"

Their high-pitched giggling stole away Ruth's answer as Ellie saw them off. She returned to her needlework, not looking up again till long after she'd bid them goodbye. The light shifted and the room was growing dark, reminding her that Ansel would soon come to take her home . . . or Daniel.

Lately Daniel had been the shadow who darkened the doorway, especially on the days Chloe came for lessons. Ellie hadn't missed the questions in Chloe's eyes, nor the sadness of her expression when he appeared. Though young, she possessed the Turlock astuteness and well knew what Daniel Cameron was about. But to her credit, she hadn't said a word.

Has he kissed you?

In the lengthening silence, Alice's probing question seemed to linger as if meant for her instead. Not since their shared awkwardness in the garden had Daniel kissed her again. She tried to imagine it a second time. More heartfelt. Less bumbling. Perhaps even . . . passionate.

Her needle stilled. The tedious embroidery before her eyes turned to midnight-blue broadcloth and callused hands, rumpled hair and hard shoulders. In the heated traces of her imagination, it wasn't Daniel who pressed his mouth to hers . . .

"Elinor."

She looked up reluctantly. How she longed to hear a simple "Ellie." She willed herself to smile, to take note of the little details she found appealing. Daniel's thoughtful gaze. His keen mind. His good name. Elinor Cameron did sound proper. Respectable. Possible.

She stood and greeted him. "You have news, obviously. Good news." He'd never looked so pleased.

"I wanted to share it with you first." He removed his hat and twirled it in his hands, eyes alight. "I've just received word I've been awarded the first pressed glass patent in America."

"Oh, Daniel!" She smiled, mirroring his delight, though she'd long been expecting it. "You—and my father—must be thrilled." Turning, she caught up her bonnet. "We should celebrate, then. 'Tis not every day one patents something."

"Your father has reserved a room at Benedict's for supper tomorrow night." Taking her elbow, he escorted her out and down the steps. "To commemorate the occasion, we're sending the president a three-hundred-piece set of engraved glass tableware, along with an invitation to come and tour the factory."

"President Monroe? Here in Pittsburgh?"

"There's more." He ushered her beyond the confectionery into bright sunlight. "We have a plan to import skilled glassmakers from Scotland and Ireland. Your father will pay the cost of their crossing and has agreed to supply free coal to heat their homes as incentive."

Ellie looked past the boatyard and glittering Monongahela to the steep wooded precipice called Coal Hill that housed the Ballantyne mining operation. "Where will they live?"

"I'll show you." Turning left, they walked down Water Street, the waning sun on their backs. The huge glassworks was in plain sight, the windowpanes in its thick walls an undeniable advertisement. Behind this were a great many unoccupied lots, all Ballantyne owned. "Though the expense will be great, we hope to have houses and small gardens built for the artisans and their families right here."

Her eyes roamed the grassy property that stretched along the street seemingly without end. She couldn't quite grasp it—the outlay, the commitment of the workers to come so

far. But her father had never forgotten his humble beginnings and sought to give other immigrants a solid start.
Though he'd had a few business mishaps, most everything
he undertook was a success. This would likely prove profitable as well.

"'Tis a promising beginning, Daniel. I'll pray all goes as
planned."

He nodded, waiting for a passing wagon before leading her
across the street to the livery where his carriage was stabled.
In moments they were settled atop the upholstered seat, leaving the smoke and fervor of town far behind.

"We've quite a bit of daylight yet. I asked your father if
he'd mind if I took you to the house site. The foundation
has finally been laid. It might be a good time to have a look."

A glance at the flawless blue horizon confirmed his words,
and she ignored her reluctance. "I'm sorry I've not been out
to see the work yet. With all the rain . . ."

"The rain? All your gentleman callers, most likely." His
smile was thin. "Peyton told me that New Hope's been over-
run since the ball."

This she couldn't deny, though she wished Peyton had
stayed silent. "I—I've not encouraged any of them."

"You've not encouraged me," he replied ruefully.

His bluntness made her squirm. She had to push past her
dismay to answer. "I'm not one to be bold, Daniel. I like
things to develop naturally, not feel . . . forced."

"Do you feel forced, then?"

Misery locked her throat and stole away her reply.

I feel . . . nothing.

His hands tightened on the reins. "I simply want to know
if there's anyone else. I'd hoped, to be honest, to announce
more than the patent at Benedict's tomorrow night."

Fixing her eyes on the fading foliage along the dusty road,

she felt a sinking she couldn't deny. Did Daniel genuinely view her as little more than a business decision, a partnership not unlike the one he'd just forged with her father? If so, her yearning heart craved far more than he was capable of.

"There's no one else, Daniel." She didn't lie. Jack was as far from her reach as the North Star. She was simply guilty of a regrettable infatuation that would fade in time. "I simply want to be certain of so lasting a commitment."

"I'll take you home, then."

The lovely afternoon turned joyless. They rode in prickly silence all the way to New Hope, Daniel staring straight ahead, his high mood a memory. Alighting from the carriage, she said goodbye, but he simply escorted her to the porch and took his leave without another word.

Mari met her at the door, taking her shawl and bonnet. "Your mother is in the garden, Miss Elinor. And your sister has gone out with your aunt, if you're wondering."

Ellie thanked her, craving the solace of the music room. The shutters were open, letting in light, the quiet promising peace. But for the mayhem in her heart. She sat down by her harp, wishing Ansel was near. After riffling through the music on the mahogany stand, she lingered on the piece they'd played at the ball. Near perfection, her father said afterward.

She'd been warmed by the enthusiastic applause that night, though in truth she only cared for one accolade. She'd looked up once while they played—a liberty that had nearly cost her her place—to find Jack listening as intently as Chloe. In that fleeting moment, her heart had overflowed, and she tucked the moment away to be savored in solitude.

Remembering, she let her fingers retrace each note, playing softly but no less poignantly, determined to ease her soreness over spoiling Daniel's delight. She tried to think of mundane matters like what she'd wear to Benedict's for the celebratory supper on the morrow.

But all she wanted was to return to River Hill.

When, Jack wondered, had Teague's Tavern lost its appeal? Cicero moved past its battered façade, a shutter still askew from the storm of months before. At the hitch rail, he spied Wade's stallion tethered alongside half a dozen other horses. Lately Jack preferred Benedict's, a more genteel establishment at the heart of town, its aspect a pleasing green, the patrons reputable, the fare celebrated.

He'd not find such accommodations farther west, and this sharpened his appreciation as he took a table by a window with a view of the street. There'd been no supper waiting at home. Mrs. Malarkey was visiting her sister in Washington County, and he'd sent Chloe back to Broad Oak that very afternoon, Ben accompanying her. It was only he and Sol and a few stable hands now. River Hill seemed silent as a tomb.

"Mr. Turlock, sir." A serving girl was at his elbow with a deferential smile, making him feel almost respectable. "What will you be wanting this evening? A meal or some ale?"

"A meal, if you will. Some cider."

She drew a harried breath. "Supper might take a wee bit longer than usual." Her tone was a touch apologetic. "We've a large party expected, and Cook has his hands full."

"No matter," Jack told her, meaning it. He had no desire to return to an empty house. His gaze halted for a brief instant on Dr. Brunot seated in a far corner. "Is the doctor dining alone, do you know?"

"Aye, that he is." She looked Brunot's way, concern darkening her plump face before she returned to the kitchen.

In the light of the sconce affixed above the table, the doctor looked undeniably haggard. Burdened. So at odds with the diners engaging in lively conversation all around him. Jack felt a tug of concern but shrugged it away as a pewter mug was set down in front of him.

He reached into his pocket and extracted a list of supplies he'd need for the journey west, some of which would be gotten at the Ballantyne mercantile. Though the keelboat he'd take wasn't Ballantyne made, it would dock at the boatyard for cargo. He knew the captain well enough and trusted they'd make the six-hundred-mile journey from Pittsburgh to Louisville and then on to St. Louis in good time, barring snags, log jams, and the like.

Turning the paper over, he reviewed a crude map, wondering if he'd gotten all the details right. Once he began the trek up the Missouri River, he'd stay clear of Fort Osage, established years before to search vessels for illegal whiskey, and proceed on to Fort Lock. He'd already secured a trading license, allowing him to enter Indian territory with the agreed-upon eight hundred gallons of whiskey, but he'd need to post a bond that he'd not sell to the natives once there.

Despite all this, the boat's deepest recesses would carry all the equipment necessary to build a distillery at the mouth of the Iowa River. Henry Turlock vehemently opposed any restrictions on the whiskey trade, operating as though none existed and expecting everyone else to fall in line. There was much at stake. The trek west would be a test of Jack's powers of deception and double dealing.

I don't care what you do just as long as you don't get caught doing it.

Weighted by his father's words, he looked out the window to street lamps burning brighter in the dusk, illuminating an impressive party on the tavern walk, the curb crowded with carriages. 'Twas Silas Ballantyne and family, a few close friends. Ellie.

He focused on her alone, going cold at the sight of Daniel Cameron clutching her gloved arm. In the glare of lamplight, she looked every bit as lovely as she'd been at the ball, dressed just as finely in a blue gown, pearls in her dark, upswept hair. He found it nigh impossible to look away from her.

The Ballantynes were the expected party, then. He heard them enter the adjoining foyer and breathed easier when they disappeared into a private room in back. That it was a celebration of some sort there could be no doubt. The betrothal that wasn't announced at the ball? Some business deal? Maybe another birthday?

He took another sip of cider as if to dampen his disquiet, hating the hunger he felt to be among them—to be one of them. For the first time since his father began pushing him west, he felt a sweeping relief he'd not have to stay on . . . and watch Ellie's courtship play out before his very eyes. He was leaving even earlier than planned, and not a day too soon.

"Jack?" The voice at his elbow ended his musings. "Mind if I join you?"

He looked up into the familiar face of Dr. Brunot. At Jack's nod, the doctor took a chair, pulled a pipe from his pocket, and lit it by the single taper at the table's center. The flame flared brighter, drawing attention to deep bruises and a chilling laceration across his left cheek.

Jack felt a startling revulsion. "You look in need of some doctoring."

Through the smoke, the weary eyes regarded him solemnly. "Unfortunately, these are only the injuries you can see."

"Someone waylaid you on the road." At Brunot's nod, he continued, "Who?"

"You're more likely to know the answer to that than I."

Jack tensed and Brunot raised a hand as if to deflect his reproving look. "I don't mean to implicate you. I'm just seeking answers."

Feigning calm, Jack leaned back in his chair and took another drink, thoughts still full of Ellie.

The doctor drew hard on his pipe, casting a look about the room. "Opposition is growing fiercer toward those of us who help fugitives—more beatings, threats, torched homes and barns. As a result, save the Quakers, we're losing support. Some have even become proslavery spies under threat. We no longer know who we can trust."

"It's a dangerous game."

"Aye, and becoming more so." Brunot kept his voice low. "There's a group known as the Pittsburgh kidnapping ring made up of professional slave hunters, city constables, and lawyers who are abducting free blacks and selling them south. Your father and brother are said to be among them."

"I'm not surprised," Jack told him, "but I know nothing about it."

"I'm asking you to find out."

Jack's resistance climbed. He took another drink, wishing for something more bracing than cider. Just when he thought he was free of Allegheny County, the Turlock taint, something new surfaced. "What good will it do?"

"We need your help. The other night when I was waylaid on the road after making a medical call, these men—all masked—demanded I furnish them with the names of local abolitionists. They specifically wanted to know if Silas Ballantyne is involved. Word is they mean him harm and will stop at nothing to achieve their ends. I refused to give them what they wanted, thus the beating."

"They mean to make an example of Ballantyne, then."

"They mean to ruin him. Silas has his enemies—those

302

who are jealous of his success and despise his benevolence, his antislavery views. Some pretend to be his friends who I suspect are part of this ring and would rejoice to see him brought low."

"He's aware of the trouble, I take it?"

"Aye, aware and steadfast. He won't turn back." Brunot leaned forward entreatingly. "Jack, you have connections we abolitionists lack. 'Tis imperative we know who we're dealing with, who may be posing as antislavers but are spies instead."

"You want me to learn what I can from my father and brother, ask around town."

"They'd never suspect you." His eyes shone with renewed vigor. "You've given them no reason to believe you're sympathetic to our cause."

None but putting a gun to Wade's head and shoving a McTavish against a wall.

"I don't know that *sympathetic* is the right word. As for Jarm and Cherry—" Jack hesitated, thinking back on the turn of events. "I had no choice but to take them in."

"You had a choice, Jack." Brunot's gaze held firm. "You chose to help. That made you one of us, if only for a moment in time. You've told no one what you've done, nor exposed the rest of us."

"I leave in three days. Little time to be of use—"

"You underestimate yourself—and leave me few options." With a sigh, he set his pipe aside. "I've been considering riding out to Broad Oak—"

"Don't." Jack felt a chill even as he said the word. He held Brunot's gaze in warning. "Don't cross my father."

The serving girl returned with a steaming plate, interrupting their unsettling conversation, but supper no longer held any appeal. He made no attempt to eat but sat and fought his rising panic that the Ballantynes . . . Ellie . . . were undoubtedly a target. Though he'd weighed and measured their motives in helping fugitives, no amount of reasoning could account for such risk.

"Why in God's name do you abolitionists do what you do?"

Brunot stood, pipe clutched in his fist. "That's just it, Jack. 'Tis done in God's name, all of it."

He moved toward the door, his slow gait indicative of his injuries. Jack watched him go, his meal untouched. No doubt, like Silas Ballantyne, the doctor would continue assisting slaves till his dying day.

No matter the danger.

29

What of soul was left, I wonder,
when the kissing had to stop?
ROBERT BROWNING

Broad Oak, framed by the fading September sunset, was awash in crimson and gold. Jack dismounted at the front of the house, but before he'd tethered Cicero to the hitch rail, Chloe came flying out the door and into his arms, nearly knocking him off his feet. Wordless, she clung to him a moment too long, and he sensed her unspoken misery, her longing to return to River Hill. His throat locked tight as he held her, one hand awkwardly patting the straw-colored braid that snaked down her back.

She looked up at him, a plea in her damp eyes. "Pa says you're leaving—sooner than planned."

"Aye, day after tomorrow."

"Oh, Jack, what will I do?" Her voice caught on the end, half cry. "I don't have Miss Ellie any longer, and now I won't have you."

"There's Sally and Ben," he said. "You can visit Sol and Mrs. Malarkey whenever you like. Go fishing, riding."

305

"But it won't be the same." Her chin trembled. "Please take me with you. I won't be a burden. I'll even mend your clothes. Miss Ellie taught me to sew, remember. We can read those books—"

"She also taught you to pen a letter. 'Jack Turlock, Fort Lock, Missouri Territory.'" Taking her by the arm, he went inside the house, eyes trailing to the stairwell ceiling, where oil-brushed angels played their harps, reminding him again of Ellie. Miserable, he looked away.

Chloe followed him out the back door, voice low. "Ma has a headache and is abed. Wade and Pa are—well, you know where. Ma says they should just camp by the stills this time of year."

He caught the derision in her tone, fueled by Isabel's dislike of the entire whiskey enterprise. Whiskey was too common, she often said. Far beneath her O'Hara roots. Though whiskey was made year round at Broad Oak, it was made round the clock during the fall run.

They approached the bustling distillery, the scent of the mash tubs, seething with fermenting grain, overpowering and ripe. He much preferred the storage houses where whiskey cooling in oak barrels held the tang of ripe apples. Taking out a handkerchief, Chloe covered her nose. Ellie's influence, likely. The smell had never bothered her before.

"Pa says it's the largest run so far," she managed through the embroidered linen.

Lights flickered inside buildings, illuminating near-ceaseless activity. A great many Turlock slaves, brought up from Kentucky, were at work, their dark faces shining with sweat and intensity. He heard raucous laughter erupt from Josiah Kilgore's office, followed by Henry's deeply resonant voice.

His mood soured, fueled by Dr. Brunot's concerns at Benedict's the night before. When he filled the door frame of the ledger-lined office, the merriment died. Chloe stood in his shadow, and he felt an odd impulse to protect her from the epithets and crassness that flowed as freely as the whiskey.

Jack hated the insolence on Wade's face. The smug complacency on his father's. An old, irrational wish buried from boyhood took hold—that the open fires necessary for producing all that whiskey would turn explosive. Fire was a constant threat, given the highly flammable nature of alcohol, and required extreme vigilance. It was his father's only fear.

"So, Jack, ready to head west?" Henry set an empty tumbler on the table, eyes narrowing in question.

"Aye, the *Independence* takes on cargo tomorrow," he answered, "and leaves the day after."

Henry refilled his glass and held the liquor, now aged a pleasing crimson-gold, to the light. "All is in order, I hope."

He meant the distilling equipment, of course, packed in crates and marked as something else entirely. The deception nettled Jack as never before.

"The plan is in place for me to join you in spring," Josiah Kilgore was saying. "I'll bring a number of carpenters and slaves to build a replica of the distillery here on a smaller scale."

Jack bit down hard on his tongue, lest he say he'd not be waiting. He'd deliver the whiskey, off-load the still farther up the Missouri, and that would be the end of the Turlock whiskey enterprise. He'd then head west unencumbered.

"By the time that first crop of wheat and rye are in, you'll be ready for a solid run. My goal is four hundred gallons—and no opposition." Henry's smile was tight. "I've just received word that Fort Lock and its commander are eagerly awaiting you."

"Blast, Jack!" Wade managed a wink. "You'll be the most popular man west of the Mississippi. Makes me wish I wasn't tied to home."

Jack fought down the sickening certainty that once he'd gone, all pandemonium would break loose. His father had other motives for sending him on this mission. Henry Turlock wanted him out of the way. Jack had been a fool for protesting early on. It had sent a red flag to his cunning, farsighted father that he had Ballantyne sympathies. And Henry, determined to bring Silas down, wanted no opposition.

Swallowing hard, he opened his mouth to utter something about Dr. Brunot being waylaid and beaten, anything that would counter the deceit and ill will that thickened the room. But a distinct check, firm as a restraining hand, gave him pause.

Say nothing.

The words were as clear as if they'd been spoken outside himself, yet were buried soul-deep. Blood pounding in his ears, he heeded the voice, though it took every shred of will not to knock Wade down and take his father by the throat. Violence had ever been the Turlock way and was all he knew.

Ira furor brevis est. Anger is temporary madness.

"You don't look well, Brother. Here, have a drink." Wade pushed a glass toward him, but Chloe sprang between Jack and the table, the look of Isabel engraved in every hard line of her face.

"You know Jack doesn't like whiskey and never has!"

At this, Henry simply refilled his own glass in smooth defiance. "Daughter, you'd do well to sound less like your mother and remember where your fortune lies."

Cowed by the stern reproof, she sought the safety of Jack's shadow as Wade's bloodshot gaze trailed after her. Jack took a last look around the cluttered office before going out without another word, Chloe on his heels.

"You'd better say something to Sally," she whispered.

But Jack's eye was on the main house and the darkened panes of their mother's bedchamber. He wouldn't bid Isabel goodbye, given her dislike of sentiment or any emotional display. And given the knot in his throat, he couldn't say goodbye to Sally either.

Instead he tarried at the hitch rail in front where Cicero waited, dusk cloaking the grounds. Everything looked and smelled old . . . faded. Like autumn. Chloe was struggling again—he could feel it, the burden of a long separation between them. She seemed like a little girl now, braid unraveling, eyes shot through with sadness.

"When will you be back, Jack?"

The vulnerability in her expression tore at him.

He wouldn't tell her he wasn't coming back. That he would finally be free. Of his past. Their family's reputation. His unrelenting anguish over Ellie. He'd keep going west, take a new name. Become lost in the wilderness, where no one knew him or cared who he was.

He reached out and pulled her to him in an awkward embrace. "I don't know, Chloe. There are a great many things beyond my control." His aching head spun with all the possibilities. "I'll write to you and you'll write to me." The promise of some tie, some link across the miles, was hollow comfort. He didn't know if letters ever reached the West. "I've been thinking, come spring, you could plant that corner of the garden you and Ellie started."

She gave a little nod.

"Sol said he'd help. Ben too." He paused, the pain in his chest building. "It would be good to think of you there, in that sunny corner, waiting for me—" His voice broke, betraying him. His hand closed about her braid. "Maybe you can make it fine again."

She bent her head, her arms tight around him. "I'll pray for you, Jack."

"Ellie taught you that too, I'll wager."

She swiped at a tear with a quick hand. "She always prayed with me before lessons. She prayed for you."

He turned away before she could read the telling wetness in his own eyes and swung himself into the saddle. Atop Cicero, he felt on firmer ground save Chloe's last, startling words. So Ellie prayed for him. He wasn't surprised, but he couldn't help wondering what she prayed for. The entreaties were endless, he guessed.

He was a Turlock, after all.

Ribbons of light lay across the oak floor of Jack's bed-chamber, gilding the contents of an open trunk and the field desk beside it. He'd taken pains to pack as lightly as he could but sensed he'd soon regret it. Leaving civilization far behind was a daunting prospect. A few things he couldn't do without—extra quills, ink and paper, his shaving kit . . . the Bible Silas Ballantyne had given him. Freshly laundered linen shirts, dark pants, wool stockings, and boots littered the worn rug at his feet. His weapons were hidden.

Morning would come all too soon. Straddling a chair by a window, he turned his back on the upheaval all around him and tried to quiet his thoughts. Through the glass, the Monongahela, ever fitful, winked at him with a blue eye as the afternoon sun began to slide west. Yet another reminder of his destination. As consuming as the coming journey was, it took up far less of his thoughts than the trouble at hand.

He'd lain awake half the night pondering Dr. Brunot's dire words, knowing he could do little to stop the coming conflict. Allegheny County was fast becoming a battleground, but what a strange battle it was. The real evil was slavery, and it drove men to extreme measures. And it would be the means by which the Turlocks and their allies brought the Ballantynes down.

Till now he'd never felt driven to his knees. Never gave way
to emotion. But there was no denying he was coming apart
inside, anguish and grief and guilt forcing him to the floor.
Once there, ignorant of how to pray, all he could utter were
a few paltry words.

*God, help . . . Stop my father and Wade. Protect the Bal-
lantynes . . . Help me get free of this suffocating desire for a
woman I cannot have.*

He got to his feet and circled the room, tossing a few
more items into the open trunk. Dusk was falling and the
minutes had slowed to a crawl. He needed to go for a ride
before stabling Cicero for good. Head into town for supper at
Benedict's. Check the cargo now loaded aboard the keelboat
a final time. But none of it held the slightest appeal.

He was so preoccupied, he failed to see the shadow darken
the door frame till Sol's voice broke over him, hesitant and
apologetic, as if sensing his turbulent mood.

"Pardon, sir."

Jack swung around and faced him. "No pardon needed, Sol."

"Someone's here to see you." He looked perplexed but
pleased. "It's Miz Ellie. I put her in the blue room. The front
parlor."

Ellie? Jack felt surprise wash his face.

"I'll keep her coachman company while you're . . . um,
occupied."

With that, he trod away, leaving Jack to ponder the impossible. Ellie here? Why? Suspecting Chloe of some prank, he
left his bedchamber and descended the stairs, noticing the
door to the parlor, usually shut, was wide open. Mindful of
his unruly hair, the rasp of beard darkening his jaw, he crossed
the wide foyer, wishing he'd made himself more presentable.

Ellie heard footfalls, and her breathing thinned, gaze riveted to the parlor door. It had taken all the courage she possessed to come here, knowing Jack had never wanted her at River Hill. Likely he'd see her as just another interruption today.

Behind her was the mysterious glass armonica. In the few minutes it had taken Solomon to fetch Jack, she'd let curiosity lead her to the corner, where she lifted a dust cloth and admired the antique instrument. How she wished she could play it. That same sweet poignancy returned as she took in the beautiful, neglected room. She half expected Chloe to bound in and throw open the shutters, transforming the darkness to light.

But it was Jack who appeared in the doorway, shoulders squared, his gaze stony.

"Ellie." His low voice sent a tremor through her. "What brings you to River Hill?"

No proper greeting. No forced small talk. Leave it to Jack to come straight to the heart of the matter. She swallowed past her awkwardness and met his eyes. "I—Chloe didn't come for lessons this week. Is she ill?"

He took a step into the room. "She's back at Broad Oak. She was supposed to send you a note."

But she didn't.

Embarrassment faded to confusion. Had Chloe hoped she'd come to River Hill and meet Jack instead? The obvious slid into place, but it no longer mattered. She was here, whatever the reason, her nerves on end simply standing five feet away from him. He was heartrendingly handsome in that roguish, careless way he had, shirtsleeves rolled up to his elbows, tousled hair looking like windblown straw.

Go, came a whisper of warning.

As she thought it, he took another step into the room, surprising her, crossing some invisible, forbidden boundary.

312

Rattled by his nearness, she let a burning question spill out of her. "Why didn't you tell me you were leaving?"

He hesitated, locking eyes with her. "Does it matter?"

"Yes."

"Why didn't you tell me about Daniel Cameron?"

"Because there's nothing to tell." Her voice shook when she said it, as if she'd crossed some forbidden threshold herself.

Reaching behind him, he shut the door.

Oh, Jack.

Longing cut a wide swath through her. She felt as light-headed as she had the day she'd fainted at his feet. Only today she stayed standing, her heart so full she felt it would shatter. He closed the distance between them till they were a handbreadth apart. Even the dimness failed to disguise the sweetness in his gaze, so at odds with his storminess of moments before. *This* wasn't the Jack who didn't want her . . .

Ever so slowly he brought her arms around his neck till her fingers grazed his linen collar and the silken fringe of his hair. Her resolve to keep her distance slipped away. His long, lean fingers threaded through her upswept curls, tilting her head back to receive his kiss. He tasted warm, almost honeyish, his mouth exploring hers as she melted beneath his hands.

"Ellie . . ." He paused, sounding a bit breathless. "I'm in love with you. I've long been in love with you. Do you believe me?"

Did she? At the moment she couldn't think . . . couldn't breathe. "I came here—I meant to see—about Chloe."

"For once I'm grateful for her conniving."

She shut her eyes, the swirl of longing too strong. "Yet you're leaving."

"Aye, at first light."

"Chloe needs you, Jack . . . I need you."

He stilled. "I wonder what your father would say about that."

"My father . . ." She paused, trembling slightly, her skin like fire where he'd touched her. "He's never spoken a bad word about you."

"He well might, knowing I've kissed you, compromised you—"

"With my consent."

"Aye, but it's another matter entirely to make you a Turlock."

"Not if I want to be one." The breathless admission, hard won as it was, set her free. All her hopes and dreams, so long denied, gathered in one heartfelt plea. "I'd be proud to be your bride, Jack."

A shadow crossed his face. "Sweet agony, Ellie. If I had my way, I'd marry you here—now."

"Then summon a judge or magistrate." Her voice came soft but sure. "There's time enough. We'll have tonight."

He drew back slightly, though he held both her hands to his chest. "Would you do as my mother did, then? Forsake a good life, her family name, and wed a man like Henry Turlock—"

"You're nothing like your father, nor Wade." She touched his cheek, felt the rough scrabble of beard, and fought down her dismay. "You're the image of the judge."

He shook his head, misery clouding his eyes. "I need to go, Ellie. You need time. Becoming a Turlock isn't something to be decided in an afternoon . . . if ever."

Her voice broke. "Take me with you, Jack."

For a moment she thought he might heed her plea till he renewed his own. "If you feel the same when I come back . . ." He bent his head, his breath stirring a tendril of her loosened hair. "Then I'll speak to your father. Bring you home to River Hill. Make you mine."

Yes. That was what she longed for. To be his and his alone. Yet in the silence of her heart, she sensed his tender words were but an impossible, hopeless promise in the face of an unknown future. She bent her head, hating her tears and the gnawing panic that whispered she'd never see him after today.

Taking her face between his hands, he kissed her again, hunger and need and longing in the taste and feel of it. Every brush of his mouth against her own, every caress, drove home the bittersweet truth that he loved her deeply.

"Chloe said that you pray for me." Wonder warmed his voice. "That must take some time."

"I ask God to bless and keep you. To bring you back to me whole-souled."

"Redeemed, you mean." He smiled, but there was something sad in it. "For as a good old Puritan observes, Christ is beholden to none of us for our hearts. We should never come to Jesus until we feel that we cannot live without Him."

She held his gaze. "You've been doing Chloe's lessons."

"Aye," he murmured. "I've always had a bookish bent."

She took his hands as she'd seen her parents often do, entwining their fingers the way she wished they could entwine their bodies and souls. "Would you . . . pray with me?"

"Ellie, I . . . don't have the words."

The vulnerability in his eyes wrenched her heart. "Sometimes words get in the way."

For a few emotion-laden moments they lowered their heads, the minutes marked by some obscure timepiece she couldn't see. Their combined "Amen" was hushed, eclipsed by the parlor clock shuddering a mournful five times.

She spoke through her tears. "'Tis your last chance, Jack, to make me your bride."

"Nay, Ellie," he said with difficulty. "Next to last, Lord willing. I've just prayed that it will come to pass."

Jack released Ellie, only to take her in his arms again before they left the house. His heart was hammering so hard, it seemed he'd been swimming the length of the river instead of the usual breadth of it. The sweetness he experienced with her was a joy he'd never known. There was something hallowed and hushed in her embrace, a refuge from the storms within and without. A promise of a better life.

He guessed they'd been in the parlor a good hour or better but wasn't sure. Time melted away at her touch, every second wedding her deeper into his head and heart, making him second-guess his decision to leave. The anguish of it was something he'd not reckoned with.

He looked longingly toward the river beyond the wide, sunburned slope of grass. Aye, a long, cold swim was what he needed, something to wash away the heat on his unshaven face and help him return to reason. Even if he didn't want to.

He took her by the elbow, and they walked to the porte cochere through a swirl of autumn leaves, the sun unbearably bright after the dimness of the parlor. There her driver waited, the coach at rest. Sweat spackled the back of his neck and dampened his shirt. Surely Sol and the stable hands could see him unraveling.

And Ellie . . . Another glance at her and he almost pulled her into his arms again, uncaring about broad daylight or who might be watching. She looked even lovelier well kissed, her lips made fuller from the brush of his own, her hair threatening to spill free of its pins. His longing collided with raw grief and the half truths he'd told her.

Never again would he touch her, kiss her. Not beyond this day. If something happened to her father at the hands of a Turlock, Ellie would be caught in the crossfire. Fear and frustration left him short of breath. Whatever transpired, he'd not be here to see it play out. She'd soon come to hate him and his family, their tie and the memory of this moment severed forever.

His heart fisted as he motioned for the coachman, who stood talking with Sol in the cavernous, hay-scented space. Once situated in the coach, Ellie smoothed her skirts, settling back on the seat, her damp eyes seeking his.

He sent up a silent plea to help stem his churning emotions, wanting to reach for her again.

Pray for me, Ellie. Never stop loving me.

He shut the door and the coach rolled away, crushing crisp fall leaves beneath its wheels. He held his breath, waiting, hoping. She turned and looked back at him through an open window, heartache in her gaze.

30

Preceded on a jentle brease up the Missourie.

WILLIAM CLARK

Ellie's return to New Hope was little more than a haze as she clung to the memories just made in the dusty, bedimmed parlor. Jack's scent clung to her, earthy and clean, her skin a bit raw from the brush of his whiskers. She'd been a little desperate at the last, wanting something tangible to hold on to—a lock of his hair, some token from his study. But all she had was the fading feel and taste of him, the words he'd whispered and those she sensed he'd held back.

She stared at the landscape without focus, relieved she'd taken the coach and no one could witness her tears. By the time New Hope's cupola gleamed above the treetops in the dusk, her damp handkerchief had been folded and tucked away. Slipping past the maids to her room would be a formidable feat. Her hopes died when the front door was flung open.

Gwyn welcomed her in, taking her hat and gloves. "Good afternoon, Miss Elinor."

Ellie tried to smile as Gwyn recited who was at home and who wasn't. Across the foyer, the study door was open and beckoning, confirming her father's presence. Indecision flickered through her. From where she stood, she could see him at a window, back to her, the unyielding line of his shoulders reminding her of Jack at the last. He had a view of the orchard and stood stone still, the way he did when pondering something. Might it be Mama? Aunt Elspeth? Some business matter?

Gathering courage, she entered and drew the door shut behind her. He turned, welcome in his eyes. Oh, why had she not simply gone to her room? She felt empty and poured out, too sore for speech, yet unable to hold all the hurt in her heart.

She looked at her beloved father, a catch in her voice, knowing how much her words might wound him but determined to speak them anyway. "I'm in love with Jack Turlock and he's leaving in the morning."

There was a breathless pause.

"I ken both," he replied, opening his arms to her.

She rushed to him like she'd done in childhood, wishing he could take away her hurt. Though she clenched her jaw till it ached, sobs tumbled out of her as his arms closed about her.

"I-I never meant to care for him. I simply wanted to help Chloe. And now I've just come from River Hill, hoping to see her again, but said goodbye to Jack instead. My feelings for him are such that I practically threw myself at his feet."

"I doubt you had to throw yourself far but that he was right there to catch you." Understanding laced his voice as he smoothed her hair with a gentle hand. "I'll wager his feelings are as strong as your own."

"I wasn't sure till today. We spoke of marrying . . . children. I told him I'd go with him. But he said becoming a Turlock isn't something to be decided in an afternoon, if ever."

"Then he's an even better man than I thought he was. I

don't know many who could withstand the temptation of a lass like you. I ken he loves you and wants to do right by you. By your family."

Shamed by her own impulsiveness, she bent her head. "I'd have broken your heart if I'd left with him. Mama's too."

"Aye, and then mended it back again by bringing home a bairn or two."

She pressed her damp cheek against the soft felt of his coat. "Jack has always behaved honorably."

"I expect nothing less, Turlock or no."

"If he goes, I'm afraid—" She stumbled on the barest thought of a long separation, sure the West would swallow him whole and her life would be one of waiting, wanting, ever wondering. "I have this terrible feeling I'll not see him again."

"Pray for him, Ellie. Pen him letters." His voice dropped a notch. "Simply love him."

Love him.

That she could do. But at such a distance?

He tilted her chin up and looked into her eyes. "You need not fear being apart. Your mother and I were separated eight long years, remember, yet nothing could dull her memory nor dampen my feelings for her. When she came back into my life, 'twas as if she'd ne'er been gone. She was even more beautiful to me—and just as beloved."

"Would you welcome Jack here at New Hope as your son-in-law?"

"I'll welcome whomever you love, Ellie. Just don't betray yourself and wed for anything less."

"I cannot marry Daniel, then." The admission, so easily spoken here in private, seemed to stick in her throat when she thought of facing Daniel himself.

"D'ye want me to speak with him?"

"No, I—I owe him an answer." But she wouldn't mention

Jack. Daniel's pride might never recover. "I'll tell him. Soon. For now I'd best go to my room."

"All right, then." Looking across the study to the mantel, he made note of the time as she stepped free of his arms. "The *Andra* docked this afternoon with a full load of cargo and a few guests. Since your mother isn't back from the orphan home yet, your sister could use your help upstairs."

A full attic, then. She nodded, latching on to being of help and forgetting herself, if only briefly. "Is that why you're home early today? Did you bring them here? In broad daylight?"

"Aye, one of the coaches has been refitted for the task."

"Like Dr. Brunot's?" At his nod, she let the fact take hold, sensing their involvement was deepening. "My, Da, but you're bold."

"The Ballantyne steel," he said.

By the time Mama returned with news that Peyton would be dining with Aunt Elspeth in town, Ellie had managed to bathe, clothe, feed, and cajole twin babies to sleep. Each was nestled in the crook of her arm as the rocking chair glided to and fro in the candlelight. Situated on the third-floor landing by a window, the attic stairs just across, Ellie studied the wee features of her charges, marveling at their uniqueness. One boy. One girl. Not ebony but the hue of coffee with cream, born of a black mother and a white overseer.

They'd had colic, the mother said, and the father had threatened to sell them or smother them if they continued to cry, so one rainy, New Orleans night she'd scooped them up and run. How Da found her, found the other five now upstairs, was a mystery. Once at New Hope, they spoke mostly of the future, not the past, and Ellie was left to guess about their tragic lives before they'd been smuggled aboard a Ballantyne vessel.

As night deepened, the anguish in her heart leapt bright as candle flame. Jack would be having his supper now, she guessed, though she'd been unable to eat her own. He'd likely wander through the empty rooms of River Hill, going from study to bedchamber, packing, checking, remembering, perhaps backtracking to the blue room where they'd kissed, wondering if it was all a dream.

Never had she traversed such heights or depths in one day. She still felt spent, the push of her foot to maintain her rocking tedious, the gentle movement lulling her toward sleep.

A sigh shuddered through her. Oh, to rearrange time . . . drain the rivers dry so he couldn't leave . . . send for Reverend Herron, who'd surely voice his objections to her wedding a rebellious Turlock when he'd expected a pious Cameron instead . . . become mistress of River Hill in the span of a blessed, passion-filled night . . . have Chloe returned to their care and begin a new life.

Lord, let it be. Someday. If it pleases Thee.

The river was a soft lavender-silver now, spreading out before her from her eagle's perch, looking endlessly long as it slipped west.

Oh, Jack, come back to me.

Jack met the misty September sunrise atop Cicero, heading not toward Pittsburgh but Broad Oak. Taking an overgrown, neglected trail, he tried not to think of Ellie. His heart pulled him to New Hope, to ask Silas for her hand and savor the feel of her in his arms again. But he stayed steadfast, bent on another place. He'd not come here for years. The memory had always come to him instead—fresh, frightening, relentless as the river at flood stage.

Dismounting, he tied Cicero to a scraggly limb of laurel

that rimmed the little glen like a fence, a trickle of creek cutting through. It had altered little in all that time. He recalled how his father, shrouded in shadows, had stood across the way, having trapped the lawman like prey. Jack remembered the horror on Cyrus O'Leary's bearded face when he realized he'd not ambushed Henry but Henry would bury him.

In that instant Jack had cried out in terror, and his father backhanded him, sending him sprawling into the late autumn leaves, their brilliance crumbling beneath his boyish weight. It was over in seconds. A fatal gunshot. Smoke. His father had thrust a shovel in Jack's hand and told him to stop crying and dig like a man. He'd vowed that Jack would share the same grave if he told. Jack hadn't said a word.

Now the first leaves of fall lay atop the lone gravesite, a bewitching amber-gold. But even beneath a foot of fallen snow, Jack would have known the place, so heavily had it lain upon his heart.

God, forgive my father, my family, for our many sins. Forgive me.

The rain pocking the pewter surface of the Monongahela reflected Jack's somber mood. A west wind was kicking up, much to the aggravation of both captain and crew, making ascending the river against the current doubly difficult, even dangerous. The *Independence*, ponderously heavy with cargo and lying low in the water, shuddered as it left the dock.

Jack gave in to a final impulse to look back at Pittsburgh. All was dappled in haunting, rain-swept shades of gray. The place they'd docked was slick and empty save the barefoot boys who'd freed the mooring lines moments before. Silas Ballantyne was nowhere in sight. Only Ansel stood on the levee as they left, raising a hand in farewell.

"Miserable weather for a departure," the captain muttered as he stood beside Jack on the quarterdeck. "And we've only just begun."

Nine hundred miles more.

Jack's gaze swept the muscular slaves at the oars, their grim faces beaded with rain and sweat, sodden red kerchiefs flattened against dark skulls. The sight soured his already queasy stomach.

"With any luck, the rain will ease." Captain Maxwell waved a hand to his second in command and ordered the sodden square sail taken down.

A low moan rippled through the rowers, and Jack's thoughts swung to the giant pot still taking up much of the hold. God help him, he'd like to lighten their load, right here in plain view of Pittsburgh. What would his father and Wade have to say about that?

Too heavy astern, the keelboat moved through the water like a wing-clipped waterfowl. It wasn't farfetched to envision the floating hulk speared by a snag or beached on a sandbar before they'd made the first landfall.

Maxwell scowled, slapping at a mosquito. "Congress has ordered the Army Corp of Engineers to begin ridding the river of debris, but I say we'll ne'er see the end of it. Can you swim, Mr. Turlock?"

"I cross the Mon and back most mornings."

"Then yer used to her fits and whims."

The vessel was at the juncture of the Monongahela and Allegheny Rivers now, widening into the Ohio, close to a mile across in places. Here the water turned a vivid, churlish green before flattening into a muddy maelstrom. The Mississippi was mostly yellow, Jack recalled, and then there was the fractious Missouri, aptly named Old Misery.

Maxwell turned to him, wry. "Care for a dram o' whiskey?

Yer father sent enough to flood the hold. I doubt the thirsty Missouri garrison yer bound for will miss a gallon or two."

"Nay, I prefer to swim sober," Jack said, voice snatched by the rising wind.

Maxwell chuckled. "So do I, though the crew might sing a different tune." Adjusting his dripping cap, he sighed. "Feel free to retire to yer quarters if ye like. The foul weather shows no sign of abating."

Jack turned away, going below to the afterdeck. Shedding his coat and hat, he surveyed the narrow cabin redolent of new lumber and small, fragrant drifts of sawdust that had escaped a brisk broom. A bunk, bench, and desk were its only furnishings save a bookshelf affixed to an end wall.

A far cry from the antique elegance of River Hill.

Homesickness seized him, made him question his course even as the *Independence* swept him downriver. He could feel the restless rhythm of the water beneath his boots. No doubt he'd be out of his wits with boredom long before he saw the headwaters of the Missouri. Or else sunk in dismal reflection, as he was wont to do of late.

Opening his lap desk, he withdrew an inkwell, then sharpened a quill. Above his head, the wind was blowing a chill rain sideways through an open window, spattering his paper with a low whine and whistle. He slammed closed the shutter, then fumbled for a phosphorus match in his belongings like the ones Brunot had given Jarm and Cherry for their journey north. The candle flamed, and Jack returned to inking his quill.

Dear Ellie . . .

He shut his eyes, stunned by the power of memory. Was it just yesterday she'd come to him? Kissed him as willingly as a bride? Her tearstained face, the softness and scent of her, seemed to linger in the blue room long after. He looked toward the slim bunk with its thin wool blanket, where he might have lain with her in his arms. If they'd wed, the tiny cabin wouldn't have held them. Yet it had taken every shred of self-control to refuse her.

Ellie Ballantyne Turlock.

The mere joining of their names sent a shiver of longing through him. Nine hundred miles of misery awaited if he couldn't think about her clearly, couldn't cut her loose from the moorings of his life like the *Independence* from Pittsburgh.

He took up his pen and aimed for honesty.

> *It only seems fair, given matters between us, that I tell you straightaway. I have decided against returning to Pennsylvania. Our separa-tion will restore all sensibilities concerning our future and reveal our brief liaison for what it was—a fleeting infatuation.*

Fleeting? Nay. Infatuation? Nothing could be further from the truth.

Still, the lie seeped from his pen, bold and black. His hand wavered, and he set the quill aside, only to take it up again and force a few final words.

> *You deserve far more than I could ever hope to give you. I'll not disgrace you with my name or my family's reputation.*

Cold. Terse. Typically Turlock. He scrawled his signature and sat back, letting the ink dry, then fisted the letter into a ball. He held it over the candle flame till it caught fire before tossing it into a nearby bucket, where it curled to ashes.

He couldn't hurt her. Better to say nothing and never return. She'd soon grow tired of waiting. Daniel Cameron or
someone else would woo and win her, holding her close as
Jack had done in the hallowed breathlessness of a late summer afternoon, daring to imagine she might be his.

Sleep finally relieved him—restless, dreamless sleep—and
then a sudden crashing outside his cabin jarred him awake.
Yanking open the door, he expected chaos, only to find that
a crew member had slipped on the rain-slicked deck and
dropped Jack's supper tray.

"I'm not hungry anyway," he told the apologetic lad with
a shrug.

The wind had shifted and grown stronger, bumping up
against him, ruffling his coat and hair as he stood at the prow,
the rowers behind him as twilight encroached. He wondered
what Chloe was doing. If the rain was coming through the
roof at River Hill or the carpenters had mended the leak.
Whether or not Sol would give Cicero to Ben as Jack had
requested or keep him at River Hill in hopes Jack would
return. And Ellie . . .

Thoughts of her raced down like rain, pelting him. Was
she thinking of him? Trying hard not to? Loving him at a
distance? Praying?

He faced the storm, feet widespread as the keelboat listed
a bit. He felt soulless. Bereft. Without anchor. Reaching into
his pocket, he withdrew George Whitefield's old journal and
turned to a random page.

The weather was cold, and the wind blew very hard; but
when the heart is full of God, outward things affect it little.

31

They that love beyond the world
cannot be separated by it. Death
cannot kill what never dies.
WILLIAM PENN

She had to tell Daniel. But now wasn't the time. The trouble was there never seemed to be a proper time. Heartbreak was best dispensed in small doses, if at all. But since Daniel didn't love her, perhaps the sting of her refusal wouldn't be so great. Still, her dread went deep. Wedged between Daniel and Mina in the Market Street Theater, Ellie paid little attention to what was happening on the stage, preoccupied with what she must say. The truth—all of it.

I cannot marry you, Daniel.

You are, and ever will be, my friend.

I'm in love with Jack Turlock.

The cold of early November seeped along the floor, chilling her leather slippers and linen-clad legs despite her froth of petticoats. If she was shivering amidst an overflowing theater crowd, what must it be like for Jack in the West? Winter was hurtling ever nearer, every day that passed a bleak reminder of how much time and distance was between them. Had it merely been two months since he'd left?

A burst of laughter returned her eyes to the stage, to the comedy performed by a traveling theatrical group from New York. The irony of the play's name didn't escape her. *The Thwarted Suitor.* Try as she might, she couldn't follow the storyline, able actors though they were. Their exaggerated antics and painted faces both fascinated and repelled her, though Peyton seemed to find them amusing, and even Ansel and Daniel were laughing. Andra and Mina were absolutely rapt, as was Elspeth, hardly blinking as the drama unfolded. It was Elspeth who had talked them into going, despite Da's quiet disapproval and Mama sending her regrets.

As her shivering increased, Ellie turned her thoughts toward warming up at Benedict's afterward with steaming cups of chocolate and late-night chatter, something to take her mind off of Jack and Chloe.

She'd sent two letters addressed to Broad Oak since Jack's leaving. Likely Isabel had intercepted them, as there'd been no reply. Ellie longed to know what Chloe was doing, if she was happy. She and Ben would have retired their fishing poles till spring. As for Jack, she'd been unable to put her thoughts to paper, unsure of where to send a letter. And she'd received no word from him . . .

A standing ovation soon freed the group from their balcony box, and they went out into the frosty night, Daniel taking her arm. Just down the street, Benedict's was as crowded as the theater, but they were soon seated and served. Distracted by customers coming and going, Ellie sipped her chocolate and listened as everyone discussed the play's highlights.

"Once I had dreams of being on the stage," Elspeth told them, her smile almost wistful. "Your mother had gone to Philadelphia to work at the foundling hospital. I wanted to join her in the city and audition. But when I arrived, the only thing I met with was yellow fever."

"It's not too late to further your ambitions, is it?" Peyton studied her in the flickering lamplight. "You're lovelier than any actress I saw tonight and just as entertaining."

"You flatter me—something I've always enjoyed." She winked and everyone chuckled. "I've since decided that all of life is one grand drama. Who needs a stage? Besides, I don't like the idea of traveling round with a company. I want to settle down."

"Are you thinking of returning to York?" Daniel broached the question they all seemed to be pondering.

"I'm afraid the smithy in York was getting a mite crowded. My sister-in-law Felicity and I never quite saw eye to eye."

"Ah, Felicity," Andra murmured as she and Elspeth exchanged a glance. "A more high-strung soul there never was."

"Pittsburgh is more to my liking." Elspeth toyed with her cup, slanting a glance about the crowded room. "I've made inquiries and have found work at a millinery on Broad Street."

"Are you fond of needlework, then?" Ellie asked.

"I'm not as gifted as your mother, but I do what I can."

"I'd be glad to help you find lodging," Peyton told her. "There's a genteel boardinghouse on Liberty Street that might suit, with a view of the river."

"Perhaps tomorrow. I'm anxious to settle in, attend church."

Church? Ellie nearly choked on her chocolate. Since when was her aunt interested in spiritual matters? Could it be their prayers for Elspeth were being answered?

"You're more than welcome at First Presbyterian." Ansel, silent until now, extended an invitation.

Elspeth smiled—that lovely, evasive smile that made Ellie wonder what was really at work in her head and heart. "I used to attend church in York . . . with your father. I'm not entirely the sinner one might think."

There was a breathless pause.

"I hardly think that," Peyton replied. "Father and Mother rarely talk of York."

"Well, I don't blame them. 'Twas so long ago."

Ellie leaned back in her chair, trying to sort through the threads of conversation. Elspeth had been in Pittsburgh for months now, living at the hotel, dining nearly daily with Peyton. Ellie suspected she'd depleted all her funds. They'd expected her to return to York weeks ago.

Lost in thought, she let her gaze drift about the crowded room, past ladies' elaborate winter bonnets and gentlemen's top hats to a man rising from a corner table. Her heart tripped. *Jack?* Same wide-set shoulders, same formidable stature.

Jack's father.

He turned around and looked their way, making Ellie want to slink beneath the table. But Henry Turlock wasn't focused on her. His gaze fastened on Elspeth and stayed fast. Andra and Peyton were sparring over something. Daniel and Ansel and Mina were talking of the glassworks. No one else witnessed the spark of recognition in Henry's face—or the answering flicker in Elspeth's. Ellie felt a bewildering dismay.

The woman on Henry's arm was not his wife. Clad in an ermine-lined cape and hat, jewels about her throat, she didn't remotely resemble Isabel.

"My, my," Elspeth remarked, unfolding a lace-tipped fan and smiling benignly at Ellie. "Benedict's is a touch crowded tonight. I was like ice in the theater and now I'm practically on fire."

Ellie lowered her eyes as Henry Turlock passed by their table. Heartsick, she resisted the urge to watch his exit. He even walked like Jack.

Ansel opened the boatyard office at dawn, feeling more rested than he had in days after a sound night's sleep. Dr. Brunot had transported the last of the fugitives two nights prior, and the attic was now empty save the maids readying it in anticipation of the next need.

Tunneling a hand through his hair, he surveyed the latest shipbuilding plans, ignoring the new copy of the *Pittsburgh Gazette* that lay folded on his father's desk. They usually read the headlines before the day began, but lately there seemed little news of note, aside from rising grain prices and an oil embargo . . . and a sudden flurry of wedding announcements. None of which were his or Ellie's.

He sensed Daniel was becoming as frustrated as Mina. No pending engagement. No wedding date. Time ticked on, and neither he nor Ellie, it seemed, had the heart to settle matters.

"Mornin', Mister Ansel."

Ansel looked up to see a dark-headed lad in the doorway, fetching in wood for the stove crackling in a far corner.

"Morning, James. You've begun a fine fire."

"Thank ye, sir." He heaved his load across the room and dumped it in the wood box. "I'll confess my mind ain't on fires and such this mornin' but the dim news wingin' about town."

"Oh?" Ansel replied absently, sharpening a stylus with a penknife.

"Aye, sir. I s'pose the paper there on the master's desk is full of it, though I ain't had time to read it myself."

Curious, Ansel flipped the *Gazette* over, then turned it around to better eye the headline.

Keelboat Sinks in Missouri Storm.

"I never figured the river would claim as fine a man as Captain Maxwell. Don't seem fair somehow." The apprentice was watching him, awaiting his reaction. "But those Turlocks, guess they got what they deserve. One of 'em, anyway."

One . . . The stylus fell from Ansel's hand and clattered across the desktop. Though his eyes remained locked on the newsprint, he wanted to fling it into the fire. A line in boldface seemed to shout the tragic story.

ALL LOST.

Stunned, he scanned the names of casualties, the little breakfast he'd eaten starting to churn. Listed below Captain Maxwell and crew was Jack Turlock. The sole passenger. *Och, Ellie.*

He shut his eyes as if doing so could staunch the pain he felt for her, for Jack. *All lost.* Lost in the icy water. Lost eternally.

"Everything all right?" His father stood in the open doorway, asking a question he couldn't answer.

James gave a somber greeting and finished tending the stove. Ansel swallowed, tried to speak. His father shrugged off his greatcoat and hung it from a peg by the door. When the lad went out, Ansel passed him the paper.

For just a moment Da's stoicism slipped. There was a flash of disbelief followed by barefaced sadness. He murmured something in Gaelic that sounded like a prayer.

Sitting down, Ansel sank his head in his hands as his father reached for his coat again.

"I need to tell Ellie. I may or may not be back."

The stone chapel wore a mantle of ivy and moss, the waning November sunlight casting a pale halo about the stone foundation. Ellie pushed open the wooden door and felt immediately at peace. Here her parents had been wed, each baby christened in the Scots tradition. She'd recently confided to Mama that she'd like to marry here as well. Mama had smiled and nodded, probably thinking she meant Daniel.

Taking a seat on the first bench, she pushed her hands deeper into her fur-lined muff, feeling the cold stone beneath her. She didn't mind the chill. It lent itself to clarity of thought, whereas her bedchamber fire lulled her to sleep. Here she could pray unhindered, without interruption. Andra never thought to look for her, and Mama never intruded on her private time.

She daydreamed as much as she prayed, dressing the little kirk with ribbons and roses as if it were her wedding day. At long last she'd wear Mama's silk dress and veil. Chloe would be best maid along with Andra, if Andra didn't protest her Turlock groom. There would be a bride's cake, a honeymoon. But none of it mattered, truly. If no one came—if there was only a small celebration—nothing could take away the joy she felt in Jack's presence.

Bending her head, she tried to quell her longing, the mere memory of his embrace making her woozy. Her every prayer was that he'd come back to her again. She felt bewildered that she didn't know just where he was. As the days passed, she fought the perplexing feeling he'd somehow moved beyond the reach of her caring. Her prayers.

Footfalls made her look up. Da? His beloved form filled the doorway, seeming strangely out of place. He rarely came here. Her smile waned at the look on his face, the grieved green of his eyes.

She stood, her muff falling to the bench as her thoughts began a wild dance. "Are you all right? Is Mama?"

He came nearer, all too silent, his arms closing about her. He rested his cheek against her loosely pinned hair. In that instant she sensed his desperate struggle, his anguished reluctance to say what he must.

"Ellie . . . there's been an accident downriver."

"An accident?" The frantic lilt of her pulse filled her ears.

"On the keelboat your Jack was traveling on."

Your Jack.

She went completely still. In the silence of her heart, she knew.

"The paper reports the sinking happened a fortnight ago. I confirmed it with port authorities before leaving town."

The words washed over her, stormy and frightening and strange. She listened to them as if from a distance. As if she were drowning too.

"The boat was caught in a storm at the headwaters of the Missouri. The cargo was too heavy and it capsized."

"All . . . lost?" Her voice broke.

"Aye, 'tis said."

Lost. What a world of hurt lay within the smallness of that word.

She felt herself fade as a tide of anguish rose inside her. *Jack! Jack! Jack!*

Her sobs filled the chapel, rebounding off cold stone walls, bringing her to her knees. If not for the hard arms around her, she'd have sunk to the stones at her feet. They stood a long time amidst her weeping, oblivious to the cold and Andra's distant call and the winter darkness pressing in on them.

Regret rushed in. She should have gone with him. Should have been there at the last. She far preferred a watery grave to life without him.

They were being so careful of her. In the days to come, everyone at New Hope seemed to tiptoe around her. Broken, numbed by a chasm of lost, she'd finally told Daniel the reason she couldn't wed him.

"But Elinor . . ." He looked down at her, his conundrum

playing out across his face. "With all respect to Jack Turlock and his passing, there's no longer any impediment to us . . . once you've finished mourning, that is."

"And you would still have me, knowing I love another." Even the suggestion seemed a compromise, a betrayal.

"I would still have you, knowing you'd stop loving him in time."

In time. Did such heartache ever ease? Or did it only deepen? Her prayers for Jack, for their future, had gone unanswered. She felt haunted. Had Jack cried out to God in the storm? Had his last thoughts been of her? She would live with the gnawing uncertainty the rest of her days.

Her tangled thoughts swung to Chloe. Who had told Chloe the terrible news? Had they done so gently? Had there been anyone at Broad Oak to hold her and bear the brunt of her hurt? Chloe loved Jack so, and he, in his own gruff way, had loved her. He'd tried to do right by Chloe, tried to give her something beyond Broad Oak's coldness and deceit.

She went through the motions of each day, trying to keep sudden, stubborn reminders at bay, but they were everywhere. The rivers turned stormy, tormenting her anew. Ansel donned a swallowtail coat, a replica of Jack's the night of the ball. A message came from Broad Oak, hand delivered by Sol, casting her back to Chloe's first note saying Jack would allow lessons.

She took the paper from Sol's wrinkled hand warily, her emotions as raw and reddened as her eyes.

"Ben asked me to bring this to you real quiet-like." His voice was low, as if sharing a secret.

Ellie thanked him, his sorrowful expression weighting her long after he'd left. She tore open the paper in the privacy of her room, her fingers trembling.

Pleez cum. Cloe sic.

Heartsick, no doubt. Had Chloe taught Ben to write, to read? It could be nothing else. With a purpose she'd not felt in days, Ellie wrapped herself in a dark cloak and bonnet and hurried to the stables. As the coach rolled away, she wondered if Andra and the maids watched her going, mystified. She'd forgotten to tell anyone she was leaving.

She'd never been to Broad Oak, daunting prospect as it was. Consumed by Jack's passing, she gave little thought to her mission, the fear she felt over arriving unannounced and uninvited buried deep. She prayed Henry Turlock wasn't at home. He frightened her in ways she couldn't fathom. Even now she recalled seeing him at Benedict's and felt a latent chill.

A dour-faced housekeeper let her in and grudgingly went to fetch the mistress. Ellie's gaze climbed the ornate staircase after her, lingering on the angelic mural overshadowing the foyer. Heaven . . . harps . . . plump, smiling cherubs. Harps aside, she didn't believe in that kind of eternity. Stilted. Shallow. The scene resurrected her deepest fear. She craved the comfort, the reassurance, that she'd see Jack again. In a place far removed from Broad Oak's stairwell ceiling.

The house was all too hushed. She latched on to the hope that Chloe wasn't truly sick but heartsick, and would come running down the steps into her arms. Her courage almost faltered when Isabel Turlock appeared instead. Clad in black, she descended the staircase slowly, without a single gem of the jewelry she was known for except an elaborate mourning ring. At the bottom, she squared her shoulders, and the enmity in her eyes erected a wall.

"Miss Ballantyne, I believe."

"I've come to see Chloe."

"Chloe is ill."

Out of the corner of her eye, Ellie saw a sudden movement. Wade had come into the hall, coatless and dressed as casually as Jack had once been, driving home his memory. The band of pain around her heart tightened. "I'd still like to see her."

"Another day, perhaps."

"Another day might be too late." Her fleeting time with Jack had taught her that. Never again would she take time, a life, for granted.

"Are you insisting, then?" Crossing her arms, Isabel withered Ellie with a look. "Of all the impudent, unladylike—"

Clutching her skirts, Ellie did the unthinkable and pushed past Isabel, anguish propelling her up the unfamiliar staircase. Isabel's shouts to stop only fueled her steps. At the very top, a great many closed doors seemed to mock her impulsiveness. Which was Chloe's? Hearing a noise, she whirled round to find Wade taking the stairs two at a time in her wake. To escort her out by force?

The heft of him, his flinty expression, stole her courage. She'd beg if she had to. But he simply stepped around her and walked to a far door before thrusting it open. Ellie rushed toward it, hearing Isabel call for the housekeeper below. Trembling, distrustful of Wade, she all but slammed the door and slid the bolt into place. Wade's footfalls faded, but his ensuing argument with his mother was far harder to dismiss.

Behind her, Chloe lay on the bed, her face lacking any color, her hair shorn short. Because of a fever? Her eyes were closed, her breathing shallow. Ellie expected to see the usual clutter left by a physician—opaque bottles and bloodletting devices—but the nearest table was bare save a guttered candle and an untouched cup of tea. No doctor . . . Why?

Dropping to her knees by the bed, she reached for Chloe's still hand. "Chloe, 'tis only me. Ben sent a note round by Sol. I-I didn't realize you've been teaching him to read and write." The simple, misspelled words were indelibly penned in her heart and head, evidence of a boy's heartfelt affection and concern. "I'm so proud of you."

To her relief, the limp fingers gave the barest squeeze.

"I heard about River Hill." Ellie kept her voice soft, afraid of taxing Chloe with too much talk. "Sol said it's yours now."

Chloe's eyes fluttered open. "I want to go . . . be with Jack . . . I miss him so."

Not only you, Chloe.

The sorrow of the moment cut deep. How was it that she had so much—a loving family, a good name, a secure home—and Chloe had so little? Why had Chloe lost the one thing that mattered most?

Ellie worked to keep her voice even and hopeful. "When you're better, we can continue lessons and plant the garden like we planned—make it pretty again. We'll even go fishing."

Cool fingers caressed her damp cheek. "Say a prayer for me, Miss Ellie . . . Say some Scripture." Chloe's eyes closed again. "Too tired to talk . . ."

A noise at the door reminded Ellie she was an unwelcome guest. She'd run out of time. Words. Hope. Chloe was holding on to life by a slender thread, one frayed by things too hard for a girlish heart to hold.

"Then just listen, Chloe love." Though she felt mired in heartache, a beloved Scots Psalm rose above her sorrow. Her father's deep voice returned to her, undergirding her much as his arms had done in the chill of the chapel when she'd learned of Jack's fate, helping her speak words of comfort and truth. "'The Lord's my shepherd, I'll not want. He makes me down to lie, in pastures green he leadeth me the quiet waters by . . .'"

In the stillness of the unfamiliar room, the Lord seemed near.

And that was enough.

32

My harp also is turned to
mourning, and my organ into the
voice of them that weep.

JOB 30:31

Ellie faced Isabel in the foyer and found that the woman was regarding her with even more hostility than before. She'd earned it, she guessed, barging upstairs like she'd done. For a few breathless moments, Ellie tried to fathom that this was Jack's mother, a woman who might have been her mother-in-law. But she could find no hint of her beloved in this irate woman who was clearly desirous of her leaving.

"Chloe is in dire need of a physician. I fear she's more ill than you might think." Ellie looked past Isabel to Wade. But Wade was regarding her in an unnerving, half-amused way, as if she was merely providing him an afternoon's entertainment. She renewed her plea, flushed and perspiring beneath her heavy cape. "Dr. Brunot will come as soon as possible, I'm sure—"

"I don't remember you having any medical background,

340

Miss Ballantyne, only a simple day school." Isabel gripped the newel post of the staircase. "And I'm insulted that you force your way into my house, uninvited, and dictate what I should do with my daughter." She motioned for the housekeeper to open the front door. "Chloe will mend. Besides, I'll not let Brunot set foot on this property, given his sentiments."

His sentiments? The words were coated with such derision there was no mistaking their meaning. "Then send for Phipps or Alexander," Ellie retorted. "They share your own misguided views, if I'm not mistaken."

At this Wade smirked. Phipps and Alexander were proslavery physicians, both outspoken opponents of Brunot. Ellie couldn't have fueled Isabel's ire more if she'd set fire to her.

"Horse doctors, the both of them!" Isabel spat. "As for you, Elinor Ballantyne, I'll thank you not to show your face here again or bestow any more of your unwanted advice."

Ellie ached to have the last word, then gave way. Shaking, she hurried out, sensing the deeper danger of encountering Henry Turlock the longer she tarried. Never had she been so glad to flee a place, yet she felt brutally torn as she got into the waiting coach.

All the way home she prayed, so undone she felt she was on the brink of falling ill herself. She tried desperately to quiet her thoughts, but the sound of Peyton's raised voice sent her spinning as she set foot in the house. It carried through the open study doorway into the foyer, heated and dismayed. Ansel spoke next, his voice equally aggrieved. Were they sparring again?

Intent on her room, Ellie's foot touched the first step when Andra's voice stopped her cold. "Elinor, where have you been?"

"Broad Oak," she confessed, her voice thick from weeping.

"Broad Oak?" The revulsion in Andra's tone cut her. "Why?"

"Chloe is ill."

Peyton appeared and motioned them both into the study, out of the maids' hearing, and shut the door. Ellie was relieved to find Ansel in the shadows. "El, are you all right?"

She could only stare at him in mute appeal, emotion closing her throat.

"You didn't see Brunot at Broad Oak, I suppose." At the shake of her head, he ran a hand through his already rumpled hair. "I'm afraid he's missing. Mrs. Brunot says he hasn't been seen or heard from since leaving for a medical call out Braddock's Road two days past."

Peyton shrugged. "He's likely attending a birth or death at some far-flung farm for all we know."

"Well, I don't have a good feeling about it," Ansel replied.

"Nor do I." Andra walked to a window, giving Peyton a sidelong glance. "And I'm tired of you making light of everything, including the equally disturbing matter of Aunt Elspeth's latest admirer."

Peyton tugged nonchalantly on the bell cord. "She has many admirers, most of them widowers."

"And one most decidedly *not*," Andra shot back, eyeing him fiercely.

"Henry Turlock's peccadilloes are well known."

"That's not the point. I lay the blame at your door for introducing them."

"I didn't introduce them. Wade did."

"So Wade had already made Elspeth's acquaintance?"

"Aye, at the theater."

Ellie stepped between them, hoping to quell the quarrel. "Where are Da and Mama?"

"Dining with friends in town," Andra told her.

Ellie sank into a chair by the glowing hearth, wanting to curl up into a little ball and go to sleep. Peyton and Andra's arguing stilled while Gwyn served tea, only to resume the moment she went out again. Resisting the urge to cover her ears, Ellie looked toward Ansel.

He took a seat beside her, sympathy in his eyes. "You didn't receive a warm welcome at Broad Oak, I take it."

"I didn't expect one." Isabel's barbs still clung to her, bitter and hurtful, but it was Chloe she was most concerned about. "Please pray for Chloe. She's very ill and heartsick over—" She stumbled on Jack's name. She hadn't spoken it aloud since the tragedy. "Isabel won't send for a doctor. I mentioned Brunot and she flatly refused."

"We can't force a physician on them, but we'll pray Chloe weathers this without one." Though his words were reassuring, the alarm in his eyes held fast. "As for Brunot, he didn't come last night as planned, and he's not one to miss a meeting. We have four friends needing transport north."

She felt a shiver of alarm yet clung to Peyton's assumption that the doctor was simply making a prolonged call. "You'll go in his stead then."

"Aye, I'll go—and gladly. But it doesn't help explain his absence."

"Be careful." Her soft words were almost lost amidst the swell of Andra's and Peyton's voices across the room. "I suppose you'll take the newly refitted coach—the one like Dr. Brunot's." At his nod, she pushed past her exhaustion. "Let me go with you—you'll need a ruse. You can't go driving an empty vehicle about the county and arouse suspicion."

"I'm hoping no one will notice."

"I'll say I'm visiting Harmony Grove. Mama and I do have friends there."

"El, it's too risky."

"'Tis far less so with me as a passenger, surely."

He studied her, his gaze heavy with indecision.

"Please," she urged, wanting to help, wishing Andra and Peyton would stop their wrangling. Lowering her voice, she asked, "What is all this about Aunt Elspeth?"

"Elspeth seems to be spending an inordinate amount of time with Henry Turlock of late. A dangerous liaison, Da says."

Dangerous seemed an understatement. 'Twas shocking. Frightening. "I recall seeing him at Benedict's," she said, remembering how he'd given Elspeth a lingering look. But in truth, her striking aunt garnered many admiring glances wherever she went.

"We can do little about Elspeth, but we can pray for Chloe and manage the fugitives as best we can." Ansel stood and looked down at her, his reluctance plain. "We'll delay a while longer in hopes Brunot will return. But we'll soon need to act. More fugitives are waiting to cross the river."

I'm in love with you. I've long been in love with you. Do you believe me?

Ellie's needle slipped. Drew blood. A scarlet drop fell onto the ivory cloth she was embroidering and melted into it, soiling the lovely fabric. 'Twas Mama's Christmas gift, but she didn't feel so much as a flicker of dismay. Her heart was not in her task. It felt as frozen as the Allegheny outside her window, ice-hardened in the fist of winter. Sometimes she doubted it would ever thaw or see spring.

A month had passed since she'd heard of Jack's death, a fortnight since she'd seen Chloe at Broad Oak. She seemed to watch the goings-on around her like a wax figure or a spectator viewing a play, with little interaction or interest.

Somehow she'd made the trip to Harmony Grove with Ansel more than once, despite Da's concerns. He'd spoken to her about reopening the day school sooner than planned, but she doubted she'd do so even come spring. That seemed a part of her past, buried with Jack.

As Christmas neared, Mama went about singing hymns and keeping the small staff busy with preparations. *Nollaig Beag*, or Little Christmas, was not to be missed, despite the pall of mourning. Mamie was immersed in the kitchen, baking an abundance of Yule bread and black bun, the fragrance rivaling the confectionery on Water Street. Swaths of holly and berries and greenery were wound round the stair banister by Mari and Gwyn, every mantel adorned with countless candles. All wished for wintry weather. Christmas without snow is poor fare, Da always said.

Ellie tried to fasten her thoughts on the things that had brought such pleasure in years past, but the darkness inside her was too deep. Her every thought seemed to be one unending prayer. For Chloe. Dr. Brunot, still missing. The fugitives in their care. Aunt Elspeth.

"Ellie?"

Mama came into the parlor and shut the door, the concern in her eyes making Ellie's heart leap with renewed alarm. "Sol is here to see you. I asked him to wait in your father's study. But if you'd rather, I can see why he's come in your stead."

Ellie's hurry to the door was her answer. 'Twas the finest Christmas gift imaginable to have Chloe well again. Had he come all this way to tell her on such a bitter, windy day? Perhaps deliver a note from Chloe herself? Her spirits lightened at the very thought.

As Mama looked on, she crossed the foyer and entered the study, leaving the door open in her haste. Sol stood facing the fire, shoulders bowed. Slowly he turned round.

Ellie's hopes collapsed at first glance. The grave look on his face negated any glad news, and she was cast back to the shattering moment she'd heard about Jack. Unable to give a greeting, she sought the nearest chair.

"I'm afraid I don't bring much other than bad tidings here lately, Miz Ellie. But I figured you'd want to know straightaway. It's about Miz Chloe . . ." He struggled for control, his eyes dark pools. "She was buried at Broad Oak yesterday."

Ellie stared at him, unable to take it in. Unwilling.

Heartache upon heartache.

"It's said she went real peaceful-like." A tear glazed his wrinkled cheek. "Sally—Ben's granny—was with her when she passed."

Sally . . . one of Broad Oak's slaves. The irony was not lost on Ellie. Despite the sickening swirl of the room, she felt deeply thankful it was Sally who'd been with Chloe. Though they'd never met, she sensed Sally was a believer. 'Twas only fitting that Chloe was ushered into the presence of the King by one who knew Him well.

"She told Sally—" Sol looked away, the hat in his hands clenched tight. "At the last Miz Chloe told Sally that she saw somebody waitin'."

Her voice, when it finally came, sounded far-off and fragile. "Somebody?"

"Aye. Mister Jack."

Jack.

And Jesus.

The church bell seemed to clang more than peal this winter's morn as the congregants hurried inside First Presbyterian to escape the chill, heads down in the sleet-studded wind. All were shoulder to shoulder in the Ballantyne pew save Andra, who remained at home nursing a cold, her place conspicuously empty. Behind them sat the Camerons—and a guest.

Ellie had seen them in the narthex moments before and still felt riddled with surprise. Whoever this woman was, she was garnering a great deal of attention in her royal purple cape and bonnet, her ebony hair as dark as Ellie's own.

Peyton leaned in to whisper in her ear, "Isn't that Penelope Cameron, the cousin from Westmoreland County?"

Penelope, Daniel's very marriageable cousin? Unsure, Ellie turned her attention to Reverend Herron instead. As the service progressed, she grew sleepy, even nodded off, her bonnet grazing the solid shoulder of her father. He looked down at her, concern darkening his gaze.

There were to be no more trips with Ansel to Harmony Grove, he'd told her gently that morning. She was to remain at home and recover from the shock of the last weeks within New Hope's walls. Hearing it, she felt a little like an exotic hothouse plant. No one seemed to understand that no matter what she did—or didn't do—her sadness failed to ebb. It rimmed her heart, cold and dark, growing deeper still.

She stood with the congregation as a Scots Psalter was sung, the one she'd spoken to Chloe at the last. Despite its beauty, every familiar note seemed barbed. She blinked back tears, surprised they always surfaced willfully, without warning.

Heads bowed for the benediction. She prayed for healing. Peace. Into the ensuing quiet crept an odd sensation—a subtle shaking. The hallowed space bore a faint rumble of thunder, followed by a great rousing roll of it. The kirk's very foundation seemed to heave. Reverend Herron's unfinished prayer hung in the air as a second pew-shaking boom rent the room, and several elders stood. The Sabbath calm turned chaotic as people began abandoning pews and rushing for doors, reminding Ellie of the spring storm and Jack and riding into Pittsburgh amidst all the mayhem.

She found herself on Peyton's arm as he hurried her and

Mama to the coach, every eye drawn east. Another rumble sent the horses bolting, almost tumbling the coachman from his seat. With Ansel's help, he brought the horses round, and they finally left the churchyard and started out of town.

Ellie felt the squeeze of Mama's gloved hand and was thankful for Ansel's calm as he took a seat opposite them. "Da and Peyton and a few constables are going to inquire about the trouble." He opened a shutter to better see the landscape. "It seems to be coming from Broad Oak's direction. I heard more of their slaves disappeared last week."

"Still no word of Dr. Brunot?" Ellie asked.

Ansel frowned and shook his head. "None, I'm afraid. He's been gone long enough to start an investigation, but the sheriff is saying little so far."

They were silent the rest of the way home, jarred twice more by near-deafening explosions, the horses frantic again. But once they'd shed their wraps and joined Andra in the parlor, all seemed to settle.

Cocooned in a quilt near the fire, her nose reddened by cold, Andra peppered them with questions before they'd shut the door. "What on earth is happening out there? Mamie said it's rattling all the china in the pantry and upsetting every horse in the stables."

"There may be trouble at Broad Oak," Mama told her, ringing for tea.

"May be? It sounds like the place has blown up!" She drew her quilt closer. "I imagine Wade is to blame. We can no longer lay the trouble at Jack's door—"

Mama silenced her with a look, expression grim. Ellie pretended not to notice but moved to an east window, her back to them. Smoke was rising, billowing and gray. A shiver ran through her. Broad Oak . . . burning? An acrid smell seemed to sneak through the window cracks, whispering of something momentous. Ash was scattering across sodden fields. Silvery-white against the cold landscape, it resembled blowing snow. Whatever had happened, she was glad Chloe was spared the calamity.

"We had a visitor in church today—Mina and Daniel's cousin Penelope." Mama steered the conversation in a safer direction. "She seems a lovely girl. Peyton seems to think so especially."

Andra raised an eyebrow. "Peyton? I'm glad you didn't say Ansel. What a strange love triangle that would be."

"I still have hopes for Ansel and Mina," Mama murmured, taking up her embroidery hoop.

"I recall the last time Penelope was here. Peyton seemed so befuddled he could hardly tie his cravat." Andra sneezed into her handkerchief. "I'll admit a wedding would be a fine thing after so melancholy a winter."

"Come, Ellie, and join us." Mama patted the sofa invitingly, luring her away from the window.

Ellie smelled the peppermint tea from several feet away and tried to look appreciatively at the tray crowded with tiny sandwiches and tea cakes that Mari had set down.

"Speaking of relatives . . ." Andra posed the perilous question as she sipped from a delicate cup. "I suppose you didn't see Aunt Elspeth in town today?"

"No, but I did see Alec Duncan." Mama began pouring tea for Ellie. "He sends his regrets that you're ill and hopes you'll be well enough to attend the Nevilles' winter ball. Apparently you promised to do that some time ago."

Andra's wan color turned dusky. "And is Mr. Duncan quite well?"

"Miss Sylvia Denny seems to think so."

Ellie almost smiled at Mama's subtlety. Reaching for her teacup, she startled as another explosion rocked the room.

The amber liquid spilled and pooled in her saucer, steaming and sweet.

"Like cannon fire," Mama said, her eyes drifting to a window. "We'll soon know the cause of it. Your father and Peyton should be back soon, or so I hope."

The afternoon stretched long and anxious. Ellie resumed her vigil by the window, the first to hear heavy footfalls at dusk. In the light of the sconce illuminating the foyer, her father's eyes were weary. Even Peyton was strangely silent. They gathered in the study after being pulled from the far corners of the house, Mamie and the maids among them.

"The biggest of the Turlock warehouses has burned," her father told them. "No one is sure how the fire started, but a great deal of damage was done by exploding casks. The distillery and outbuildings—and the house—were spared. There's a river of whiskey surrounding the place, but thankfully no loss of life."

"Perhaps one of their runaways started the fire." Peyton shrugged off his coat and handed his top hat to a chalky-faced Gwyn. "Their overseer, Marcum, is as hard a man as I've ever met. I'll not forget what he did to Adam and Ulie. It's hard to have sympathetic pangs for any of them at Broad Oak."

Supper was served, but few had an appetite and conversation was meager at best. Afterward Andra entertained them on the pianoforte while Ellie looked absently at her harp. She'd not played a note since Jack's passing. There seemed to be little music in her soul that sorrow hadn't crowded out.

"Come, Ellie, play for us." Her father was regarding her thoughtfully, his eyes kind.

She took a seat at his bidding, fingers poised on the strings, trying to dredge up a melody from memory. But lately her thoughts were so muddled she struggled to recall the simplest things.

"D'ye want me to accompany you?" he asked.

She looked up in surprise. "Yes . . . please."

He went to a case and selected one of the violins in their collection, a Bergonzi from Italy. Its varnish glinted a pleasing crimson in the candlelight. Tightening the bow, he turned back to her. "Bach's *Adagio*?"

She nodded. 'Twas a beautiful, soothing piece, a favorite of theirs, one she knew by heart. They began in perfect accord. She was relieved he hadn't asked her to repeat the sonata from the ball. As she thought it, long-denied images of Chloe and Jack rushed in with such bittersweet clarity her fingers slipped from the strings. Though she bit her lip till it nearly bled, all her self-possession crumbled and she couldn't regain her place.

Getting up from her seat, she mumbled an apology and fled the room, wishing she could escape her heartache as easily. But it followed hard on her heels, as sure a presence as her worried mother, who came up the stairs after her.

33

*The look of love alarms because 'tis
filled with fire.*

WILLIAM BLAKE

On Christmas Eve morn, New Hope awoke to a foot of snow. Ellie lay awake in the predawn hush, remembering Mama's plan to deliver gifts to tenants and staff before settling in for a special supper and family devotions at twilight. The gifts they'd readied for Sol and Ben waited near the hearth. Books and sweetmeats, wool scarves and mittens. It would be a sad time for them without Jack and Chloe. She wanted to bring them a little cheer if she could, and perhaps be cheered in return.

When Mama and Andra hadn't returned by early afternoon, a second, smaller sleigh was brought round, its bells and brass trim tinkling and glistening as the runners slid to a silent halt at New Hope's entrance. Ansel helped her onto the seat, arranging her lap robe and checking to see if a foot warmer of hot coals was beneath her feet.

"You'll make a fine husband one day, being so solicitous." She pressed a kiss to his ruddy cheek, touched by his concern.

"I'm off to River Hill. I want to thank Solomon for his kindness to me, leave a little something for Ben."

His eyes held hers in question. "Do you want me to go with you?"

"No, I have an escort and won't be long," she reassured him. "I'll be back before you mind the light." She cast a glance upward to the snow-shrouded dome. Now that the attic had emptied, the cupola would shine again. Never was there a better time for hope and Christlike kindness than at Christmastide.

The sleigh was far faster than the coach, borne along by a surefooted horse that seemed glad to be free of the stables. Few were out on such a day. The snow, shaking down lightly when she'd left, was tumbling so fiercely by the time they neared River Hill she considered turning back. Her spirits fell to find the gates closed, but the groom soon had them open, then shut them again in their wake.

Everything was a glistening, blinding swirl of white. Even if Sol wasn't here but at Broad Oak, she was glad she'd come. She wanted to look on the old house a final time. Frame it in her head and heart and bid it goodbye. Make peace with all that might have been. It would soon pass into other hands—just whose, she didn't know. She envied them.

As the sleigh neared the stables, she spied Sol outside in the courtyard with another black man she'd never met. Surprise lit Sol's aging features, and he gestured for her groom to pull beneath the porte cochere. "Miz Ellie? That you?" He came closer. "Nigh froze to death, I fear."

"Not quite," she said, though her smile felt locked in place. "'Tis good to see you again, Sol. I was worried with all the trouble at Broad Oak."

"We be fine—me and Ben and Sally—though the ash and smoke over there is still smolderin' somethin' fierce."

She reached down, feeling for the gifts beneath her lap robe. "I wanted to wish you all a blessed Christmas." She passed the packages to him, moved by the shine in his eyes. "And I wanted to see River Hill again."

He nodded in understanding, then squinted at the sky. "Why don't you come inside a few minutes and still your shakin'? Have some tea? By the time you warm yourself, the snow might ease. Your poor horse could use some oats before you go out again."

At her nod, her groom made for the shelter of the stables, and she followed Sol down a shoveled path past brittle lilacs wreathed in snow.

"There's a fine fire in the study. I've been going through some papers and belongings for Broad Oak, trying to set things in order for Mister Henry." The confidence was almost apologetic, spoken in a whisper. "Miz Malarkey quit her post, so it's been somewhat lonesome. Just me and the stable hands, mostly."

Once inside the foyer, she faltered. Jack's presence, his beloved, masculine scent, seemed to pervade every inch. Tears gathered in her eyes, yet Sol seemed so pleased to have company she didn't have the heart to deny him.

"Some hot tea will take the chill away, and then you can go on home again."

He excused himself to go to the kitchen, shutting the door to the study so the warmth of the room wouldn't lessen. She was thankful he'd not taken her to the blue parlor, where the memories were so thick and sweet they'd likely overwhelm her. As it was, she fought against fresh heartache when faced with the room Jack had used the most.

Here his fishing rods were visible, angled against a paneled wall. His spectacles—had he forgotten them?—lay atop a ledger. And his books, so many of them—who would read and treasure them now?

354

Lord, help. She shut her eyes, clinging to the tiny scrap of faith that things would be better in time.

Beyond the nearest window, snow layered a deep sill, and a tiny redbird perched like a bit of holiday whimsy. It began to sing, easing her a bit. Careful to avoid Jack's desk, she sought a chair by the fire and listened for Sol's footfalls. He seemed to be taking a long time.

The warmth of the hearth . . . one too many sleepless nights . . . the deep shadows of the room lulled her. Eyes closed, she surrendered to the welcome haze of sleep.

"Ellie, love."

The words seemed to come from a great distance. Was she dreaming? Someone had hold of her hand. Coming slowly awake, she focused on the firelit silhouette of a man kneeling in front of her. Broad of shoulder. Head slightly bent.

Her whole world shifted and gave way.

Jack.

In the turmoil of the two months since the flatboat's sinking, his memory of her had become muted. Now her nearness stole Jack's breath. The sight of her, so vulnerable in sleep, so fragile-looking in the largeness of his Windsor chair, wrenched his heart. Her head was bowed like a broken flower stem, as if her fur-lined bonnet was too heavy, her gloved hands folded in her lap. He was reminded of how fragile life was, how everything could sway and slip away at the slightest instant.

He'd not wanted to scare the wits out of her, but there was no way around it when she'd thought him dead. And so he came back to her as gently as he could. On bended knee. By the light of the fire. Taking hold of her hand.

"Ellie, love."

Her eyes met his, brilliantly blue and disbelieving. Afraid. Reaching out ever so slowly, she touched his bristled jaw as if to make sure she wasn't dreaming. "Jack?"

Throat tight, he caught her fingers in his own, tugging off her glove and planting a kiss on her palm. "Aye, Ellie. I've come back—but I couldn't tell you."

The pain etched across her face cut him. "But I thought—the keelboat's sinking—"

"It happened, just like the papers said." He looked away from her, still haunted. Even the memory of the wind and the waves was terrifying. "I should have died that day on the river. Only two of us survived." Somehow he'd slept through the start of the midnight storm that fateful eve. Failed to hear the frantic activity outside his cabin, the call to abandon ship. Unbelievably, he'd just slept, unaware of the storm and the bitter irony of it all.

He'd been sleeping through the storm his whole life.

When he'd finally come awake, it had nearly been too late. He'd grabbed the black oarsman flailing nearest him in the raging water and begun a desperate swim to the ice-encrusted shore.

"It was my second warning. The first was in the woods last spring, when a tree almost crushed me along the turnpike." He swallowed hard, amazed at the clarity of hindsight. "A man only has so many chances."

She looked stunned, clearly trying to grasp all that he'd told her. "How did you come so far? You must have lost everything in the sinking—"

"We relied on the goodness of strangers along the way, sought refuge at farms and other places. I told no one who I was. Only you and Sol—and the slave I saved from drowning—know I'm alive."

"The man I saw with Solomon at the stables? No one else?"

"Dead men arouse no suspicions. And that's how it has to remain."

Her eyes registered alarm. "Are you involved with what's happened at Broad Oak, then? The fire? The runaways?"

"Aye, I'll not lie to you. I forged free papers for all those at Broad Oak willing to run and set fire to the warehouse. Sol acts as my eyes and ears during daylight hours, and I move after dark."

"But—why?"

For a moment he couldn't speak, his anguish was so fresh. "Chloe haunts me day and night. The very hour she died, my father and Wade were drunk in town, and my mother pleaded a headache and locked herself in her room. Only Sally sat with Chloe till the end."

She looked at her lap, tears streaming down her face.

"And then there's Brunot."

Her head came up, her damp gaze searching. "Dr. Brunot?"

He let go of her hand. He'd already said too much. Chloe's loss alone clawed at him. Coupled with the doctor's, it caused the rage churning inside him to burn bright, hardening him and turning him into his father. Ruthless. Cunning. Relentless. Not the new man in Christ he had become. Not at peace but at war. He stood, stepping away from her as she got to her feet.

"Jack, please. You're not only destroying Broad Oak . . . what you hate . . . you're destroying yourself. I beg of you—"

"Go home, Ellie. Go back to your safe, sane life. I'm naught but a Turlock with the Turlock taint, and it's all I'll ever be."

"That's a lie!" She faced him, fury framing her features. "You may bear the Turlock name, but Christ has made a different way for you—you're to walk as He walked. You lose nothing by being quiet and leaving all to Him. Don't dishonor Him or Chloe's memory—" She broke off, stumbling over the beloved name. "Don't destroy my love for you. I'll gladly be your wife, bear your children, stand by you. But I can do none of those things if you're de—"

"Dead, Ellie? I'm glad you have no illusions about how this will play out."

"And you would choose that over a full life? A blessed life?" Her gaze held his. "Then mayhap you're not the man I thought you were. The man I told my father I wanted to marry."

He went completely still. "You told him? About us?"

"I needn't have said a thing. Somehow he knew, as all wise fathers do."

"And will you tell him about today? Finding me alive and well?"

"Alive? Yes. But not well. And I'll not leave here till you promise you'll do no more harm to Broad Oak or yourself." She glanced out the window, more distraught than he'd ever seen her. "'Tis snowing harder, and my father and Ansel will soon come looking for me. What will you do then? You can't hide forever." She extended a hand to him entreatingly. "I don't want to lose you again, Jack. I can't bear it a second time. Burying Chloe was heartache enough."

Inwardly he reeled, her pleas chipping away at his resolve. He'd come back fully expecting to find her wed to Daniel Cameron. Instead she was here. Proving her love for him. Staying steadfast. He reached for her with the same desperation he'd felt in the icy water to stay afloat, holding her so close the rhythm of her racing pulse felt like his own.

"Promise me, Jack."

He rested his cheek against the silk of her hair, and all the light seemed to leech from his soul. He could promise nothing. "It's not safe for you to be here any longer, Ellie. There are things happening at Broad Oak and elsewhere you know nothing about."

He felt dazed. Bone weary. The days and nights since the sinking had been an endless blur. *Kindle a candle at both ends and it will soon go out.* The Irish saying returned to him, full of worry and warning. Stepping away from her, he opened a desk drawer and removed some papers and a small box, feeling time tick against him.

Ellie watched his sure movements, marveling that while she couldn't stop trembling, Jack showed an unnerving calm. Firelight gilded his hair and his winter-tanned features, calling out deep shadows of sleeplessness beneath his eyes.

"If something should happen to me, if my father comes upon these papers, he'll destroy them. I want you to take them to New Hope and keep them there."

Confused, the pain in her heart building, she took the documents, her reluctant gaze making out the lettering of a will and deed of property.

"Your father approached me months ago about the sale of River Hill. I'd meant it for Chloe but have since made it out to him. I want it to be his—yours—if it can't be mine."

She felt a strange resistance override her surprise. Her father had approached him? Why?

River Hill means nothing to me without you. Though she tried to hold them back, her tears spotted the papers, making the ink blot and run.

Laying the documents aside, he took something from his pocket.

She spoke past the catch in her throat. "A posy ring?"

"Aye, the one my grandfather the judge gave his bride." He slipped the ring on the third finger of her left hand, a near-perfect fit. The width and weight of it seemed to carry a promise. His voice was oddly rough, as if the words came hard for one unused to tender things. "With this ring, I'm asking you to be my bride. To live here and make a better life. A faith-filled life. To turn River Hill into what it once was—a place of beauty. And peace."

The words seemed solemn as a wedding vow. She stood on tiptoe and pressed her mouth to his, sealing a covenant wrought in words, if not in church. Though she'd tried to forget the wonder of his kisses, their sweet roughness stole her breath all over again. And then, without another word, he took her gently by the arm to the waiting sleigh.

From his perch in the cupola, Ansel could make out the dark lines of Ellie's cutter slicing a new path across the white-washed landscape toward New Hope. Relief tempered his anxious mood. He'd wanted to go after her as the winter light dwindled and she'd not come back.

Once home, she'd likely shed her wraps and go into the study. She'd been spending a lot of time there, not talking much but reading, as if she sought the comfort of their parents' presence and the escape of books.

She'd become so fragile since Chloe's death. And losing Jack Turlock seemed a blow she couldn't recover from. Ellie's feelings ran deep once her heart was won, much like his own. He felt the need to get her alone, confide in her about Sarah Nancarrow. The letter from England rested in his breast pocket and was fraying around the edges, he'd read it so many times. But Sarah would have to wait.

Now it was dusk, and the maids had been busy for half an hour, turning the house bright, bringing dozens of tapers to life. The scent of beeswax, pine, and spices was particularly heady. He could hear Mari's high Welsh lilt in greeting and Ellie's soft answer as she came into the foyer.

Bowing his head, he breathed a prayer of thanks and a petition for any who'd been waiting for him to light the signal lamp. The rivers were nigh frozen now and could be walked across without great risk, or so he hoped. Just two winters past, a young mother, her baby bound to her back, had crossed the Monongahela near River Hill. The river's center had turned fragile, spilling them into the icy current, and she'd had to claw and crawl her way across. Hands and feet bleeding from the passage, she'd finally collapsed on shore.

Thankfully, Sol had found the mother and child and brought them to New Hope. Judith and little Tice had stayed for months before they'd been well enough to go north. The Ballantynes had considered letting them stay on, but bounty hunters had turned vigilant—and more vicious—bringing an end to the matter. Ansel recalled his mother's weeping at their leaving, as she so often did when fugitives moved beyond the relative safety of New Hope.

Despite the fear shadowing him, his hands were uncommonly steady of late when he lit the cupola. Tonight he prayed the ice would hold. That Ellie's broken heart would mend. That no more cryptic notes would be sent to him, warning, threatening, just like Brunot had received at the last. The doctor had become a hunted man . . . a haunted man.

And so had he.

Ellie came up the staircase, so shaken by Jack's reappearance she felt the news was written on her face. Voices filtered down from overhead. Was the attic full again? If she ran into Andra or Mama, she could simply blame the cold for her red cheeks and trembling.

She reached the second-floor landing as Andra and Peyton started down from the third floor. Hurriedly she made it to her room, slipping inside and shutting the door as quietly as she could. She leaned against it, willing her thoughts to be still, wishing her heart would follow. But she could do little but fall to her knees by the crackling hearth. For long minutes she sat locked in prayer, her petitions a muddle of joy and disbelief.

And terrible fear.

34

To him that you tell your secret you resign your liberty.

PROVERB

The dining room, bedecked with greenery, shone softly with candlelight, the best china and French crystal luminous. Mamie had outdone herself with one course after another, keeping them long at table. Ellie spooned her Christmas pudding at meal's end, feeling stuffed with secrets as much as holiday fare. Beneath her bodice, the posy ring dangled on a thin slip of silk ribbon, an ever-present reminder of Jack. If not for that small token, she would have sworn she'd dreamed up that snowbound hour at River Hill the day before.

Her gaze roamed the room, resting on Peyton. Her older brother seemed absolutely besotted. Beside him, Penelope Cameron was clearly enjoying his monopolizing, cheeks red as the holly berries adorning the mantel. Next to her, Andra was eyeing the mistletoe—and Alec Duncan—warily. Ellie's heart twisted for him . . . and Mina. Ansel, usually attentive, seemed preoccupied, even distant, tonight.

Her spirits sank further when she came to Elspeth. Her enigmatic aunt was being her most charming, centered between Daniel and his father. Would that she attend to the widowed Cullen instead of the married Henry. Ellie felt a nudge of sympathy for Isabel, who was surely aware of her husband's dalliances. Perhaps this explained the deep bitterness Ellie had sensed in her at Broad Oak.

"Elinor, may I?" Daniel was looking down at her, extending an arm. She gave him a small smile, thinking how shocked he'd be—how shocked they'd all be—if they knew Jack was back.

Once dinner was over, they gathered in the parlor where the Yule log was lit, and Ansel took up his fiddle, giving Ellie a questioning look as if wishing she'd join in. But she simply sought a seat on the sofa nearest the hearth as he tightened his bow. Soon the firelit room resounded with a lively Scottish jig.

Thankfully, Daniel wouldn't ask her to partner with him, as she was still mourning Chloe, if not Jack. Her dress, usually so festive on Christmas Day, was a deep purple, almost black, and served as a reminder. With twelve of them present, Daniel wouldn't lack for partners, at least. Mina was dancing with Alec Duncan now and looking more animated by the minute.

Her parents passed in front of her, and Ellie felt the brush of Mama's brocade gown. Mama was smiling at something Da had said, regarding him intently when they slowed to a waltz, in perfect time with his steps. The way her father was looking at her mother reminded Ellie of Jack. There was fire and steel in his gaze, tempered by tenderness. She'd witnessed their quiet exchange for years but had never understood the depths of it till now.

Watching them, she wondered without end how Jack was spending his Christmas. If he would honor her plea. He should be here in this very room, having partaken of their fine supper, daring to dance with her, experiencing the joy of family and friends in ways he'd never known. Oh, what a cold, comfortless Christmas it was likely to be at River Hill with him in hiding . . .

At the anguished thought came the faintest rattle of glass like the tinkling of a chime. And then, in another breath, a tremendous boom seized the room. The dancing ceased. Ansel's bow slid off the strings. Ellie's pulse picked up in rhythm, strenuous as the reel he'd just abandoned. Absently she put a hand to her bodice, feeling the posy ring beneath.

Her father looked west. "Broad Oak, mayhap."

Ellie felt a sickening certainty it had to do with Jack. She took a deep breath, fumbling with her fan, afraid her own culpability was splayed across her face. She so wanted to share the joy of Jack's return as well as the burden it wrought. That he was bent on ruining Broad Oak—foiling his father and Wade—she now knew without a doubt. The Turlocks' legacy of violence and misdeeds spanned generations and seemed unstoppable.

Elspeth settled on the sofa beside her, arranging her pea-cock-blue skirts to their best advantage. "Elinor, you look so very pale."

Ellie swallowed down a sigh. The fact that she was sitting knee to knee with Henry Turlock's mistress restored her color, surely. "You're kind to take notice, Aunt," she said politely, nearly flinching in anticipation of the next boom.

"I saw that you ate little at dinner. I'm afraid not even all this commotion can put a dent in my appetite." Mamie had come into the room, serving syllabub, and Elspeth reached eagerly for a cup. "Peyton tells me your dear papa may be whisking you away to Scotland ere long."

"Oh?" Surprised, Ellie looked to where her father had been standing, only to find he'd left the room. "I'd love to see the land of his birth, Highland Perthshire especially. There's said to be a portrait of Niel Ballantyne and his fiddle in the great hall of Blair Castle . . ." Her voice trailed off. She'd not wanted to confide such things, but Elspeth's presence always rattled her beyond reasoning.

"That might be just the remedy for what ails you." Elspeth's voice turned silk soft in consolation. "New vistas, new memories. Even my short trip from York to Pittsburgh has done wonders for me."

Ellie said nothing to this, relieved when Ansel resumed playing, this time a slow air. Thankfully, no other noises rattled the windowpanes. She looked toward the wavy glass to the snowy world beyond and said another silent prayer, trying to latch on to the wonder of Christmas.

Joy to the world.

The next day brought high winds and blowing snow—and word that another of Broad Oak's costly Irish stills had exploded on Christmas Day, shutting down the entire operation. The *Pittsburgh Gazette* shouted the story in bold black, telling how the great numbers of livestock there, fattened on the spent mash left over from the distilling, had gotten loose and were running amuck over Allegheny County.

Peyton had chuckled when he'd read the news aloud, envisioning the inebriated animals unsteady of foot. Even the waterfowl about Broad Oak were said to be flapping drunkenly, and there were precious few slaves left to restore order. Ellie was not amused, her scattered thoughts pinned on Jack.

Now in late afternoon, curled into a Windsor chair by the study fire, Ellie reread the opening lines of *Pamela* twice, three times. But the passionate love story failed to hold her. The scratch of her father's pen stole her concentration, as did Mama's soft humming as she sewed across the room.

In the past she'd always welcomed winter, if for no other reason than it freed her father and brothers from the demands of boatyard and mercantile. With the rivers frozen and every boat locked in ice, they'd not see the spring thaw till March. By then she hoped to be a bride. Settled at River Hill. Perhaps expecting a child.

Or in Scotland, if Da had his way.

Jack's posy ring lay warm against her skin. She longed to slip it on her finger, slip free of the secrecy of hiding it. Her prayers to either confess Jack's reappearing or stay silent clamored inside her without answer. Now the silence, the nearness of her parents, seemed to call for a confession. She cleared her throat and set her book aside, beset by misgivings. Would she betray Jack by doing so? Or help him in some way?

She started to speak as a timid knock sounded. When the door opened, Ellie shed her resolve. A worried Gwyn appeared, eyes on Da. "Pardon, sir, but the sheriff is here to see you."

More news from Broad Oak? Breath held, Ellie uncurled from her knot, smoothing her skirts as her father stood and Mama looked up from her sewing. Sheriff Ramsay's ponderous form filled the doorway, several aldermen behind him in dark greatcoats and hats.

"Sheriff . . . gentlemen," her father said in greeting. "What brings you out in this weather?"

There was the slightest pause. "I wish I had a better reason than this . . ." Ramsay hesitated, his expression almost apologetic as he gave a nod to Ellie and her mother before turning back to the man looming large behind his desk. "As acting sheriff of Allegheny County, I have a warrant for your arrest."

Ellie took a step back as if buffeted by the words, her dress hem brushing the dog irons. But she barely noticed the heat scorching her linen stockings. Her gaze ricocheted between

Mama's shocked features and her father's stoicism, his expression never wavering.

Ramsay took out a paper—the warrant? "We also have reason to search the premises, beginning with the house."

"On what grounds?" Da asked quietly.

"Harboring slaves." Ramsay's tone turned cold. "Not only harboring but equipping them with firearms, a federal offense." He reached into his breast pocket and withdrew something wrapped in linen. Uncovering it, he held a pistol aloft. "We have the slave in custody who named you as the source of the weapon. You well know the penalty for arming fugitives, Ballantyne."

Suddenly nauseous, Ellie fastened her gaze on the pistol—the very one she'd secured beneath the chaise seat that fearful day on the back road. 'Twas Mama's weapon, rarely used. The pearl handle and markings couldn't be mistaken even from several feet away. "I was last in possession of that pistol." Her voice, maddeningly feeble in her alarm, was directed at Ramsay, though her eyes sought the safety of Da's own.

Her father turned toward her, bade her stay silent with a single piercing look.

The sheriff's expression hardened. "Then perhaps I should take you both into custody—"

"Nae." The stern word erected a wall as her father cast a grim glance at the men. "Do what you will with me, but leave my family alone."

Stepping aside, the sheriff motioned to an alderman bearing shackles.

Ellie's heart clenched and didn't let go. Did they think her father posed a threat? Might run? All seemed to freeze as a commotion erupted in the foyer.

Andra pushed past the throng of men, stiff with fury as she stepped into the room. "Shackles?" Her voice swelled with censure as she leveled Ramsay with a look. "Are you insane? Or simply stupid?" She snatched the shackles away and flung them into the hearth's fire, where they clattered noisily against the grate. "This is a Ballantyne, *not* a blackguard! Not a Turlock!"

There was a stunned silence. Ramsay's gaze became a glare of ice. Undaunted, Andra stood between their father and the men, only retreating when he spoke a few terse words in Scots.

"Caumie doun, dochtor."

The quiet admonishment touched Ellie, but she was drowning in too much dismay to heed it. While two of the men began to open doors and search the study and ground floor, another two hastened upstairs. Fear left a sour taste in Ellie's mouth as she watched their ascent. The attic was full of slaves—three had come Christmas Eve, the fourth Christmas Day.

Desperate, she looked toward Ansel. His restraining hand was on Andra's arm as the sheriff escorted their father outside to a waiting coach, its black lines forbidding, the horses' breaths pluming in the cold.

Mama was standing alone in the study doorway, her head bent. Was she praying? Silent tears coursed down her cheeks. Ellie groped for a handkerchief in her dress pocket, her own face wet.

The foyer was closing in now, whirling and blackening. Her father's sturdy form disappeared into the coach's confines, swallowed from view by the sudden shutting of the door.

"What the devil is happening here?"

'Twas Peyton's voice, as aggrieved as Andra's had been, resounding to the rafters as he came in the back door. Ellie latched on to the strength of it even as her own was ebbing. But the darkness proved too deep, and she let go, tumbling into an inky abyss.

The pungent scent of smelling salts brought Ellie round, but it was more shame over her weakness that propped her upright. Ansel hovered over her where she lay on the study sofa, concern etched across his handsome face. The room was empty. The house was empty. She felt it—and feared it.

"El, I need you, never more than now." He raked a hand through his hair, eyes darting to the study door as if expecting the sheriff to reappear. "Peyton and Andra have gone to town with Mother to the jail. A few aldermen are searching the grounds, starting at the river's edge."

She listened, breathing in hartshorn and camphor and the scent of cloves, her head coming clear.

"I want you to ride to the mill right away." Glancing away, he called for Mari and asked her to fetch a cape before lowering his voice again. "The runaways are hiding there—"

"They weren't found in the attic, then? By the sheriff's men?"

"Nay." His features hinted at impatience. "There's no time for questions. Ride to the mill and tell them to slip through the woods and cross the creek, heading north to Ferry Road. They're to wait in the brush and watch for a wagon bearing hogsheads. The driver will conceal them and take them to safety, Lord willing."

He helped her to her feet, enfolded her in the cape Mari brought, and fastened the braided collar. "Your mare is saddled and waiting behind the stables. I won't be here when you return."

The cryptic words swam round her head, silencing the queries that sprang to her lips. Without a look back, she hurried toward the stables, shivering, stumbling.

The journey to the mill took twice as long with sleet spattering her face and the wind working to tear her hood free. Fear beat a suffocating rhythm inside her all the way. Would the sheriff's men follow?

At last the old edifice rose up, its dark timbers starkly ugly against the melting snow. Likely the poor, shivering souls within were huddled behind the secret door in back of the wheel. An eerie silence hovered as she tethered her horse to a laurel bush and fought the tremor of apprehension that urged her to flee.

A tentative push to the door left her overcome by the odor of old grain and dampness and the drip of water. When a rough hand clasped her arm, pulling her inside, she gasped. Something hard and cold pressed against her temple.

"P-please," she stuttered wildly. "I-I mean no harm."

She heard a terse oath as both hand and pistol fell away.

"Ellie, forgive me—I couldn't see who approached."

Jack.

Her surprise was so great she fell against him. Clutching his coat with shaking hands, she tried to steady her voice as Ansel's instructions spilled out of her. "You must hurry—the sheriff's men are searching the property as we speak."

In moments, without another word, he'd opened the trap door behind the giant wheel. Four fugitives shuffled past by the light of a lone lantern, each clutching blankets, making her think they'd left the attic hours ago. Ellie stood silent as they passed, emotion closing her throat. When they'd almost reached the door, Jack asked them to wait.

Bending his head, he began to pray. Haltingly. Brokenly. Though the words seemed wrenched from his very soul, a sense of wonder pervaded the still place, beginning in Ellie's thankful heart. "Almighty Father, you created all men equal, and for that liberty we give you heartfelt thanks. These fugitives are in your faithful hands. Guide them safely to freedom and lives spent in Your service. For this we plead Your everlasting mercy."

It was a prayer she'd heard uttered by Dr. Brunot many

times in the last few months, before he'd gone missing. While she pondered it, Jack said "Amen" and led the group out, leaving her to murmur her own prayer on their behalf.

In minutes he returned, shutting the door soundly. His beard scraped her cheek as he took her in his arms. "What's happening at New Hope?"

She shut her eyes, still woozy. "The sheriff and his men came with a warrant and a pistol—the one the bounty hunters took from me that day along the back road. They claim my father gave it to a slave, so they've arrested him. I feared when they searched the house—"

"Ben overheard Wade say the sheriff was planning to arrest your father today, and he told Sol." His arms tightened about her. "I rode over in the night to give a warning. Ansel asked me to bring the runaways here in his stead. He felt his absence would arouse suspicions if the sheriff came."

She could only imagine Ansel's shock at Jack's appearing. As if reading her thoughts, he murmured, "I had a rough go of it convincing him to trust me—and making sure no one else saw me. We transferred the runaways soon after."

"You've been here since last night?" Beneath her hands he felt chilled to the bone, his clothes seeped with cold.

"I'm only concerned about the fugitives . . . your father." He brushed back a stray curl from her face. "You."

"My father—" Her voice broke. "What will happen to him now?"

"Your father has been incriminated on false evidence. He's done nothing wrong except shame those who are cowards about their convictions, who won't make a stand against slavery. There's a proslavery ring in Allegheny County that is working to undermine abolitionists. Ramsay and other city leaders are among them. My father and Wade are said to be the founders of the group."

"Then Da has little chance—"

He put a finger to her lips. "I'm doing what I can to distract them at Broad Oak and elsewhere. And I'm privy to their plans."

"But if your father or Wade realize you're alive . . ." Overcome, she pressed her cheek against the smooth wool of his coat.

"I'm simply giving them a taste of their own medicine. And I have no fear for my own life. Not since coming to Christ. As the old saint Whitefield said, we are immortal until our work is done." He took her gently by the shoulders. "Go home, Ellie. I've more work to do. Pray for your father. The fugitives. Pray for me."

35

Love can hope where reason would despair.

LORD GEORGE LYTTELTON

Nearly dawn, it was the day of Silas Ballantyne's arraignment. So wary the hair on the back of his neck bristled, Jack positioned Ben at the edge of the clearing to act as sentinel. Though Jack had yet to disturb the soil, the shovel was heavy in his hand and sweat slicked his brow. A band of sunlight stretched across the silent meadow, promising to melt the remaining snow.

His breathing quickened as he turned the shovel over on its side and scraped free a sheen of ice. The grass beneath was missing, and mud met his gaze. A fresh grave, just as he'd suspected. Not only the lawman's of old.

Brunot's.

Heartsick, he thrust the shovel into frigid ground. His father must have been hopelessly drunk to have planted both bodies in the same place. And a hurried job it had been. Casting a look at Ben to make sure he was acting as lookout and was spared the grisly sight, Jack began to dig.

374

For all its gilt and glitter, Sloane's Boardinghouse had a slatternly reputation, its posture on the edge of Pittsburgh a reminder of its removal from polite society. Though a far cry from the Palais-Royal or the Château-Gontier Jack's father frequented when in Paris, its lush, whiskey-laden rooms boasted courtesans just the same. Till today, Jack had never been inside, though one step into the foyer shook him to the core. He spied a prominent attorney's profile as the man disappeared for a tryst in an upstairs room.

He'd planned his visit carefully, knowing his father and most of Pittsburgh would be in court for Silas's arraignment. Wade and Isabel would have gone with Henry, not wanting to miss the glorious descent of a man so many respected, even revered. Jack wagered Elspeth would shun the courtroom drama and remain behind at Sloane's. Henry would likely join her here once the proceedings were over. Elspeth Lee provided a welcome distraction from all the chaos swirling around them.

His father, flummoxed and furious over the destruction at Broad Oak, had hired bounty hunters to track those responsible. He'd also ordered another still from Ireland and sent Marcum to Kentucky to bring up more slaves. Henry Turlock was not a man to be daunted for long.

Jack removed his hat and dangled it in one hand while running callused fingers over his beard with the other. The gilt mirror opposite reflected a well-dressed man, slightly gaunt, his whiskers a handy ruse. Shadows rimmed his eyes, bespeaking one too many sleepless nights and a great deal of mischief. He was growing weary of playing the game, and he couldn't hide forever. Someone might well recognize him here and the news would spread like fever.

A sudden movement from a side parlor caught his eye. Silk skirts rustling, a woman came forward, rouge marking high cheekbones the color of her ruby gown. Madame Sloane? "Welcome to my establishment, Mister . . . ?"

Jack ignored the question. "I'm here to see Elspeth Lee."

"Miss Lee?" She seemed surprised, slanting him a shrewd glance and reaching for a bell on a marble-top table. "Is she expecting you?"

The appearance of a maid spared him an answer. When Madame turned back to him, a question in her eyes, he said, "I won't be long." But in truth, he'd be here as long as it took.

"Very well, then. If you'll wait in the red parlor, Anna will escort her down." She began a slow, unnerving walk around him. "But I must ask that you leave all weapons at the door or in my safekeeping while you're here." Extending a hand, she waited as he reluctantly withdrew a pistol from his greatcoat and a knife from his boot.

In moments, he was hemmed in as the maid closed the parlor's double doors and Elspeth Lee stood facing him. Though he'd only seen her at a distance, he knew she was a handsome woman. But the similarities linking her to Ellie's lovely mother ended there. The sisters simply bore the same remarkable eyes, as blue as the Monongahela on the clearest day, and the same lushness of figure.

"Have we . . . met?" She was taking his measure, her gaze warming with unmistakable interest.

"I'm Henry Turlock's son Jack." He felt the same reluctance of old at the admission.

Her brows arched. "The one who drowned at the headwaters of the Missouri?" She was smiling at him slightly, as if privy to some secret joke. "Well, I must say, you're in fine form for a dead man."

He nearly smiled back at her as she sat down upon a near sofa and smoothed her skirts, her gaze swinging back to him warily.

Taking the chair opposite, he set his hat aside, gaze roaming a room made darker by several shaded windows. "I'm here to talk about your future," he began thoughtfully, remembering all that Ansel had told him. He chose his words carefully, not wanting to rile her but simply back her into an uncomfortable corner. "I thought you'd want to know that my father will soon be in the Allegheny County Jail on charges of murder—"

"Murder!" She seemed amused again—and disbelieving—though she cast a quick look at the door as if fearing someone might be listening.

He kept his voice low. "Murder, aye. A far cry from the charges of petty thievery against you." He let the words take hold, rued the slight hardening of her features. "Since Madame Sloane likes to be paid on time, you'll soon be out on the street without my father's backing. You can't return to York, as your brother has a warrant out for your arrest. Even now your transgressions there are circulating in the papers."

He reached into his coat pocket, removed a copy of the *York Gazette*, and placed it on the table between them. "The money you stole from your brother's smithy has no doubt run out, making my father's offer to keep you here a very convenient, if temporary, solution. You'll get no help from the Ballantynes, as there is still the matter of a fire and the death of your infant son between you—"

"How dare you!" She lashed him with the words, all levity gone. "That was years ago! Nothing was ever proven, no charges filed."

"All sins cast a long shadow, as the Irish say. My father is no exception. Whiskey and women have ever been his downfall." He leaned back in his chair and studied her, feeling her own alarm was but a mirror of his own. The lovely Elspeth Lee was clearly trapped, as was he. He'd taken a terrible risk talking about his father. Elspeth could tell Henry everything before the day was out, and he'd hunt Jack down and kill him. Or have someone else do it in his stead. Even now his father's warning of years before turned him to ice.

If you tell a soul, you'll share the same grave.

Since the sheriff was in league with Henry and Wade and those who comprised the Pittsburgh kidnapping ring, Jack doubted an arrest would be made. He had to act quickly. Stay hidden. Everything hinged on the response of the woman facing him.

"There's a remedy to all this." He forged on, aware of the rush of heat beneath his damp collar. "I'll repay your debt to your brother in York and provide you a handsome allowance, enough to live on comfortably the rest of your days. But you'll have to cooperate with me."

Her chin lifted. "What makes you think I can be bought?"

"What makes you think I'd think otherwise? You have no history of doing things out of the goodness of your heart."

At his rebuke, she turned her face away, staring into the hearth's fire. "The truth is, no matter what I've done, I'm fond of my nieces and nephews. They've shown me more kindness than most—and precious little judgment."

"Then you need to help their father."

"Help him? How can I?" She sank back on the sofa as if all the fight had gone out of her. "Your father is determined to bring the Ballantynes to ruin. He told me so within these very walls."

"I'll wager he told you a great deal more that can be used in the Ballantynes' favor."

"Only that he forced a free black man to lie about the pistol or else be sold south—the very gun Elinor was carrying along the lane when he sent his slave catchers after her. Apparently the sheriff is all too willing to believe the ruse."

"I want you to testify against my father. And the sheriff."

"What?" The fear in her face almost smote his resolve. "You must be mad! You'd actually betray your father?" Her gaze turned smoldering. "You're certainly no saint to be speaking to me of my sins."

"I never claimed to be. But God in His mercy has forgiven me. And I'm bound by Him to tell the truth." Jack reached for his hat. "You have until the Ballantyne trial begins to make up your mind. My offer to repay your debt and shelter you stands. But not a word to anyone."

She stood up, her demeanor still far from obliging. "How will I know when the legal proceedings start?"

"I'll send word to you here when I find out."

If my father doesn't silence us first.

"Your mouth—it's bleeding." Ansel's concern barely dinted Ellie's misery as he fished a handkerchief from his coat pocket.

She'd bitten her lip repeatedly, trying to quell the emotion that roiled inside her. Each step into the filthy jail was like a blow. Even in winter, the chill failed to suppress the stench, making Ellie glad she'd eaten nothing at breakfast lest she lose it on the straw-lined floor.

Mama had gone first, into a small anteroom off the sheriff's office. Sand sifted through an hourglass on a crude table by the barred door, marking what little time remained. At the last moment, no doubt brought on by the incident in New Hope's parlor, Ramsay had denied Andra entry, and she remained outside in the coach with Peyton.

When Ellie saw her father bound from ankle to wrist, the long chains grinding and dragging at his barest movement, something broke inside her. He was unshaven, clad in the same clothes he'd had on when arrested four days prior, terribly disheveled, and seeming a stranger. Shackled so tightly his wrists were raw and bleeding in places, he couldn't embrace her, and she sensed his keen regret. With a little cry, she threw her arms about him as Ansel stood by silently.

"When all this is over, we'll go to Scotlain, aye?" His lilt settled over her, his words sure and steadfast. "Home to the Highlands." He pressed his bristled cheek to hers. "Ye ken what the Buik says. 'The Lord is my rock, and my fortress, and my deliverer; my God, my strength, in whom I will trust.'"

"I ken." Her voice was small as a child's. Her faith felt just as small. She longed to tell him about Jack, upon whom she'd pinned her hopes, but she was checked by a startling thought. Who was her Savior at such a time? None but Christ. The message in her father's eyes was unmistakable.

Fear not.

"Time is up." Ramsay was at the door. Unsmiling. Cold.

Ellie's hands slid down her father's wrinkled greatcoat. She was unable to leave him with a smile or a reassuring word.

Ten o'clock in the morning. Court proceedings had begun. Seated in a hired coach parked in an alley by the courthouse, Jack flexed his cold hands and wished he could stretch his cramped legs. The coach curtains were closed, denying him the view he craved—the sight of Elspeth Lee's arrival. She was to meet him here in the alley and they would enter the courtroom together. Excruciating minutes ticked by, confirming what he feared.

She wasn't coming.

He'd have to face his father alone without a shred of evidence to back him up save the gravesites. Decomposed as Brunot's body was without benefit of a casket, the authorities might well dismiss it altogether. Given so many were in league with his father, he didn't doubt it. His own life was in danger the moment he stepped from the coach. Elspeth Lee had likely told Henry everything.

He clasped the door handle and gave it an aggravated turn as dread pooled in his belly. *His mischief shall return upon his own head, and his violent dealing shall come down upon his own pate.* The Scripture, unbidden, solaced him not a whit.

Ellie kept her eyes down, hands folded in her lap. As with the jail, she'd never been inside the courtroom, and its austereness stole her breath. Not even the presence of two hundred or more onlookers—many shoulder to shoulder in the gallery above—could warm the large space. This was the place of hardened criminals. Not her beloved father, who sat in a wooden box at the front of the room as if guilty of some contagion, a bailiff nearby.

Beside her, Peyton whispered about the proceedings as if to ease her, but anxiety left her struggling to breathe beneath too-tight stays.

Mama, clear-eyed and firm of gaze, was to her left, hemmed in by Andra and Ansel. Behind them sat the Camerons and Reverend Herron. Ellie kept her eyes on her father, wavering only once when the Turlocks entered the room. Henry and Wade escorted the black-clad Isabel up the aisle to sit opposite the Ballantynes, creating a stir. Ellie suppressed a shudder. The only Turlock she longed to lock eyes with was missing. She'd last seen Jack at the mill six days past.

The bang of a gavel seemed to shatter her heart. Someone was asking her father his plea to the charge of arming a slave. *Not guilty.* Despite his unkempt appearance and several days' growth of beard, Da sat straight of shoulder and was remarkably strong of voice, as calm as if in kirk.

His legal counsel huddled in a tight knot to the left of Judge Treadway, the sheriff and a great many aldermen in the front row facing the jury. Too sore to watch, Ellie lowered her head, eyes fastened on the beaded reticule in her lap as the Negro who'd incriminated her father was led out and seated. At once the room grew hushed. The man appeared so beaten down, so careworn, Ellie felt a tremor of pity when she lifted her head to look at him.

The attorney stood several paces from him, as if reluctant to get too close. "Your name?"

The man stuttered and wheezed as he began. "My name is Mose, sir. I come up from New Orleans on one of Mister Ballantyne's boats."

"Can you tell the court the name of the steamer you were aboard as a stowaway?"

There was a pause. "Yes, sir—it was called the *Elinor*."

The exchange continued on for several endless minutes, sounding stilted and rehearsed. Ellie had never seen this man in her life, nor had he ever darkened New Hope's doors. When the sheriff presented the weapon, she felt a sickening dismay.

"Is this pistol familiar to you, Mose?"

He nodded vigorously. "Yes, sir. Mister Ballantyne—he give me the gun. Said to use it to help me gain freedom."

The irony of his words tore at Ellie's heart.

"And did Silas Ballantyne urge you to any action besides escaping your owner and arming yourself with this weapon?"

He hesitated, swallowed, gaze falling to his lap. "He asked me to do violence to a man named Brunot."

Brunot? Ellie held her breath as audible gasps sounded all around her. Peyton reached out a hand and clasped the bench in front of them till his knuckles whitened. Ellie expected

Andra to leap to her feet in agitation, but she simply shifted in her seat, arms crossed.

"Can you point to the man who gave you the gun?" the prosecutor asked. "Who urged you to do this violence?"

A tremulous finger pointed to Da's straight figure.

"And what did you tell him in response?"

"That I never killed no man before. That I don't know nothin' 'bout shootin' nobody. Slaves ain't allowed guns."

"But Ballantyne kept insisting you harm Dr. Brunot?"

"Yes, sir. He said he'd bring my wife and children upriver if I killed him. But I was afraid, so I told the sheriff."

"Did Ballantyne tell you why he wanted you to do this violence? A long-standing grudge, perhaps? Some other matter?"

The man's ebony eyes shone. "He said the doctor was trying to hurt slaves like me, not help 'em. That Brunot was posin' as one of them abolitionists but was really a slave catcher in disguise. Ballantyne feared Brunot would turn him in—"

"That's a lie!" A shout sounded from the gallery, firm and full of heat. It rolled to the far corners of the courtroom, drawing every ear and eye. "Silas Ballantyne neither armed this man nor killed Dr. Brunot. Henry Turlock did both."

Feeling ice-cold to her toes, Ellie braced herself for the fight to come. Jack stood looking down at them, face tight with fury, eyes fastened on Henry, who'd come to his feet. With a little cry, Isabel bent her head and leaned into Wade, stricken as much by the sight of the son she'd thought dead as by his damning accusations, surely.

"Henry Turlock is the murderer of Theo Brunot, just as he was the murderer of Cyrus O'Leary eighteen years ago, in my very presence. They share the same grave."

Henry stood, swayed. The court was in an uproar now, the din rising above the judge's pounding gavel. A door slammed shut, and Ellie caught a flash of purple out of the corner of her eye. Elspeth? Her aunt was rushing to the front of the courtroom like a woman possessed, to the very box her father sat within. Would she harm him? In defense of Henry?

Chest rising and falling beneath her cape, Elspeth swung round and faced the court. "Silas Ballantyne is indeed innocent of all charges. And this man, Mose"—she gestured toward the stunned witness—"is a free Negro who's been threatened with slavery by Henry Turlock if he fails to accuse Silas Ballantyne. Not only he himself but his wife and six children."

Ellie's focus veered between Jack still in the gallery and her aunt. Elspeth needed no theatrical stage upon which to perform. She was at her finest in a cold courtroom filled to the brim with astonished onlookers.

"Mose is a free man, bullied by authorities in Pittsburgh like *you*." She stabbed a finger toward the sheriff. "And *you*." She gestured to another man. "And the three of you." She cast a dismissive hand at a trio of aldermen before turning toward the judge.

Ellie watched her father's gaze cut to Henry Turlock, whose rugged features had turned a frightening crimson. Isabel sank back onto the bench, the brim of her bonnet concealing her face, while Wade—

"Nay!" Ellie leapt to her feet as Wade withdrew a pistol from beneath his greatcoat, resolve hardening his every feature. But the thunder of the gun's discharge snuffed her cry of warning.

Smoke powdered the air, and Da was jarred backward by the impact. Ellie felt herself sinking, her legs giving way, as Wade aimed a second pistol at Elspeth. With a strangled cry, Jack leapt from the gallery like something feral and knocked Wade to the courtroom floor.

Aldermen swarmed forward to restore order, Reverend Herron in their wake. Benumbed, Ellie watched as Peyton began catapulting over benches toward the front of the room, past hysterical women and frowning men, not caring who he pummeled to reach their father. Next to her, Ansel and Andra hovered protectively around their shaken mother.

Relief sang through Ellie. Though her father clutched his shoulder and blood was turning his coat scarlet-black, he did not appear seriously injured. The bullet meant for Elspeth had lodged in the judge's bench.

As for Jack . . .

He was looking at her across the teeming room, his relief as potent as his smile.

36

*Whatever our souls are made of, his
and mine are the same.*

EMILY BRONTË

"You ken what the Scots say about marrying in January."
Andra's voice dropped to a distressed mumble as she but-
toned the back of Ellie's gown. "We'll all catch our deaths
in the chapel today."

"Only a few guests have been invited to the short ceremony.
Far more will come to River Hill for the wedding breakfast
and reception." Ellie took a deep breath to quell the flutter
inside her, thinking of all they'd had to do in the fortnight
since the courtroom fracas. River Hill had been turned on
end in preparation and come to new life.

"You might at least have waited till Da's wound healed.
He's determined to play the Shaimit reel and might well re-
injure himself fiddling so vigorously."

"I don't think it's the cold or Da's condition that troubles
you . . ." Ellie turned round and took her sister's hands in
her own. "But my groom."

Andra's eyes were grieved. "I do wish you'd confided in me about him. Here I was thinking Jack had drowned and you'd eventually wed poor Daniel. Never in my wildest imaginings would you choose a Turlock, even if he did come back from the dead!" Slipping free of Ellie's grasp, she reached for the wedding bonnet with a little sigh. The attached veil cascaded through her hands like a frothy waterfall, the rose point lace exquisite.

"Jack is a fine man," Ellie said softly. "And Da's given his blessing."

"I ken you'd wed him, blessing or no." Carefully Andra placed the bonnet on Ellie's head and began tying the chin ribbons. "I must admit his heroics in the courtroom curried some favor, though I feared he'd break his neck jumping from the gallery like he did!"

"Feared—or hoped?" Ellie teased gently.

"No matter." Andra's eyes were a wash of green. "You'll soon melt his heart, little sister. You've never looked so lovely."

"Nor has your groom ever looked so handsome." Mama stood in the open doorway, a joyful smile aimed at both daughters, a lush bouquet in hand. "Jack is below with your father in the study. Elspeth and Isabel are keeping company with Reverend Herron's wife in the parlor."

Ellie's stomach somersaulted in surprise. "Well, wonders never cease!"

Andra's sly smile stole away her poignancy of moments before. "I'm sure that canary of mine is being duly entertained—or is providing some entertainment."

"Singing his heart out," Mama confirmed, passing Ellie the bouquet.

"Roses . . . in January?" Awed, she buried her face in the blooms, marveling at the sweet scent and rich hues. From deep crimson to pale pink, there were two dozen or more—and a sprig of white heather for luck.

"You should see the chapel," Andra said. "Filled to the brim with every hothouse flower in Allegheny County!"

Ellie looked up at Mama. "I have you and Da to thank for that, I suppose."

"'Twas your father's doing. As soon as the ceremony is over, they'll be taken to your new home. Our wish is that you'll make River Hill's garden glorious again and the old place will be like it once was." Her smile turned wistful. Opening a gloved hand, she revealed a cameo. "Isabel asked that I give you this."

In her palm nested a girl in dark ivory relief, her profile unmistakable within the elegant oval frame. On the reverse side, set in pink milk glass, was a lock of hair held in place by tiny pearls representing tears.

Chloe.

Ellie's heart ached anew. Since she'd awakened that morning, her thoughts had been consumed as much by Chloe as Jack. She wanted Chloe here. She wanted her near. Chloe's girlish hopes had brought about this day. She'd loved Jack deeply.

"'Tis yours," Mama told her. "Isabel wants you to have it. She seems quite . . . changed."

"With Henry and Wade both in jail, I don't doubt it." Andra's brows arched as she fussed with a stray thread on Ellie's skirt. "I'm surprised she's even here."

"Jack insisted," Ellie said softly. "And I agreed. Though she'll only stay for the ceremony."

"We'd best go below—'tis almost ten o'clock." Taking her by the shoulders, Mama turned Ellie toward a full-length mirror. "I daresay you're more beautiful in this gown than I was."

As delectable as a bride's cake, the heirloom dress was white tulle over pale blue silk, the full skirts adorned with rose and ribbon embroidery, cascading to her ankles in shimmery splendor. Would Jack be pleased? She'd soon see the answer in his eyes.

"I believe I'm ready." Ellie stepped away from her reflection, her bouquet trembling slightly in her gloved hand.

"Shall we pray?" Mama asked, as if sensing Ellie's need.

Joining hands, they bowed their heads, the silence sweet and expectant as the mantel clock chimed the wedding hour.

Jack stood at the front of the chapel, barely aware of the chill, overcome by a blessed intoxication that had naught to do with spirits. The heady scent of roses clung to the wintry air, and the stillness, save the hushed pattering of feet as guests arrived, felt holy. With Silas to his left and Reverend Herron to his right, he was in fine company. Even Peyton's occasional appraising stare from a front pew rolled off him like river water.

Clad in the suit he'd worn to the Ballantyne ball, Jack felt well-dressed, if a bit self-conscious. Sol had fussed over him endlessly that morning, whistling all the while, expressing his delight that everyone would descend on River Hill in the hours to come. Truly, the old house had never looked finer, and he had Sol and a great many hired help to thank when all was said and done.

His gaze rose to the chapel rafters, set in place the century before. Winter light spilled through narrow stained-glass windows, and candles were a-shimmer on every stone ledge. Here Silas Ballantyne had wed Eden Lee and had every Ballantyne baby christened in the Scots tradition. Instead of feeling out of place, Jack had an inexplicable sense that he'd come home.

His mother sat in a side pew, causing him a moment's worry. He'd wanted her to come, hoping the day's joy might ease her sadness. She met his eyes, her face half hidden beneath her darkly veiled bonnet, and he tried to smile past the tightness in his chest. Despite everything, she was his mother and he loved her. And in her own way, she cared for him.

A sudden stirring at the door caused every head to turn. Ellie stood framed in a ray of winter sunlight, looking more like an angel than a bride. His heart picked up in rhythm as she glanced his way. Silas went forward to bring her to him, joining their hands as Ansel began a hallowed air at the back of the chapel. Ellie looked up at him, eyes luminous, the lovely cameo pinned to her bodice his undoing.

He swallowed hard, felt the strengthening squeeze of her hand. The posy ring, gotten back from her the day before, was warm in his fist, the inscription circling round his head. *Keep faith till death*. And death it had nearly been. Twice.

Reverend Herron's tone was solemn yet warm with pleasure. "Do you, Sean Ciaran Turlock, take this woman, Elinor Louise Ballantyne, to be your lawfully wedded wife?"

Jack felt a sudden bumbling at Ellie's slight, questioning smile. In the excitement of the past few days, he'd forgotten to tell her that Sean was the Gaelic equivalent of Jack. "I do."

She echoed the words before they said the traditional Irish vow together. "By the power that Christ wrought from heaven, mayst thou love me. As the sun follows its course, mayst thou follow me. As light to the eye, as bread to the hungry, as joy to the heart, may thy presence be with me, oh one that I love, 'til death comes to part us asunder."

A tear slipped down her cheek. He longed to brush it away. Kiss it away. Maybe at the wedding breakfast, if there were more tears. Or tonight when they were alone. He felt befuddled as a schoolboy as he brushed back her lace veil to kiss her, contemplating what was to come. For now her nearness wrapped round his senses and made him wish the coming hours away.

The traditional Scottish wedding psalm was sung, Silas's deep voice ringing out in benediction. Reverend Herron kissed Ellie's flushed cheek as guests clapped and nodded. "A Scots custom, if not an Irish one," he said with a smile.

Raising her ringed hand, Jack kissed the third finger where the posy rested, wishing with every fiber of his being that Chloe could see their happiness.

But perhaps, somehow, she did.

When the fiddling ceased and the last guest had gone home, Ellie found herself standing in the middle of Jack's bedchamber—*their* bedchamber—listening for his footfalls. Alone in the unfamiliar, masculine room, she felt at sea. But for his distinctive clary-sage scent . . . the discarded swallowtail coat . . . the Bible atop the nightstand.

Someone had drawn the shutters and curtains, lit a fine fire, and turned down the bedcovers. Countless flowers, looking as fresh as they had in the chapel that morning, adorned vases about the firelit room, their fading fragrance subtly sweet.

Sitting down on a stool, she slipped off her shoes and wriggled her stocking-clad feet. Andra wasn't there to help her undress and manage her many layers. She supposed she'd have to hire a lady's maid. For now she had . . . Jack. He was leaning into the door frame, watching her, hands clasped behind his back as if faced with the temptation of treacle or marzipan.

"Are you feeling homesick, Ellie?"

She smiled at him. "I *am* home, Jack."

With a look of relief, he shut the door, stirring the air so that the candle flame danced. He crossed slowly to where she sat, took her hands, and gently brought her to her feet. The top of her head grazed his clean-shaven jaw. "I'm sorry there's to be no wedding journey, Ellie."

The regret in his tone bruised her. He meant till the trial was over. As a witness, he couldn't leave the county till his father was sentenced. He'd only narrowly escaped prosecution himself, given the explosions at Broad Oak.

She touched his cheek, thinking how little a honeymoon trip mattered. "We'll stay snug at River Hill till spring. Then the rivers will be navigable again and we'll take a steamer to New Orleans like we planned."

"On the *Elinor*."

"Indeed." She began untying his cravat, the intimacy of the moment making her feel very married. "With you by my side, Da won't deny me the dangerous pleasure."

Leaning in, he kissed the bare hollow of her shoulder. "He's already talking of christening a boat for a grandchild."

"Oh?" She knew it to be true. Her father hadn't stopped smiling all day. "'Twill be at least nine months till that happens."

His eyes were roguish. Merry. "I'd hate to disappoint him and be a day late." Reaching out, he doused the candle flame with his fingertips before returning her to his warm embrace. He kissed her as he'd not done all day, though the strength of it told her he'd wanted to. Badly.

"Ellie, love . . ."

She softened like wax beneath his hands, every inch of her flushed with love and longing. She felt she'd come home. She was Jack Turlock's bride. And tonight, at least, she never wanted to leave River Hill, wedding journey or otherwise.

Epilogue

Man's yesterday may never be like his morrow.

The *Elinor* docked on a fair May night studded with starlight, its great bulk borne along on a stiff westerly breeze. Ellie stood at the hurricane deck railing, Jack by her side, their wedding journey of two months behind them. Though it had been the happiest time of her life, her hungry gaze scoured the moonlit dock for signs of her father and brothers. But only a few roustabouts scrambled to secure the mooring lines and ready the stage planks in the lantern-lit shadows.

"Are you disappointed, Ellie, love?" Jack threaded his arms round her waist, his lips brushing the back of her neck where her chignon slipped free of its pins. "They'd not recognize you anyway."

She smiled at his teasing and remembered his gentle words the next morning when she arrived at New Hope and faced Andra in the foyer. Her sister circled her as if she were a museum specimen on exhibit, a look of wonder on her face. "Are you feeling well, Elinor? You're so . . . prodigiously big!"

Peering down from the stair landing, the maids giggled. Ellie gave them an awkward smile, draping her hands over her expanding middle. "'Twas a secret till now," she said, thinking how small her waist had been on her wedding day. "I'm more than four months along. I simply wasn't showing when we left for New Orleans."

"Well, I didn't think it was all that shrimp remoulade and crawfish bisque you'd been writing home about!" Andra motioned Ellie into the parlor, giving a backward glance at Mari and Gwyn and requesting tea. "We're in need of some good news, aside from Peyton and Penelope's betrothal, that is."

"So there's to be another wedding?" Ellie raised her brows in surprise, her own glad news forgotten. "Truly?"

"Supposedly, though our dear brother keeps postponing the date. Penelope is proving very patient."

"A postponement? Why?"

Andra rolled her eyes. "Business, ye ken."

"But there'll always be business." Ellie took a seat, already feeling ungraceful with her added bulk. "Perhaps I can help move things along now that I'm home."

"Good luck." Andra took a chair opposite, darting a look at the door as if impatient for tea. "Enough about weddings— or the lack. I'd much rather hear about your trip."

"Oh, New Orleans was wonderful. Jack is wonderful." Feeling a nudge to her middle, Ellie placed a hand there. "I've brought gifts for everyone. Cashmere shawls for you and Mama, a Tourte le jeune bow for Ansel—"

Andra's pinched expression stopped her midsentence. "A great deal has happened since you've been gone. I hardly know where to begin." Reluctance wove across her face, heightening Ellie's alarm. "Da wanted to be the one to tell you. But he's in town with no inkling you're here, and Mama is meeting with the Ladies' Aid Society."

"Well, go on."

She gave a nod. "First the good news. Aunt Elspeth has settled into a genteel boardinghouse in town, thanks to Jack's generosity. She's certainly redeemed herself since Henry Turlock's trial and has even been coming to church. As for Wade, he was released from jail a month or so ago after Henry was sent to the penitentiary in Philadelphia to begin his sentence." She hesitated as Gwyn served tea, waiting till the door was closed before continuing. "As for Ansel . . ."

Ellie waited, fears mounting.

"He's been gone a fortnight."

"Gone? I don't understand."

"No note was left—not a word at the last. We aren't sure if he went of his own accord or . . ." Tears glimmered in Andra's eyes. "Da cautions us against despair, but we aren't sure what has happened. There were some papers found—some threatening messages sent to Ansel prior to his disappearing. My fear is that Wade is involved, wanting revenge, but we have no proof."

Ellie's hand shook, sloshing tea over the delicate rim of her cup, the joy of her homecoming a dim memory. Andra's own distress was so evident, Ellie feared the situation was even worse than it seemed. Was Andra withholding anything? Or simply being mindful of her condition?

Setting her cup aside, Ellie moved toward the foyer, the sudden stitch in her side hardly slowing her. Passing the maids, she hurried up the stairs, praying Andra wouldn't follow.

Ansel must be there somewhere, mayhap playing a trick like he'd done in childhood. Not gone. Not missing. Nor worse.

She pushed open the door of his bedchamber and stood on the threshold, craving his voice, his reassuring smile, the easy bond between them. The emptiness was profound. The dark room bore his unmistakable scent—the disarray of a man too preoccupied to put his hat and boots away, or who'd meant to do that very thing but never would again. Whispering his name, she caught up his greatcoat from the back of a chair, burying her face in its familiar folds, her heart shattering over and over.

He wouldn't go without telling her. He'd have left a last note for her. Said some sort of goodbye.

Unless . . .

Author's Note

When I began researching this novel, I was soon rocked by my misassumptions about slavery and the Underground Railroad. As a student of Kentucky and Ohio history, I found that the slavery issue in Pennsylvania was even more complex than I had first thought. In the words of author David G. Smith in *On the Edge of Freedom*, "Every single fugitive slave escaping by land east of the Appalachian Mountains had to pass through Pennsylvania, which is why the state, its laws, and the attitudes of its citizens was so important."

I had always believed that Pennsylvania was indeed a free state and little slavery existed within its borders in the early nineteenth century, given the Pennsylvania Assembly's passage of a gradual abolition bill in 1780 and other antislavery legislation. Yet despite valiant efforts by Quakers, free blacks, and abolitionists, slavery persisted, especially west of the Susquehanna River, until 1840. Tragically, slaveholders and anti-abolitionists like the Turlocks found ways to thwart the law.

Every name and incident involving slaves in *Love's Awakening* is taken from the historical record. The Ballantynes' legacy as abolitionists is inspired by courageous people like William and Phoebe Wright of Pennsylvania, passionate antislavery activists who are credited with assisting hundreds of fugitives to freedom. Yet it should also be said that many fugitives—men, women, and children—passed through Pennsylvania with no help from northern whites, relying solely on themselves or free blacks.

While some abolitionists were open about assisting slaves, much of the Underground Railroad activity in Pennsylvania was so secretive it is still unknown today.

I am most indebted to these sources for their candid, moving accounts of the Underground Railroad and the slavery issue: *Underground Railroad in Pennsylvania* by William J. Switala; *On the Edge of Freedom: The Fugitive Slave Issue in South Central Pennsylvania, 1820–1870* by David G. Smith; *Bound for Canaan: The Underground Railroad and the War for the Soul of America* by Fergus M. Bordewich; and *Across the Wide River* by Stephanie Reed.

Acknowledgments

Since I was small and became lost in the wonder of words, it's been my desire to honor the Lord with my writing. My stories are not my own but His. It's a marvel they ever saw print. My prayer is that each one reaches the hands and hearts they were made for.

Unending thanks to each of you who've come alongside me with an outpouring of love via email, snail mail, prayers, gracious reviews, and more. You've encouraged and blessed me in ways you'll never know short of eternity.

*Take a sneak peek
at the next installment!*

The Ballantyne Legacy, Book 3,
by Laura Frantz

Available Fall 2014

Prologue

*The fear of death follows from the fear of life.
A man who lives fully is prepared to die at any time.*

MARK TWAIN

ALLEGHENY COUNTY, PENNSYLVANIA
DECEMBER 1825

So this was how it felt to die.

Warm and sticky. Sudden. Hazy. The bullets tore into his back, his knee, crippling him midstride. Pain exploded inside him, and his frantic grip on the baby's blanket went slack. Wren's terrified wail was worse than the anguish shuddering through him. Not yet a year old, his daughter stiffened in his arms as smoke cloaked them in powdery waves.

"Ansel—hurry!" Sarah's voice sounded choked . . . strangely distant.

Strength ebbing, he pushed his wife into the coach, nearly throwing the baby in after her. On his heels was his apprentice. Turning, he called to the lad as another shot rang out along the wooded road. Ansel's hands threaded through the smoke and darkness toward the boy and felt a bloodied limb.

God, no . . . God, help.

He'd been wrong to return home to Pennsylvania. Wrong to think the trouble over slavery had died down. The thought lambasted him as he thrust the lad into the coach and started to climb in after him.

"Away! Away!" he shouted to the coachman, his hoarse cry meeting with another gunshot.

The driver slumped atop the high box seat in answer, his whip dangling from a limp hand. With an overwhelming burst of stamina, Ansel slammed the coach door and climbed upward, dragging his battered leg atop the box, steeling himself against the searing ache.

Grabbing hold of the whip, he braced himself as the vehicle lurched into the rain-soaked night and tried not to flinch as the cold weight of the coachman's body shifted against him.

He was shaking. Praying. Preparing to die.

'Twas a bitter end to a long-awaited homecoming.

1

*Soon after, I returned home to
my family, with a determination to
bring them as soon as possible to live
in Kentucky, which I esteemed a
second paradise.*

DANIEL BOONE

CANE RUN, KENTUCKY
JULY 1850

Papa had forsaken his black mourning band.

The shock of it stole through Wren like ice water. For two years her father's shirtsleeve had borne a reminder of her mother's loss, as telling as the lines of grief engraved upon his handsome face. Not once had he taken off the black silk. But today, on this glorious July morn, it was missing. And Wren ached to know what stirred inside his russet head.

It had all begun with a letter from far upriver. From New Hope. She'd paid the post the day before, wonder astir inside her as she studied the elegant writing. *Ansel Ballantyne, Cane Run, Kentucky.* They received a great deal of mail, mostly from Europe and the violin collectors and luthiers there, or from Mama's family, the Nancarrows in England. Not Pennsylvania, with the Allegheny County watermark bleeding ink on the outer edge of the wrinkled paper.

She ran all the way home and arrived at the door of their stone house flushed and so winded she could only flutter the letter in her fingers. As it passed from her hand to her father's, she measured his expression.

Pensive. Surprised. Reluctant.

Sensing he craved privacy, she turned on her naked feet and fled, climbing the mountain in back of their home place till her lungs cried for air.

There she sank to her knees atop a flat rock and drank in the last colorful bits of day.

The river before her was framed by fading light, no longer blue but liquid gold. Wide and unending, it cradled a lone steamboat with fancy lettering on its paddle box. Wrapping her arms around her legs, she breathed in the sultry air, not coming down again till her father's husky voice cut through the mountain twilight, calling her home.

The supper that Molly, their housekeeper, had made was waiting. She darted a glance about the kitchen. No Molly. No letter in sight. Just cold cups of cider and deep bowls of hominy stew and cornbread drenched with butter.

"*A bheil an t-acras ort?*" Papa stood in the doorway to the parlor, speaking the Gaelic he'd used with her since childhood, warm and familiar as one of Molly's hand-sewn quilts. *Are you hungry, Wren?*

Hungry, yes. For mourning bands and Mama and explanations of strange letters from upriver. She nodded, sitting down and waiting for grace. Tears touched her eyes when he prayed. The words were Mama's own, ushering in her sweet presence again.

"I've news from Pennsylvania." Swallowing some cider, he gestured to the mantel where the letter rested.

"From the Ballantynes?" Wren nearly choked asking it, the grit of cornbread crumbs in her throat.

"Aye. It's been awhile since they've written. Longer still since I've visited. Things there are changing . . ." Misery rose up and clouded the blue of his eyes. He took another sip of cider and then pushed up from his chair, nearly sending it backwards. "I fear I've been away too long."

Tossing aside his napkin, he limped out the back door, his old injury tugging at her as he disappeared among fruit-laden trees. In the heat of the kitchen, she was left alone with her clamoring questions.

All her life she'd wondered about their family in western Pennsylvania. She'd heard the romantic tale of how her Scots grandfather, Silas Ballantyne, had come over the mountains the century before and built a fancy brick house for his bride. She was sure the glimmers of gossip whispered by Cane Run folk had been embellished over time. Some sort of trouble had driven Papa away from there more than twenty years before. But that was a puzzle too.

She picked up his bowl of stew, set it in the hearth's embers to keep it warm, and placed his plate of cornbread atop it. Though he'd gone outside, his profound disquiet lingered. She'd not seen him this upset since Mama's passing.

Darting a look at the mantel, she sighed. The letter that started all the trouble seemed to taunt her, the black mourning band coiled beside it, rife with mystery.

Birdsong nudged her awake, just as it had for twenty years or better. Wren could smell coffee—and varnish. Someone was in the workshop situated across the dogtrot at the south end of the house. The instruments seemed to dry better there, soaking up the sun through the skylight in the vaulted ceiling, the room's brightness calling out the rich pine and maple grain of the finished fiddles.

She dressed hurriedly and donned an apron, then wove her hair into a careless braid, tying it off with a frayed, rose-colored ribbon. It jarred sourly with her moss dress and navy shoes, giving her the look of a crazy quilt. She never fussed overlong about her mismatched wardrobe, not caring how she looked. A spill of varnish or a chisel gone awry had wrecked more dresses than she could count.

The workshop door was open wide, and she saw the long rack stretching the length of the room, jewel-toned violins strung like beads on a necklace. The smell of varnish wafted strong but not unpleasantly so, competing with the tang of freshly cut wood. Lingering on the door stone, she swept the shop in a glance. Papa? No. Only Selkirk, Papa's apprentice. Straddling a bench, he was carving the scroll of a violin from a piece of pine, his back to her.

"Morning, Kirk."

"Morning, Wren." He didn't so much as glance up, keeping his chisel true to the wood, a dusting of sweet shavings across his breeches.

"The McCoy bow is finished. I rubbed it with pumice powder and oil just yesterday. But you'll need to test it first." She'd lost count of the bows that didn't pass muster. The instruments they made had to be nearly faultless. Papa's reputation as luthier depended on it.

"I won't be making any deliveries today." Selkirk's tone was low. Thoughtful. "Your father's left for Louisville. Something about booking passage upriver to Pittsburgh."

She went completely still, nearly forgetting how strange it was to be alone with Selkirk without Papa present. Just outside, Molly was stringing laundry on the line joining house to shop. *Mute Molly*, Cane Run folk called her. When small, she'd been choked by a slave trader and robbed of her voice.

Wren fought the catch in her own throat as she fastened her gaze on the instruments adorning the sunny room, not just fiddles but mandolins and dulcimers and psalteries, the work of their hands and hearts. "Pittsburgh sounds right far."

Kirk shrugged. "Just a few hundred miles. Easily managed by steamer." He looked up, his chisel aloft. "Don't you want to meet your Ballantyne kin, Wren?"

Did she? In truth, she rarely thought about them aside from Christmas when Grandmother Ballantyne sent lovely, impractical packages downriver. An enameled jewelry box. A cashmere shawl. An ivory-handled parasol. Things far above Wren's raising. "Mostly I forget all about them."

Kirk gave a chuckle. "Well, they've not forgotten you. Fact is, they've named a steamboat in your honor. She's called the *Rowena*."

"You don't mean it."

"Aye, I've seen her taking on cargo in Louisville. A fine steamer she is too, well deserving of your name."

Her backside connected with the nearest stool. "But . . . why?"

"Because the Ballantynes are rich. Because they name all their steamers after the petticoats—er, ladies—in the family."

"I'm hardly a lady," she replied, glancing at her stained apron.

"You might be by the time you come back here."

The very thought made her smile. She reached for a finished bow and newly strung fiddle, launching into a lively jig as if it could drive the ludicrous thought from the room. But it simply ensnared Kirk, keeping him from his work.

His mouth quirked with amusement. "If you tickle their ears with your fiddle, they might well forgive you for Cane Run. The truth is, Wren, you don't belong here. Not like the Clarks and Landrys and Mackens who settled this place. Your mother's people are of English stock, aye? And your father, for all his humility and homespun, is still a Ballantyne."

"I misdoubt I belong there either."

"How will you know unless you go?"

Because some things the heart just knows.

"If someone named a boat after me and begged me to come upriver, I'd be the first aboard." Kirk traded one chisel for another. "It's a bit odd your father seldom speaks of his kin. Makes me wonder what drove him to Kentucky to begin with."

She rested the fiddle across her knees. "All I know is that Papa left Pennsylvania when he was young as you and sailed to England. He took up with the Nancarrows—Welsh luthiers—and wed my mother. When I was born they came to Kentucky."

"Bare facts, Wren. You'd best be finding out before you go."

She fell quiet, pondering the sudden turn of events, the steamboat *Rowena*, and Louisville, a place she'd never been. "When will Papa be back?"

"Tomorrow or thereabouts."

She was used to his absences. His violin hunting often took him away for months. Sometimes Mama had accompanied him, but never Wren. Since Mama had passed, Papa hadn't gone anywhere at all.

Why on earth would he now want to return to Pennsylvania?

Laura Frantz is the author of *The Frontiersman's Daughter*, *Courting Morrow Little*, *The Colonel's Lady*, and *Love's Reckoning*. A two-time Carol Award finalist, she is a Kentuckian currently living in the misty woods of Washington with her husband and two sons. Along with traveling, cooking, gardening, and long walks, she enjoys connecting with readers at www.LauraFrantz.net.

Meet
Laura Frantz

Visit LauraFrantz.net to read Laura's blog
and learn about her books!

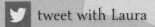 see what inspired the characters and stories

enter to win contests and learn about what
Laura is working on now

tweet with Laura

"*Stunning. Heart-wrenching. Breathless.*

Not since *Gone with the Wind* have I read an
epic novel that has stolen my heart, my breath, my sleep to
such a jolting degree."

—JULIE LESSMAN, award-winning author of the
Daughters of Boston and Winds of Change series

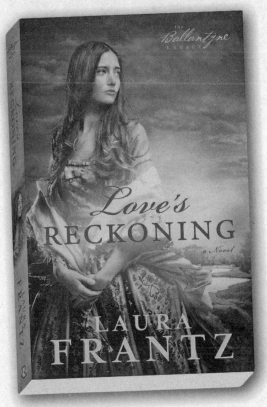

In this sweeping family saga set in western Pennsylvania, one
man's choices in love and work, in friends and enemies, set the
stage for generations to come.

"You'll disappear into another place and time and be both encouraged and enriched for having taken the journey."

—JANE KIRKPATRICK, bestselling author of *All Together in One Place* and *A Flickering Light*

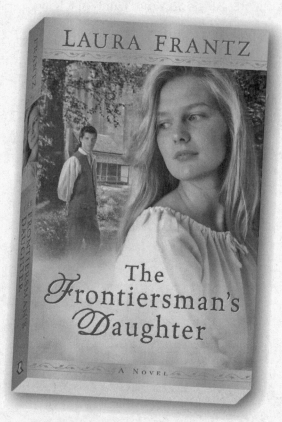

This epic novel gives readers a glimpse into the simple yet daring lives of the pioneers who first crossed the Appalachians, all through the courageous eyes of a determined young woman.